A Stolen Kiss

A Stolen Kiss

KELSEY KEATING

A Stolen Kiss

Young Adult Fantasy

Cover design by Jenny Zemanek at www.seedlingsonline.com
Typesetting by Chris Bell with Atthis Arts LLC at www.atthisarts.com
Ebook formatting by Kella Campbell with Ebooks Done Right at www.ebooksdoneright.com

Published by Swanifide Publishing
Visit www.swanifidepublishing.com for more information.

ISBN (paperback)   978-1-943923-00-7
       (ebook)   978-1-943923-01-4

Visit the author at www.kelseykeating.com,
on Facebook at www.facebook.com/authorkelseykeating,
or on Twitter @kelseyraek.

To all my swans.
Thank you for your endless support.

Chapter 1
CHANGE YOUR FATE

. . . .

"Once upon a time, blah blah blah," Sarah groaned and lay back on a pile of hay.

Derric Harver laughed and continued to unload bales of hay from the cart. History never held her interest for long.

"You're supposed to be studying that book, not mocking it. You know how upset Father will be if you don't pass your history exam. You need that merit if you ever want to move up from lady's maid."

"So what if I don't." Sarah shrugged. "It's not like I'll ever be nobility; that takes a royal order. No matter how much money my mother collects, she still hasn't been made a noble—why should I be any different? Besides, I could always come here and work in the stables with you." Her face lit up, and she bounced forward. "Oh, I like that! Think of how much fun we'd have!"

Derric let out a genuine guffaw and dropped his bale of hay. "I love you, little sister, but we both know you wouldn't last a day in here. You may not be nobility, but your blood is high society; mine is peasant. The only thing my life is good for is working here in the stables."

"No, it isn't!" Sarah glared at him, one hand on her hip while the other balanced her history book. "It's what my mother thinks you're good for. I know better. You could be the highest scholar in all the kingdom if you'd just let everyone know how smart you are."

Derric ignored her and gestured to the page still open in the book. "This one's fun. It's about a girl in a red cloak who outsmarts a wolf. You remember? What happened and in what year?"

"Ugggggh." Sarah let out a whine and plopped the book back down on the hay. "Can't I just do this later?"

"Don't you have duties in the castle? You could be attending to those instead of studying."

"No. Maria's sleeping. I have my morning off to spend with you, but I might leave if you keep making me recite history." Sarah winked and twirled around, her skirt stirring up loose feed.

"You know you need this. Don't fight it." He grinned despite himself. "Stop that—you're going to get your dress dirty."

"Know what we should be doing? We should be helping you get out of these stables and into the palace guard. It's not as good as a scholar, but it's something!"

Derric shot her a withering look as he pulled the last bale from the cart, but Sarah was undeterred. "We have to get you a new position. You're so strong! You'd be a fantastic guard."

"I'm not welcome in the castle, as you very well know, so how could that ever work? I told you—I'm fine here."

"What happened wasn't your fault," she said. "Your mother was the one who—"

"Let's not talk about it." Derric turned his back on her. He hated speaking of his mother. It always made his stomach squirm. Sarah didn't understand—not really—everything that had happened . . . or how much Derric missed his mom.

"It's not fair," Sarah said. "It's not like you *asked* her to curse the princess. Besides, no one knows she's your mother. No one knows who you are."

Grimacing, Derric shook his head. No, he hadn't wanted what happened. Worse, he'd tried to fix it and only messed things up more. A flood of memories made him shudder. There would be consequences for his actions. He knew it.

"We could give you a different name, just to be safe," Sarah suggested. "We could change your fate. Make you new."

Her words stung—they always did on this topic—like a knife in his chest, one that never dulled. When he was eight, their father signed him over to the stable and never looked back. Sarah, then five, never gave up on him. Over the last nine years, she'd continued to come visit him, always looking up to her big brother, never knowing the whole story.

"Der . . . Dare . . . Dan . . . Daniel!" she said, tapping her chin and chuckling. "You could say you're from another kingdom! No one would ever know who you were. Daniel of Dellsby."

"Sarah, I don't have time for this. I'm working. What happens when the princess wakes up?"

"She won't." Sarah waved the remark away. "They gave her a draft to make her sleep so she'd be well rested when *Prince Humphrey Degalt of Dellsby* arrives." Sarah turned up her nose and raised her eyebrows in a mock solemnity as she pronounced the prince's name.

At the mention of the sleeping draft, Derric tensed. Once again, his mind flashed back nine years—to the day he made the biggest mistake of his life.

"She's been given a sleeping draft. Poor dear, never sleeps a wink at night. She'll wake when she's ready."

"What's the point of being the princess's lady's maid if you are always here with me?"

"I'm not always here with you." Sarah smoothed out her petticoat made of finer fabric than Derric would ever be able to afford. "I'm only here every spare moment I can be." She grinned and threw her arms around his waist, squeezing him tight.

"You're here more often than you're home with Father." He extricated one arm and wrapped it around her tiny frame.

"Maria doesn't mind. She knows I come and see you."

"The princess doesn't forbid it?" Derric eyed her through slitted lids.

"Well, she doesn't know who you are." Sarah released him and sat back on the bale of hay, drumming her fingers on her thigh. "She knows I have a brother, but she doesn't know it's . . . you. Like I said, no one knows your name—they just call you the stableboy."

"I have been erased from memory," Derric said with a soft sigh.

"Exactly! That's why you should show them how much you can do, move up in the world!"

Derric had opened his mouth to rebuff her again when they both froze at the sound of someone outside the stable.

"Sarah!" The feminine call was hushed, secretive. "Sarah, are you in here?" A young woman peeked around the corner, spotted Sarah, and gave a soft shriek. "I knew it!"

Mouth dropping open, Derric gaped at Princess Maria Regalla of Opea. It'd been nine years since he'd seen her up close. Flawless curled locks cascaded about her shoulders, framing her heart-shaped face in curtains of raven silk. Dark eyes lit up at the sight of Sarah: eyes larger than any Derric had ever seen before—with lashes thick, long, and black as her hair.

"My lady, I thought you were sleeping." Sarah reached out her arms and accepted the princess's embrace.

"I faked the draft." Maria winked at her. "I hate that stuff. I sleep at night, but they won't believe me."

"I thought the curse kept you awake at night." Sarah frowned, and Maria shook her head.

"Living with a curse means learning to *live*. I figured out how to sleep ages ago. I'm never tired in the morning." She glanced past Sarah to where Derric stood, still gaping at her. "Is this your brother?"

"Yes," Sarah said with a smile, turning to face him. Maria stepped forward, eyeing him with unguarded interest.

"I've heard so much about you from Sarah," she said, her voice taking on a hint of reverence. Even though he was a foot and a half taller than she was, he felt small before her.

"Your Majesty," he mumbled, bowing and losing his balance.

"Rise." She made a dismissive gesture with her hand, and he did so. For a moment, she studied his face. "It's strange you're here when your sister works in the castle. Why the stables, Master Digson?"

The use of his sister's last name put him off balance, but he stammered a reply.

"I—I. That is . . ." He shook his head and adopted a simple tone. "I'm not equipped for a position in the castle, m'lady. I haven't the wits for it."

"You seem bright enough to me. You're tall, you look strong, and you've got a nice chin. I bet you'd make a good guard."

"That's what I said!" Sarah exclaimed, hopping to Maria's side. "I never noticed his chin, though. Is it nice?"

"Oh, very." Maria nodded, reaching out and tugging at Derric's sleeve. "You see how it's sort of square and strong? He has a rather nice face all over—very attractive." She snatched her hand back, shocked at her forwardness. Clearing her throat, she turned back to Sarah. "He'd do well in the guard."

Derric stared at the princess, uncertain how to react. She studied his face with interest, and though he struggled against the redness creeping up his neck, he appreciated the moment to study her as well.

Soft. That was the word that came to mind. Maria looked like she'd be soft to touch, with her beautiful skin reminiscent of cinnamon. Her lips pursed as she turned back to Sarah to answer a question Derric hadn't heard, but they still held their full shape. Everything about her said petite and royal, from her perfect nose, to her manicured eyebrows. What on earth she could find attractive about him, he didn't know.

Something isn't right. The tiny voice came unbidden, and he brushed it aside. For once, he'd accept a compliment and keep it.

"I need to sneak back upstairs before anyone comes to check on me," Maria said, her gaze back to the stable entrance. "Come with me."

Sarah obeyed at once, Derric forgotten until they reached the stable door.

"Master Digson." Maria turned toward him.

"Your Majesty?"

"I'll see what I can do about your position. I'm sure you'd much prefer the guard—far more interesting than the stables."

Derric nodded but said nothing, knowing it wouldn't make a difference. He'd never leave the stables. Even if he pretended to be someone else, he'd never be able to escape his past. One thing was certain—the princess could never know the truth. He couldn't imagine her horror if she found out what he'd done.

Chapter 2
A Royal Flush

Maria exited the stable with her chin held high, squashing the jumbled nerves that zinged around inside her. *You are the princess. Act like the princess.*

"Do you really think you can get him into the guard?" Sarah asked, walking a few steps behind Maria.

"What? Oh, yes. I'm sure that can be arranged." Maria swallowed hard, glad she didn't blush too easily.

"Are you all right?" Sarah bounced a little closer as they walked through the main hall of the castle, her light brown eyebrows knitting low across her brow. "Your face is flushed."

All right, maybe I do blush. "I'm fine."

A knowing grin spread across Sarah's face. "You're nervous, aren't you?"

"Nervous? Why would I be nervous?" She couldn't push the face of the stableboy from her mind. She had to clear her thoughts of him. Now wasn't the time to dwell on the face of a peasant—even if that peasant had hair the color of sunshine, eyes as green as the grass, and a mouth like . . . *no!*

"For Prince Humphrey to arrive." Sarah let out a little giggle. "I'm excited and nervous too!"

"Oh, that. Yes. That is exactly what I'm thinking about." Maria let out a breath of relief. "There's much to do before he arrives. We'd better get a move on."

"I think you look fantastic," Sarah said, cocking her head to the side to assess the final result.

"Exquisitely beautiful, Maria," Lady Deserey, one of her ladies-in-waiting, said with a curtsy. Maria fought an eye roll. None of her ladies cared a lick about Maria's happiness. The queen had selected each of them from the highest ranking nobility in all of Opea, not just the capital city of Edleton. They knew nothing about Maria, nor did they care to.

"Ladies, would you please give me a few moments to finish?" she asked in her sweetest tone. "Sarah will help me. I'll see you below." The three girls curtsied in unison, and exited the room on dainty feet. With a huff, Maria dropped to the floor and covered her face with her hands. "I don't know if I can do this."

"Of course you can! You can do anything." Sarah dropped down beside her, her sweet face beaming with its ever-present smile. "You are Maria Andelle Regalla, and you're about to meet your betrothed."

"What if he doesn't like me?" Maria wrapped her arms around herself.

"What's not to like?" Sarah stood and offered Maria her hands to help pull her up. "Only a fool wouldn't fall in love with you at first sight."

"But if he doesn't," Maria argued, "then he won't want to break the curse and I'll be stuck lying—lying awake thinking about it." She finished without looking at Sarah, hoping her near slip went unnoticed.

"He will break the curse." Sarah pulled Maria over to her full length mirror. "You'll have your happily-ever-after to go in the history books right after your parents' story. I'm sure of it."

"You know," Maria said, placing her hand on Sarah's shoulder. "I don't know what I'd do without you. Half the time you act more like a big sister than my maid. Sometimes I forget how much younger than me you are."

"Only three years." Sarah smiled and turned to the mirror, fluffing the petticoat of Maria's dress. "Well? What do you think?"

Maria examined her reflection. Every hair was in place, pulled into an elegant updo. Her features were embellished, and the dress complemented her figure.

"I wish they'd stop making every dress I own in red." Maria twisted, taking in the side view and as much as she could see of the back. Her bustle brought out the rear of the dress, shrinking her waist in comparison.

"Most women can't afford red fabric. I'd love to have a red dress."

"You can have mine." Maria sighed. "I should be wearing purple. It's the royal color of Opea." A twinge of pain flickered in her heart. "It just shows they don't see me as the future queen—a marriage prop and nothing more."

"Prince Humphrey will see you as beautiful." Sarah wrapped her arms around Maria's waist and rested her chin on Maria's shoulder. Maria frowned at the contrast of Sarah's lighter skin to her own.

"Why is your brother so pale?"

"What do you mean?" Sarah stepped away.

"He's pale. His skin is . . . is pink. It's not like ours or that of anyone I've met in Opea. Your skin is lighter than mine, yes, but it's still far tanner than his."

"He spends too much time in the stables, I expect."

Maria frowned. That wasn't a good enough answer. Why would a brother and sister look so different? Even though Sarah's hair was a light maple, butterscotch color, it wasn't anywhere near as golden as her brother's.

A knock at the door interrupted her thoughts, and Maria called out for them to enter.

"My lady." Durton, a male servant, bowed low before her. "Your parents request your presence. His Highness Prince Humphrey and the Queen and King of Dellsby have entered the city gates."

Her stomach flopping like a baby rabbit unsure on its feet, Maria nodded. Sarah gave her two thumbs up and bid her good luck.

Caviar? Really? Maria stared down at her plate, stomach churning. Her parents wanted her to make a good impression, didn't they? Expecting her to stomach slimy little fish eggs wasn't a good first step.

"So, um, Maria." Humphrey cleared his throat, drawing her attention to where he sat on her right. "Do you . . . do you like . . . fish?"

She turned to him and noticed the glisten of sweat on his forehead. Seeing he looked as uncomfortable as she felt improved her mood. "Um, I actually don't. No. Do you?"

He nodded. "We have a lot of fish in Dellsby. The sea provides our most profitable goods: fish, shells, plant life. And we love to swim in the waves."

"I don't swim much," Maria admitted. "I've always wanted to, but I've never been a strong swimmer."

"Maybe you'll learn." His smile was genuine and kind, though not the beatific smile of a man besotted with love for her.

"I'd like that." She returned the grin, knowing hers wasn't any more romantic.

From the moment he'd entered the castle hall, Maria had liked Humphrey. She knew his cordiality only bespoke proper princely training, but his easy smile and handsome appearance didn't hurt anything either. Short, dark, wavy hair—not a single strand out of place—graced his head like a crown all its own. Large, white teeth decorated every smile, and his chocolate skin appeared free of any blemish.

In fact, Humphrey's eyes were his only surprising feature. They contrasted so drastically from the rest of his appearance; it felt as though he could see right through her. Several times since his arrival, Maria had noticed Humphrey glance at his parents and receive a curt nod in return. This, she understood. Her father would squeeze her hand when he wanted her to stop or start talking.

Parental approval—the crutch of every well-mannered child.

After dessert, Maria's mother stood, glass in hand. "Perhaps we ought to retire to one of our sitting rooms? Rubelle, Darian, would you join Patrick and myself? No, Maria dear, why don't you give Humphrey a tour of the castle?"

The glimmer in the queen's eyes left no doubt of what was expected next. To confirm her suspicions, Maria glanced at the King and Queen of Dellsby. Both stared as if trying to force their son to hear their thoughts, eyebrows raised in expectation.

"Yes, uh, um. I'm sure I'd love a tour." He stood and held his arm out for Maria to take. As expected, she did so. Once their parents were gone, Humphrey's whole body relaxed. "Phew, that's a relief. Do you ever get used to them staring at you like that? I don't."

"I guess not." She laughed, gesturing in the opposite direction their parents had taken. "I can show you to your room if you like. We can pretend we had a full tour, and you could get some rest after your long journey."

Humphrey jerked back in surprise. "I hadn't taken you for a rule breaker. We may actually get along. The gentleman in me insists that after you show me where my room is, I walk you to yours and bid you goodnight. Technically, the space in-between can be counted as a tour."

"Perfect plan." Maria pointed at the staircase. "We can go that way. Your bedroom is in the east wing, and mine is in the northernmost tower."

"Why? Are you a fan of heights? Parents afraid you'll Rapunzel yourself out of here if you aren't up high enough?"

Maria shook her head. "No, it isn't that. They were pretty … upset … when I was cursed. They put me up there to be away from prying eyes. It helped, though, being up there. Easier access to the sky."

"I'll pretend like that made sense." Humphrey followed as she led the way, two servants trailing behind them as chaperones.

"And so concludes our tour," Maria said, holding her arms out to one side to show the staircase up to her tower. "I will bid you goodnight and see you in the morning."

"Maria!" Sarah came around the corner. "I didn't expect you back so—" She caught sight of Humphrey and froze. "I—I'm so sorry, my lady. I didn't realize …"

"It's fine. Humphrey, this is my lady's maid, Sarah Digson. Sarah, Prince Humphrey Degalt of Dellsby."

Sarah dropped into a curtsy, and Humphrey nodded in return.

"Maria," Humphrey lifted her hand into his. "I suppose we both know what's to become of us, but I'd feel better about it if we did this the old fashioned way." He knelt down on one knee, and Maria's stomach flipped, a mixture of excitement and dread. "Will you marry me?"

She opened her mouth, ready to accept and secure her country's safety and a husband for the rest of her life. All she needed was one little word …

Chapter 3
A Failed Night

Prince Humphrey's procession began a few hours after Sarah and the princess left the stables. Derric watched it from his place beside the horses, marveling at the rich outfits even the lowest servants wore. The King and Queen of Dellsby weren't visible in their carriage, but the son, riding behind on his white stallion, announced his presence with a dazzling white smile and gentlemanly wave.

Prince Humphrey was what Derric expected him to be: majestic, handsome, and no doubt charming. He looked like Maria with his dark hair and skin, though nothing about him seemed soft, not even the way he held his horse's reins. To the untrained eye, he appeared confident and at ease, but Derric could see his knuckles whiten as they gripped the leather straps.

He's nervous. Derric watched the prince's jaw clench and unclench. *Then again, I'd be nervous too if I was meeting my fiancée for the first time.*

The procession passed out of sight through the gates of the castle, and Derric returned to his work.

As night fell, Derric tended to the horses. Nights were cold as winter drew near, so Derric brought blankets out for each of the royal steeds. Thumper, one of the large workhorses, was the last to be draped for warmth. As was his custom, Derric draped Thumper, grabbed his own blanket, and lay down next to the animal to keep warm as he slept. The stables were cold most nights, even in the summer, and Thumper never seemed to mind Derric's company. He had raised him from a colt, and since Derric had no place to call home, Thumper's stable was as good a place as any to make his own.

Derric had been lying down for scarcely ten minutes when a loud clattering noise in the dark stable brought him leaping to his feet.

"Derric!" Sarah called, and more noise filled the stable as she let out a shriek of pain. She'd no doubt stumbled into the feeding buckets. "Derric, I need you!"

"What is it?"

"You have to come with me. Now," she ordered, locating and tugging at him.

"Why?"

"Maria needs you! Maria and Prince Humphrey."

"Me?" Derric froze, fear gripping him. "Why do they need me?"

"Something's happened. Something bad, but I don't know what it is. You will. It has to do with ... with the curse," Sarah whispered, and Derric's anger spiked.

"No! No, I'm not helping with anything to do with my mother's magic."

"You have to! You know more than anyone else about curses and spells. You're the only one," she lowered her voice, almost inaudible, "*who knows about magic* left in Opea. You'll know how to fix this."

"But it's dark out," Derric argued. "Maria should be *in* her curse right now."

"No, she says it starts at midnight," Sarah said as she walked behind him and pushed with all her might to make him move. "You're coming. That's that."

"How am I supposed to help?"

"You'll see when you get there. They won't know who you are. I just told Maria you knew a lot about the history of spells, okay? This is a royal order!" She threw all of her weight against him.

"Fine." Derric stepped sideways, and Sarah fell forward, Derric catching her before she hit the ground and letting out a little chuckle.

"Ouch! Nice. Come on."

As they entered the castle, Derric's breathing constricted. He hadn't stepped foot in the building since a year after his mother disappeared. Like it had only been yesterday, Derric's memories rushed in, and he was nine years old again.

The spell had been cast a year before, and no one had been able to locate his mother. As a healer, his father had been brought to the castle, his wife at his side. The king and queen, aware of some connection between them, had questioned Master Digson about the sorceress's whereabouts while the children sat outside and waited. From the moment his mother cast the curse, Derric lost all favor with his father. In a fit of insane desperation, Derric ran up to the tallest tower—to Maria's room—and burst inside.

Nine years old, Maria lay fast asleep on the bed in the middle of the day. No one ever knew the details of Maria's curse, and Derric was shocked to find she was under a sleeping spell. It wasn't Gilda's style of magic. The dark-haired little girl didn't stir as he approached, but Derric had known she wouldn't. With bravery beyond himself—and a little relief he hadn't needed to slay any dragons—Derric fulfilled his pledge to end Maria's curse and win back his father's affection. Steeling himself, he did the grossest thing a nine-year-old boy could do.

He kissed her.

Nothing happened.

Mortified and embarrassed, Derric realized he was no knight, no prince, and no hero. Either his mother had added a Royalty Clause, or he just wasn't strong enough to break it. Dejected, Derric returned downstairs to where Sarah sat playing with jacks in the hall. As he slumped against the door to the throne room, he heard the most disturbing conversation of his young life.

"Perhaps if I saw the princess, I could—" His father's voice.

"She's sleeping," the king replied.

"It's a sleeping curse?" Sarah's mother guessed.

"No, it's something that comes on her at night," the queen had said. "She's been given a sleeping draft, poor dear. She doesn't sleep a wink otherwise."

A momentary thrill filled him—he hadn't failed, he'd only misunderstood. Derric didn't realize then the importance of this conversation. It wasn't until he was older, lying in the stable late at night, when he realized what he might've done.

"Here we are. Okay. Stay calm—they don't know who you are." Sarah brought Derric back to the present as she stood on the uppermost stair of the tallest tower. Pushing open the door, she beckoned Derric through. As if in a dream, Derric stepped across the threshold into the place he'd sworn to never return.

Chapter 4
No, Nope, and Never

• •

"Sarah." Relief washed through Maria as they entered the room. "Thank goodness you're here." She looked up at the young man she'd met that day in the stables and pushed away the same swirl of attraction. "You know about spells?"

"A bit, you see I'm—"

"There isn't time." Humphrey waved his hand, his eyes bleary and his perfect hair mussed from running his hands through it. "We need your help now."

Maria frowned at his rudeness. Of course the prince found this whole situation frustrating, but Master Digson had come to help them after sunset and, so far, without any request for repayment.

"What's going on?" he asked, frowning between the prince and princess. Humphrey glared at Maria, and she blushed.

"Tell him," Humphrey demanded, a quiver in his voice. His tone set everyone on edge. Maria saw Sarah's brother clench his fists at his side. His loyalty emboldened her.

"I can't." Maria glared back at Humphrey. "It's all too humiliating."

"Humphrey proposed to Maria," Sarah jumped in, "but she can't say yes."

"What do you mean she can't say yes?"

"They mean she keeps refusing me and then pretending like it isn't her fault." Humphrey stared at the ground, refusing to even look at her. "It's not like I asked to come here. I didn't seek you out to have you throw my offer in my face."

Sarah stepped up beside Maria. "No, she wants to. She keeps trying, but it comes out as 'no' or 'nope' each time."

Maria winced and dropped her gaze to the ground.

"Propose to her again." Master Digson gestured to Humphrey with more authority than would be considered proper, but it made Maria want to laugh. "I need to see it happen."

Rolling his eyes, the prince turned to face her. "Princess Maria Andelle Regalla, will you marry me?" His tone and his face were in perfect harmony—he didn't want to be there.

Sucking in a steady breath, Maria opened her mouth, intent on saying yes, telling herself she *could* say it. "Yeeee-no." At her failure, she groaned and turned away from them all.

"One more time," Master Digson said, gesturing at Humphrey. "But this time, get down on one knee and try to mean it."

"Excuse me? Who says I didn't mean it that time?"

"We all know you didn't mean it," Maria snapped, her eyes shining with unshed tears as she bit back what she really wanted to say.

"I'm just trying to suss out a few things. I need to see a romantic proposal."

Though he sighed in aggravation, Humphrey won a few steps back into Maria's good favor as he focused his attention on the task at hand. As he drew a calming breath, the prince's demeanor changed. He slicked back his hair, smiled with stunning white teeth, and knelt down on one knee before her. Sarah let out a sigh of contentment, her hands clasped above her heart.

"Maria, I know we haven't known each other long." Humphrey held her hands in his. "I know also that we're expected to marry. We've been groomed for it. As the youngest of three sons, I'm not in line for my throne, but I would be honored to help you rule your kingdom."

Maria closed her eyes and pursed her lips to keep from scoffing. Clearly this prince leaned more toward logic than romance.

"All this is true," Humphrey continued, perhaps sensing he'd strayed from the storybook proposal. "But those aren't the reasons I want to marry you. In our short acquaintance, I've been bewitched by your beauty, ensnared by your wit, and enchanted by your—" he faltered, his gaze falling below her neckline and resting on her breasts for several awkward seconds. "Er, uh, heart. Enchanted by your heart."

Maria blushed, feeling exposed. Though she tried to tug her hands away, he clamped down harder, his sincerity returning.

"For these reasons, amongst many others, I want you to be my wife. Would you do me the honor of marrying me?"

This time she was certain she could say yes. She wanted to say yes. Humphrey was everything she'd ever wanted when she was a child. He was the man of her dreams—her mother had told her so.

"Prince Humphrey Reginald Degalt, it would be my honor . . . that is, I would love to not marry you."

Humphrey grinned and then paused, his brow furrowing. "Sorry, but did you say *not* marry me?"

"Did I?" Maria turned to Sarah and her brother, who nodded. "Damn! Oh, my apologies. I mean, oh dear."

"I can only take so much rejection." Humphrey stood. "Do you know what's wrong, or is this some colossal joke at my expense?"

"Princess," Master Digson fixed his gaze on Maria. "When he asks you to marry him, what do you want to say?"

"I want to say yes," she said, unable to look at Humphrey. "I want to say I can already tell we'll be close. I want to marrrr him. Marrr. I want to be his wwwwwiiirrrnooo." Frustrated, Maria let out a shriek and dug her fingers into her hair. "Why can't I say it?"

"Princess, if I may." Master Digson held out his hand. Her heart rate spiked at his offer. Quieting her sudden giddiness, Maria placed her hand in his. His fingers closed over her dainty fingers, and she felt the calluses of his daily work life, so different from Humphrey's soft unworked hands.

"Your Highness." Master Digson reached his other hand out to Humphrey, who seemed unnerved by the idea of holding another man's hand. "Please. It's necessary."

Maria bit her lip to keep from giggling as Humphrey dropped his hand in Master Digson's. Sarah hovered just behind her brother, and Maria saw the concern in her maid's expression. What was he was about to do?

"Hmmm." He rubbed the top of Maria's hand, his eyes closed in concentration. "Yes. There's a block."

"Brother, dear, what are you doing?" Sarah hissed from a few steps away, but he didn't acknowledge her.

As quick as lightning, Master Digson released their hands, his eyes opening. "It's a clause."

Chapter 5
THINKING FAST

. . . .

Derric held the princess's hand in one hand and the prince's in the other, trying to think. There was no way he could figure out how or why the princess couldn't accept Humphrey by doing this, but he felt the need to show some mysticism in response to Humphrey's skepticism.

The difference in the two royals' hands threw him off a bit. He was holding another man's hand, and it felt weird. Maria's hand, in contrast, felt silky and welcome. He rubbed the smooth skin on the back of her hand.

"Hmm." *Think fast. Think fast!* "Yes. There's a block."

"Brother, dear, what are you doing?" He heard Sarah's hiss behind him, and he fought back a laugh. Sarah called him "dear" when she was irritated with him.

What could stop Maria from saying yes? She said she wanted to, and he didn't think she'd lie. She should be able to.

Unless . . . it had to be!

He dropped their hands, his eyes snapping open. "It's a clause."

Chapter 6
Be-clause You Can

. . . .

"It's a what?" Humphrey and Maria said together as Sarah brought a hand to her head and said, "Of course, a clause!"

"A curse, or rather any spell," Master Digson began, "is essentially a contract."

Maria blinked. "A what now?"

"The sorcerer, by using magic, writes an internally binding contract with the subject—in this case, *you*. Like any contract you might have with a blacksmith or a builder, there are often clauses written in to avoid someone taking advantage of you."

Maria glanced at Humphrey to see if he understood what was being said, and found comfort in the confused arch of his brow. Master Digson noticed, too, and returned to plain speech.

"A curse like yours has rules. All spells have rules, much like a genie's lamp does. Otherwise, magic would be abused by those in possession of it. For example, neither a genie nor a sorceress can bring someone back from the dead—the power required is too vast. A sorceress can create a love potion, but a genie can't force love. And, to keep a sorcerer from running amok, there are rules that restrict a love potion's usage.

"Curses are the same. You were cursed at a young age, which limits the severity allowed on the curse. An adult can be cursed with something far more dangerous than a child. Curses have clauses in regards to how they're broken. They can't disappear just because ten years have gone by, like a spell can. Curses must be broken, or they can be removed by the one who cast them."

"Right. Right, okay, that makes sense." Humphrey started pacing, and Maria sat down on her chaise, trying to focus on the impromptu lesson. "So she can't say yes to marrying me because of her curse? I thought marrying a prince would break it, and therefore, she should marry me?"

"It depends on the rules in place. A Marriage Clause would work, like you said, but then she should be able to say yes. I'm guessing there's a Kissing Clause. The only question is what kind."

"There's more than one kind of Kissing Clause?" Maria's shoulders slumped, feeling things had gone too far. Perhaps if she were honest about her curse, they could stop the whole charade.

But then, if she told Humphrey the truth, it still wouldn't explain why she somehow couldn't agree to his proposal.

"There's a standard Kissing Clause and a True Love's Kiss. Standard's the easiest to work with. A kiss will end the curse. True Love's Kiss," Master Digson grimaced and shook his head, "is far more difficult to find. In fact, most stories from *The History of Fairy Tales* are actually inaccurate. Almost all of them had Standard Kissing Clauses—hence why princes could wake up the princesses without ever knowing them."

"Right, because you can't fall in love just by looking at someone." Humphrey nodded in agreement, soaking up everything Master Digson said. Maria shot him a glare, but the prince didn't see it.

"So if you have a Kissing Clause, all it would take is—"

He stopped talking, a dazed, faraway look contorting his expression. Humphrey turned a concerned eye on Maria, who looked to Sarah for understanding.

"Brother?" she said as they all watched several unidentifiable emotions pass over Master Digson's face.

"All it would take is a kiss to break the curse." Though

he finished his sentence, Maria couldn't help but notice the worrisome way his brows knit together.

"So maybe I just have to kiss her!" Humphrey gave a jovial clap of his hands and threw his head back with regal sophistication. "Come, Maria." When she blanched, he grinned. "It was bound to happen sooner or later. After all, we're to be married."

"But what if it's True Love's Kiss?" Sarah interjected, frowning at her brother.

"I have a plan for that already." Humphrey pulled Maria up off the chaise and encircled her waist with one arm. "Maria, I don't believe in love at first sight."

Well, we're getting off to a great start, she thought, but he continued.

"However, I've known since the age of twelve that I was betrothed to marry you on your eighteenth birthday next month. Because of this, I have dreamed of you over one thousand times." Humphrey's glittering smile crinkled the corners of his eyes, and for the first time, Maria felt he was being genuine.

"Without ever meeting you, I've spent many hours by your side. When I was gifted your portrait three years ago on my eighteenth birthday, I kept it with me always. I used to pretend to have long conversations with you about our likes and dislikes and how we'd raise our children."

Blushing, Maria dropped her gaze, but Humphrey used his free hand to tilt her chin up.

"Without a doubt, I can say I've loved you for ages. Now I ask for your permission to place a kiss upon your lips."

Overwhelmed by joy and her own growing feelings of affection for him, Maria nodded and opened her mouth to declare her love for him as he leaned in.

"I love you, too, Derric."

Chapter 7
WHO DO YOU LOVE?

Humphrey's kiss found its mark just as Sarah spun around to Derric, her mouth open in silent horror.

Did she just say my name?

As though it dawned on the prince in the same moment, he jerked back, halting the kiss.

"I'm sorry, but did you say—"

There was a loud popping noise, and Maria vanished. Sarah let out a soft scream, her hands flying to her mouth.

Where the princess had been standing, a large, beautiful, sleek black swan sat, shaking its feathers out. All attention fixated on the swan, which bobbled its head and blinked several times before looking up at them.

"Well, that was unexpected," the swan said with Maria's voice. "How'd you all get up there?" Maria the swan dropped her gaze to her feathered body and screeched. "A swan? No! Not again! I'm not supposed to be a swan!"

Her cries turned into panicked honking as Sarah tried to calm her down. If the two of them weren't in such hysterics, it might have been funny—a girl chasing a swan around the room with cries of "Oh, my lady" every few seconds.

"A swan! A swan!" Maria screeched, flapping her wings and rising into the air. Humphrey and Derric ducked low, and the prince reached into his pocket and drew out a watch on a chain.

"How odd, it's not midnight yet."

"That's what's odd?" Derric asked, losing his battle with laughter and snorting helplessly.

"Did you hear what she said? I don't think it was 'Humphrey.'"

"We'll figure this out. Sarah! Hang on, I have an idea. Princess, you need to calm down."

The swan, now spouting glorious silver tears, dropped back down to the ground and curled into herself, tucking her head back behind her wings.

"Excuse me, Maria?" Humphrey approached his future bride with tentative steps, and she peeked out from behind her wing. "Whom did you say you loved?"

With alarming speed, Maria reared up and launched herself at Humphrey, pecking at him as he ducked for cover.

"You turned me into a swan! You did this, and you ask me what I said? I AM A SWAN!"

"Whoa!" Derric launched forward, scooping Maria away from the prince. All at once, she grew heavier, and Derric found his arms wrapped around the princess, human once again.

"What on earth?" Derric released Maria at once.

From where he still crouched a few feet away, Humphrey peered through his arms, still raised, guarding his face. "Maria?"

"Does this mean the spell's broken?" Sarah asked, stepping up to Maria's side and guiding her back to the chaise. "Was that it?"

Derric watched Maria's face as she followed his sister. The pale and pinched expression suggested fear, not relief. Something wasn't right.

"Let's find out." Humphrey said, ever optimistic, dropping down to one knee before Maria again. "Marry me, Maria, because I love you."

"I will marry you, Derric. Because I—wait a minute."

"Who is Derric?" Humphrey cried, throwing his hands in the air and rising. "I'm going mad. I know it! Is my name Derric? No. No, it isn't!"

"Well, it isn't my fault!" Maria snapped, facing off with her prince. "I don't know who Derric is. Maybe your name should be Derric!"

Their argument continued as Sarah shoved Derric from the room, her face livid.

"What did you do?" she hissed as soon as they were out of earshot of the princess's chambers. "Why is she saying your name in there?"

"Is she saying Derricus? No, I think not. For all we know, there are hundreds of Derrics in the kingdom."

"You know she's saying *your* name. Now spill! What did you do? What's going on?"

"I didn't do anything!" Derric lied, his heart beating so fast he was sure Sarah could hear it. "This can't be my fault. It can't!"

Sarah squeezed her eyelids shut and pressed her fists against her temple. "There has to be a precedent of something like this in the histories."

"Sarah!" Maria's call drew their attention back to the chambers they'd left. "Sarah, I need you now!"

The two siblings returned to the royals, both of whom were red in the face and fuming.

"Tell him I don't know anyone named Derric. Tell him!"

"His name is Daniel," Sarah said, pointing at Derric, her eyes wide in panic.

"I don't care what his name is." Humphrey threw his arms into the air. "I want to know who Derric is."

"Why can I only say I'll marry Derricus Harver when I—" Maria stopped midsentence and rested her hand above her heart. "Oh dear heavens."

"What is it?" Humphrey's anger evaporated as Maria stumbled. Sarah rushed to her side and supported her.

"Harver. That's the name of the one who cursed me."

Derric's blood ran cold, and he stood still as Sarah shot him a warning look.

"You mean the sorcerer cursed you so you would only be able to marry him?" Humphrey gave a great sigh of disgust. "What a lowly devil."

"No, a sorceress." Maria frowned down at her hands.

"But I think she had a son, if I remember right. They fled after she cursed me and were never allowed to come back."

"Aha! She made it so you'd have to marry her son as a way to usurp the power of the kingdom!" Humphrey slapped his knee and nodded while Derric's world crumbled around him.

Had she done that? Or was it his mistake that had led them to this?

If it had been a Standard Kissing Clause, Derric's kiss when they were children would have broken Maria's curse, but it wouldn't have bound her to him. Had his mother planned on using him to obtain control over the kingdom?

"It's a binding, then," Sarah said, not meeting Derric's eye. "Daniel, my brother here . . . Daniel is his name . . . he's told me all about them."

Derric gritted his teeth, but Maria and Humphrey didn't seem to notice Sarah's odd behavior.

"A binding is the reason I'm turning into a swan?" Maria asked. The room grew quiet as all attention turned to her.

"Don't you always turn into a swan?"

At Sarah's question, Maria's face flushed, and she didn't make eye contact with any of them. "Of course. Yes. I've always turned into a swan. I just meant, is it a binding or a curse?"

"It's kind of like a clause," Sarah explained, as Derric watched Maria fidget with the sleeves of her dress.

"A binding is a curse that ties you to another person. It's much harder to break. In fact, it's nearly impossible."

"Nearly, but not completely impossible?" Humphrey resumed pacing the room. "What do we have to do? Find this Derric Harver and kill him?"

"No!" Sarah and Maria said together.

"That's a method that sometimes works," Derric said, feeling honesty might be his only option. "But the sorceress probably thought of it. If the person you're bound to fulfills the Happily-Ever-After Clause, you'd be set free."

"That means he'd have to fall in love and get married to someone else," Sarah clarified.

"Neither of those things seem like options." Maria rubbed her temples and sighed.

"Well, there are always loopholes."

Maria looked up, hope shining in her eyes. "Loopholes?" At his hesitation, she pressed him. "Maste—Daniel, whatever it is we need to do, I'll do it."

"You'll need to find the sorceress and have her remove the curse."

A Stolen Kiss

Chapter 8
A Broken Curse

. . . .

The momentary balloon of hope rising in Maria's chest deflated. Find the sorceress who cursed her?

"You're joking."

"I'm afraid not." Daniel didn't seem keen on the idea himself. "With magic this powerful, you have to have it undone from the source. You'd need to find her and either get her to tell you how the binding is meant to work, or have her remove the spell."

"She's not just going to remove the curse," Sarah said, folding her arms across her chest.

"She might. It would depend on why she cast it in the first place. Do you know?"

"I don't," Maria confessed. "No one's ever known why she targeted me. Do you think she'd tell me? How would I even begin to find her?"

"She was last known to be heading west. We could go with you and help. De—Daniel knows everything there is to know about magic and potions. He could help us find her by reading the magical footprints." Sarah beamed, but Maria saw Daniel shoot his sister a glare.

"It's settled, then." Humphrey clapped his hands together, his mouth twisting into a determined smile. "We'll leave first thing in the morning. I'll tell my parents you accepted, and we'll slip away before anyone can stop us. Daniel, you work in the stables? Have the horses ready by sunrise. Sarah, have the princess's bag packed and gather food from the kitchens. I'll get the necessary defensive equipment. My love," Humphrey bowed with gallant grace before her, "we'll find a way to end this curse."

"Yes, well . . . midnight is approaching, and we want to get as much sleep as possible." Maria ushered the men toward the door. "I'll see you in the morning. Goodnight!"

With the door closed, Maria rested her forehead against the polished wood. Behind her, Sarah rummaged through the armoire in search of traveling clothes. The sound of searching ceased.

"Maria?"

Maria twisted around, still resting against the door, and slid down it. Sarah abandoned her packing and knelt before her.

"We're going to figure this out. My brother has the knowledge, and Humphrey has the courage. Please don't be upset."

"I know. I think I'm just tired. Would it be possible to pack in the morning before we go?"

"Of course. Let me help you into your nightclothes, and then you can be off to sleep."

Once Sarah shut the door behind her, Maria let out an exasperated cry and fell face first onto her bed.

No. No. No. No. NO! How could this be happening?

All her life, she'd been patient and kept up appearances, only to have her hopes dashed against the jagged rocks of despair. What had she ever done to deserve this? Nothing!

Okay, maybe not nothing . . .

Maria rolled over onto her back, blowing a mess of stray strands of hair away from her face. Midnight ticked ever closer, and with each passing second, her stomach twisted. Would she turn into a swan again, as she had earlier? Had she gotten herself into this ugly mess with her lies? She'd forgotten how horrible and strange it felt to be a winged creature.

A Stolen Kiss

After all, she hadn't transformed in nearly nine years.

Midnight came and passed, and still Maria lay in human form. Exhaling the breath she hadn't realized she'd been holding, she shoved up from her bed and moved to the doors of her balcony. Though the night had cooled, she still felt warm as she surveyed what little she could see of her kingdom in the night's darkness.

Not a swan.

Why, then, had she transformed earlier?

The last time she could remember sprouting feathers, she'd been nine years old. That horrible year, each sunset meant she'd turn into a hideous little cygnet. Hating it as much as she did, she'd begged her parents to never let anyone be with her when she changed. Then one night, the sun set, and nothing happened.

Elated, Maria ran the length of the castle to the queen's chambers. Her mother's door stood ajar, and as Maria nudged it open, she overheard her mother and father speaking.

"We should be thankful," her mother said. "This curse has been a gift from the heavens. We have offers pouring in from all the neighboring kingdoms. Once we announced Maria's eligibility, princes were throwing their crowns into the ring."

She heard her father speak next. "Who knew a curse could save our kingdom? Once we choose a prince and they're both of age, he can break the curse, and we'll have a future king prepared to rule. It's the first sigh of relief I've been able to breathe since discovering the only child we'd be able to have was a girl."

"Such a shame," her mother agreed. "I guess we can see it as a blessing, then. If Gilda was going to curse us to have no more children, at least she made the child we had of use to us."

"You know, you might be on to something there, dear. Though I wish she would have told us why she was so angry. Might have saved us all of that banishment business we went through. It is rather aggravating to not have a royal sorceress anymore."

"Mm, quite. No way of getting her back, though. She didn't leave a forwarding address."

"The lynch mob might have prevented it," the king agreed. "Ah, well. No matter. When Maria turns eighteen, this will all be sorted out, and no one will have to worry about her being born a girl."

Crushed, Maria had returned to her room, locked the door, and wept into her pillow. Her parents hadn't wanted her, and she'd been cursed because they weren't happy with a girl. She wasn't good enough to rule the kingdom on her own. The curse would save her and her people.

A terrifying thought flitted through her young mind. If the potential princes knew her curse was broken, they wouldn't want to come and break it. No prince meant no king . . . and no king meant her parents might chuck her out as a useless failure for getting rid of the curse by herself.

From then on, Maria kept up the pretense. Each night, she shut herself away in her room and locked the door, pretending the curse still worked its magic over her. It wasn't until Humphrey arrived that things fell apart.

Now, everything was a giant mess, and she'd turned into a swan again. Restless, Maria pulled on her robe and swung her leg over the balcony edge, her toes finding purchase in the thick vines climbing the castle wall.

Tonight, she wanted to be free of her tower.

A Stolen Kiss

Chapter 9
Humphrey's Burden

. . . .

Derric stared down at the half-filled satchel. He'd stuffed everything he owned into it and still had more than enough room to double what was already in there.

"Do you think they'll come after us once they realize we've gone?" Sarah asked from her usual position on top of a hay bale. "And how long do you think it will take them to notice we aren't coming back?"

"There is no 'we.' You'll stay behind and tell the royals whatever Maria tells you to tell them." Derric said, closing up the satchel. "We'll be gone by first light, so I'm sure they'll notice when she isn't seen at breakfast."

"Maria never goes down for breakfast. She's under her curse until at least ten in the morning."

Derric paused, and a disbelieving smile twisted his lips. "Ten in the morning?"

"Yes. Why? What's so funny?"

"Nothing." Derric scrutinized the horses' saddles. "It's just, I've never heard of a curse lasting from midnight until ten o'clock in the morning. Curses like the princess's are almost always sunset to sunrise."

"Well, hers isn't."

"Then how are we supposed to leave at first light? Won't she still be a swan?"

When Sarah said nothing, Derric went about his work. Silence settled around them until Sarah yawned.

"I'd best be getting to bed. I have to get up early to finish packing for Maria. See you at first light, *Daniel*."

"You aren't coming," he shouted after her and turned to

make a final check of the saddlebags. With the food Sarah brought and the maps he had on hand of the lands of Opea and nearby, they'd be able to care for their needs. His mother had often gone over the maps with him, teaching him the herbs and spices that could be found for whatever ailment a man might have. He tucked them in his satchel and pushed aside the memories of his childhood.

"Master Digson?"

With a start, Derric turned around. Prince Humphrey stood in the stable doorway, his shoulders slumped and his mouth downturned.

"Your Highness." Derric bowed, and once again the prince waved him off.

"None of that. I don't particularly care for it. Please call me Humphrey, Master Digson."

Derric ground his teeth against the name. "In that case, you should call me . . . call me Daniel."

"Very well, Daniel."

They stood there in awkward silence, Derric watching Humphrey as his gaze moved around the stables.

"Nice place, this," he said after a while, his lips twitching. "Cozy. Horses. Like 'em?"

"Yeah, I suppose I do." Derric shifted his weight and folded his arms across his chest. "Is there something you needed?"

All at once, the prince crumpled. His face scrunched up, and he dropped down onto one of the crates near the door. Though no tears flowed forth, Humphrey let out a ragged, dry sob and shook his head.

"Need? Yes. I need to know if I'm doing the right thing. Am I doing the right thing?" He didn't wait for Derric's answer before continuing, "I'm the youngest of three sons. Maria's parents picked me from the lot of those vying for her hand. It's expected of me to become king over her land. I didn't even want to *be* a king! Mumsy and Dad have always pushed for that, but I wanted to be an actor! They want me to break this curse, but what if I can't? What if I'm a horrible king? What if I'm the least popular king ever, and every one of my subjects hates me? Would you want me as your king?"

Humphrey jumped to his feet and started pacing. "I'm expected to marry a girl I just met and live happily ever after with her. We were supposed to fall in love at first sight, right? But the thing is, I don't even know if I like her much right now. She attacked me! Look at the bite marks!"

Derric held still, perplexed as Humphrey waved his hand in front of his face. He wasn't sure what to say. Even if he did know, the prince wasn't stopping long enough to give him a chance to say anything anyway.

"I know princes are chivalrous and kind. I know a knight would do anything for his lady. I *want* to help Maria, but is it possible? You're the one who knows all about magic. Tell me, are we on a fool's errand, or do we stand a chance?"

The prince's energy had expended itself. He sagged, dropping back down onto the crate, and turned his basset hound gaze onto Derric.

"We're doing the right thing." Derric wasn't sure if he meant it or if it was just what Humphrey needed to hear. "I would do anything to help my princess."

Humphrey passed a hand over his face. "You're right. Even if I don't know how I feel about Maria, she needs our help. Man, I would hate turning into a swan every night. That has to be the worst."

"I don't know." Derric settled down next to Humphrey. "She could have turned into a badger. I think that would be worse."

A loud, booming laugh erupted from Humphrey, who leaned away and slapped Derric hard on the back. "A badger! Good one! That *would* be worse."

"You know," Derric said, a grin tugging at one corner of his mouth. "For not even being sure if you like her, you fooled me today with your speech. I think you even had my sister weak in the knees."

Humphrey gave a modest toss of his head. "I'm an actor. It's what I do."

"Maybe that's our problem. Maybe it still is a True Love's Kiss Clause. After all, magic can always tell if you're acting."

"It can? Damn. I thought I'd been convincing enough."

"No, magic always knows what's in the heart." Derric tapped the place above his own, and Humphrey nodded.

"So either I actually fall in love with Maria, and we see if that works, or we go find the sorceress and get her to sort this out."

"Right."

"Well then, I suppose there's no use waiting around to fall in love. Let's get to finding a sorceress." He clapped Derric on the back and stood. "Thanks, mate. I feel better. I'm not used to traveling without my own manservant, but he married last month and is off on his honeymoon. The one they gave me here at the castle is a right ol' curmudgeon. Not the one to share a heart-to-heart with. Anyway, see you in the morning."

With that, Humphrey turned on his heel and strode out of the stables. Derric sat in stunned silence. Maybe being royalty didn't make someone much different from him after all.

Chapter 10
WATER FOUL

. . . .

Maria ducked out of sight behind a low stone wall as Humphrey made his way back to the castle. To her horror, he stopped just above her and leaned against the wall, looking out over the pond bathed in moonlight.

"I'm doing this for you, Maria," he said as he hurled something out toward the pond. It hit the water with a soft plop and sank. Heart hammering, Maria pressed harder against the wall, certain he didn't know she was there. With a sigh, Humphrey rested his forearms against the wall, his fingers dangling just above her head.

After what felt like an eternity, Humphrey moved away and headed back into the castle. Maria pulled away from the wall and headed toward the stables. She had to tell *someone* her secret before they started on their journey—she needed an ally. Part of her wanted to tell Sarah, the closest friend she had, but she already felt guilty enough for lying this long. Somehow, the thought of coming clean felt worse than continuing the lie.

Telling Sarah's brother, though, made sense. He knew the most about magic, and he might know why her curse would come and go. Besides, knowing all of the facts might help him figure out why she couldn't say yes to Humphrey—maybe they wouldn't even have to leave at all. Butterflies tumbled in her stomach, betraying her uncertainty about visiting a young man she wasn't betrothed to.

Taking a deep, steadying breath, she raised a fist to knock on the stable door and gave a gasp of surprise. No fist, but feathers.

When did I change? Maria glanced behind her, as if she'd see a shimmer of magic or a place in the ground where her tread turned from footprints to webbed prints. On such a dry night, not a trace could be found.

With an indignant huff, Maria dropped down to the ground, tucking her feet under her and tapping her beak with her wingtip. She could head into the stable as planned, but would it do any good to go to him now and claim she hadn't turned into a swan in years?

The glimmering pond caught her attention. A little flurry of excitement swirled in her stomach. It'd been ages since she'd been for a midnight swim.

Resolving to have a conversation with Daniel first thing in the morning, Maria flew off to the pond. As her feet touched down on the cool water, a shiver ran through her body. Oh, the luxury of a pond! Maria kicked her webbed feet and soared around the length of the pool. As she rounded for another lap, something twinkled in the moonlight beneath her. Through the clear water, Maria could make out something resting at the bottom of the shallow end of the pond.

Was this what Humphrey threw? Glancing swiftly around to ensure she was alone, Maria sucked in a breath and plunged face first into the water, her feathered rear end poking up above the surface. Stretching her neck as far as it would go, she strained for the little glimmering thing, the water just murky enough to obscure it.

She clamped her beak around it, surprised to find it flat and hard. As she pulled her head back, water flooded her mouth and nose, causing her to choke. Something heavy wrapped around Maria's legs, dragging her down into the water. Panic swelled as she fought to reach the top, swinging her arms in wild motions.

Arms?

Her face broke the surface, and she pulled the object from her mouth to expel a mouthful of water and suck in a shuddering gasp of air. Hair wrapped around her face, obscuring her vision, and she tried to give a shout for help as she was pulled under again. She'd started in the shallower end of the pond but had somehow been dragged further north into the deep waters. Her robe weighed heavy on her, tangling up in her legs and erasing any hope of treading water. Maria tugged at the ties even as her lungs burned for lack of oxygen.

Dark shadows pricked the edges of her vision, and everything turned hazy. Just as Maria felt her will to fight slipping away, a loud splashing noise awakened her sense of survival. Arms wrapped around her, pushing off of the muddy ground and sending them both skyward. Lungs aching and head spinning, Maria fought to hold her breath just a few seconds longer.

Almost.

Almost.

Cold air stung her face as she broke the surface, her rescuer still holding her tight and dragging her backward to the shore. Part of her still-whirring brain urged Maria to help, kick her feet or something, to expedite the process, but she couldn't bring herself to move.

With little to no tenderness, her savior heaved her onto the grassy edge and collapsed beside her. Maria stared up at the starry night sky, still trying to understand what had just happened, all the while relishing the taste of the clean night air—even if it did cause her to cough and her lungs to burn as it repaired her addled brain.

"What . . . the . . . hells were you thinking?" she heard her savior ask, his voice full of frustration. "Why did you jump into the water in your nightclothes? Are you mad? Do you have a death wish?"

Still wheezing, Maria tried to find her voice, tried to explain what she'd been doing, but fatigue claimed her tongue. How long had she been in the water? It had felt like both a single second and an eternity. He leaned over her, a grimace etched into his lips. Maria blinked, trying to remember why she knew him.

"Maria? Can you hear me? Great, you're as cold as death. I need to get you out of here."

With little effort, he lifted her from the ground and carried her back toward the castle. To her surprise, he veered left, away from the stone palace, and headed toward the stables. Recognition clicked into place.

That's right. He's Daniel, the stableboy.

Daniel carried her through the stable door and stood her on her feet. "You need out of this robe."

She watched as he fumbled with the knot, tightened from its time in the water. She was struck with an absurd urge to giggle, and as the chuckle escaped her lips, Daniel's face flamed red. Without saying a word, he disentangled the knot and peeled the soaking wet fabric from her icy skin. Still ignoring her gaze, he draped a blanket over her shoulders and secured it before settling her down against one of the sleeping horses—her sleeping horse, Verona. He woke the beast up and instructed her to lie down so Maria could rest against her.

The heat from Verona's body seeped through the blanket, reviving Maria's awareness. For the first time, she realized how cold she'd been, and shivers wracked her body. Daniel knelt before her, rubbing the blanket around her arms in an attempt to generate warmth. His jaw quivered with cold, and it dawned on her that, amidst his care for her wellbeing, he remained soaking wet.

"Y-you need a blanket," she said, sitting up straighter and peering around the stable.

"I'm fine."

"You are n-not!" She craned her neck in search of warmth for Daniel, but aside from what already draped the horses on such a late, autumn evening, there didn't seem to be much else. Frustration rising, Maria turned back to Daniel. "Where do you live?"

Her question caught him off guard, and his eyebrows arched up toward his dripping sandy blond hair. "Here, Your Highness."

"Here. The stables?" When he nodded, she had to hold back a snort of angry disgust. "Well then, where's your bed? Your blanket? You must have one."

"I do, my lady."

"Then where is it?"

A smile pulled at the corner of Daniel's mouth. "You've got it."

A moment passed as Maria stared at Daniel, his words sinking in. Not only had he saved her from the depths of the pond, but he'd given her his own bedding to keep her warm while he sat shivering in front of her.

"Well then," she said, losing steam as she felt blood rush to her face. "Thank you." They sat in silence for several seconds more, holding each other's gaze.

"May I ask why you went into the pond in your nightclothes?"

A smirk tugged at Maria's lips. He'd calmed down and no longer felt the need to swear at her it would seem. "I didn't."

Daniel's eyes widened, and his brows formed a hard line. "Did someone throw you in? Who? I'll get the guard right away and—"

"No, no. Nothing like that. I wasn't in my bedclothes when I went into the pond." The look on Daniel's face kept her talking, afraid he had the wrong impression. "I mean, I was a swan. I was taking a nighttime swim in my feathers, and I dove in to grab something on the bottom, but I changed back into myself."

"You changed back?" Daniel sat back on his heels, a quizzical expression settling on his face. "Why do you keep changing back?"

It was obvious he wasn't addressing her, and for the first time Maria realized she still held whatever it was

Humphrey had thrown into the pond in her right hand. Daniel continued to mutter to himself as he moved away from her and started searching for something. Pulling her arm out from the blanket, Maria inspected what turned out to be a tiny silver-framed portrait.

Behind the waterlogged glass, a lovely young woman stared up at Maria with wide, amber eyes. Her hair had fiery hues with darker lowlights, and while she had a sweet smile, something secret hid behind her twinkling gaze.

Who is she? And what was she to Humphrey that he would dispose of her portrait. What had he said just before? That he was doing it for me?

Maria opened her mouth and looked up, hoping to ask Daniel's opinion, but her words died on her tongue as she watched him. He'd removed his wet shirt and tousled his sandy hair. His fit physique and square shoulders were distraction enough, but it was what he was doing that kept her silent.

Daniel's eyes were closed, and his mouth moved, uttering silent words. Each arm occupied itself with pointing and gesturing, as if Daniel mapped something out only he could see. His eyebrows scrunched low in concentration as his gesticulations gained steam, and he started to pace back and forth.

"But if she wasn't a swan, then the curse would be broken. She's a swan sometimes when she's supposed to be and sometimes when she's not. But why? What about a kiss would do this? And which kiss? The first kiss or the second kiss?"

"We only kissed once," Maria reminded him, snapping him out of his reverie. Daniel jumped, eyelashes fluttering as he returned to the present.

"I'm sorry. I was just . . . just thinking."

"Yes, but Humphrey only kissed me once." She stood and pulled the blanket from her shoulders, handing it back to him. The portrait, cold against her skin, still rested in her right hand. Daniel accepted the blanket and draped it over one arm.

All at once, Maria considered what this would look like if an outsider entered the stable to check why there was a light burning within. There she stood in her nightgown with a young man in his breeches. Horror filled her, and she ran for the door, scooping her wet robe up as she went.

"I've got to go. Thank you for saving me!"

"Wait, I'll walk you back. You shouldn't be alone at night." Daniel moved to join her, but she let out a soft shriek.

"NO! I mean, no. It wouldn't be appropriate. You're uh . . . and I'm . . . well. We can't be seen like this."

Daniel glanced down at his bare torso, and his head snapped up, eyes wide. "Princess, I'm so sorry."

"Don't be sorry," Maria snapped, peering out the stable door to make sure no one was around to see her. "You saved my life. And for heavens' sake, call me Maria. I do think you've earned the right after tonight. Goodnight, Daniel!"

Quick as she could, Maria sprinted into the cold night, suppressing another exclamation as the frigid air whipped about her. Even as she climbed the vines back to her tower, cursing herself for her foolishness the whole evening, a secret thrill fluttered through her chest.

Humphrey might have his secret portrait—something she'd get to the bottom of—but as she changed into a dry nightdress and climbed into bed, Maria couldn't help but relish the adorableness of Daniel, shirtless, trying to work out her curse for her.

Chapter 11
WESTWARD BOUND

. . . .

The horses stood ready just outside the stable as the first beam of sunlight snuck into the darkness, casting an orangey-pink hue on the overcast clouds. Derric forwent sleep after Maria left, his mind tumbling over different ideas and possibilities. Few things were solid in the murky bog of magical intrigue they floundered in. Derric pulled out parchment and quill and spent the wee hours of the morning chronicling the important points:

1. ~~MOTH~~ GILDA HARVER CURSED MARIA.
2. GILDA BOUND MARIA TO ~~THE~~ DERRIC IN ORDER TO RUIN HER CHANCES AT BREAKING THE CURSE (SO SHE COULD GAIN ACCESS TO THE THRONE?).
3. MARIA IS TURNING INTO A SWAN, BUT IT SEEMS FAULTY AND INCONSISTENT.
4. ~~MY MISTAKE HAS NOTHING TO DO WITH ANY OF THIS.~~

Blushing, Derric crossed off the final point and drew a line in order to make a list of the things he *didn't* understand.

1. MARIA DOESN'T STAY A SWAN—WHAT IS CAUSING HER TO CHANGE BACK AND FORTH?
2. WHAT WAS GILDA'S MOTIVATION? SHE WASN'T EVER THE MALICIOUS TYPE.
3. WHY DOES GILDA WANT DERRIC TO BE BOUND TO MARIA?
4. WHERE IS GILDA HARVER?

Derric sighed and folded the note, slipping it in snug with the maps in his bag. A sound behind him turned his attention to Maria, Sarah, and Humphrey—only the latter looking wide awake and ready to ride.

"So, which way are we going?" Humphrey asked, keeping his voice low.

"You're asking me?" Derric turned to Sarah and Maria. Both of them were watching Derric in eager anticipation.

"Of course!" Humphrey's grin broadened. "You're the brains of this operation. You're the one who can . . . what did you say it was, Sarah? 'Follow the magical footprints'?"

"Right," Derric said, falling into thought. Where *should* they begin? Quiet conversation continued behind him as he moved to his bag and removed the maps his mother gave him so many years ago.

Edleton was the royal city of Opea. Opea sat at the center of four countries, with Dellsby to the south and east, Braskey to the north, and Kyleria to the west. Dellsby, though the largest and the easiest to hide in, already had a royal sorcerer and many more throughout the villages. Braskey wasn't accessible, blocked by the Tranchet Mountains.

She wouldn't go to Braskey. The thought sprang forward as soon as he entertained the idea. *Dellsby is too friendly with Opea. She's in Kyleria.*

A chill ran down his spine, and he shuddered. For nearly a century, Kyleria and Opea had balanced on the brink of war, teetering like a boulder on a cliff's edge— waiting for one tiny push to knock it over. Thirty years of strained peace lay between them now, a silence honored on both sides. The princess of Opea and a prince from Dellsby wouldn't be welcome in those lands.

But that's where she'd go—somewhere no one from Opea would follow. This thought tingled with magic, and Derric knew it showed him the way. To enter Kyleria, they would have to be stealthy, and the path wouldn't be easy. After all, one of the reasons the two countries never went to war was the treacherous terrain between them.

"...all of the time."

"How long before he comes back?"

Derric blinked and looked up. His three companions watched him. Sarah shook her head with a smile and moved to her horse. "Okay, he's back. Let's go."

"Whoa, whoa, whoa." Derric moved to block her path. "I told you—you aren't coming. You're fourteen, and this might be dangerous."

"You're eighteen, and you can't tell me what to do."

Derric gripped her shoulders. "I'm serious. You can't come. Father will be furious if he finds out I let you—"

"Like you care what Father thinks. You don't even like him." Sarah pulled away from Derric's grip. "Besides, I'm not afraid."

"You should be."

"A woman can do anything a man can do." Sarah straightened, her chin in the air.

"You sound like your mother."

"No." She stared straight up at him, a fierce glint in her eyes as she whispered. "I sound like *yours*."

He gaped at her, realizing she was right. Sarah never aimed to be like her own mother, often feeling as detached from her as he felt from their father.

"Daniel, I need Sarah." Maria moved up to his sister's side. "I want her along."

He grimaced, but gave a curt nod. A little thrill shot through his heart at the thought of having her along—they never had enough time together. Sarah gave a triumphant grin and stepped past Derric to her horse. It occurred to him he'd gotten four horses ready—not three.

Maria and Humphrey still stared at him, Humphrey's head cocked to the side. Blushing, Derric moved to Thumper and pulled up onto the workhorse's saddle. Humphrey, once mounted, rode up beside him.

A Stolen Kiss

"Where to?"

"West."

Humphrey's eyebrows arched, and he gave a soft nod of his head. "West." He cast a final glance over his shoulder, and when Derric followed his gaze, he saw nothing but the castle pond, glinting in the first rays of sunlight.

They rode for eight hours without conflict, engaging in casual conversation and laughter. Sarah teased Derric, while Humphrey remarked on the different sights of Opea he wished he could have enjoyed. Maria remained silent, casting a shrewd gaze at the countryside as they passed through two separate villages. Stomachs rumbled just before they exited the second town, and they stopped to buy food at an inn.

"You can't go in," Sarah told the royals. "You'll be spotted."

"What's wrong with being spotted?" Humphrey asked. "We left notes last minute saying Maria was going to show me about and not to expect us until late. All very clever, if I do say so myself."

"Perhaps, but if anyone comes here to ask questions, it would be best if there weren't any locals who could say which way you went. Ride on to the grassy outskirts of town, and we'll meet you with the food."

Derric stifled a laugh when he heard Humphrey mutter, "She's rather bossy" as he took his leave.

"I don't see why we couldn't have just used the food we brought." Sarah flipped her caramel braided hair behind her. "Isn't that the reason you had me bring all that food from the kitchens?"

"That's for when we're in the middle of nowhere without a town to camp in. While there's food to be bought and royals with moneybags as large as you are tall, we'll buy our meals."

Twenty minutes later, they sat amongst a pleasant picnic in the grassy hills of the western countryside.

"We're going west." Maria didn't ask, but stated, as her gaze narrowed at Derric.

"Yes, that's true."

"Why?" Maria's tone wasn't welcoming or curious, but hard as steel.

Derric glanced at Humphrey, whose eyes widened. He shook his head, declining to offer any help as he bit off a large bite of his chicken leg and gestured to his loaded mouth as an excuse not to speak.

"The magic leads us west," Derric said, opting for short honesty rather than drawn out explanations.

"West as in western Opea? Because there are very few villages left between here and the border, so our journey will be a quick one." She pursed her lips in challenge, and Derric sighed.

"Your Highness—"

"Maria."

"Maria, we're headed to Kyleria."

Silence fell heavy upon them as Sarah and Maria processed what Humphrey and Derric had already come to terms with.

"But," Sarah began, "isn't that dangerous? It's hardly a place to take our princess—something horrible could happen!"

"This journey never claimed to be an easy or safe one," Humphrey reminded her, having swallowed his food. "Anything worth having is worth struggling to achieve."

"Maybe for my brother, or even for a prince, but this is the future queen I'm sworn to serve! We can't go traipsing about dangerous forests, bogs, and swamps! Let alone gallivanting into foreign and hostile territory and asking for an inn to stay the night, 'And oh, by the way, we're looking for the sorceress who fled here after ruining the princess of Opea's life. Have you seen her?'"

"Fine." Humphrey gestured to the horses. "Go back. Daniel and I will continue on, and, assuming we find the sorceress, we'll just have to figure out a way to capture her or convince her to return with us, since she'll need to be in Maria's presence to remove the curse."

"How can you allow this?" Sarah turned to Derric. "She's your princess, too. How can you expect her to put her life at such risk? Or any of us for that matter?"

"I told you not to come! Did you think it would all be a picnic?" Derric shot back. "You're all for women doing everything men do, little sister, but as soon as that thought is tested you turn tail and run."

"That's not what I meant—"

"We're going with them."

All attention turned to Maria. She didn't look at any of them, but picked at the hem of her simple day dress.

"Maria," Sarah began, but Maria shook her head.

"It seems fitting my enemy would be in enemy territory," she said, a rueful smile playing on her lips. "It wouldn't be right for me to remain at home and let others fight my battle. Daniel's right. I believe in order for a woman to be taken seriously—especially a woman who is destined to become queen—she must first be willing to cross whatever bridge she needs to. No one in Kyleria knows what Humphrey or I look like, so we won't be in danger of being recognized. No, the danger we'll face will happen long before we cross into a Kylerian town."

Her grin widened as she raised her head to look at them. "I, for one, have been dying for a bit of adventure."

Humphrey straightened where he sat, beaming at her like a proud father. Sarah stared at the princess in open awe and veneration. Derric, on the other hand, nodded to Maria, approval flitting across his face.

"To Kyleria," he said, raising his drink. The other three raised theirs in response.

"To Kyleria."

Chapter 12
PRIDE AND PANTS

. . . .

They decided to rent rooms at an inn when they reached a village on the outskirts of the wilds. An hour of sunlight remained, and Maria wasn't about to waste it.

"Gentlemen, please get us appropriate lodgings. Sarah, come with me."

"Where are we going?" Sarah asked, whirling around as the inn's stablehand led the horses away.

"There's a tailor across the street here. We're going to see if they have any pairs of pants for young men that might fit us."

Sarah's mouth popped open, her eyes going wide. "We're going to do what?"

Frowning, Maria repeated herself, and Sarah emphatically shook her head until the princess growled in agitation.

"Sarah, I am not going to trek through the wildlands in a dress. Between Fangralee Forest and the Mortal Marsh, a dress will only hinder us. We'll spend more time being weighed down or held back than we will moving forward."

"But . . . but . . . " Sarah stared around to Humphrey and Daniel for help. "It's unladylike!" When Maria only raised an eyebrow, she pushed on. "You're the princess of Opea. You aren't meant to wear men's clothing."

"And yet I'm going to. I'm the princess, so I get to decide what I wear. I decide to wear pants."

Sarah grunted in frustration. "Fine, you choose to wear pants, but you're still royalty. A common tailor won't have anything suitable for you. They won't have the fabrics you're accustomed to. You aren't used to wearing linens and rough wools. That isn't what the royal tailor uses for your clothing. You'll be uncomfortable."

A small smile twisted Maria's lips. "Are we talking about me or you? I might have to adjust, but this trip is already far from comfortable. I have a feeling it's going to get a lot worse before it gets better. Besides, we need to save our dresses for when we reach Kyleria."

Quieted for a moment, Sarah pursed her lips. "All right. Yes, I admit I don't want to wear pants. I am *a lady's maid*. I didn't take a job at the castle to wear commoners' clothes. If that makes me a bad person, I'm sorry."

Maria laughed, pulling Sarah into a hug. "Oh, my dear friend. I don't think it makes you a bad person."

They pulled apart, and Maria caught Humphrey looking at Sarah with something that hinted strongly at disappointment. Daniel busied himself checking the bags.

"You're offended by commoners' clothing?" Humphrey asked, his lip puckering out and his brows knit together. His gaze flickered to Daniel and then back to Sarah.

"Girls don't wear pants unless their families can't afford dresses. Besides, the poorer the class, the itchier the fabric—nobody likes to have itchy pants. I'd think we're better than that."

"You think ... you think you're better than your brother?"

Daniel stilled over the last bag, facing away from them. Maria could see his shoulders stiffen, and she placed a hand on Sarah's shoulder. For a moment, everything was quiet.

"I'd never thought of it that way," Sarah said, her voice hoarse. "Of course not. I think he is the best person I know."

Humphrey nodded, though his brows remained furrowed, and he turned away to join Daniel on his way into the inn. Maria looped her arm through Sarah's and gave her friend a sympathetic smile.

"Come on. We'll go get a few pairs of trousers each—for me to wear while we're in the wilds and for you once you realize I'm right about the advantage of wearing trousers." When Sarah didn't perk up at the joke, Maria gave her a little shake. "Don't fret. Humphrey and Daniel will have forgotten this conversation before we return. Daniel knows how much you love him."

"Are his clothes made of itchy fabric?" Sarah's tone was pinched as if she fought back tears. "Is that what he's been forced to wear in the stables?"

"If he wants new pants, we'll buy him new pants. Would that make it better?" She patted Sarah's soft hair, giving the younger girl another squeeze. "It's never a bad idea to buy someone a gift."

When they returned, Maria and Sarah had two pairs of trousers each and another two for Daniel. The tailor and his wife had found pairs intended for a young man, not much larger than they were, who had died in a plow accident the week before. Before they left the store, Sarah acquired the name of the boy's family and asked Maria if they'd be able to send some money or a gift of condolence to them.

"I just think something from the royal family might . . . might ease their pain."

"That's a lovely idea, Sarah. We'll do it first thing in the morning before we set out. They would receive the same sort of treatment if they came before my father in the throne room if the accident caused them financial hardship. Why not take care of it ourselves!" She glanced up at the sky as they exited the shop. "Oh my, let's hurry. The sun's almost set, and I'd rather not turn into a swan in the street."

"I thought you didn't turn until midnight."

Maria pretended she didn't hear, running back toward the inn, dragging Sarah along in her wake.

A Stolen Kiss

Chapter 13
WILLING TO LOSE

. . . .

erric and Humphrey turned in after the girls left for the tailor. After traveling for fourteen hours—and riding for over twelve of them—their bodies were feeling the exhaustion. Derric was accustomed to hard labor, but the soreness in his legs from straddling the horse all day zinged into his thoughts.

Humphrey, while used to long journeys on horseback, wasn't adjusted to the less-than-pampered ride. Still, after hearing Sarah complain about fabrics and commoners, Humphrey did everything in his power to not utter a word of complaint. Noting Humphrey's self-restraint, Derric did his best to be a serviceable valet.

Humphrey insisted he'd visit the tailor first thing before they left in the morning. "I'm certain my clothes would stand out like a sore thumb amongst the commoners in Kyleria. If we're caught, we'll all be in trouble. Maria and Sarah's day dresses will blend in, but this," Humphrey held up the silk cravat, "will obviously denote my nobility. It even has the family crest on it. No, I need new clothes."

"Then perhaps we ought to go to an actual shop," Derric suggested. At Humphrey's confused look, he explained. "Tailors make clothing custom. In a shop, you can buy premade clothing and then, if you have the money, take them to a tailor to fit them to you."

"Perfect!" Humphrey pulled back the covers on his bed. They'd acquired two rooms with two beds each. He paused just before slipping in. "Do you think we ought to check on the young ladies to make sure they're safely in their rooms before we go straight to sleep?"

Derric blinked and nodded. "Yes, I . . . I guess. Here, I'll do it. I'm still dressed." He headed for the door. This prince continued to surprise him; Derric wouldn't have thought to check on Maria and Sarah—a side-effect of his many years on his own in the stable, perhaps. Humphrey wasn't as stuck-up or lofty as Derric had assumed when he saw him ride past the stable yesterday.

Yesterday.

Derric shook his head as he stepped into the hall. It'd been some time since the girls had left, and with the sun dropping, he had no doubt they'd be back soon. Sure enough, he saw them rushing through the main entrance as soon as he reached the open staircase. Each held a brown paper package in her arms as they sprinted up the steps.

Maria let out a shriek of surprise as she hit the top step and noticed Derric for the first time. Sarah collided into her from behind, and both went flying, sprawling out at Derric's feet in a fit of giggles.

"You scared me!" Maria rasped between peals of laughter. "Hurry! Help us up."

"We got our pants." Sarah rolled about beneath him like a drunken loon. "We got you some too!"

"Help me up. I'll be in feathers soon."

Derric complied, hooking his arms under Maria's and lifting her to her feet. He repeated the routine with Sarah and gestured towards the room next to his and Humphrey's. They started through the door and jerked backwards almost at once, their shrieks of laughter returning.

"What?" Derric bolstered them both as they nearly fell over once more.

"My . . . dress . . . is . . . caught," Maria said with tears in her eyes. "On the door."

Sure enough, a few threads on the hem of her skirt hooked around the hinge. Derric crouched down to remove the hitch, but it disappeared before he could reach it.

"What in the—?" He jerked back. On the floor just

inside the room, Maria the swan sat with a sigh, black feathers ruffled.

"Oh my." Sarah rushed forward and crouched down before the swan. "Is the transformation painful?"

"Honestly, no. I don't even feel it."

"What happens to your clothes?" Derric asked from the door, his gaze moving back to the hinge her dress had caught on.

"They change to my feathers. Transformation all in one. At least the sorceress—"

"Gilda. Her name's Gilda." Derric winced as soon as he realized he'd corrected her.

"Yes, well, Gilda the sorceress was at least kind enough not to leave me in my bare skin each morning when I transform back."

Frowning, Derric nodded. "That is a kindness. I've never heard of the clothes transforming with the cursed. Usually, a curse is meant to embarrass the individual as much as possible." He straightened and took a step back. "Well, I'll see you both early in the morning. We'll head out before the sun takes its morning height. Humphrey wants to check in at a shop before we go to acquire a few less obvious pieces of clothing."

"Wait!" Sarah pulled open her paper package, holding up a pair of trousers far too large for her slight frame. "We got you these—well, Maria got them for you. They're really nice, not itchy at all!"

"I only paid for them. Sarah picked them out from the tailor's stock of 'no-shows' after giving your measurements."

Stunned, Derric accepted both pairs. They appeared to be made from cotton—the material most of Sarah's dresses were made from. "Thank you," he said, unable to think of much else to say. Sarah rushed over and threw her arms around him, giving him a tight squeeze.

He entered his own room to find Humphrey staring straight up at the ceiling, mouthing something. At Derric's entrance, he turned his head and gave him a look so serious it reminded Derric of when he got into trouble with his father as a boy.

"Daniel, do you think it is more important to give everything for your country, or do you think a man is entitled to his own life, regardless of what station he's born into?"

Derric closed the door behind him and dropped onto his own bed. For a few moments, he contemplated the prince's question. Was he on this path for his country or to assuage his own guilt?

"I think—I think a man must decide for himself. What's most important to him? Is it his country? Then he should do what's best for his country. The question is what he's willing to lose in order to have what he wants."

Humphrey nodded. "You're right. What is he willing to lose?"

A honk sounded, and they both jumped. A fit of giggles followed through the paper-thin walls. As the giggles died down, Humphrey asked in a much quieter whisper, "Have you figured out the whole swan/princess thing? Why she turned into a swan when I kissed her?"

Derric shook his head as he ducked under the covers and blew out the candle. "I think this is the strangest curse I've ever heard of. The rules aren't clear, and there seems to be more than one hidden clause. If I had to guess, I would think there's more than one thread of magic involved."

"What do you mean?"

"Well, a standard spell—even with a True Love Clause—has to follow the rules. For Maria to change into a swan when you kissed her makes me think there might be two conflicting magics at work. But I'm not sure yet. It's hard to tell this early."

"Two magics? Like another sorcerer?" Humphrey sounded angry. "Do you think Kyleria could have taken advantage of Maria's cursed state?"

"It's likely. They have more sorcerers per capita than

anywhere I know, and we suspect they granted Gilda asylum when she fled Opea. The thing is, a sorcerer would have had to get close to Maria to curse her a second time. It would have to have been a discreet mission."

"If we can find Gilda," Humphrey whispered, making a sound like he'd rolled over in his bed to face Derric, "and she removes the curse, would we be able to break the second curse on our own, or would we need to find whoever cast it?"

"We should be able to figure it out on our own."

"Good. I'm not sure how long we can traipse around the world for the sake of Maria's feathers before I tell my parents to go stuff themselves so I can marry—" Humphrey broke off, and a tense silence filled the air. "Marry someone who doesn't need saving," he finished, though Derric could tell that wasn't what he'd been about to say.

"We'll figure this out. Everyone will get their happily-ever-after just like in the history books." Derric heard Humphrey give a soft snort and decided not to ask.

"I suppose we should get some sleep. Goodnight, Daniel."

"Night, Humphrey."

Chapter 14
Sarah's Dolly

. . . .

Maria and Sarah woke early and went about filling a nice basket to take to the family who had lost their son. Confident the royal guard would never think to look so close to Kyleria, Maria didn't feel guilty that they weren't setting out from the little village of Brent right away.

Sarah went into the first shop on her own, Maria still waiting for all of her feathers to disappear. She'd forgotten how often a few would remain behind, needing to be plucked before she felt presentable. They perused the second and third shops together, creating a large basket teeming with breads, meats, cheeses, and a new dolly Sarah picked out for the little sister.

"I got one of those when Derric's mother—" She froze mid-step, and Maria jerked back when the basket they were both carrying halted too.

"Did you just say Derric?" Maria's heart sped up, and she let the basket drop the short distance to the ground. "Derric as in Harver?" Sarah had a terrified, guilty look on her face, and Maria narrowed her gaze. "Sarah? I insist you tell me right now what Derric's mother has to do with you getting a doll."

Silence prickled Maria's nerves as Sarah struggled before speaking. "Derric—Derric Harver's mother is the reason D-aniel's mother isn't here anymore."

Maria blinked, taken aback. "What? How? Wait, you and Daniel don't have the same mother?"

"No, we don't." Sarah stared down at her feet, brows

furrowed. "I shouldn't have said anything. He doesn't like people to know."

"Who would understand better than I would? Please, you must tell me."

Chewing on her lip for a moment longer, Sarah seemed committed to silence. Just as Maria bent down to grab hold of the abandoned basket, Sarah spoke.

"Gilda Harver is the reason Daniel doesn't have a mother anymore. It happened when he was eight and I was almost five. I don't remember all of the details, and he won't talk about it, but it had something to do with magic."

She said it in such a rush Maria almost missed it. When Sarah finished, she reached down and grabbed her handle of the basket. For a while they didn't say anything to each other.

"If Daniel's mother didn't die until you were five, how is it you were ever even born?"

"Our father never married Daniel's mother." Sarah spoke in a light tone, but Maria felt the shame of such a statement and regretted asking. Sarah pressed on. "He was bewitched—by her beauty, I mean—but it was short lived. They were young and foolish for a few weeks one summer. By the time he found out about Daniel, when Daniel turned one, he'd already married my mother. Daniel's mother raised him, but each Sunday he would come dine with us. Those were my favorite days. I think that's why Daniel and I are so close, because it was always a treat for me to see him."

"And he came to live with you after she died?"

Here, Sarah hesitated once again. "At first. He still came for Sunday dinners, at least for a while, but Father sent him to the stables to learn a trade."

"Your father sent an eight-year-old boy?" Maria asked, trying to hide her shock and disapproval. It wasn't un-common for boys as young as ten to begin learning their father's craft, but to send an eight-year-old just after his mother died? And to the stables, no less?

"Well, Father wanted us both to be able to make our way in the world and especially for us to do so in the castle. With my mother's connections, I was able to become one of your lady's maids. My brother, though, had no such connections. I think Father always hoped he would find his way into a grander position through hard work. It just hasn't happened yet."

"It will." Maria gave a curt nod. "I will make sure of it. We'll have him recruited into the King's Guard as soon as we return."

"Oh, my lady. He would love that so much!"

"Quit calling me 'my lady,' Sarah."

"But we're in public." Maria shot her a quelling look. "Yes, Maria."

Dropping off the basket gave Maria such a warm feeling of accomplishment. She knew, as soon as she returned home curse-free, she would start handling throne room matters and meeting with her subjects. No longer would she hide away the way her parents had forced her to. No, she would embrace her people and hope they would love her in return.

Never in all of her life had Maria been hugged so tight as when Martha, the mother of the young man who had died, wrapped her in her arms.

"Oh, my ladies," she said through teary sobs. "Thank you. Thank you so much. It's been horrible without him. Every day I wake up, and, for a few moments, I think it's all been a bad dream. And then I remember, and the grief is all new." She hugged Maria again, and the princess's heart broke for the poor woman.

She and Sarah hardly said anything as they made their way back to the inn. They'd need to leave soon, but Maria felt she was taking a piece of Martha's pain with her. As she walked, she thought of Daniel. What would it have been like to lose your mother so young, or at all? Her parents weren't the warmest of souls, but they loved Maria in their way. It was the silly little things, like the way the king would bring her a painting from wherever he'd traveled or the way the queen would wink at her whenever one of the nobles did something boring or stuffy.

Her heart ached for Daniel. In truth, she knew next to nothing about him, but the pain he'd suffered—being ostracized and alone at such a young age—felt like something she could understand. He never said much, and what he did say always seemed to be for someone else's benefit. She'd never talked to him, not really. As they rounded the last corner turning onto the inn's street, Maria resolved to do just that—to have a conversation with Daniel focused solely on him. A warm, fluttery feeling bounced around in her stomach, the same feeling she'd had after first meeting him. With her lips pulling into a small smile, Maria looped her arm through Sarah's and walked a little quicker.

Chapter 15
Derric's Diary

. . . .

Derric went with Humphrey to a shop that sold men's clothing while the girls went on mission to find a basket, whatever that meant. While Humphrey examined trousers, Derric studied his maps in an effort to discover the path of least resistance. Swallowed whole by his project, he didn't notice a thing until Humphrey tapped him on the shoulder.

"Prince to Daniel. Hellooooo, Daniel?" Humphrey grinned as Derric blinked and looked up. "My word, man. Didn't your parents ever tell you it's impolite to ignore royalty?" He chortled at his own joke, and Derric smiled.

"No, they didn't."

"Come on. You mean to tell me your mother doesn't harp on you every time you go off to wherever it is you go?"

"I don't have a mother." Derric said it so automatically he almost laughed at the irony of it: to claim he didn't have a mother when the woman they were hunting down was the very woman he claimed didn't exist.

"You don't have a—but Sarah said just yesterday on our ride that she dines with her mother and father every Sunday and won't be missed until then."

"Yeah, she does, with *her* mother and our father."

"Oh." Humphrey glanced around the shop, worrying his lower lip in concentration. Derric could almost feel the prince's struggle with his duty to be polite. "So, what happened to *your* mother, then?"

"She's gone. Has been since I was eight years old."

"Does that mean Sarah's mother raised you? I'd think she could be called your mother if she—"

"Sarah's mother hates me," Derric said in a flat tone. "She never had anything to do with me beyond the dinners I used to go to on Sundays."

The subject dropped as the shop owner wandered over to them and started asking Humphrey questions about sizing and material. Once the prince had been loaded down with several pairs and led behind a coromandel screen to try them on, the topic resurfaced.

"Why does she hate you?"

Derric held back a grimace. It wasn't the prince's fault, but Derric had been living a solitary life for so long, he wasn't sure how to talk about things with other people.

The dark curls poked up over the screen, followed by a pair of clear blue eyes. "You don't have to tell me, you know."

For some reason, this made Derric want to do the opposite. "My mother met my father when she was very young. They shared interests, wanted the same things—she loved him. Instead of marrying her, they began an affair—all while he was courting a woman of the higher class."

"Sarah's mother?"

"Sarah's mother." Derric nodded even though Humphrey couldn't see. "When my mother found out she was pregnant with me, she told my father. He chose to end things with her instead of seeing them through. He married Sarah's mother before the truth got to her well-connected family. My mother then raised me on her own."

A snort from behind the screen bolstered Derric's own anger. It felt good to have someone know what his father was like and to agree.

"When Sarah was born a girl, my father returned to my mother and tried to obtain custody over me. The damage had already been done, and she refused. But, I was allowed to join them every Sunday for dinner. For a while, things went smoothly, but the older I got, the crueler Sarah's mother became. By the time I was six, she didn't make any attempt to hide her true feelings. For two years, I put up with the abuse in order to see my father and sister, even though my mother said I could stop going at any time.

"After she . . . it happened when I was eight. With nowhere else to go, I went to my father's home. My first night, I heard Sarah's mother arguing with my father. She told him if he allowed me to stay, she would make his life as miserable as possible. I didn't belong there anyway, since there wasn't any proof I was actually his. The next day, my father signed me over to the stable master."

Derric looked up as he finished his story and found Humphrey standing outside the screen, staring at him with undisguised disgust.

"He just let you go? Just like that?"

"Just like that."

Humphrey shook his head, still working his way through what he'd heard. "If you were eight when your mother died, how do you know all of this?"

"My mother told me stories about my father whenever I asked. She never hid the truth from me—said that would make me ashamed of who I was. After she was gone, I found a diary amongst her things. I hid it with my own so no one would take it from me. It had enough written in it to fill in the spots I was missing." He didn't add that there were several spells and plant guides in the diary, or that the book almost seemed to change, to adapt, to whatever Derric needed to find.

"That's the worst story I ever heard." Humphrey gestured to the storeowner. "And I've heard awful things from my manservant. His father used to hit him, but at least he sobered up and repented his evil ways. This doesn't seem to have a happy ending. Is this why Sarah is a lady's maid, and you're in the stables?"

"Yeah. Sarah's mother pulled strings to get them into consideration for classification as nobility. She isn't of noble blood, but she's just a step down."

"Yes, I'd like to buy these." Humphrey gestured to the pants he wore as well as two other pairs he held in his arms. "You can keep the ones I came in with. They won't do me any good where we're going."

They paid for the trousers and headed back to the inn. It occurred to Derric he ought to show a similar interest in Humphrey's life, at the very least to be polite.

"Does your mother ever harp on you for anything?"

"Mumsy? Do you have an hour?" Humphrey laughed and shook his head. "Let me tell you about the time I was caught sliding down the stair railings of our grand hall when I was supposed to be in my music lessons. She reddened my backside so badly I couldn't sit comfortably for at least a month ..."

And so it went, with Humphrey regaling Derric for the better part of a half hour before the young ladies arrived and they could saddle up, on their way to the western wilds of Opea.

Chapter 16
Last Night of Safety

. . . .

The western wilds weren't a gradual change of land. They didn't sneak up on you and lull you into a false sense of security. No, Maria realized, her heart thrumming as she stared off into the distance, the western wilds trumpeted their arrival.

Large and thick, black and angular, and all without a leaf between them, the trees of Fangralee Forest—also known as the Foul Forest—jutted up into the sky, which faded from blue to grey as soon as it hit the tree line.

"Is it enchanted?" Sarah asked in a low voice, as if the forest might hear her from a mile away.

"It has to be." Humphrey glared at the scene before them, his swarthy skin paling.

"It isn't enchanted," Daniel said, as he spurred his horse forward. "It's enchantment."

"I'm sorry, it's what now?" Humphrey gave a soft kick to his own horse to catch up with Daniel, and the girls followed suit.

"It's enchantment," Daniel repeated. "It hasn't been magicked. It *is* magic. All sources of magic come from Fangralee. Magic courses through each and every tree, right down to its smallest root. It all originated here."

"Proof all magic is evil." Maria glared at the forest, trying to push aside the fear it instilled in her, but Daniel shook his head.

"Magic isn't evil, not at its core. It's neutral. The user is the one in control, just as with any other power source, like money or nobility."

"Then why is Fangralee so . . . so . . ." Sarah trailed off, gesturing toward the blackness growing ever closer with their horses' steps.

"Dark? Sorcerers did this—sorcerers and those they work for."

"How?"

"By using magic for gain. In every kingdom except Opea, there are sorcerers and sorceresses. Each possesses an inconceivable amount of power as a sort of birthright. There are rules, of course, but these beings can do what others cannot. Most sell their abilities for monetary gain and prestige, and others use it for revenge or to instill fear in others. A handful wield it kindly, to help and to heal. Magic was meant to be used for the good of all, not the greed of a few."

"They're not supposed to make money with their magic?" Maria asked, thinking it a rather unfair stipulation. Even sorcerers needed to make a living.

"It's not about making money. It's about exploitation and greed. In the beginning, magic folk would trade their services for what they needed, or maybe charge basic fees depending on the level of magic required of them. Now, though, even the simplest spell will cost you your firstborn."

Maria shivered. It all rang true. She knew of people who paid with their first child in order to have something magical. At least, there had been stories before her father banned all sorcery from Opea.

"And their misuse has turned the forest black?" Humphrey asked.

"Yes. The balance is off. The forest—all the wilds—reflects the way magic is used. Fear, greed, anger, and death. That's what we'll find in most of the wilds."

"Most?" Maria turned to Daniel, who didn't look at her. "But not all?"

"If there is a single sorcerer or sorceress who still uses magic for the good of others, there will always be a light in the wilds. The trick will be finding it."

"We have to find it?"

"I think if we can, we should. The light will be the safest place for us to camp. Traversing the forest alone is more than a week's journey, and I fear sleeping amidst the trees might be the last thing we do."

"What if we can't find the light?" If Humphrey was afraid, his voice didn't betray him. Maria felt a little prickle of pride for him; he *would* be so brave when she felt like a puddle of fear.

"I suppose we'll have to figure something out."

"Maybe we'll be able to keep watch," Sarah suggested. "Have night watches, and that way not all of us will be sleeping and vulnerable at once?"

"Maybe." Daniel frowned, considering it. "I'm not sure what we'll be facing. We won't know until we go in."

Right, Maria thought as they rode on in silence. *That makes me feel better.*

At Humphrey's insistence, they made camp just as the sun started to fade.

"I'd rather tackle this in the daylight. Besides, it's best if Maria isn't defenseless when we first see what we're up against. I mean, she has quite a fierce bite, but what if whatever's in there eats swans?"

Maria opened her mouth to thank Humphrey, but Daniel cut her off.

"If it eats swans, it probably eats people, too. Regardless, let's have one last night out of danger."

Humphrey set up a tent while Daniel started a fire. Sarah dug through the food bag to find an adequate ration for dinner, and Maria turned into a swan.

"I'm worried about our water rations," Sarah said as she pulled the waterskins from her horse. "Will there be safe water to drink when we're in the forest?"

"I have no idea," Daniel admitted as the tent collapsed on Humphrey for the third time. He moved to help.

Maria turned to Sarah. "I'll know if the water is safe or not."

"You?" Sarah and Humphrey said together, and Maria glowered at them.

"Yes, me. When I'm a swan I can always sense healthy water. I don't know if normal swans can do that—maybe it's my magical power or curse side effect. Right now, I can tell you a freshwater stream is," she sniffed at the air, "just a quarter mile into the woods."

"Amazing." Humphrey grinned at her. "That's the type of thing that will come in handy. Well done."

When they'd eaten and the tent no longer looked like it could collapse any second, Sarah and Maria were ushered inside.

"Don't you worry," Humphrey assured them. "With Daniel and I out here, nothing will come harm you. At least, not tonight. I can't make any promises once we're inside the forest."

Sarah laughed, and Maria gave him a honk of appreciation. Inside, Sarah climbed into her bedroll, muttering about her bed back home, and Maria settled on top of her roll, wondering why they'd brought it at all. She stood on one leg and tucked her head under her wing.

Though Sarah tossed and turned for some time, her breathing evened out, and Maria knew she was asleep. Despite being exhausted from their journey, sleep refused to come to her. When she'd had enough of pretending, she poked her head out from under the tent flap, wondering if she might take in one last night of stargazing.

By the fire, a figure sat with his back to the tent. Maria waddled out to him, unable to see who it was from his shrouded back. As she moved closer, the firelight cast an eerie glow on the profile of their guide. For a moment, Maria contemplated Daniel's features. Unlike

Humphrey's angles, Daniel's were rounder. His jaw was still strong, but his nose wasn't quite as straight and sharp. It pointed up just a touch at the tip. Rounder, too, were his face and his lips.

Humphrey gave a loud snore from the other side of the fire, and Maria giggled.

Daniel started, his hand falling to the hilt of his dagger. "Oh, it's just you. You know, as a black swan, you shouldn't creep up on people in the dark."

"I'm sorry. I couldn't sleep. Couldn't you?"

"Not yet. I've been thinking about the forest and what we might face in there."

"How do you know so much about it?"

"My mother taught me."

He seemed to regret the words as soon as he said them. He glared at the fire and didn't look at her when she next spoke.

"Sarah told me about your mother. She died when you were eight, isn't that right?"

Daniel shrugged, and she took that as assent. "She seems to have taught you a lot in those few years. I don't think I was even reading that well when I was eight."

"She started teaching me these things when I was two. She told me living in a world with magic meant I had to understand every bit of it, or else it might take advantage of me. Of course, that was before the ban on sorcery. The knowledge seemed sort of useless after, well, you know."

Maria nodded, aching to ask a question she'd been wondering ever since speaking with Sarah earlier in the day. "Was . . . was your mother . . . did she have magic?"

For a long time, Daniel didn't respond. He seemed to consider his answer, and when he did speak, it was in a measured tone. "She was well-learned in the way magic worked. She understood it better than most actual, proclaimed high wizards. After she was gone, I found a diary of hers, and it continued to teach me the things she knew."

A Stolen Kiss

Maria laid a hand on Daniel's arm and lightly ran it up and down in an effort to show comfort. "I'm sorry you lost your mother."

Daniel started and leaned away from her. Maria jerked back, embarrassed and confused.

"What?"

"You're—you're human."

Maria closed her eyes, threw her head back, and released a cry of frustration. "Why does this keep happening to me?" She opened them again. "Wait, does this have something to do with you?" A flutter leapt in her stomach.

He considered her for a moment. "I don't think so," he said. "If it had to do with me, you wouldn't be turning into a swan at all. My presence would be enough to keep you human."

"What is it then? What keeps turning me from swan to woman? And why did I turn into a swan when Humphrey kissed me?"

"The real question is," Daniel began, eyeing her with narrowed gaze, "why weren't you already a swan that first night?"

"What?"

"Sarah brought me to you after sunset. You should have already been a swan. And why did you tell Sarah your curse was from midnight until ten in the morning?"

Maria blanched and looked away. "I—I don't know."

"Yes, you do." When she didn't respond, he reached out and gripped under her chin, forcing her to look at him. "What aren't you telling us?"

A flicker of fear passed through her, and her resolve caved. "I went eight years without turning into a swan."

All at once, the story tumbled from her lips. How she'd stopped being a swan when she was young, but hadn't told her parents because she'd overheard how pleased they were they could use her curse to get a king for the kingdom. She told him how she faked her curse each night and locked herself up. How she'd told Sarah it started at midnight the one time Sarah had been with her past sundown. She told him how the other night was the first time in a long time she'd become the feathery version of herself.

"When Humphrey kissed you."

"Yes, when Humphrey kissed me."

"How strange." Daniel blinked and shook his head. "It did the opposite of what it was supposed to do. Almost like your curse had somehow grown latent and he revived it. But what made it latent? Unless . . ." Daniel retreated into deep thoughts he didn't bother sharing with her. After a long bout of silence, Maria stood and made her way back to the tent.

"He's a good guy, you know."

"Excuse me?" Maria turned around to find Daniel looking at her.

"Humphrey. He's a good guy. We'll figure out what's gone wrong with your curse, and when we do, I think you and Humphrey will make great rulers."

"He might, but I'm a liar and a coward."

"Maria," he said, pushing himself into a standing position and approaching her. "We're all liars in our own way. It's a despicable thing, but we lie to protect ourselves. You did what you thought your parents would want and got in over your head. We'll fix it. I promise I'll help you solve this, or I will die trying. Then, when you're free, you can marry Humphrey and live happily ever after like all the history books say."

"You think we can?" she asked, wanting to step closer to him, feel his touch.

"I know it. I've never had a friend before, but I think even if I had twenty, Humphrey would be the best of them all. He's a pretty cool guy. I know you guys have had a rough start but . . . I think it'll all work out."

Cold washed over her, despite being so close to the fire. If Humphrey was so wonderful, who was in the portrait

A Stolen Kiss

he'd thrown away? Was that woman someone he'd left behind to fulfill his duty to her? And if so, would he ever *really* be able to love her?

Would she be able to love him?

Looking up into Daniel's earnest face, she smiled for his sake and pushed down the feelings threatening to overwhelm her. "I'm sure it will. I expect we'll be very happy."

Tell one truth, cover it up with two more lies.

Chapter 17
Fangralee's First Foe

. . . .

Sarah woke Derric at first light the next morning. He sat up in his bedroll, bleary eyed and foggy, and gave a hearty yawn.

"Shh." She swatted at him with one hand, the other pressed to her lips in a sign for quiet. "Quick, before the royals wake up."

Rubbing his eyes, Derric nodded to show he understood.

"Good. Okay, quick update. I told Maria your mom died when you were eight, and that's why we have different moms."

"I know," Derric grumbled. "We talked last night when she couldn't sleep. Humphrey knows too—that we're half-bloods."

Sarah sighed and smiled. "That's good. It makes me feel better, like we're hiding less."

With a snort, Daniel stood and cast a glance at the remnants of the fire. "I think we're hiding more now than ever. Pull out a few of those muffins for breakfast. We will want to be in Fangralee before the sun gets too high."

Humphrey woke with the start of one trained for, but not accustomed to, combat. He grabbed Derric's arm as he was shaken awake, and thrust a clumsy right hook out of his bedroll. Though untrained in any form of combat, working with horses had given Derric enough reflexes to move out of the way.

"Oh! Daniel. Sorry mate, you startled me. Not used to being woken by someone else."

"How do you wake up back home in your palace?"

"One of the servants opens the curtains, and I wake

up when I please." He pushed himself all the way up and groaned. "And I miss my bed. Oh bed, some day we will meet again, my love."

Derric laughed and moved away from the prince. "We need to get going. Fangralee stands before us."

Humphrey glowered at the towering forest, not ten minutes' ride from where they'd slept. "Ah, yes. Today we face the beast. Or, the first beast, rather. What lies beyond Fangralee?"

"The Mortal Marsh," Derric said with a sigh. "And beyond that, the third piece of the wilds. Tranchet's Pass."

Humphrey groaned again, though this time not from his aching body. "That pass is a demented web. It starts all the way up in that northern country. What's it called again?"

"Braskey."

Humphrey groaned. "It starts all the way up there, weaves through mountains that span three or four separate countries, and comes out at Kyleria. It's ridiculous. If we don't know which way we're going, we're as like to end up in wherever-the-hells-that-is as we are Kyleria."

"We'll find the right way." Derric didn't know where his confidence came from, but he knew he'd have no trouble winding through the pass.

"How?"

"Magical footprints, remember?" Maria said.

Derric and Humphrey turned to see her standing behind them. Her confidence in him made Derric grin. "You trust my ability, then?"

"I have complete faith," Maria said with a softness that made Derric's stomach flip. She walked right by him to Humphrey's side, gazing up at her future fiancé. "Now, are we ready to go, my prince?"

Surprised by her attention, Humphrey gave Derric a goofy grin. "What do you say? Time to go?"

"Time to go."

At the base of the forest, with trees standing so tall they weren't able to see the sky above them and so thick they only allowed a single file line of horses, they entered the blackness.

The moment Thumper crossed the threshold, it was as though evening had descended. The sunlight remained behind, leaving only a hazy glimmer guiding the way. Derric needed the first half hour to adjust to his surroundings, to grow accustomed to the pressing silence, and to gain his bearings in such a light-forsaken place.

Questions filled his mind, and despair clawed at his soul. Would they ever make it out of this foul place alive? Could they even find the bit of light in the darkness? Would he be able to protect Sarah amidst all of this? What dangers lurked ahead that he couldn't see?

You will fail, the voices murmured to his spirit. *You'll never again see the light of day. Just like your mother, it will consume you. You will fail. You will hurt your friends. You will lead them to their doom.*

No, Derric thought, closing his eyes for a moment to reorient himself. *No. We won't fail. We have each other. I'm not alone.* The melody of a song his mother used to sing flitted into his thoughts, and he felt calmer and lighter.

"How do we know we're going the right way?" Sarah asked in a whisper that echoed around them, ending two full hours of silence among the travelers. Derric wondered if they—like him—needed time to sort through the sudden onslaught of darkness.

"Daniel?" Maria rode right behind him, with Sarah behind her, and Humphrey at the rear to protect their flank. She sounded scared.

"Stop here." Derric slid off of Thumper's back and stepped away from their procession.

"What are you doing?" Sarah whispered, now sounding as panicked as Maria.

"I need to figure out where to go from here." He closed his eyes and knelt down into the mulchy dirt. Steadying his breathing, he let the silence of the forest disappear, forgot the trees, and quieted his mind. He placed one hand into the dirt in front of him and then the other, feeling the cold earth around his fingers.

Magic pulsed like a beating heart beneath him. At first it was faint, a light thrumming against his fingertips. Steadily it grew until the drumbeat reverberated within his bones and threatened to shatter him apart. Just as he almost lost his senses to the maddening vibration, a familiar chord echoed, and he grabbed hold of it with his thoughts. The thread, light and buzzing, tugged at his right hand.

Gilda, he thought, plucking the chord and listening to the resonance. Yes, it was his mother's, left behind so long ago yet still so strong, as though it linked him right to her. He would feel the pull anytime he wished now, having found the right thread.

A loud snapping noise broke his concentration, and his eyes flew open. The sound of a steel blade being pulled from its sheath came from behind, and every muscle in Derric's body tensed. In seconds, Humphrey stood at his side, his blue eyes fixed on the blackness off to their right.

Beyond their vision, something large stirred in the forest.

"Where's your blade?" Humphrey asked in a whisper so quiet it almost couldn't be heard.

"All I have is this," Derric mouthed back, pulling up his dagger. He'd sharpened it before leaving, but it couldn't stand against much more than a rabbit or a badger.

Humphrey nodded, the muscle in his jaw tightening. Derric mimicked Humphrey's crouched stance, waiting for whatever lay beyond the darkness to attack.

Another twig snapped. Then three more, followed by

what sounded like running. Humphrey sprang into the air to meet the approaching adversary.

From the blackness emerged a lynx, larger than any Derric had ever seen. Its yellow eyes flashed as it met Humphrey's blade with sharp and agile claws, long as daggers. Horrified, he watched as the prince struggled to battle the cat, which fought with the precision of a well-trained swordsman. Behind Humphrey, Maria and Sarah cried out each time the lynx's claws came too close to Humphrey's throat.

Something isn't right. The thought forced its way to the front of Derric's mind, and he raced through what he knew. *This cat battles like a man. In Fangralee Forest, what is it? In Fangralee Forest, even the creatures are not what they appear.*

With a strong backhanded swing, the lynx knocked Humphrey's sword out of the prince's hand. It soared several feet away, Humphrey falling to the ground as the cat's body wound up for the final deathblow. It leapt into the air.

"No!" Derric moved before he realized what he was doing, planting himself between the lynx and the prince with arms outstretched.

Something powerful expanded between them like a shield, throwing both Derric and the lynx backward in opposite directions. He landed on his back, the wind knocked from him as pain shot through his body. Fighting for breath, Derric pushed to his feet, Humphrey at his side looking just as dazed as Derric felt.

The lynx, having fallen ten feet from them, shook its head, the yellow gaze coming to rest on Derric. All fear left him as he watched the cat tentatively move closer. It wouldn't hurt them now.

"Who are you?" it asked, and Derric heard everyone gasp around him.

"D-Daniel Digson," he lied, not breaking the connection of their eye contact.

The lynx's mouth twitched, and Derric knew at once

it had caught the lie. He held his ground as the cat drew nearer, and as Derric focused on the glittering eyes, he thought of a wolf.

All at once, the creature shifted. Instead of a lynx, a large grey wolf approached him.

"What on earth?" Humphrey muttered, but Derric kept his attention on the creature before him.

"Who are you?" he asked, one hand on the dagger just in case.

The wolf's brows rose. "Who? You ask *who* I am and not *what*?" When Derric said nothing, the wolf let out a soft chuckle. "You know respect, horsemaster. It will do you well."

Behind him, Derric heard Sarah whisper, "How did it know he works with horses?"

"I know many things, girl," the wolf said to Sarah, still staring at Derric. "I am many things." Without any warning, the wolf transformed into a man in a hooded cloak, his features hidden except for his mouth. "I am all things. You," he circled Derric, "are many things, too." As the creature walked around Humphrey, it changed into a red haired young woman. Humphrey sucked in a breath, and to Derric's surprise, so did Maria.

"I know your secrets," she said as she swept her gaze over all of them. "I know your lies."

"Who are you?" Derric repeated, knowing he mustn't be swayed by the creature's double-talk.

"I am Ellis." The creature blinked as though stunned by its admission.

"A shapeshifter."

"Yes." Ellis smiled with the woman's mouth. "A shape-shifter." Changing back into the lynx, Ellis came to sit on its haunches before Derric. "But what are you?"

"A man."

The lynx chuckled. "A man. Are you sure? I think I see much more in you. So many secrets, *Daniel.*"

Derric felt as though the blood in his veins turned to ice, his whole body going cold as Ellis continued to laugh at an inside joke.

"What do you want from us? Why did you attack?" Derric didn't know a lynx could show haughty affront, but Ellis managed it with ease.

"You came into my forest. Humans have no place here—no right. This place belongs to magic and those who wield it."

"We're seeking a sorceress." Humphrey's words drowned out Derric's next question. "This is the path to where she is, and we have to find her."

Ellis cocked its head to the side. "Why do you seek what you already have? Ask the sorcerer for help."

"There aren't any in Opea." This time it was Maria who addressed the lynx. "They were banished after the sorceress we seek cast a curse."

"Ah," Ellis said with a soft sigh. "You seek the one who cursed you, princess. You seek in vain, but I will not stop you. I am not the worst you will face, and I won't be the last."

Derric's eyes narrowed as he surveyed the cat. "You're letting us go?"

"Do I have a choice?" Ellis asked. "I can draw no closer." To prove its point, it took several steps toward Derric and was forced backward by something invisible.

After a few moments of stunned silence, Humphrey spoke. "Right. Well then . . . we'll be off now, won't we?" He turned to Derric, who nodded despite his misgivings. "All right. Goodbye, shapeshifter."

As the prince made his way back to his horse, Derric returned his attention to Ellis. "What is this barrier?" he asked. "And how long will it last?"

Ellis's eyes glittered with mischief. "That's up to you, Derric," it said in a voice so low no one else would hear. "It will remain as long as you let it."

"Is it a part of the forest's magic?"

"It's magic, but it doesn't belong to the forest." Ellis sighed. "If you don't know who's protecting you, I'm not going to tell you. That would spoil all the fun for me. You have an interesting future, Derricus Harver, and I want to be there to see it all play out."

Before Derric could say any more, Ellis vanished on the spot.

"Daniel? Let's leave while we still can, before whatever that shield is fades."

At Maria's call, Derric turned away from the spot where Ellis had been sitting, but he couldn't shake the eerie feeling as he got back into his saddle.

Someone was protecting them? Who? He thought about the magical thread he could still feel as he directed their party northwest, the thread that bound him to the woman they sought.

Could she be protecting them? Would she? Derric pushed on through the darkness, sure the next danger was right around the corner.

Chapter 18
Darkness and Light

. . . .

Maria felt she'd never be warm again. The blackness pressed against her, and the encounter with the shapeshifter frayed her nerves. She could still see the woman from the portrait making her wide circle around Humphrey. Her future fiancé, so intent on getting them out of danger once he'd realized the shapeshifter wouldn't harm them, hadn't said a word. Sarah chattered nonstop with Maria, no doubt to keep the silence from overwhelming them as it had before.

"I just think Dellsbian silk is so much lighter than Opean, don't you?"

"Oh yes, I agree." Maria tried to focus on the mundane conversation, but dark thoughts kept pulling her mind elsewhere. Over and over she saw Humphrey lying on the forest floor with the lynx about to strike, Daniel stepping into the way. But the memory devolved into terror as the image shifted and the lynx dropped Daniel to the ground, mauling him with vicious strikes.

If she pushed thoughts of the lynx away, the redheaded woman appeared, jabbing a knife into Humphrey's side before turning to finish Daniel off.

Over and over she saw these visions, all the while trying to keep up conversation with Sarah. Daniel didn't speak either, but from where she rode behind him, he appeared lost in thought, the same as Humphrey. She suspected he focused on getting them out of the forest or, at least, finding the light area he'd been sure was in here somewhere.

After a while, Sarah fell quiet, having run out of things to say. As soon as her lady's maid's voice vanished, the dark thoughts circling Maria descended. Every negative thing she'd said, done, or had done to her came flooding back. Pictures and images of things that hadn't happened yet poured forth and clouded her vision. Death felt more welcome than survival.

You left home for nothing. You'll die out here. You'll watch as your friends die slow and painful deaths before succumbing to the darkness yourself. You'll die alone, unloved, cold and broken.

A loud groan sounded behind her, and Maria jumped. Swiveling in her saddle, she watched Humphrey jump off his horse and drop to his knees.

"I can't take it anymore," he said, grabbing fistfuls of hair. "Make it stop."

In front of her, Daniel twisted around, his brow furrowed. "Humphrey? What is it?"

"These thoughts. They won't go away. Everything bad I've ever done—everything that's ever happened or could happen—it keeps running through my mind no matter what I do."

Maria snorted, though she couldn't fathom where the anger came from. "You're a prince, what could possibly have happened to you that was so bad? You've led a charmed life."

"You're one to talk," Sarah said.

Maria rolled her eyes. "Oh, please. You've been blessed by fortunate circumstances while your brother's worked hard all of his life. You don't know what's gone on in our lives. It's not always easy being royal."

"Oh, I'm sure." Sarah let out a harsh laugh as she glowered at Maria. "It must be impossible to have others wait on you, and care for you, and tend to your every need. How difficult it is to have to wake up when you feel like it or wear jewels and nice clothes."

"And be cursed or be expected to live up to expectations beyond you," Humphrey shot back at Sarah. "To be expected to give up everything for your people, for the greater good, and not be able to do what you want most or be with whom you love."

"Oh yes, you poor prince." Maria sneered at Humphrey, her eyes stinging with tears that threatened to spill out any moment. "You're stuck with me in order to become king of one of the richest and most fruitful kingdoms in all the lands. You've suffered so, leaving behind some commoner, no doubt, who only wanted you for your riches."

She couldn't believe the words she was saying. They didn't sound like her; they didn't *feel* like her. She tried to pull back, away from the venom spilling from within.

"Besides, Daniel's the one here who should be complaining. He's poor. He's almost an orphan. Out of his own goodness, he's agreed to take us through this hellish place in order to break my curse."

"If you feel so strongly about your darling Daniel, why don't you marry him instead of me?" Humphrey said through gritted teeth. "Oh, that's right, because you're in love with the villainous Derricus." He stood to his feet, his face darkening. "Don't speak to me like you've been waiting all your life for my love when we both know you want nothing of it."

"Stop!" Daniel stepped into the fray, and a dark cloud lifted. Maria realized she and Sarah had gotten off their horses at some point during the fight, though she couldn't remember doing so. The look on Daniel's face scared her—scared her because she saw fear in his eyes.

"Everyone, please, calm down. This isn't you talking. It's the forest."

Maria blinked. *The forest?*

"How would you know?" Sarah asked, baring her teeth at him. Even as she did it, Maria knew it wasn't right, wasn't Sarah.

"Clear your heads. You have nothing against each other. It's the forest working its magic on you. None of it is real."

Oh, it's real, Maria thought, eying Humphrey with sudden dislike. *He doesn't want me and never did. He's marrying me because he has to for "the greater good."*

"Why aren't you affected?" Humphrey asked, taking a step back away from Daniel. "Or are you a shapeshifter?"

"A what?" Daniel pulled back in surprise. "Why would you think that?"

"Ellis thought you were more than a man. Remember what it said?" Humphrey turned to Maria and Sarah. "When Daniel said he was a man, Ellis asked if he was sure and said there were so many secrets in him. What if he's lying to us? What if he's a shapeshifter and is leading us into danger?"

Maria felt her heart beat harder. Humphrey spoke truth, and now her eyes were open to it. Daniel was her enemy. She stepped away from him, closer to Humphrey. Sarah alone looked like she had any doubts about Ellis's words.

"No. No, he's my brother. He's always protected me. I would know if he was something evil."

"Would you?" Maria asked, and Sarah frowned.

"Why isn't it affecting him, this . . . this darkness?" Humphrey jerked his chin at Daniel. "What makes him different from us that he isn't feeling what I'm feeling right now?"

"What are you feeling?" Daniel asked, his voice steady.

"Like my head might split apart. Like maybe I'll never know happiness or warmth again."

"That's how I feel too," Sarah whispered, shivering.

"I did feel that way," Daniel said, meeting Humphrey's accusing stare. "I felt sure I was leading us all to our deaths, but then it changed. I started thinking of this little song my mother taught me when I was young, and the thoughts went away."

"What song?" Maria asked.

Daniel started to hum, soft but audibly. Once he started

singing the words, a weight lifted off of Maria's shoulders, and she sucked in a full, deep breath, realizing for the first time how constricted her chest had felt.

Though the winter winds blow fierce and cold,
And all my love has gone,
I will be both brave and bold.
Yes, I will carry on.

When darkness sets its grip on me,
And fear starts to descend,
I'll hold on to the light of old
Until the very end.

I will bid the darkness flee,
And tell death to be gone.
It hasn't strength nor hold on me.
My light will carry on.

It was as if a light bubbled within her. Even the darkness around them lessened, and she could almost sense the sunlight just beyond the thick canopy of trees above them. When Daniel finished, the warm feeling remained. Maria looked at Sarah and Humphrey and saw they'd brightened as well.

"It's a spell," Humphrey stated, grinning at Daniel. "Your mother taught you a spell. Fantastic."

Daniel shrugged. "She used to sing it when I was young and had bad dreams. After she was gone and I was alone in the stables, I would sing it to myself to keep from being scared."

"Brilliant. Absolutely brilliant. All right, let's go." Humphrey marched back to his horse with a new spring in his step, and Maria laughed as she followed suit. Everything felt fine, beautiful, even in this dark and decrepit forest. It was strange how the song seemed to work deep into her heart. She felt cheerier than she could remember feeling in a long time.

A Stolen Kiss

"It's a marvelous spell." She heard Sarah say dreamily behind her. "Simply marvelous."

Daniel cast them all an odd look that hinted at unease, but Maria paid it no heed. What right did he have to feel uneasy about anything when the world lay before them? Confidence swelled in Maria. Yes, they'd get through Fangralee with ease, pass through the other wilds, and be in Kyleria in no time. Nothing would stop them.

Coming down from the spell's high, however, did just that.

Chapter 19
Island Sanctuary

. . . .

Derric waited for what he knew would be inevitable. The instantaneous cheer the other three felt after he sang the song unnerved him, and there was no doubt Fangralee's magic had something to do with it. Back home with his mother, it'd been a small talisman against bad dreams. Here in the heart of darkness, it felt like a ball of sunshine went with them.

Sarah, Maria, and Humphrey talked and laughed without care, buoyed by the light. Derric kept his wits about him, waiting for the other shoe to drop. They made noise and carried on, and all the while he kept an eye on their surroundings as he followed Gilda's magical thread.

Hours. Days? Derric knew it couldn't have been more than six or seven hours since they'd entered the forest, but everything felt wrong. A sudden quiet pressed against him, and he peered back over his shoulder.

Gone were the smiles and the gaiety from his companions' faces. Instead, looks of confusion and disappointment met his questioning stare. At once Derric realized Fangralee had ebbed the magical tide of the song's peace. To fall from a height of that magnitude would leave them tenfold more susceptible to the darkness of the forest.

"Though the winter winds blow fierce and cold, and all my love has gone," Derric sang, drawing their attention again. "Come on. You'll have to sing with me. The forest is trying to get into your heads. Sing."

"We don't know the words," Sarah said, panic alight in her eyes.

"Then I'll sing until you know them."

And he sang. His wasn't the voice of a minstrel, but he could have blended in with a choir. He kept the words flowing, returning to the beginning as soon as he finished. Humphrey caught on quickest and surprised them all with an angelic voice that melded with Derric's.

Maria joined next, her voice much like a seagull's caw, but it didn't lessen the effect. "Why don't I feel as good as before?" she asked as the tune ended for a third time.

"Because the forest wanted you to feel that way the first time. It was making easy prey for when the magic wore off. You'll be even more susceptible to the darkness now, having known joy like that. You don't have to sing the song out loud. Now you know the words, have them playing in your head whenever you start to feel hopeless."

"Why didn't you feel it the way we did?" Sarah asked.

"Probably because I've been singing it since childhood. Spells cast over and over again aren't as effective as the ones cast once in a while. They still work, but not with the same power. I've built up a resistance to it that even Fangralee couldn't get by."

"I feel tired."

"I'm hungry."

"Oh! Lunch!"

Derric sighed and shook his head. This wasn't a place to stop for a meal, but hunger was a novelty to the royals and Sarah, none of whom had ever waited for a meal, let alone missed one altogether.

"It isn't safe here. We ride until nightfall."

Sarah gaped at him. "That's too far away! How will we even *know* when night falls in here?"

"Maria will turn into a swan."

"How will she eat dinner as a swan?" Sarah argued, and Maria let out a small huff.

"Swans have mouths, you know. They can eat food."

"There, problem solved." Derric continued on. His sister continued to pout while Humphrey put on a brave face.

"It's best if we save our rations, anyway. If we were to run out, we'd starve!"

"But I'm hungry," Maria said, as though shocked anyone could *remain* in this state.

"There are apples in Sarah's bag," Derric said through gritted teeth. "If she can get to them without stopping, you can each have one."

Maria said something under her breath, and Sarah snickered and replied in kind. Though he couldn't hear it, he knew it was about him. Annoyed and stung, Derric retreated into his own thoughts as he focused on the forest around them.

The shapeshifter bothered him most. Something about the encounter left an ashy taste in his mouth, like he'd missed something important. Ellis's riddles had to have meant something. What did he know about shapeshifters? Something . . . there was something he'd missed.

He plucked without thought at the strand of magic he had tethered himself to. It rang out, and he adjusted their course. They needed to find a safe place to camp, and soon. Night in Fangralee would be ten times more dangerous than the day. Ellis's presence only scratched the surface of what lurked in Fangralee, and if they didn't find a secure location, there was no telling what might attack.

Where do I find safety?

Go left.

Derric blinked, breaking out of his thought pattern and noticing the sounds of the others munching apples, his sister repeating what she'd asked.

"Did you want the fourth one? It's the last."

"I, uh, not right now. Save it." Why hadn't he brought more than four apples? Derric pushed this thought aside and went back to his musings.

Why would I go left? Left of what? We're hardly following a path.

Left. Here. That tree—the one with the knot that looks like a cow's face.

Derric peered ahead into the darkness. Sure enough, a gnarled tree with an oddly shaped protrusion stood steadfast before him. He pulled on the reins, and Thumper slowed.

If I go left, he thought, *I'll be leading us away from where the magic-tether is taking me.*

Go left, and you'll be out of Fangralee faster. You can make up the time in the marsh.

Despite misgivings that he might be listening to an unfriendly entity, Derric directed them left at the tree. As he did so, a sudden peaceful bravado swelled in his chest as though to comfort him and let him know he'd chosen wisely.

Several hours passed without incident, leading Derric to wonder if they remained under the shield's protection. Night would be on them soon, and still he waited to understand why going left had been so important.

"Will we have to ride the entire journey? Do you think there might be any walking involved? I'm not sure I can take any more of this. I'm sore!" Maria groaned behind him, and Derric glanced around to see her shifting in her saddle.

"Me too," Sarah said. "This is so uncomfortable. How long until we stop?"

"We can't stop until we find what we're looking for," Derric said, turning back to face forward.

"And what are we looking for?" Humphrey asked, his tone one of mild curiosity, as though riding all day didn't bother him.

"That." Derric stopped Thumper in his tracks, a laugh bubbling up from deep within him. Amidst the dark, dank forest of Fangralee, surrounded by murky waters, an island of pure golden light called out to them.

"Oh my," Sarah murmured in awe.

"Is it real?" Humphrey asked in a reverent whisper.

"There's one way to find out." Derric spurred Thumper ahead, and the horse needed no help in knowing which way to go. This solidified Derric's confidence, as animals always sensed evil before humans. If Thumper trusted the area, so did he.

The island wasn't much larger than Maria's chambers back in Edleton Castle, but it would fit them all for the night. There was a soft popping noise behind him, and, as Derric swung around, he saw a swan falling off of Maria's horse.

"Looks like we're just in time," Humphrey said, jumping down from his own steed to scoop the dazed swan into his arms. "You need rest, my dear."

"I didn't realize I wouldn't be able to stay in the saddle," Maria said as Humphrey led his horse forward by the reins, walking beside it with Maria secure in his other arm.

They reached the water's edge, and Derric hesitated. Would it be safe to cross? It didn't look deep, but they had no way of knowing, and though the island looked safe, the water might be dangerous.

"Maria?" Derric asked, turning to gaze at the black-feathered beauty. She sniffed the air before fluttering out of Humphrey's grasp and landing next to Sarah's horse.

"It doesn't smell dangerous." She sniffed again. "It's clean and drinkable, but I don't know how deep it is. Hang on."

She hopped into the water and ducked her head below the surface. They waited for her to resurface, and Derric had a wild, panicked image of a creature coming up from the depths and throttling her.

"Maria," he said with a hint of urgency. She popped back up and shook her regal head.

"It's not too deep. The horses should be able to get across if they give it a good swim. Can they do that?"

"As long as they don't panic, we should be fine. It isn't a great distance."

"Wait, so do we have to swim?" Sarah asked, eyebrows rising. "Is it deep?"

"It's over your head, yes." Maria paddled around, and Derric had the distinct impression she was being smug.

"So off with this dress, then," Sarah said. She'd forgone the trousers for one more day, but it seemed she'd run out of options. "Humphrey, don't look."

The prince turned away as Derric unbuttoned Sarah's simple dress and helped her step out of it. She stood before him in bloomers and chemise.

"You'd better make it quick," Derric said, wadding up her dress and stuffing it into his bag. He ignored her protests against wrinkles.

With a final glare for her brother, Sarah took a running jump into the water, launching herself halfway across before plunging below the surface.

"All right," she called. "Now you two can cross, and I'll come out once you've reached the other side."

"This all seems highly unnecessary," Humphrey muttered under his breath as he directed both Sarah's and his horses into the water. "Come now, old chap. There you go."

With the prince leading two horses, Derric directed Thumper and Maria's horse, Verona. As he ushered them to the water's edge, Thumper's body tensed, his ears twitched, and Derric swung around to face the forest in response.

A large, hairy *something* lurked just beyond the trees. Derric could make out its bulk, but nothing specific. Fear seized hold of him, and his mind worked faster than he'd remembered it ever working before.

Get the horses into the water. Get the others across. The island will be safe. MOVE!

"Swim to the island, now." Derric kept his tone calm despite the panic warring against his senses. With the gentle touch he'd learned at a young age, he calmed Thumper and kept the two horses moving forward.

"Daniel?" Maria had picked up on his panic. "What is it?"

"Do as I say. Get to the island. Humphrey? Come get the reins here."

The splashing behind him told Derric they were doing as he asked. The prince reached him as the water reached Derric's waist. He handed off the reins without looking, his gaze focused on the forest.

"Go. Now," he whispered, reaching down and pulling his dagger free from his hilt.

"But you're not—" Humphrey began.

"I said go!"

As if Derric's shout was what the creature had been waiting for, it leapt out into the clearing. The horses whinnied in panic, rushing into the water and dragging Humphrey with them. Derric held his ground, taking in the sight of it.

Large and bearlike, it had fangs the length of Derric's palm and red, beady eyes—six of them. The wiry, black hair stuck up in all directions, branches matted into most of it. The thing snarled at Derric, pawing the ground with one of its five legs.

"Daniel!"

He wasn't sure who called for him, but he ignored it. With the creature focused on him, the others had made it across. He, however, didn't have that luxury. He couldn't swim fast enough to get across before it'd be on him.

The beast charged, and Derric crouched down, preparing for the attack.

Chapter 20
DEATH BECOMES HIM

. . . .

Maria, Humphrey, and Sarah stood helpless on the golden island as Daniel squared off against the giant *thing*. As it lunged, Sarah cried and turned away, Humphrey grabbed his sword and waded back into the water, and Maria . . . Maria decided to be useful.

With a loud honk of protest, she leapt into the air and flew as fast as she could toward the beast. The sudden approach of an oversized black swan didn't seem to be on the monster's agenda. Caught off guard, it swerved and passed Daniel in order to chase after the new prey.

"Daniel! Get to safety!" Maria called, flying just low enough to remain interesting, but not so low as to be caught by one of the five clawed paws.

Instead of heeding her command, Daniel leapt forward and slashed at the beast's side. With a loud roar, it forgot the swan, and two paws knocked Daniel to the ground. He shoved his dagger up into the creature as it leaned over him, and it squealed, clawing at him again.

"Daniel!" Maria dropped down and pecked as hard as she could at one of the six red eyes, then the next, and then the next. Absorbed by her vicious attack, Maria didn't see the immense rat-like tail until it hit her from above, dropping her to the shore.

Crumpled beneath the behemoth with no way of escape, Maria stared up into what would be her end. If it stirred fear in her from above, the view below drenched her in terror beyond imagination.

Behind its two fangs, the yellow, jagged teeth looked

like thousands of needles crammed into a maw of black, putrescent sludge. Its breath was hot and foul—the smell of the dead. More eyes glowered at her from under its belly as it made its descent. Maria heard someone call her name from what seemed like far away, but she had one last absurd thought.

This is it. After all of this, I'm going to die as a swan.

All at once, things changed. The eyes shifted their attention away from her, the creature gave a high-pitched wail of pain, and everything went dark.

Dark, but not unconscious. Maria grunted in an attempt to breathe beneath the body of the grotesque carcass. She tried to move, but the weight of the creature kept her from making much headway.

"Maria! Maria, are you okay?" Humphrey's voice sounded muffled.

"Get me out of here!" she cried, the lack of oxygen making her head feel funny.

A lot of grunting sounded beyond the muffled wall of fur, and in a flash, the golden light of the island just beyond the water broke through her darkness. Strengthened by the sight, she waddled out from under the body. Humphrey let it drop the moment she was free.

"You're alive," he said as he wrapped her up in his arms in the strangest yet most comforting hug she'd ever received. "Oh, thank the heavens."

"You killed it?" Maria asked, pulling her long neck back to look at him. "You killed that thing?"

"Don't sound so surprised," he said with a smile. "I've been training with a sword since I could walk."

"What about—?" Maria's gaze fell beyond where Humphrey knelt, over his shoulder, where a body lay unmoving in the dirt. "Daniel!"

Humphrey turned in alarm and dropped her to rush to his side. "Daniel? Daniel! Come on, mate. Wake up!"

Maria hovered beside Humphrey, and a sound off in

the forest churned her anxiety. "Humphrey, we have to get to the island. *Now.*"

"But how can we get him across if he's—" Humphrey began just as Daniel stirred with a groan.

"No. Maria," he said, and then his eyes popped open, and he sat up. "Maria!"

"I'm fine! I'm right here!" she said as Humphrey restrained Daniel in his panic. "We have to get to the island. Can you do that?"

"I can—ow." He sucked in a breath, and she followed his gaze as it dropped to his arm. Three slashes dripped blood where the beast had clawed him.

"Humphrey, help him swim across. I'll see if Sarah knows how to dress a wound."

Sarah stood at the island's edge, her face white and her eyes round with fear. "What's wrong? Is he all right?"

"He's been cut by that creature. It'll need to be dressed once Humphrey gets him over here. Do you know how to do that?"

"Yes, of course—but the bandages might be wet. I didn't even think of taking anything out of the saddles when the horses crossed."

"We'll have to figure it out and make do."

It took Humphrey a while to get Daniel across the short stretch of water, as the prince had to swim while the stableboy back-floated. Maria paced, and Sarah laid out the miraculously dry bandages. The herbs Daniel had brought were also somehow dry. In fact, Maria had been shocked to discover, everything in Daniel's bags seemed untouched by the water, despite the outer fabric of the bag being as soaked as the rest.

"Here. Careful, don't move it too much," Humphrey ordered as he sat Daniel down near the horses. Sarah moved to tend to him, and Maria spoke to Humphrey.

"We should probably—"

She stopped speaking as Daniel slapped Sarah's helpful hand away.

"Daniel." Sarah leaned back, just as taken aback as Maria. "I have to dress your wounds." She approached him again, but the moment her fingers brushed his skin, he shoved her away. "Hey!" she cried. "What are you doing?"

"Don't. Touch. Me."

Maria's feathers ruffled. Something about the tone of his voice felt wrong. Sarah sensed it too, and she leaned away from her brother.

"Daniel?"

"Stop calling me that," he spat, glaring at Maria. "Don't you ever call me that again."

"Please, let us help you. You're hurt." Sarah gestured to his arm.

He sneered and pushed himself to his feet. "Hurt? What would you know of hurt? Of pain? Any of you?" He tilted his head to the side until his neck cracked. "What do any of you know about anything?"

"Hang on a second, here," Humphrey said, standing and approaching Daniel. "Don't tell me I know nothing of pain. Don't act like you know my life. You need to calm down, sit down, and let your sister dress your wound."

With a bark of laughter, Daniel moved away from Humphrey. "You? Know pain? Not too long ago you told me the saddest story you'd ever heard was what my father did to my mother—to me. If that's true, then you've led a sheltered life, *Your Highness*." He punctuated the last two words with a mocking bow, smiling up at Humphrey through haunted eyes.

"Please, this doesn't sound like you." Sarah stepped up and placed a hand on his shoulder. He shook her off.

"Stop touching me! Why do you always have to be mothering me? You aren't my mother!" Daniel grabbed fistfuls of his hair and grunted, muttering more about his mother under his breath.

"Let us help you," Sarah said, her voice strained.

"You can't help me. No one can help me! Don't you see? It's too late. I've done too much. There's too much wrong. I'm unwanted. No good. Damaged."

"You aren't damaged," Humphrey ventured, casting a wary glance at Sarah while Maria stayed back, unable to do anything in her swan form. "There's nothing wrong with you that we can't fix if you just let us look at your arm."

"They left me."

His whisper was so quiet they almost missed it, and Maria sensed something deeper in whatever ailed their guide.

"Who left you?"

"They did. They left me. They didn't want me, neither of them."

"Who?" she repeated.

"My mother." The broken note in his voice sent chills through Maria. "My father."

"Your mother died. That wasn't because of you."

Daniel turned to face her, and the look in his eyes didn't ease her feeling of fear. Before he could say anything, Sarah spoke.

"You can't say that. Your mother is gone, but Father didn't abandon you! I didn't abandon you. You still have family that loves you."

"Hah!" Daniel's bark of laugher held no humor. "Father has no love for me, and you know it. He couldn't even stand keeping me for a day."

Sarah's brows furrowed. "A day? You lived with us for a while before you went off to start your apprenticeship at the stables."

"*One day!*" Daniel yelled, holding up his pointer finger. "One day after I walked into his home, he *sold* me to the stablemaster. I was eight years old, Sarah. Do you know what it's like to be sold by your own father?"

"What do you mean sold? Father signed you over to be his apprentice, just like they got me my position as Maria's—"

"How old were you when you started working in the castle?" Daniel interrupted.

Sarah hesitated. "I-I was twelve."

"Twelve. And how much money do you take home for your work?"

"I hardly think this is the time to discuss my pay," Sarah snapped, but Daniel laughed.

"But you do get paid." When Sarah nodded, he straightened. "I make no money. I take in no pay for my work in the stables. I belong to the castle." His gaze shifted to Maria. "I am property of Her Royal Highness."

"That can't be true," Sarah said, though Daniel didn't take his eyes off of Maria.

"Tell them, Highness. Tell them it can be true." Daniel quirked an eyebrow when she said nothing. "Tell them that, as long as my father was paid a fair price for me, I can be property of the royal family—I can live there until I die with no hope of freedom. He signed a contract and everything, binding me to them, taking away my freedom."

Daniel turned his gaze back on his sister. "Now do you wish to tell me Father loves me? That he cares? He won't even claim me as his own. He made me a slave!" Daniel screamed and lunged toward his sister, but Humphrey blocked him.

"Something isn't right. He's not himself." Sarah clutched the bandages close to her chest, her tear-filled gaze on her brother.

"Oh? Am I not myself? Perhaps this *is* my true self, little sister. Perhaps for the first time I'm voicing *my* opinion on things. After all I've done, all I've been through, I think I've earned it."

"You're right." Humphrey drew Daniel's attention back to himself while motioning behind his back for Maria and Sarah to back away. "You're entitled to your opinion, but you have to let us treat your wounds. We'll start a fire, cook dinner, and you can rest. We're safe here on this island."

Daniel's brows rose, and he considered Humphrey. "You'd like a fire?" He held out his hand, and flames burst forth into his palm.

With a cry of surprise, Humphrey leapt back. Sarah, too, moved away. Daniel turned his attention back onto his sister.

"Surprised? Should you be? Haven't you always wondered—always whispered?" The flames grew larger in his hand as he stepped toward Sarah. "After all I've done and all of your whining, is it any wonder I'd be sick of it? Sick of you?"

"Sarah, look at his feet." Maria stared down at where Daniel stood. The golden brightness of the island disappeared where he stood, circling him in black. "Something's wrong!"

Daniel turned on Maria, but before he could so much as act, Humphrey hit him from behind with the butt of his sword. Daniel dropped face first onto the ground, the fire in his hand extinguished.

"What in the hells just happened?"

Chapter 21
IN THE DARK

othing felt right. Rage, confusion, and a power he had never known and couldn't explain coursed through his veins. He'd never wanted to hurt someone so badly. A tiny voice in the back of his mind whispered this wasn't right, wasn't natural, but the all-encompassing power drowned it out.

He could do anything.

Hurt anything.

He could destroy the world.

The fire in the palm of his hand intoxicated him—he'd created it by his own sheer will. He turned on the familiar girl with light hair and skin who clutched bandages. He knew her, but that didn't matter. As he advanced, he had only destruction on his mind.

And then everything went black.

Chapter 22
Ellis Returns

. . . .

Daniel's crumpled body lay at their feet, and the sudden departure of his senses made less and less sense.

"He's a sorcerer," Humphrey said, awed.

"I don't know." Maria peered down at his injured arm lying twisted beside his prone form. "What if whatever that thing was poisoned him? After all, platypuses have venom in their claws."

"I think that's actually a stinger on its hind leg," Sarah said, kneeling down next to Daniel and checking his pulse. "I hope the blow to his head doesn't do any damage. Head wounds are dangerous."

"How do you two know all of this?" Humphrey asked in exasperation. "Platypi and head wounds? We have to figure out how to fix him before he wakes up!"

"Is it platypi? I thought it was platypuses."

"Hang on, maybe there's something in his mother's journal." Sarah moved to Daniel's bag and rummaged through it. "Ah, here it is. Oh no, I don't even know what we're looking for."

"Ask it," Humphrey suggested, kneeling down beside her.

"Excuse me?"

"Ask it for help. If Daniel's a sorcerer, his mother was too. I've seen sorcerer's journals before. They always find whatever it is they're looking for, but since we don't know, maybe we can ask."

Despite the frown furrowing Sarah's brow, she spoke to the book. "We need help."

She cracked open the book, and Maria waddled over to peer over her shoulder.

A sketch of the creature sprawled across the top half of the right-hand side of the journal. Above it, a single word. *Beornach.*

Maria tested the word out. It felt foreign on her tongue and sent a shiver down her spine, like an ancient language for an ancient evil. Sarah read the writing beneath the sketch.

"'The beornach or *Beornatichus Latrodectus* is a tri-beast found in the deepest heart of Fangralee Forest. Born of the darkest magic in the days of the Shadow Trials, the beornach combines the size and brute strength of a bear, the many eyes of a host of spiders, and the bloodlust of a hyena. Among its magical properties, the beornach can see in the dark and has a two hundred and seventy degree span. It's vulnerable from behind.

"'Beware the beornach's claw. Ten times more dangerous than death, the venom found in the creature's talons has properties more magical than physical. Exposure to the venom isn't painful, nor does it lead to physical grief. Instead, the magic will attack the soul of the victim, turning it black.' Black? That must be what's—"

"Sarah, keep reading," Humphrey ordered, doing his best to bandage Daniel's limp arm.

"Oh, right. 'If untreated, the poison will adhere to the core of the victim, and he or she will—will lose the essence of their being, replaced by a darker version of his or herself.'" Sarah looked up from the reading to stare at her brother. "Wow. They . . . they really don't cushion the blow do they?"

"So whatever is wrong with him, if we don't fix it, he'll stay this way?" Maria asked, frowning down at the page again. "It looks like there's an antidote. Turn the page, Sarah."

"Do you think it's the poison that gave him the power to create fire?" Humphrey asked, voicing what Maria had been wondering. "Does it make the person an evil sort of sorcerer?"

"Maybe."

Sarah turned the page and glanced over the antidote. "It looks like we'll need root of the dragonfire plant, essence of the mandrake leaf, and crushed aglaophotis. We mix it in clean water and boil it over a hot fire, stirring three times every hour with the feather of a swan—where on earth are we going to find a swan feather in the middle of Fangralee?"

Maria cleared her throat and drew Sarah's attention. The girl blushed and gave a small laugh. "Oh yes, right. Well then, I know my brother packed mandrake leaves and dragonfire plant in his supplies before leaving, but the aglaophotis? That won't be easy."

"Why not?" Humphrey, having bandaged Daniel's arm, moved to tie his hands behind his back. "Where does it grow?"

"I don't know. It's really rare and looks similar to a few other peonies. It's used to ward off evil, so I'm not so sure Fangralee will be abundant in it since," she gestured at the darkness around them, "you know. He would be the one who'd be able to find it, and I don't think he'd be willing even if he were awake."

Maria was already reading the next page of the journal open in Sarah's lap. An indiscernible creature shrouded in black had been sketched with the word *Shapeshifter* written across the top.

> *Of all the creatures of darkness, the shapeshifter is the most mysterious. Neither evil nor good, creatures of this kind work for their own gain and survival. No one knows what a shapeshifter looks like in its true form, nor is anyone aware of when the shapeshifter first spawned into being. They've always been and always will be.*

No other living thing on earth knows more than the shapeshifter. It can see inside heads and hearts. It knows your secrets, your lies, and your fears. It can help to realize your hope or plummet you into the depths of despair.

Beware the shapeshifter's tricks, but know this—its true self is its most protected asset. If, by chance, the shapeshifter is lulled or forced into revealing its name to those who understand its power, they will have command over it.

A shapeshifter knows all things. Use its knowledge well.

A shapeshifter knows all things ... all things? She came back to the conversation Humphrey and Sarah were having.

"... keep watch, and the other two could go into the forest to search for the plant."

"At night? That would be madness, and we can't wait until the morning—what if it's too late?"

"What was the name of the shapeshifter?" Maria asked.

"What?" Sarah turned to her. "What did you say?"

"It was ... I don't know. Started with an E?" Humphrey said with a shrug. "Why?"

Maria groaned. "Why can't I remember? Was that seriously just this morning? E ... Eaton ... Elton ... Ell ..."

"Ellis," Sarah said, not looking up from the book.

"Ellis! Ellis, I need you!" Maria cried, flapping her wings in a mixture of excitement and desperation.

A shadowy figure appeared before her, taking shape to resemble the dreaded redhead from the portrait Humphrey had disposed of.

"Did you want to hear my secret?" she said, batting her long lashes.

"I know your name. It's Ellis. That means you have to

do what I ask," Maria said gesturing to the journal with her wing. "It says so right there."

"Well, aren't you a clever little duck," Ellis said, a smile plastered on the redhead's pretty face. "What is your request?"

"A beornach poisoned our friend, and we need to make the antidote, but none of us know how to find the, uh—"

"Aglaophotis," Sarah supplied, her eyes wide and transfixed on Ellis.

"Yes, the . . . that. I want you to find it for us. You know all things, which means you would know where it grows. You, great and powerful Ellis, could get the plant and be back before we even start a fire."

"A flatterer, how charming." Ellis cocked its head to the side and considered her, unblinking. In fact, with the exception of the exaggerated batting of its lashes, Ellis didn't seem to need to use its eyelids. "It is true. I could get the plant and return without harm coming to myself, but why should I?"

"I know your name, Ellis, and I invoke it."

"Silly girl, I admire your tenacity, but I didn't give *you* my name. I gave it to him." Ellis gestured to Daniel's prone form. "He alone may *invoke* my name. You know, normally we just say 'call my name.' No need to be so dramatic. However." Ellis steepled its fingers and pressed the tips to the redhead's lips. "I am intrigued by your cunning and even by your desperation. Why do you want him cured?"

"Because we don't want him to be evil!" Sarah exclaimed, but Ellis held up a perfectly manicured hand.

"Tut, tut, Sarah. I'm not speaking to you. Hush, child."

"M-many reasons," Maria said, faltering in confusion. "He's our friend and Sarah's brother. We want to save him. We need him to help us get to Kyleria."

"No you don't, and no he isn't. You could solve all of your problems right here in this forest as well as you can in Kyleria. As I told you before, your quest is futile. There's nothing to save. He's not dead, nor will he die. No, he will be more powerful than any of you ever dreamed if you allow him to be as he is and succumb to the poison."

"We want him to be the young man we know," Maria said through clenched teeth. "We want him to be the one we care for."

"*Ah yes,*" Ellis said with a catty grin. "The one you care for. You don't care for this version? He's rather honest, though, isn't he? Or are his truths like mine—unwanted? You want the pretty package, the stablehand with the heart of gold. You don't want the baggage that comes with it."

"We don't want the lies that came out of his mouth while under the effects of the poison." Sarah, having pushed herself to her feet, moved toward Ellis, her eyes bright with anger. Humphrey leapt up and pulled her back, but didn't say a word.

"No lies, child. Everything your darling brother said while under the magic of the beornach is true. He *is* a slave. Your father never did want him. Want to know what else, little girl?" Ellis transformed into the shape of a man Maria recognized as Sarah's father, though she'd only met the healer a few times.

"Stop it." Tears shone in Sarah's eyes, and she struggled against Humphrey's hold on her. "Stop it! Change back!"

"My darling, Sarah," Ellis said. "Do you want to know the truth about your father? Your father wasn't seduced by your brother's mother. Oh, no. He strayed of his own will, and she used it against him."

Sarah shut her eyes, and the tears spilled forth, running down her cheeks.

"Better yet," Ellis continued. "Your father was a betrothed man—engaged when he decided to take the other woman into his bed. He didn't want his fiancée to know—lied to her, and Daniel's mother agreed to keep the secret on one condition: that he take care of her son. He cast aside his paramour and ruined her life. The day after

Daniel arrived, young and helpless and desperate to know everything would be all right . . . he sold the child into the last known form of slavery in our lands—to be owned by the Crown.

"He broke his promise, but Daniel's mother wasn't there to defend her son. She couldn't return and enact the revenge your father deserved. His wife went on in blissful ignorance and petty hatred, never knowing your father was a slimy louse, willing to trade his dignity for his affluent connections." To Maria's surprise, Ellis reached out and brushed Sarah's cheek with a gentle caress.

"That's enough," Humphrey said, glaring at Ellis and turning Sarah away from the shifter. She leaned against Humphrey, her body shaking with emotion.

In a blink, Ellis transformed back to the redheaded woman. "Careful, or we'll tell your story next."

"Ellis, will you help us or not?" Maria asked.

"Because you know my name, and because you, dear girl," it reached out and stroked Sarah's hair before Humphrey could stop it, its eyes still on Maria. "I look forward to keeping an eye on . . . I will make a deal with you. I will get you your plant in exchange for something else."

"What would that be?" Something told her it wouldn't be anything good.

"A favor."

"I will agree, as long as that favor isn't my firstborn, second born, or any offspring or family member."

Ellis reared back in mock surprise, but smiled. "How truly remarkable. You *are* cleverer than I first saw. Yes, I think it will be quite fun watching you on this journey. Agreed."

Without another word, Ellis disappeared. It reappeared within minutes, a large chunk of plant pulled out by the root in its hands.

"You'll need more than just tonight's share." Ellis dropped the bundle before Maria. "I would get that swan feather sooner than later, or you won't have it at all."

"What do you mean?" Humphrey asked, as Maria plucked one of her own feathers with her beak.

"By the time he's awake and ready to fight you off, she won't be a swan for long after." Ellis leaned down next to Maria so just she could hear. "Watch that heart, Your Highness. It will give you away in the end."

With that, the shapeshifter vanished into the night.

Chapter 23
A Taste of Madness

. . . .

Derric woke on his stomach with his head pounding and mouth dry. Anger hit him first, followed by frustration as he realized his hands had been bound.

"Release me." The sound of his own voice had a rich, authoritative depth, and it pleased him.

His three captors looked around from where they'd been focused on a small pot in the fire. The prince continued to stir whatever they were cooking.

Of course, Derric thought with a flash of disgust. *They would be worried about their hungry bellies.* He wriggled around in an attempt to get free, but whoever had tied him up had known what he was doing. Somehow, the culprit had managed to tie his hands in a locked position, preventing him from doing magic.

Humphrey.

"You think you're so clever," Derric said, glaring at the prince, who appeared sideways from this angle. "Where did you learn to tie up a sorcerer?"

"You know," Humphrey said, his calm tone setting Derric's teeth on edge. "It's like you all keep forgetting. In Dellsby, those who practice magic are free to do so. However, those who misuse their powers are still arrested and imprisoned just as any common lawbreaker would be. We know how to subdue a magical being."

Derric snorted and rolled over onto his back with difficulty. His own body weight pressed his hands into an even more uncomfortable and awkward position behind him. He let out a grunt of pain and tried to flip back over. Sarah, he noticed, seemed troubled by his suffering.

"Help me," he said, gaze fixed on his sister. "Please."

"I won't untie you," she said in a firm tone he didn't believe. "But I'll help you sit up. Okay?"

Instead of responding, he dropped his face into an innocent and accepting frown. Sarah drew near and, despite her petite form, was able to shift him into a sitting position, his back against a boulder.

"Sarah," Derric said under his breath so the other two wouldn't hear. "Sarah, what's going on? Why am I tied up like this? Did something happen?"

Doubt flickered across her features, and she blinked. "D-don't you remember?"

"I remember the beast—a beornach wasn't it? It was coming at me and then . . . and then, nothing." He widened his eyes for emphasis. "What's going on?"

"You were injured. It did things to you. You really don't remember?"

"What things?" Derric congratulated himself on the subtle panic he'd infused into his tone. Sweet, simple Sarah now searched his face with an open mouth.

"Derric?" she whispered, glancing back at the other two. "Derric is that really you?"

"Don't let them hear you call me that," he said with a quirk of his lips. "Might not go over so hot if I've already somehow gotten myself into trouble."

"It is you!" Sarah turned with bright eyes to the royal duo at the fire, ready to call out to them.

"Wait! Don't tell them."

"Why not?"

"First you have to . . . you have to tell me what I've done. I have to know what I did that was so bad they tied me up in the first place. I just remember everything going dark, and I didn't feel like myself again until . . . until you started to help me up. Sarah, it must have been your touch that saved me. The love of my sister must have been what I needed."

A Stolen Kiss

A sheen of tears glittered in Sarah's eyes, and she smiled, her lips wobbling. She would burst into tears any moment now.

"Untie me and tell me what's happened so I can start fixing this."

Sarah knelt down beside him. His heart pounded ever harder as her fingers inched closer to the ties that bound him, so loud he was sure she'd hear. Just before she touched the rope, something loud, large, and feathery attacked.

"Sarah, get away from him!"

Derric grunted as he fell sideways, hitting the ground hard. A person lay on top of him, her dark hair clouding his vision.

"Maria! What are you doing?" Humphrey called from by the fire.

The princess shoved herself off of Derric and moved back, standing in between him and Sarah, who sat in the grass just beyond.

"He was pestering Sarah to set him free. Sarah, whatever he told you is a lie."

"But Maria, it's him. I could tell. He's back to normal again. He said—"

"Lies, Sarah. He's still under the influence of the poison."

"How do you know that?"

"Look at him, Sarah. The ground beneath his feet is just as black as the rest of Fangralee. The *real* Daniel told us the blackness of Fangralee comes from the dark misuse of power."

Derric cursed and rolled onto his knees, maneuvering himself into a kneeling position before her. "Well done, Your Highness. The mistress proves her superiority yet again. But tell me, what is it about me that turns you back into your human self?"

Maria didn't even flinch. "If your presence counteracted

my curse, I'd never turn into a swan. You told me that, remember?"

Rage bubbled in him as he glared up at her, a cocky smirk plastered on her face. Somewhere in the back of his mind, a dying voice admired her courage. He squashed the feeling.

"Then perhaps it's my touch, Mah-ree-uh," he said, emphasizing every syllable. "It seems any time I've touched you while you've been a swan, you've become a princess again. Now isn't that funny?" His dark eyes glittered with humor as he saw the first hint of concern cross her face. "Wouldn't it be grand if the touch of a stableboy—a slave, no less—could turn the princess on or off."

His innuendo wasn't missed, and Maria's caramel cheeks flushed. "How dare you speak to me this way!"

"Yet, you don't deny it. Come, Princess, wouldn't you like to touch me again? To find out if I really have power over you?"

"Stop it!" Sarah called, pushing herself to her feet and coming to stand by Maria.

Of course she wouldn't want him to say any more. She *knew* what kind of power he had. All he had to do was say his name, and all would be revealed. Maria was bound to him, thanks to his thoughtful mother. With one word, he could make her do whatever he wanted. However, bound up as he was, the prince would put an end to Derric's life before he even had a chance to defend himself. The image tasted sour, but with it came a new, far more amusing idea.

"Have you noticed, Humphrey?" he asked, eyeing the prince hovering over whatever dinner he was concocting. "How Maria changes back when I touch her? Have you wondered about that?"

Humphrey paused over the fire, turning ever so slowly to look at Derric. Oh yes, he had him.

"Also, I've been meaning to ask why you never questioned Maria waiting to turn into a swan that first night until you kissed her? But every night of our journey, it's been *sundown* when she's changed. And didn't she first tell you the change happens at midnight? How strange, don't you think?"

He watched in triumphant glee as Humphrey's attention turned to Maria, a suspicious glint in his eyes.

"That's true," the prince said, turning back to his dinner. A moment later, he rose to his feet. "Maria?"

"Now is *not* the time to discuss this," she said, a tremor in her voice belying her brave front.

"Oh, I think this is a very good time." Humphrey moved to stand beside Derric, who knelt before him. "Why weren't you already a swan that first night? Why does Daniel's touch change you back every time?"

"Not every time!" Maria cried, taking her eyes off of Derric. "I changed once in the pond when he wasn't anywhere near me."

"But I did save you when you almost drowned," Derric mused. "Some thanks I get, carrying your cold body back to the stables, dressed in nothing but your nightgown—which is partially see-through when wet, by the way," he added with a smile at Humphrey.

The prince sucked in a breath, his face reddening. "You were alone with him at night?" He didn't move, but his anger made him seem larger, more intimidating. "Why didn't you turn into a swan that first night, Maria?"

"Who is the red-haired woman, *Humphrey?*" she snapped back, taking a step forward. The question caught the prince off guard, and he hesitated. "It seems I'm not the only one keeping secrets, *dear.*"

"Maybe you'd be better off with the slave, then?" Humphrey shouted, and Derric laughed.

Something hot and slimy poured into Derric's open mouth, choking him. It tasted like dirt and seared his throat as he spluttered. He swallowed desperately. Almost at once, his insides began to writhe in pain, and the cuts on his arms burned in agony. He let out a terrible scream and fell sideways.

"What have you done to me?"

"I gave you a taste of your own medicine." Humphrey held up a wooden cup Derric hadn't noticed.

"I will burn you all for this," Derric hissed, his body spasming again.

"There's nothing you can do to us now," Humphrey said, his voice calm and assured again. "You're done."

"That's what you think. ELLIS!"

Chapter 24

LOOPHOLES AND LULLABIES

. . . .

Maria's world moved in slow motion, and yet everything happened too fast to comprehend. Anger turned to confusion as Humphrey shifted, mid-argument, and poured the contents of a wooden cup into Daniel's laughing mouth.

The fight had been a ruse? Humphrey wasn't mad at her? She couldn't wrap her mind around it. Daniel screamed in agony and fell sideways, and his cry chilled the blood in her veins. "—Ellis!"

No, Maria whirled around to see Sarah, stark white and wide-eyed. Undoubtedly, she realized what this meant: Ellis was obligated to do whatever Daniel ordered.

He could kill them all before the potion did its work.

Ellis appeared before Daniel in lynx form, its feline eyebrows raised in vague curiosity.

"You called?"

Daniel curled up into a ball as his body shook with a new wave of pain. Sarah rushed forward to his side, unable to stand helplessly by. Ellis, however, yawned.

"How long will this take?" Sarah cried.

"They poisoned me!" Daniel said to Ellis through gritted teeth.

"We didn't poison you," Humphrey said, though his brows knit together in concern. "We're saving you."

In response, Daniel screamed again. A shiver ran up Maria's spine. "Ellis? Did you switch the plants?" Fear prickled her skin. They wouldn't have known if he had. "Did you poison him?"

Ellis rolled its eyes. "Of course not. I wouldn't be able

to collect my favor if I'd given you the wrong plant. Besides, I can't kill him—it's part of the rules."

"Rules," Maria muttered in annoyance. "What's with all of these stupid magical rules?"

"Ellis," Daniel grunted. "Kill them. Kill them all!"

The lynx turned yellow eyes on the three of them, the glimmer of a true hunter lurking in its gaze. "Kill them? That could while away the hours, I suppose." It sighed and turned back to Daniel. "But no. I don't think so."

"You have to obey me! You gave me your name!"

"How does he even know that?" Humphrey asked in frustration, moving to stand in front of her and drawing his sword. "Maria discovered that while he was unconscious!"

"He always knew—it was in the back of his mind. The evil inside him just decided to remember," Ellis said to Humphrey before turning back to the writhing young man on the ground. "And no, that's not exactly true, is it? I didn't give *you* my name."

"Yes, you did," Daniel hissed, sweat breaking out on his forehead.

"Tell me," Ellis said with a hint of amusement. "Is your name Daniel?"

"No!" Daniel spat, glaring at Ellis. "You know I am far more powerful than that name."

"Ah, yes, but see," Ellis grinned, showing sharp feline teeth. "I gave my name to Daniel, and you aren't him." The grin turned into a sneer as the lynx glowered down at its master. "You ought to remember who you're dealing with before you summon me again."

Without giving him a chance to respond, Ellis laid a large paw on Daniel's head. Daniel's eyes fluttered closed, and his body went limp.

"What did you do to him?" Sarah asked, clutching at her brother's shoulder and leaning her head down to his chest to check for a heartbeat.

A Stolen Kiss

"He's alive. I put him to sleep. When he wakes, the cure will have run its course."

"Why did you help us?" Maria asked. The lynx turned its imperturbable gaze on her. "Why did you choose the loophole and take our side?"

Ellis blinked. "Purely selfish reasons, I assure you. I could see the darkness in him would be stronger than any power I've encountered. It's been far too long since a beornach poisoned someone with such latent ability. While I don't mind a great evil in this world, his dependence on me would mean I'd never get another moment of peace." The lynx flicked its stubby tail in agitation. "I am no man's slave. When he is back to his normal, boring, good self, he'll call me only when in need of my particular greatness."

A small smile cracked Maria's lips. "And here I was thinking you'd taken a liking to us. Shame." She grinned at the cat, and its lips twitched. "Regardless of the motivation. Thank you."

"A liking? To you?" Ellis's gaze flickered between them all, landing on Sarah with a glare. "No, I don't think so." The cat vanished, and Maria moved to Sarah's side.

"Let's unbind him. I think he'll be miserable enough when he wakes."

"You're sure he'll be safe?" Humphrey asked, crouching down beside her.

"If Ellis says so. I believe Ellis."

"You know, it isn't wise to trust a shapeshifter." Humphrey smiled, one eyebrow raised.

Maria stared up at him. "I'm sorry for what I said—I didn't realize you were just creating a diversion."

Humphrey shook his head. "Don't worry about it. I noticed our first night away from the castle that you change at sundown, not at midnight. I figured you'd explain yourself when you were ready."

I'm ready now, she thought. Without a moment to allow second-guessing, she launched into the explanation of how she'd stopped turning into a swan for so many years up until the moment he kissed her.

"Daniel said maybe the spell had somehow gone dormant and, because I've been bound to someone else, your kiss woke it up."

"To emphasize it's not a Kiss Clause?" Humphrey suggested.

"Maybe. Or maybe it was Gilda's cruel way of making me think I was free, only to have the world come crashing down just when I meet my prince."

Humphrey laughed. "It sounds funny when you say it like that. Like we're from the history books and I've rescued you."

"Isn't that what you're doing here?" she asked with a smile. "I've always dreamed of Prince Charming coming to save me in some way or another."

"Yes." Humphrey shifted, looking awkward and glancing past her to Sarah still sitting close by with Daniel's head in her lap. "But that's why we're all here. I think Daniel is just as intent on rescuing you as I am."

"Oh, Daniel." Maria turned to look at his sleeping form. Sweat still glistened on his face, and he shifted in his sleep as though in pain. "I hope he doesn't remember all of the awful things he said."

"We can't hold any of it against him," Humphrey said, tucking into a saddlebag the rope Sarah had removed from his arms and hands. "He won't have meant it."

"He meant some of it," Sarah whispered, stroking her brother's blond locks. "He meant everything he said about our father and about being a slave."

They all sat in silence for a moment, watching Daniel writhe in fitful sleep.

"Still though," Humphrey said with a wry smile. "I kind of like knowing he isn't perfect."

"What?" Sarah and Maria asked together.

"Your brother is the essence of goodness, Sarah. He's

practically incorruptible. Everything he's done—leaving the castle, guiding us here, taking on the beornach. It's all been selfless."

"He is obnoxiously good-hearted," Sarah agreed. "He's never been selfish, and he never gets cross with me—or, well, he gets cross with me all of the time, but he doesn't act on his anger."

"It's good to know he has a dark side, even if it has to be magically induced." Humphrey paused in contemplation. "Ellis said Daniel was someone of 'such latent ability.' Do you think that means Daniel *is* a sorcerer and just doesn't know it? His mother's book is magic, so it's not difficult to imagine it being in his blood, after all."

"I caught that, too. I think he might be." Maria said.

"So, when he wakes up, if he can't remember, do we tell him?" Sarah asked. "Anything? Everything?"

"I think it'd be best if he didn't know what he said to us. To any of us," Maria said, her cheeks warming just at the thought of Daniel's suggestions of the relationship between them. She wanted *that* to be buried and done with.

"But then, do we tell him he conjured fire? That he might be able to do it again, and do more?"

"I don't know." Humphrey stared off at the fire. "We have to make sure he's back to himself." He stood and turned toward the fire. "Sarah, will you help me make dinner? I'm afraid I'm starving but haven't a clue how to cook what you packed."

"I will. Maria? Will you stay with him? I'll get one of my handkerchiefs wet, and you can use it as a cool cloth on his forehead."

The last thing she wanted to do was be near Daniel. Knowing Daniel wasn't perfect was a comfort in a way, but Maria wondered if that hadn't made the poison's effect all the more powerful. The things he had said still crawled around in her brain, and even though she knew it'd been the evil in him saying it . . . it didn't make it any less true.

She moved into Sarah's place, allowing Daniel's head to rest in her lap, and accepted the damp handkerchief when Sarah returned with it. Even covered in sweat and with all his muscles tight with pain, his beauty was undeniable. It wasn't like Humphrey's obvious, striking good looks. The prince had the sort of face one wanted to paint a portrait of—physical perfection. One look would strike a girl breathless, and she could envision him wielding a sword or wearing armor and riding a white horse.

Daniel's softer jaw, wider mouth, and little button nose held a different sort of charm—the sort that made one think of a man nurturing a lamb after it lost its mother, or perhaps a man who would get down on the floor and play with his children, even after a long, hard day of work.

Daniel's back arched, and he groaned, pulling her from her thoughts. With tender care, Maria ran the cool cloth over his face, mopping up his perspiration, before allowing it to rest against his forehead. When he didn't relax, she cupped his face in a gentle caress to keep him from rolling off of her lap, and started humming the song he'd taught them that morning.

A few bars in, Humphrey's voice joined in from over by the fire, taking over with his melodic tones. Daniel relaxed, and Maria stroked his brow with her free hand and brushed back his hair with her fingers. She knew so little about him, but found herself drawn to him in every way; not romantic feelings per se, but inexplicably drawn to him. He kept himself so closed off, and what little she knew wasn't a happy story.

Throughout their journey, she'd found herself wondering about him—his hopes, his dreams, his wants. Did he want a family of his own? Did he think he could have one after his father had sold him? She'd already vowed to free him on paper the first chance she had. Perhaps then he could do as he liked. Did he have a young maid or seamstress who loved him, whom he loved in return?

A Stolen Kiss

The idea turned her onto a much darker path. Shocked, she banished the new thoughts, and once again wondered about the poison that had overcome him. It had changed him in drastic and rapid ways. If it could do that to someone so good, what would it have done to her? To Humphrey? Neither of them was innocent: Humphrey with his red-haired woman, and Maria with her lies. Her lies and her feelings for—no. No, she wouldn't entertain them, not even as she brushed his lips with her thumb.

Chapter 25
Derric's Return

. . . .

Black dreams plagued Derric's sleep. Over and over he faced the beast and fell, surviving just long enough to see the creature slay Humphrey, Sarah, and Maria. The dream shifted to Derric standing alone in Fangralee, a woman dressed in black before him. She'd pull back her hood to reveal his mother's face—then shoot him full of lightning.

Next he'd stand over a kingdom, a familiar man shrouded in shadow beside him. The blood-red sky roiled with black clouds, and the man spoke.

"If you don't join me, you'll watch it burn."

"You'll burn it either way," Derric replied, and, as he spoke, the land before him went up in flames as terrible screams rent the air.

Just when he thought he couldn't bear to watch the kingdom burn again, everything changed. The sky turned blue, the grass emerald green, and the shadowy man became Maria, laughing as she rolled down the hill, calling for him to follow her.

The dream changed again, and now he lay in the grass beside a calm stream. The sun kissed his face, and birds chirped with chipper abandon. Something tickled his cheek, and he opened his eyes. Dark hair cascaded down beneath a crown of gold. Maria's eyes sparkled with laughter as she propped herself up beside him.

"Are you happy?" she asked, brushing his hair back.

Happy? What was happy? Derric considered the way he felt. It was new and warm, and he never wanted to leave.

"I am. Are you happy?"

"Deliriously." She leaned in and kissed him, and he savored the taste of her lips.

As she pulled back, Derric drank in her presence. "I love you."

"I can wait."

"What?"

"I'll eat when he wakes."

Derric blinked and pushed himself up. "I don't understand."

"Save enough for Daniel. I'm sure he'll be famished," Maria said, still smiling.

"There's plenty," a voice said from behind, and Derric turned to see Humphrey standing not too far away. "Sarah really can cook."

Something's wrong here.

And then he woke up.

Derric sat up so fast his head spun, and he dropped back down with a groan. The owner of the legs his head landed in gave a shout of surprise.

"He's awake!"

When Derric opened his eyes again, he saw Maria leaning over him, her brows knit together in concern.

"Daniel? How are you feeling?"

Sarah's and Humphrey's faces joined Maria's above him.

"Everything hurts. Why does everything hurt?"

"It might be because of the antidote we gave you. You don't remember?" Maria's frown deepened.

"Antidote? Antidote to what?" Derric's muscles tensed, which hurt more. A foreboding feeling coursed through his aching body.

"To the beornach's poison," she said, glancing up at where Sarah and Humphrey sat by the fire.

The words were a dagger to his heart. "Beornach?" It felt like he'd been doused in ice water. He sat up again, slower this time, and turned to face them all. For a moment he stared at them—then realization set in. "What did I do? Say? You have to tell me—No, wait . . . maybe I don't want to know."

He knew what the poison would do to a person. Hazy memories mixed with nightmares, fighting to return to the surface. Shoving them aside, he addressed his friends.

"Give me the basics. What did I do?"

Sarah cleared her throat. "You tried to get me to set you free by lying to me, and you told me everything about Father selling you to the stables."

Derric closed his eyes—he'd never wanted Sarah to know. One of them ought to have had an unblemished relationship with their father.

Maria spoke next. "You were inappropriate and tried to convince me you had power over me and my curse. Then you tried to create a rift between the two of us." She gestured to Humphrey, and Derric turned to him.

"You didn't faze me much, mate," Humphrey said with a shrug. "I knew it wasn't you talking. You tried to tell me Maria was keeping secrets, but I already knew that. We all have secrets. I poured the antidote down your throat and then—"

They all exchanged a look, no doubt trying to decide whether or not they should tell him something.

"Then what?"

"You tried to have Ellis kill us all." Sarah tried to remain casual as she pulled at her tunic, not meeting his eyes.

"And at one point you conjured fire," Humphrey added in the same tone Sarah had used, as if they were discussing a picnic Derric had missed.

"I . . . I did what?" Derric sat back and found it hard

to breathe. "Ellis . . . Ellis gave me its name. That's right, shapeshifters are controlled by their names. Then—wait, how are you all still alive?"

"Ellis found a loophole and didn't kill us," Maria said with a small smile. "Apparently for selfish reasons, but it felt gallant."

"And I conjured fire. Real fire?"

"Real fire." Sarah nodded. "But we figured that happened because of the poison—that it gave you those dark powers."

"Oh, right," Derric whispered, passing a hand over his face. He didn't feel now would be the right time to tell them a beornach couldn't give someone magical powers. Especially since he wasn't even sure what it meant. Glancing up, he saw Maria studying his face, and he rearranged his features.

"Are you going to be all right?" she asked, a hint of suspicion in her eyes.

"In time. I—I'm so sorry for what I said and did." They all murmured their understanding, but he cut them off. "I know you know it was because of the poison, but it's deeper than that. The beornach brings out darkness that's already in each of us and magnifies it, allowing it to feed off of itself."

Those things he said had to come from somewhere within, amplified and twisted. He wanted them to know— they *had* to know. It couldn't be excused or blown off. Ever since he'd found out Maria's secret lack-of-swanitude, he'd felt like he was lying to Humphrey. And hadn't he felt the pang of frustration every time Sarah spoke dotingly of their father? As for Maria, well, Derric cringed. He knew how she made him feel, and that wasn't something he ever wanted to resurface.

His words affected them all in a different way. Humphrey nodded, his lips pursed as he observed Derric. Sarah let out a mixture of a sob and a laugh, and threw her arms around him. Over Sarah's shoulder, he saw Maria staring at the ground, the firelight showing a crimson flush in her cheeks. He closed his eyes against it, but the look on her face remained burned into his memory. Part of him wanted to ask what he'd said to her, but he knew it wouldn't be anything worth reliving.

"Why don't you eat, and then we'll all get some rest. Tomorrow we won't have the comfort of this island." Humphrey moved to the fire. Derric accepted the plate handed to him and settled into his own thoughts while Humphrey set up the tent.

Difficult as it was to tell night from day in Fangralee, and with Maria's morning transformation rendered unnecessary once again, the group woke at some point the next day—the exact time, none of them could pinpoint. Derric remained quiet as they packed up camp. Not long after waking, he realized, despite their nonchalance the night before, they felt uneasy around him.

Sarah kept throwing him piteous looks with large puppy-dog eyes. Whenever he caught her gaze, she'd smile the way one might at a dying relative. Humphrey kept one hand on the hilt of his sword when he wasn't otherwise occupied, and more than once Derric noticed his suspicious glance flit from Derric to Maria and back.

As for the princess, she pretended as though Derric didn't exist.

"Where to?" Humphrey asked once they'd led the horses off the island and back onto solid Fangralee ground.

Derric, having lost the trace while under the beornach's influence, dropped to the ground once more and located his mother's familiar thread. "We'll head this way," he said, gesturing on through the trees toward what he assumed was the west.

A Stolen Kiss

"You're sure?" Humphrey asked, as Derric mounted Thumper.

"Do you doubt me?"

The prince held Derric's gaze for one long moment before shaking his head. "Of course not."

Without another word, Derric rode forward, the three of them following. For a while he feared he'd suffer their silence for the rest of the journey, so when Humphrey did break it, Derric jumped at the chance to speak.

"Are there other beornachs we need to be aware of? How do we know we aren't going to be attacked out of the blue? What else is in this forest?"

"There's more of everything here. However, since you killed the one that attacked last night, the remaining beornae won't attack without assessing the threat. I don't think they were ready to face a swan and a prince."

"What else is in this forest?" Maria asked, as Humphrey gave a triumphant whoop and threw his fist into the air.

"Well, we've faced shapeshifters and beornae," Derric said. "That just leaves snakes, gargantupedes, hippogriffs, centaurs, chimeras, and, of course, very large spiders."

"How large is very large?" Sarah asked, with unmistakable fear edging into her voice.

"The size of a chimera."

"Why must they always be so big?" Sarah said, more to herself than to the group. Derric knew his sister had no love for spiders, and he hoped they wouldn't see any of them nor the rest of the creatures he'd mentioned for that matter.

Chapter 26
Chimeras and Centaurs and Hippogriffs—Oh My!

. . . .

They saw the chimera, but the hippogriff caught them off guard.

Maria half listened to Humphrey and Sarah's endless argument about the plural form of the common language.

"Why is it *beornae* and not *beornachs*?"

"Maybe it's like *platypuses. Platypi.* Did we ever decide which it was?"

She watched as Daniel buried his nose in his mother's journal, his shoulders hunching more with each turn of the page. Without seeing his face, she had no way of knowing for sure, but his tense form made her think he didn't like whatever he'd found in there.

Guilt sank into the pit of her stomach like a rock. She hadn't been on her best behavior since Daniel returned to them. Her feelings for him weren't to be explored, but that wasn't why she'd pushed him away. Something Ellis had said wriggled around in her brain, and she'd spent most of the morning wondering how to voice it. Perhaps if she—

A piercing scream broke through her train of thought, and Maria whirled about to see Sarah pointing off to the left.

A beast almost as large as the beornach watched them from not fifty paces away. With the head and body of a lion, it had a goat's head growing out from its middle, the horns tinged red with blood. Instead of a tail, a long-fanged snake hissed at the other end.

The sounds of blades being removed from their sheaths filled her ears, but another noise accompanied it.

As Daniel and Humphrey moved to face the chimera, something large knocked Maria backward off of her horse.

She hit the ground hard, leaving her breathless and unable to call out. A beast loomed over her, difficult to see at first, but the eagle's head and giant wingspan soon came into focus as the creature pinned her to the ground with a long-taloned claw.

"Maria!" Sarah cried, still atop her steed.

The hippogriff cocked its head to the side, examining Maria with a large golden eye. A roar let her know the chimera now stood a few paces away from them, no doubt crouched and ready to pounce.

In a fleeting moment of panic, Maria wondered where the giant spiders were.

"Leonidas! Cercies! Heel!"

The hippogriff above her jerked its head up and backed away, freeing Maria. Sitting up, she saw the chimera follow suit, sitting on its haunches and looking out into the woods beyond them.

Sarah, having climbed down from her horse, helped Maria to her feet. Her horse was nowhere to be seen.

Both girls scanned the dense forest, searching for the bodiless voice, but they found no one. Humphrey moved to their sides, his blade drawn. Daniel remained further away, near the tri-creatured chimera.

Soft clopping noises drew Maria's gaze to the right, her heart leaping as she saw a horse—no, not a horse—a centaur step out onto the visible path. Horse from the waist down, she was all woman up top. Her wild hair reminded Maria of an unkempt horse's mane, black and mussed. The long tendrils fell down over her chest, covering her breasts. Her features were sharp and intelligent, with high cheekbones and a long, pointed chin. Her dark eyes, larger than any normal woman's, watched them as she approached.

"Well, well, what have we here? Trespassers in my forest? We don't take kindly to unwanted guests."

"Oh, Nysa, let me have the dark one." Another female centaur stepped in from their right, this one with a coat of auburn, the hair atop her head cut short and covering nothing, her feminine torso exposed.

Beside Maria, Humphrey let out a strangled sound as he stared wide-eyed at the newest centaur.

"Perhaps I shall." Nysa turned her attention to Humphrey. "How would you like to belong to Drusilla? She's very good to her pets."

"We're not pets. We're people." Sarah stepped out in front of Humphrey and Maria, glowering up at the centaurs.

"And yet you keep horses for pets." Nysa pawed the ground with her hoof. "So is it really strange to think we would keep humans?"

"You'll have to kill us first," Sarah said, squaring her shoulders. Humphrey shot Maria an impressed look over Sarah's head.

"I take it he belongs to you, then, filly?" Nysa said to Sarah, gesturing to Humphrey.

"No," Drusilla said with a wicked grin, mimicking Sarah by squaring off her torso and showing off her prominent bare chest. "She's protecting her lady. I like her spirit. She will be a force to be reckoned with one day."

As the centaur approached, Maria couldn't help but feel miniscule by comparison. Drusilla stopped just in front of Humphrey, who froze and stared at the ground. With a soft snicker, she ran her fingers through Humphrey's dark hair. Maria watched him tense and close his eyes.

"I think I'm going to like him," Drusilla said in a singsong voice, her doe-brown eyes large, giving her the appearance of innocence.

"Leave him alone!" Sarah shouted, shoving Humphrey back and staring up at Drusilla.

The centaur hissed at Sarah, lunging at her neck. Thumper reared on his hind legs and forced Drusilla back, stepping between the centaur and Sarah. Before either Nysa or Drusilla could act, another voice called out.

"There's another one! Here."

Maria whirled around and saw a dappled female centaur approaching near the chimera. Daniel stood where Thumper had been, his mother's journal clutched to his side. At the sight of his calm demeanor, Maria relaxed.

"Only cowards hide," Nysa said with narrowed eyes as she turned to address Daniel. Maria watched her expression change to one of surprise for an instant before she altered to cool indifference.

"I am no coward," Daniel said in a tone as serene as his countenance. "And we mean you no harm. We're just passing through."

Nysa gave a disinterested shrug of her broad shoulders. "Your business is no business of mine. I care not why you're here but that you *are* here."

"You say we've trespassed in your forest, but you know we have every right to be here."

"Perhaps you have the right, but they—"

"Are with me," Daniel finished for her, raising an eyebrow. Nysa's eyes narrowed, and Maria saw Drusilla draw back as Daniel stepped closer. The dappled centaur kept her distance as well, watching Daniel with open fascination, her grey eyes twinkling with interest.

After what felt like an eternity of silence, Nysa broke the eye contact, and Maria saw the corner of Daniel's mouth twitch.

"Strangers are of no use to us, even one such as yourself. I should order my drove to attack you now and have done with you."

Maintaining his detached persona, Daniel sighed. "I have only just recovered from the bite of the forbidden creature, and I'm sure there are still remnants of its poison in my veins. I am also the keeper of a shapeshifter's true name. If the drove attacks, I will fight back."

Nysa reared and stamped the ground with her hooves. Drusilla and the dappled centaur did the same. Beyond the trees, in the darkness, Maria heard more clopping and fearful whinnying.

"What is it you want from us, Great One?" Nysa asked.

Confused, Maria turned to Humphrey and Sarah, both of whom had furrowed brows, just as perplexed as she.

"We are on our way to Kyleria. I request safe passage for ourselves and our steeds, as well as an escort as far as you can allow."

Maria held back a snort of surprise. There was no chance in all the hells Nysa would grant them anything beyond getting out of there alive. To her astonishment, the lead centaur dropped down into a bow with a bend of her front knees.

"As you wish, Great One, so it shall be." When she straightened, Nysa threw back her regal head and let out a call in a high-pitched language Maria couldn't understand. In response, more than a dozen other centaur females appeared out of Fangralee's darkness. At the sight of so many, Maria felt the true weight of what Daniel had so coolly accomplished.

"We shall escort these humans to the Mortal Marsh," Nysa announced to her drove. "They will come to no harm or violation while in our care. Briskelle, bring forth the missing horse."

A blonde centaur with long hair in many braids came forward holding the reins of Maria's horse, Verona. She passed the reins to Maria, who heard Drusilla speak to Humphrey behind her.

"You can ride me, if you'd prefer."

"Drusilla," Nysa called, warning in her tone.

"It was just a suggestion." Drusilla petted Humphrey's head and leaned down to whisper something into the prince's ear. His face flushed, and he turned away to mount his own horse. The others followed his actions, and Maria noticed the dappled centaur remained close to Daniel and Nysa, listening to his every word with interest.

Sarah positioned herself between Drusilla and Humphrey, glowering at the brazen centaur as Maria took her place behind Daniel. On their mounts, they stood as tall as the centaurs. For the first time, Maria wondered why there were only female centaurs around them.

"The males are back at our dwellings," the blonde mare who had returned Verona said, coming up to walk beside Maria. At the quizzical look Maria gave her, the centaur laughed. "Yes, I knew what you were thinking. No, I don't read minds. I just had a feeling. That's what centaurs do. We aren't as knowledgeable as shapeshifters, but we do know things."

When Maria didn't say anything else, the blonde centaur continued. "Males of our species are the domestics—the homemakers. We are the hunters." She gestured to her fellow females. "We were out hunting when Leonidas caught your scent."

As if he'd been waiting for his name to release him, the hippogriff appeared at Maria's other side, staring at her with those great golden eyes.

"He won't harm you," the blonde said. "He's drawn to you out of kinship."

"Kinship?"

"He senses your swan half. He feels you are a kindred spirit. Birds of a feather, if you will." She laughed at her own joke and then seemed abashed. "Oh! How rude of me. My name is Briskelle." She stretched out her hand, holding it palm down at an awkward angle, a crease forming between her eyebrows. It was Maria's turn to laugh as she took Briskelle's hand and righted it into a proper human handshake.

"It's a pleasure. My name is Maria."

"Maria." Briskelle grinned as she prolonged the handshake. "What a strange yet lovely custom you have. How long does one human do this to another before they stop?"

"Not long." Maria released Briskelle's hand. "What's the customary greeting for centaurs?"

"The females head-butt or lock hooves, but the males paw the ground and bow, much as Nysa did to your Great One there."

"Great One—why do you call him that?"

"There is greatness in him. It's quite obvious he is a powerful being. Can't you see it?" She cocked her beautiful blonde head, blue eyes curious.

"Powerful?" Maria looked at Daniel, who now spoke with Nysa as an equal.

"Powerful." Briskelle confirmed. "Also handsome, virile, and honest. You can see it in his eyes. He hides things because he wants to keep others from harm, even at the cost of his own happiness. His soul is goodness itself. Not many can survive the venom of the forbidden creature without their soul being tainted."

Maria murmured her assent and fell silent, contemplating, allowing Briskelle's continuing words to pour over her unheeded.

What are you hiding, Daniel?

Chapter 27
A Centaur Escort

The minute he'd heard the centaur's call to the chimera, Derric dropped behind Thumper and cracked open his mother's journal. His frantic whisper for help turned the pages to an excerpt on centaurs. Derric focused all his attention on the words before him, half-aware of the voices arguing around him.

> *Centaurs are knowing creatures and have a good sense of what others are thinking without reading minds. Their power feeds off of emotion, sensing the troubles and truths within a turbulent soul. A calm demeanor is your best defense.*

So far those words continued to hold true as he rode alongside Nysa, the centaur chief. Nysa asked as many questions as she answered, her respect for Derric palpable.

On his other side, a silver haired, grey-eyed, dappled centaur listened with wide-eyed attentiveness. Though her coloring reminded Derric of what he'd seen most on older women, she was one of the youngest in the hunting party, smaller than all the rest. When he'd asked her name, she'd mumbled something that sounded like "Ygritte" before blushing and turning away.

"Your power is evident, even if you do not understand it yet, Great One," Nysa said, throwing her head back and shaking her mane of dark hair.

"So there is power, then?" Derric kept his voice low, though he felt certain the others weren't listening.

"In you? Haven't you realized it yet? You've tamed a

shapeshifter, survived the poison of the forbidden one, and showed no sign of fear in the face of our drove. What more do you need to see?"

"The shapeshifter gave me its name without much fight, and I survived the poison because my friends made me an antidote."

"No, the poison of such a creature is not so easily destroyed with an antidote. The host must first be able to survive as his dark self. Most are driven mad and claw at their own skin, itching to be free of the fire inside."

At the word "fire," Derric flinched.

"Yes, your feelings betray you." Nysa grinned, her dark eyes twinkling. "No ordinary being can create fire—it is a feat most sorcerers cannot accomplish." She gazed intently at him a moment. "I sense a familiar magic in you, Great One. A magic that reminds me of another who has crossed my path."

"You don't need to call me 'Great One,'" Derric said, his cheeks flushing. "My name's . . . Daniel."

"No, it's not." Again, Nysa's eyes sparkled with knowledge. "Your hesitation is evidence enough. I know who you are, and I know from whence you come. What I don't know, Great One, is why you're helping them."

A shriek of laughter drew Derric's attention behind him. Leonidas, the hippogriff, nuzzled Maria with great affection, his eyes closed in contentment. Verona didn't seem as pleased as her mistress. The horse tried to edge away and bumped into the blonde centaur on the other side, causing another round of giggles.

Derric's lips twitched in amusement as Maria's laughing eyes met his. Beside him, Nysa made a noise in the back of her throat.

"Perhaps I do see," she said with the raise of one black eyebrow. "You wish to undo what's been done to her. Her happiness means much to you. This I did not expect— the most powerful man I've ever met is infatuated with

A Stolen Kiss

a simple human girl? You could have anyone, and you choose her?"

"I don't choose her," Derric said as he returned to his placid tone and expression. "She's going to marry the prince."

"Not if Drusilla has anything to say about it." Ygritte's voice startled him. "The prince doesn't love her. His heart seeks another—Drusilla can see it. That is why she taunts him."

Derric turned to Ygritte, chewing on his lip as he stared into her open, beautiful face. "Do you see who it is?"

Ygritte blinked, and her face furrowed in concentration. "A woman of fire, of autumn, yet also of winter."

"And he left her to marry Maria?"

"No." Ygritte shook her silvery mane. "The story is sadder. His heart is the one broken, but he doesn't know the truth." She looked to her leader, face brightening. "Am I right?"

"Very close, my foal." Nysa dipped her head with aristocratic grace. "He is grieving, though his troubles are not for the reasons he believes."

"You won't give me a straight answer even if I ask, will you?" Derric said, a smirk twisting his lips, and Nysa laughed.

"No, Great One, we won't. We could, but that would be a waste. All will be revealed in the proper time. You will be the one to sense it when it comes. Your powers are not yet honed enough. They will be."

"And they will be great powers?"

"They already are. You must stop pushing them down. Do not be afraid of them; they won't turn your heart black. Her path is not yours."

Derric straightened, his heart pounding. "So you have met her, then?"

"Many years ago, yes. She came through our forest alone, seeking our protection. She, too, has felt the sting of the forbidden creature and survived the poison, though her dark days were more frightening than anything Fangralee has seen since."

"Did she receive the antidote?"

"She received it once we found her. It's fascinating, really. Such similar stories but different fates. Where she can be tamed, you cannot. Remember that, Great One. Your power is purer."

Derric fell silent, mulling over their words. Eventually, he pulled out Gilda's journal and delved deep once again in hopes of finding understanding there.

Once again, they knew nightfall when a soft honk announced Maria's transformation into a swan. Derric watched as Leonidas bounded around the black swan, cawing and nudging the ground.

"How sweet," Drusilla said, trotting past Maria. "Nysa, you may have lost your pet to a new mistress. He's quite fond of her. She'd be the first master who could fly with him since he hatched."

"We're almost to our home. Tonight you'll rest with us, and tomorrow we'll take you safely out of Fangralee." Nysa gestured through the darkness ahead where pinpricks of light could be seen.

"We're that close?" Derric asked, his heart swelling at the thought.

"No. But we happen to know how to undermine the forest's power."

They broke through the trees soon after, and a large clearing opened before them. Derric's heart skipped a beat at the sight of stars above them—he hadn't realized how much he'd missed them in their short time away from the open sky.

A wall of rock jutted up into the heavens on the far side of the clearing. Small dots of firelight lit up the structure, and Derric could see it was riddled with caves. The centaurs' dwellings, he realized, as several faces peered out from them.

"They're back!" a deep voice called, followed by a veritable stampede as the males rushed out to greet their women.

"Our hunt has been a success," Nysa called as family members reunited. "We bring game and new friends." She gestured to Derric mounted beside her. Unlike the initial suspicion and threats they'd faced with the females, the males moved forward with open curiosity and warm smiles.

"Welcome," a sleek, dark-skinned male said as he stopped beside Nysa. "Our home is your home." In hushed tones, he said to Nysa, "You couldn't have sent a scout ahead? Our cave is a disaster. I would have cleaned up one of the spares for them to stay in."

Nysa dropped her chin and gave him a sheepish grin. "I'm sorry, my love. It didn't occur to me."

The dark centaur sighed, clasping his hands together as he turned to Derric. "We are honored to have you, Great One. If you give us a bit of time, we'll have a cave ready for you and your friends. I am Drisk, mate of Nysa." He turned and started giving orders to the other males in the same breath he'd used to welcome them. Nysa watched her mate with amused adoration before returning her attention to the humans.

"Come. We'll feast together, and then you must rest."

"Aren't you worried being out in the open like this will draw other creatures to you?" Maria asked, perched on Leonidas's back.

"Our night guards are fierce warriors," Nysa replied. "Though I do think your presence may increase the dark creatures' interest in our land. We will protect you."

"It's not me I'm worried about," Maria said, her

feathers ruffling. "If our presence puts you in danger, we ought to leave."

Nysa considered Maria for a moment before speaking. "You are nobler than you first appear, Princess. You will remain with us, but you have earned our gratitude for your concern."

"Perhaps you could stay in my cave," Drusilla suggested to Humphrey. Sarah snorted, and Drusilla looked offended. "I meant all of you."

"Sure you did."

Drusilla let out a sigh and drew her head back as though wounded. "It pains me to have you speak so. I might play with little prince, here, but I do mean well." She reached out and tapped Sarah on the nose. "You must find a way past your judgment, little sister, or you won't make it through this trip unscathed."

Without another word, she trotted off toward the other centaur females who were laying out the game they'd caught. Male centaurs were already taking the animal carcasses and preparing them for cooking.

"Ygritte, Briskelle, take the three humans and show them around. I will keep the Great One with me." Nysa made a dismissive gesture, and the blonde and dappled centaurs ushered the other three and their horses forward, Leonidas going with them.

"Is . . . is there anything I can do for you?" Derric asked Nysa when they were alone. "Is there anything my power can do to keep you safe?"

"The thought is kind, Great One, but we will not need it. Rest your mind, for tonight we celebrate the journey behind and ahead. Come, I'll introduce you to my foals."

Chapter 28
A Taste of Truth

. . . .

They dined around a large bonfire and sat in the grass, the success of the hunt celebrated with music played on pan flutes by two females, while two males cantered in the firelight to a dance Briskelle called "the warrior's triumph." Much like the island, the clearing was imbued with a golden hue, a safe haven amidst the black of Fangralee.

Maria, having once again lost her feathers for who knows what reason as she was digging in her bag, clapped along when fitting and laughed at the gaiety of the celebration. Never in all of her years in the palace had she experienced a party with such life and enthusiasm. The dinner party her parents had thrown in honor of Humphrey and his family's arrival had been a stilted and awkward affair.

At the thought of her parents, Maria's stomach lurched. What was going through their minds at this very moment? Were they searching for her and Humphrey? Did they fear the worst? She pressed the thoughts away and noticed Sarah sitting by herself, her face drawn in thought.

"Are you all right?" she asked, moving to sit beside her friend. "You've been quiet ever since we arrived."

Sarah chewed on her lip and didn't say anything for a moment. Just when Maria considered giving up and rejoining the fun, Sarah spoke so fast her words blurred together.

"Doyothnmjudgemental?"

"I'm sorry, what?"

"Do you think I'm judgmental?" Sarah said with deliberate care.

Maria's brows arched, and, for the first time in a long time, she was reminded of how young Sarah really was. "Are you asking me because of what Drusilla said?"

Sarah drew her knees up to her chest and wrapped her arms around her legs. "She said if I don't change, I won't make it through this unscathed."

With a sigh, Maria leaned back, spreading her fingers in the grass. "I don't think any of us are going to make it through this unchanged. Look at everything your brother has already endured. He's faced the worst of it and is still smiling."

Sarah followed her gaze to where Daniel and Humphrey stood on the other side of the bonfire. The male centaurs were trying to teach them how to do the dance of "the warrior's triumph" on two legs.

"We all have our shortcomings," Maria said. "I don't think there's any way to get through this without them coming to light."

"You don't. You're perfect. I mean it," Sarah pressed as Maria scoffed. "You're doing all of this, risking your life to remove a curse so you can follow your duty and marry Humphrey—even though you don't love him. You were so determined to do what your parents want, you didn't tell them when the curse hibernated. You put Opea above your own safety and happiness."

"You don't think I'll be happy with Humphrey?"

"I think he's wonderful, and I'm sure you two will learn to love each other." Sarah looked straight into Maria's eyes. "But a lesser woman would forget about Humphrey and run off with the man they are bound to—even if it is a curse. You're so much stronger than that."

"Not really. I have no idea what I would do if I actually *met* Derric Harver. It's easy to ignore that part of the curse when I have no idea who he is."

Sarah dropped her gaze to the ground and said nothing. For a moment, Maria wondered at the way the other

A Stolen Kiss

girl always squirmed at the mention of Derric, but she pushed the thought aside.

"Sarah, I'm not perfect. I'm getting rid of a curse and putting three other people into danger to do so. That isn't selfless."

"We chose to come with you."

"More yet," Maria continued, raising her voice just enough to drown out Sarah's argument. "I never even considered having a choice about marrying Humphrey. It's not as though I grew up thinking, 'I could choose for myself, or I could marry the prince my parents want me to marry.' No. I assumed I didn't have a choice. But now, I don't even have the ability to say yes to anyone!"

She shook her head and leaned back to stare at the glittering sky, trying to stem the surging tide of emotion. "I can't say yes to Humphrey, and it's given me time to think about whether or not I even *want* to. I've been able to evaluate my own life and wonder what it would be like if there had been no Gilda and no Humphrey."

Across the way, Daniel threw his head back in laughter as Humphrey tried out a new dance move. She couldn't hear what the prince said, but in response, Daniel moved his hips in imitation, causing uproarious laughter to break out amongst the centaurs.

"If I could choose whomever I wanted, I don't think it would be Humphrey. I think it would be someone different from myself. I would choose someone who loved me because he wanted to, not because he had to. I think Humphrey would do the same."

"You won't choose though, will you?" Sarah asked, shifting to face Maria again. "Once we find Gilda and break the curse, you'll marry Humphrey."

"Yes."

"Why?"

"Because both of us are bound to our people and expected to do what's best for them. A marriage means uniting Dellsby and Opea. It better protects our kingdoms from war and other tragedies."

"When you're queen, will you lift the ban on sorcery?"

Surprised, Maria allowed the question to sit for a moment before responding. "I—I don't know. I hadn't thought much about it. Why?"

Though Sarah's tone remained casual, Maria noticed the calculated air with which she spoke. "Well, Humphrey comes from a land where those with magic are welcome. I thought perhaps he'd want a royal sorcerer. Or that maybe this experience has changed your mind about magic."

Maria snorted. "Oh, yes. Between that poison giving Daniel dark powers, which he tried to kill us with, and my curse having a mind of its own, I've quite grown to love magic."

"What about G—the journal my brother has? It's been very helpful to us. And Ellis? It saved our lives."

"True," Maria conceded. "But I have yet to see anything that *really* makes me think Opea would benefit from lifting the ban on sorcery." A thought that had been bothering her formed on her lips. "Sarah, what do you think Ellis meant when he said he gave his name to Daniel, and Daniel said that wasn't his name?"

As though she'd been turned to stone, Sarah stiffened, frozen in place for several seconds with wide, blank eyes. "I—I don't know," she said, turning with excruciating care. "Perhaps when the poison was making him evil, it was corrupting his true self. Maybe if he'd been taken by darkness, he would have chosen a new name and been someone else."

"Maybe," Maria agreed. Sarah relaxed, and it piqued the princess's suspicion. Sarah knew something, but whatever it was, blood would be thicker than crown. Sarah would keep Daniel's secrets. And what of his mother's clearly magical, highly knowledgeable journal? Could it be Daniel had power and hid it to keep from being banished? Maria chewed on her lip and contemplated the possibilities.

A Stolen Kiss

When the festivities died down, they were led up the mountain path to an unused cave. The cave felt homier than Maria had imagined. A small fire crackled near the front entrance, and a pile of animal pelt bedding warmed nearby. Briskelle promised them a safe sleep and left them alone.

"When we left Edleton less than a week ago," Humphrey said with wide eyes and a half-cocked grin. "I never would have expected to end up under the hospitality of centaurs."

Maria murmured in agreement as Daniel distributed their bedrolls. Sarah and Humphrey accepted their sleeping mats and moved to find a comfortable place, but Maria watched as Daniel turned to the horses. He murmured to each one, leading it to one of the pelts. All four horses fit into the cave with them, and still ample space remained. Daniel wrapped a blanket over each steed—the nights grew colder with each passing hour. Soon autumn would be winter.

As he put the last horse to bed, Daniel caught her watching him. Embarrassed to be seen staring so, Maria turned away to join the others, and found Humphrey watching her, an unreadable expression on his face.

Face flushing, Maria dropped her gaze and studiously arranged her blankets. No one said anything as they crawled into their bedding, and Maria wondered if they, like her, were processing troublesome thoughts stirred up by their journey's struggles.

Flickering firelight caught her attention, and she shifted to look toward the front of the cave. Daniel wasn't nestled in for sleep but had moved closer to the firelight, his mother's journal cracked open once again. He rested against his horse, Thumper, and turned a page.

What was it that held his attention so? What could he be learning from that book? She watched as his lips moved while he read. From the sound of it, he muttered the same thing over and over. It had a familiar rhythm, but she couldn't understand the words.

Curiosity getting the better of her, she slipped out of her covers and moved across the cave to sit beside him.

"What are you reading?" she asked. He stiffened as she settled next to him. "Well, I know what you're reading, I guess. What does it say?" When he still said nothing, Maria sighed. "Come, Daniel. You don't need to be so nervous around me. I don't blame you for what happened last night. Please. I can't bear the thought of you not talking to me anymore."

He cast her an uneasy glance. "I was trying to find out if there was anything in this book that might help us protect ourselves the way the song my mother taught me did."

"You mean like spells? Ones we can say?"

"Yes. I figured, if the song worked for all of us, then some spells must work for everyone even if they don't have magic in their bones."

"That's clever of you," Maria said, impressed by his forethought. "Have you found any?"

"Not exactly. This page here has something about returning what was lost, but I'm not sure what that means. Also, I have the feeling it won't work for just anyone. It says here 'only true power can bring back what was lost,' so I think that means magic."

Before she could talk herself out of it, Maria blurted out her next question. "But you're magic, aren't you? You're a sorcerer?"

Daniel stilled, his brows knit together in consternation. "Sorcery is banned in Opea."

It was neither a denial nor an admission. Maria turned to him and placed her hand over his as it rested on the journal in his lap. Daniel's gaze rose to meet hers. Her stomach

A Stolen Kiss

flipped, and she wondered if she'd ever noticed how green his eyes were—like sage with flecks of gold.

"I will never think less of you for being a sorcerer," she said, her chest constricting. She felt breathless. "After everything you've done for me, all the dangers you've faced, how could I be anything but grateful? Besides," she added, the corner of her mouth twitching in a smile, "I'm not sure you even realized it until recently. I saw your face when you found out you'd conjured fire."

"I want to protect you. I don't want anything I've done to keep you from your happily-ever-after."

He spoke with such earnest sincerity, but she didn't understand. He hadn't done anything to her. Being so close to him felt heady, and she wondered when her face had gotten so close to his. The urge to brush her fingers against his lips was overcome by the desire to press her mouth against them instead.

"I don't want my magic or anything from my family to hurt you," he said, his voice low.

"You haven't hurt me. You've been nothing but kind and gentle and . . . " She trailed off, leaning in to close the gap. In the second before his lips touched hers, a scream rent the air, and they jumped apart.

"What was that?" Humphrey asked, bolting upright and staring wildly about the cave.

"What's going on?" Sarah's question followed as she, too, sat up.

"I don't know." Daniel moved to the mouth of the cave as a loud trumpet rang through the night. Galloping rumbled all around them, feeling like an earthquake in their cave. One final call in Nysa's voice sent chills up Maria's spine, and then all hells broke loose.

"Warriors assemble! We're under attack!"

Chapter 29
A Fear of Spiders

. . . .

Humphrey joined Derric at the front of the cave, both gazing out into the darkness. A cold knot of horror twisted in Derric's stomach and spread through his veins like a venom, paralyzing him as he watched the oncoming horde.

Black masses advanced upon the clearing. Six thick, yet spindly, legs protruded from bulbous, coarse-haired lower bodies, giving them terrifying speed and agility. Attached to the insect-like abdomen where a thorax should have been, a human torso the color of charcoal rose erect. In contrast with the spidery lower portion, the human half lacked any hair but seemed cracked and charred. He felt the shudder run through Humphrey, who stood close beside him.

"What in all the hells are those?"

A moment passed before Derric found his voice and could answer. "Arachnae."

Behind him, someone sucked in a breath and whimpered.

"I—I thought those were a myth." The quiver in Sarah's voice matched the quake in Derric's knees.

"Apparently not," he whispered, his hand moving to his dagger.

Below them, centaurs returned the charge, weapons in hand. The multi-colored drove met the blackened horde with clangs, fangs, and hooves. Beside him, Humphrey set his jaw and grabbed his arm.

"Come on, they need our help. You two, stay in the cave."

Before he could even think, Derric found himself dragged out of the cave and down the mountain path behind Humphrey.

"How are we supposed to help?" Derric asked, tripping over a rock in the darkness.

"However we can! After all they've—Drusilla!" The auburn-haired female stopped in her tracks just ahead, turning toward them.

"What are you doing? Get back to safety!" she called, her attention torn between them and the arachnae advancing on her fellow warriors.

"No! We're here to help. I'm an experienced swordsman. Here, crouch down so I can climb up."

"Excuse me?" Drusilla's eyebrows shot high, and Humphrey held her complete attention.

"The two of us will be stronger together than alone. You move swiftly, and I can fight from your back. Let me up." Without argument, Drusilla knelt, and Humphrey swung himself up, thrusting his sword into the air. "WE RIDE!"

Off they shot toward the fighting mass, bellowing their war cries and leaving Derric clueless in the darkness. Loud screeching and screaming echoed from the arachnae, words spoken in their ancient language pierced Derric's eardrums. Heart thrumming, he spun around in search of something to do.

I have a dagger! What am I supposed to do with just a dagger and no experience?

"Great One!" Ygritte galloped toward him, her silver hair flowing behind her.

"Ygritte! What are you doing? You can't be old enough to be out here."

"I'm as old as you are," she said, lifting her chin and holding up the bow in her arms. A quiver of arrows hung from her side, ready for use. "Besides, we need your help. Your skills."

"What skills? I'm a stablehand!"

Her snort of annoyance sent a thrill of aggravation through him. "Use your powers! You're the Great One!"

"I don't know how. I've never used them on purpose."

She stood over him, her grey eyes fierce as she glared at him. "Figure it out. Without you, my kin will die. Don't think; just act."

Before he could respond, an arachnae broke past the front line and scuttled toward them with breathtaking speed. Derric froze, but Ygritte leapt into action. With a swift and practiced air, she pulled an arrow from the quiver, nocked it, and let it fly. Landing true, the projectile pierced the seared skin of the arachnae's shoulder. It screamed, but the wound only propelled it forward, its six legs skittering along the dark ground with ease.

Two more arrows sank into its body, but still the creature advanced. Grasping just her bow, Ygritte didn't stand a chance when the creature came into combat range. She dodged a swipe of the arachnae's dark axe but shouted in pain as the next swing caught her by the shoulder.

"Ygritte!" Derric rushed forward, slashing at the creature's spider half with his dagger and drawing blood. Howling, the offender turned on Derric and grabbed him by the throat, lifting him off his feet. Unable to breathe, Derric kicked out, but the creature laughed.

"Human," it said in a raspy foreign accent. "It iss your turn to be sstepped on."

Black spots appeared at the edge of Derric's vision, but a familiar voice—the same one that had urged him toward the golden island—whispered somewhere in his thoughts.

Grab its wrists. Grab its wrists. Make it burn.

Derric did as he'd been told, grabbing his attacker's wrists and wildly thinking of fire. After a second or two, the creature screamed and released him. Crumpling to the ground, Derric gasped for air. His hands felt hot, and he pushed himself up to see the creature backing away, staring at its arms in horror. Fire engulfed them, spreading to the torso and growing until the creature's whole body was alight.

The moment he felt sure on his feet, Derric rushed to Ygritte's side. Her shoulder bled, and though she fought to pull back the string of her bow, she couldn't summon the strength.

"Here," Derric called, reaching up to her shoulder. She leaned sideways so he could place his palm flat against the bloody gash. Knowing it was the right thing to do, Derric murmured the spell to return what had been lost until his hand tingled and he felt the flow of magic through him.

When he removed his blood-covered hand, the skin beneath was whole. Eyes wide with wonder, Ygritte smiled. "I knew you were the Great One." Without waiting for a response, she kissed him full on the lips before cantering off toward the fight with new fervor, shooting arrows into the night.

They don't like fire, the voice of wisdom said to Derric. *Use it against them. Set them ablaze.*

A small feeling in the back of his mind questioned the violence of the suggestion, but the centaurs needed help and needed it fast. He didn't have time to wonder about the ethics of his powers. A thrill ran through him, and his mouth twisted into a smile. This was something he could do.

With a cry like Humphrey and Drusilla's bellow, Derric rushed forward into the fray.

Chapter 30
Fire Ends the Fight

. . . .

Maria watched in horror as Humphrey and Daniel left the cave and bounded down the mountainside. Straightening her shoulders, Maria moved to follow.

"Whoa!" Sarah caught her arm and pulled her back away from the mouth of the cave towards the campfire. "They said to stay in here!"

"It's our fault they're being attacked. Nysa said they would be in more danger because of our presence. We have to go help them!"

"What on earth could we do against arachnae?"

"We have to try!"

"No, we don't." Sarah gripped Maria by the shoulders, her eyes wide. "We don't have any weapons. They told us to stay here; that's what we need to do."

"Sarah, it's not the centaur males out there fighting—it's the females. Haven't you learned anything from them? I don't want to be cooped up or fragile anymore. I want to help. I want to fight!"

She turned to leave the cave but scurried back as a large black body descended into the opening. The arachnae male crawled in across the cave's ceiling, and Sarah released a blood-curdling scream as the horses whinnied and ran to the back.

Maria's bones turned to jelly at the sight of the grotesque creature as he scaled down the wall to face them upright.

Its multitude of red eyes reminded her of the beornach, and pointed, black fangs jutted out from between its ash-grey lips. Wiry, black hair—the same as covered his lower half—sprouted atop his head. The sharp lines of his face compounded his already grotesque features. When he spoke, his words were raspy, and his laughter crawled with strange clicking noises.

"Look what Nero's caughts in his web. Little humansss with skins so fine. I think I'll take you back and share you with my mates. They loves the females. So tender and weak."

A surge of bravery wiggled through Maria's terror, and she bent down, picking up a log from the fire. One end blazed, and Maria held it like a torch, waving it before her. Nero hissed and pulled back as she drew closer.

"We. Are. Not. Weak," Maria growled, lunging and startling Nero into a momentary retreat.

"Perhaps not you, Princesssss," Nero said, causing Maria to pause. "But the maid is none so brave. Afraid of spidersss, dear? Ah yessss. Centaurs might be knowing, but we sees. I sees your fear, Sarah. I sees your failure. Princessss, I sees your loves for the son of the dark lady. I sees Derricusss Harver. I sees all."

"No!" Sarah followed Maria's example and grabbed a torch from the fire. She pushed forward, and the two of them took steps, waving their fire to keep Nero back.

"You haves no power. You leave, I kill your horsesss." Nero jerked forward, startling them. Maria pulled back, but Sarah screamed and threw her torch. It hit Nero and caught his coarse body hair, setting him aflame. With a shriek, he backed out of the cave.

Maria ran forward, watching in horror as Nero's flaming body rolled down the mountainside and into another group of arachnae, spreading the conflagration among them.

"Well done," Maria whispered, grinning at Sarah's pale face.

"I panicked."

"It worked. We know they don't like fire. Come on, let's go."

Without waiting for Sarah, Maria ran down the mountain path with her torch in hand. If she found another weapon along the way, so be it. Behind her, she heard Sarah calling for her to wait up as she, too, ran down the path. Maria didn't wait as she hit level ground but ran off toward the fray.

Two arachnae skittered past her, halting her progress. She watched as a young man atop a centaur bounded after them, both laughing triumphantly and brandishing swords.

"Back, you beasts!" Humphrey called. "Ride, Drusilla. RIDE!"

"Taste our wrath, putrescence! Leave our forest!" Drusilla galloped off, Humphrey still laughing, one arm holding her shoulder for balance.

A chuckle escaped Maria's lips. Though caught by surprise, the centaurs were by no means losing this battle. She saw fallen arachnae everywhere, and her spirits lifted.

Until she heard the piercing call and felt the rumble of the ground.

"My brothersss! Come to usss! Defend the dead! Make the nags pay!"

From far away in the darkness, more black bodies of the horde exited the forest. Maria's heart plummeted in fear, and she saw Nysa nearby, calling for all to charge. Up ahead, one lone figure ran at the oncoming army as fast as his two legs would carry him.

"Daniel! No!" Maria raced out after him, nowhere near fast enough to keep up with the centaurs galloping before her. Soon she lost sight of Daniel amidst the galloping legs as she fell behind.

Screams filled the air, more horrible than any Maria had ever heard. Her steps faltered, and she watched openmouthed as the night went from black to red, dark to light. Flames exploded into the night, and centaurs fled in Maria's direction. As they ran past, someone knocked Maria to the ground. Through the madness and chaos, she saw the majority of the horde ablaze but soon realized not only arachnae but centaurs were caught in the fire. Their writhing bodies and pain-filled shrieks churned her stomach, and she retched. With a shiver, she wiped her mouth and forced herself to look again.

Amidst the intense glow, one man stood with his palms facing out at his side, his silhouette rippling with the heat of the fire. As she watched, he turned. The glorious smile on his face left her cold, despite the night's sudden warmth. The urge to vomit returned, and she gagged. He'd done this. She could see it in his eyes—he'd used his power to do this.

When he caught sight of her, Daniel's smile flickered and then vanished, replaced with one of concern and confusion. He turned his back on the fire, and Maria pushed herself up, stumbling backward away from him. Her foot caught, and she fell down. He ran forward and knelt beside her. Whatever she'd seen on his face before was gone.

"Maria? Maria, are you okay?"

"How—how?" she stammered, pointing at the fire. The flames danced in Daniel's eyes, and his skin paled as he realized what had happened. She watched his Adam's apple bob up and down as he tried to swallow. The smell of burning hair and flesh stung at her nostrils, but Maria couldn't bring herself to lift her hand up and cover her nose and mouth. She couldn't tear her gaze from Daniel.

"There are . . . those are—" He faltered, a sheen of tears filling his eyes as he shook his head, shutting out the image before him. "What have I done?" he whispered, turning away. Whatever darkness she'd seen in his eyes before disappeared, and her protective feelings for him surged back in its wake.

"It's okay. Shh, don't . . . don't. You've stopped them." Maria pulled him into her, wrapping her arms around him and laying her cheek against his hair. He shook in her arms, and Maria watched several centaurs as they tried to put out their fellow warriors who had been caught in Daniel's fire.

A Stolen Kiss

Chapter 31
CRYING IN THE AFTERMATH

Burned bodies of the arachnae lay on their backs, legs curled inward. Three of the centaurs lay dead from the fire, with twelve others severely burned. The fight had ended, and now Derric watched the male centaurs as they brought buckets of water to put out the remaining blazes. Bodies littered the campground, mostly those of the arachnae horde, the few survivors having fled back into Fangralee.

Maria remained at his side, but Derric couldn't look at her. He still felt his magic pulsing inside of him, and despite the knowledge he'd saved many by his actions, he felt a growing uncertainty about how he'd let his magic go unchecked. In the height of his power, he'd forgotten himself and lost control. Because of him, centaurs were dead.

"Great One!" He turned to see Ygritte trotting toward him. "You must come straight away."

He followed her, numb and barely able to lift his feet from the weight of his guilt. Maria walked steadfast beside him, and after a while he realized she held his hand in hers. A small spark somewhere marveled at her touch but came crashing down as soon as he remembered the binding. As they neared their destination, he released her hand.

"You can help her, can't you?" Ygritte moved aside, and Derric saw why he'd been brought.

Drusilla lay on the ground near the base of the mountain, her face ashen. Blood covered her torso, trickling from a wound at her side. Sarah applied pressure to it with what looked like Humphrey's shirt. The bare chested prince had Drusilla's head in his lap as he stroked her hair.

"Great . . . One . . ." Drusilla gasped, her lips twitching in an attempt at a smile. "Do you . . . see? I f—finally won over my . . . my . . . little prince."

"Shh," Humphrey whispered, tears spilling down his face. He didn't bother with them, unashamed as they splashed onto his chest.

"What happened?" Derric asked, kneeling down beside them.

"She saved our lives." Sarah's words were choked. She, too, cried freely, her body shaking.

"I fell from her back during a nasty brawl. Sarah came to my aid, but before she could get me up, one of the horde descended on us. We'd be dead if—" He broke off, caressing Drusilla's cheek.

"She dove into the way. It cut her deep, but by then, Humphrey was on his feet, and he killed it."

"I thought maybe you could do what you did for me, for her." Ygritte gestured to her shoulder, drawing curious glances from the others.

"I can try." Derric removed the fabric from Drusilla's wound and had to force himself not to retch. This wasn't just a cut. He could see parts of her insides that should never show. Placing his hands over it, he spoke the spell and concentrated all of the magic he had onto Drusilla's wound.

Nothing happened.

Derric repeated the action and the words, but Drusilla placed her cold hand over his, speaking through gritted teeth.

"Stop. It—it won't . . . it won't . . ."

"It won't work."

Derric turned to see Nysa, her eyes on Drusilla, who gave her a wan smile.

"Why not?"

"You don't have enough power."

"I thought I was the Great One?" Panic swirled in Derric's gut. He had to do *something*.

A Stolen Kiss

Nysa smiled, but it didn't reach her pained eyes. "You will be, but you don't know how to wield that power yet. It is Drusilla's time, and she has made peace with that. You can't bring back the dead."

"She's not dead yet!" Humphrey cried, glaring up at Nysa.

"But she will be, young prince. This wound is mortal, and only the greatest power can return life to the vessel it has left."

"I'm so sorry," Derric whispered to Drusilla, whose eyes slid in and out of focus.

"This is . . . a warrior's death. I . . . I am . . . am . . ." She exhaled one final breath, and her body fell limp, the light gone from her eyes.

"No," Sarah sobbed, leaning over Drusilla's horse half. "I'm so sorry. So sorry."

Maria moved away from Derric, settling between Humphrey and Sarah. She placed one hand on her handmaiden's back and the other on Humphrey's, gently rubbing up and down in an effort to comfort.

Derric turned a weary gaze to Nysa, who still watched the body of her kin. "Nysa, I—"

"Not now. I know," Nysa sighed. "You must be careful, Great One. The forbidden creature has left a darkness in you—an internal scar. If you aren't careful, it can overwhelm your power. You must be diligent. Come, Ygritte. We have rituals to prepare."

After one final disappointed look at Derric, Ygritte shook her mane back and followed Nysa away from Drusilla's body. Humphrey hummed a Dellsby song of mourning as he closed Drusilla's eyelids

"What did you do for Ygritte?" Sarah asked, tearing her gaze away from Drusilla.

"I healed her shoulder after she'd been cut by an arachnae's axe."

Humphrey's song stopped mid-hum, and Sarah's eyebrows shot up in surprise.

Maria didn't seem fazed. "Did you use the lost spell?"

Derric nodded, and Sarah turned her attention to Maria. "The what now?"

"The lost spell. He was reading it before the attack."

"You have magic?" Humphrey asked, but Maria answered before Derric could.

"It's like that song we all sang. Some spells work for everyone."

Derric stared at her, knowing she knew full well what he was capable of. Something like butterflies swirled in his stomach as he realized she was protecting him. Again he reminded himself the binding made her feel this way. He also realized he couldn't keep hiding forever.

"No, it's not like the song." He turned his gaze to Humphrey and met the prince's gaze, "I'm a sorcerer. I healed Ygritte's shoulder, and then I set the oncoming horde on fire with nothing but my hands."

Silence fell over them as Humphrey stared at Derric, and Derric stared back. He couldn't even bring himself to blink, watching as a muscle in the prince's jaw twitched. Humphrey shifted Drusilla's head out of his lap with excruciating tenderness and stood up. Derric remained kneeling on the ground as Humphrey stood over him.

"You caused that fire. You, all by yourself?"

Derric jerked his head in affirmation. Releasing a sigh, Humphrey held out his hand and pulled Derric to his feet. They stood face to face now, an inch or two difference in their height. The little voice Derric no longer trusted whispered at him.

He's going for his blade. Be ready. Fight him if you need to.

No, a stronger voice said, and Derric held his ground as Humphrey pulled his bloody blade from his hilt.

"Do you think there's a spell to get my sword clean? I tried wiping it off, but the arachnae blood is like glue or something." A grin cracked Derric's lips, and Humphrey chuckled. "I had you for a minute there."

A Stolen Kiss

"Yeah, you did."

Humphrey's smile faded, and he glanced down at Drusilla, then back to Derric. "Don't take this on yourself, mate. She was a warrior. Like she said, this is how she would have wanted it to end. There's nothing you could have done." He sighed and assessed Derric with his gaze. "I guess now we know why they call you Great One."

Sarah let out a long breath she'd been holding, and Derric felt sure she'd been worried about the same thing he had—that his secret would finally be out. Oddly, though, having both Maria and Humphrey accept this part of him troubled him. Lying to them no longer felt right or safe, but telling them now would just cause them pain.

"Come on," Humphrey said, bending down by Drusilla. "Let's find out how centaurs mourn their dead so we can help them with the sendoff. Does anyone know how many we lost?"

"Seventeen." Drisk stepped out of a nearby cave, his eyes on Drusilla. "Eighteen if Briskelle does not make it."

"Briskelle?" Maria stepped forward, a catch in her voice.

"She was caught in the fire. Her burns are severe. There is no saying if she will make it through the night."

Chapter 32
Maria's Plea

. . . .

Tears sprang to Maria's eyes. Not Briskelle. She spun around to face Daniel, her shoulders set in determination. As though he read her mind, he shook his head.

"I can't. It won't work."

"You have to try."

"But—"

"No." Gripping him by the shoulders, she shook him. "No! You can't let your fear of what you can do or what you can't do keep you from trying. You have to try. Please. For me."

At her last words, he met her gaze. The butterflies returned to her stomach, somersaulting and fluttering about and reminding her of their almost-kiss in the cave. The storm clouds she could see behind his eyes told her he was thinking of the same thing.

"Daniel," she breathed, daring to take a step closer. "I know you can do this. You can do amazing things."

When she said his name, he flinched and broke eye contact. Maria held her breath, waiting for him to decide. Her focus shifted from Daniel to Humphrey. The prince also watched the sorcerer, his brow knitted together and his jaw set in such extreme concentration, Maria could almost feel Humphrey mentally telling Daniel to try. Whether or not the sorcerer could read minds, she didn't know.

Daniel lifted his chin and turned to Drisk. "Take me to her."

Chapter 33
Combining Magical Threads

. . . .

Drisk turned without word and trotted back into the cave. Keeping silent in turn, Derric followed, and Maria fell into step behind him. He heard Humphrey and Sarah discuss in whispers who should stay with Drusilla. When heavy footfalls sounded on the cavern floor behind him, he assumed his sister stayed behind and the prince now took the rear.

The smell of burning flesh met his nostrils almost at once, though they walked for some time through the winding cave. Light signaled the end of their trek up ahead, and when they reached it, Derric sucked in a sharp breath.

Over two dozen centaur bodies lay out on animal skins, some groaning in pain as they were tended to, others still as the grave.

"If they still draw breath, they will live. Many will never fight again, and still more are not out of danger, but with care they should survive." Drisk gestured to a writhing centaur female that fought her caregivers as they stitched up a wound, no herbs to numb the pain. He made no commentary on the lifeless bodies they passed, though he made a motion over each before continuing.

Derric, sensing it was a sign of respect and part of the ritual of a life passing, repeated the action at each. The stench grew stronger as they neared the end of the twisting cavern. These centaurs had legs and arms burned by Derric's fire, but his eyes traveled to the farthest corners, where the charred bodies no longer squirmed.

Briskelle's blonde hair no longer announced her

presence. Her flaxen hindquarters were scuffed with black patches, burned through to the skin in some areas, but not anywhere near as bad as her torso. Most of her skin had red angry burns covering it, and her long braids had been eaten up by fire. On the right side of her face and right shoulder, black skin bubbled, mirroring the arachnae they'd sent back into the forest.

Stomach souring, Derric turned away from the sight. His gaze landed on Maria. Though her face was ashen, she didn't turn away. She moved to Briskelle's side, taking the centaur's hand.

"Briskelle?" Her voice wavered. The blonde centaur turned her head toward the sound of her name, but her eyes didn't focus on Maria's face. The princess turned to him. "Daniel, please help her."

Derric cast a sideways glance at Humphrey and saw the prince's mouth in a grim line. No doubt he wondered if Derric would be able to do anything at all. The little voice returned to Derric's mind.

You could have help, you know. You don't need to do it alone.

He paused with his knees bent, halfway down to Briskelle's side.

Ask? How would I ask? He wracked his brain for ways to get help.

You know whom to ask.

"Ellis?" He said it aloud, and in an instant the shapeshifter stood before him.

"You are a very needy soul." Ellis, in the form of the red-haired woman, raised an eyebrow as it glared down at him.

"I need help."

"Obviously. You're rather incompetent." Ellis glanced around, taking in Humphrey, Maria by Briskelle, and the many other injured centaurs. "I see. They know a bit about you now? Took them long enough. As for the healing help you request, it isn't me you should be asking."

A Stolen Kiss

"But—" Derric began. Ellis raised a hand and spoke over him.

"You don't think, you know. You immediately assumed I would be your only magical access, but it isn't, is it?" Ellis stared at Derric, brows raised. When the latter didn't respond, Ellis released a breath in a huff. "The magical thread you've been chasing . . . can you find it again?" Derric nodded. "Then do. Find as many as you can. Now I must go—your sister could use my help."

Without waiting for him to understand, Ellis disappeared. Derric, now kneeling beside Maria, placed his palm flat against the ground and closed his eyes.

When he'd first performed this bit of magic, he'd been able to find one familiar thread amidst the thrumming magic. This time, as he closed out the world around him and focused on the magic, he found himself in another state of being.

Instead of kneeling in a cave, he knelt on a flat, dull plane, surrounded by the drumming music he associated with magic. He stood at the center of a small circle made of pure light. From the circle, thousands of magical threads extended out in all directions like sunbeams, each a combination of up to three colors.

Most of the threads were cerulean, crisp and clear as the purest body of water, followed by a hard, intimidating onyx, shiny and black as night. The fewest in representation were a glowing white gold similar to the circle he stood in. They stuck out like bright stars peeking through on a cloudy night.

From his position, Derric could reach out and touch any of the thousands of threads, but somewhere inside he knew he mustn't take more than necessary or given. With ease, he located Gilda's thread. Its familiar thrumming made it vibrate with more force. Plucking it from the masses, he saw it, like many of those in the web, was a striped mixture of two colors: onyx and cerulean. The colors shifted and swirled, each attempting to gain dominance over the other.

As he watched, a soft ringing mingled in with the drums, calling out to him. He turned and saw one thread wiggling about not far from him. Small and thin, it looked as though it had little, if anything, to give—yet, as he plucked it, its strength proved true. This one, unlike his mother's, shone blue with strands of golden white wrapping around it. At his touch, it latched onto him, singing with delight at having been noticed.

Well, he thought with a smile, *I won't deny the help.*

All at once, the image dissolved around him.

Derric blinked, readjusting to reality as the torch-lit cave materialized around him. Everyone watched him with a mixture of curiosity and fear.

"Where did you just go?" Sarah asked from behind him, making him jump.

"When did you get in here?"

"I've been here for ten minutes. You were glowing."

Derric's mouth opened, and he stumbled over his words. "I . . . wait what?"

"It was pretty small, but we could definitely tell. It was like you were made of light." Humphrey shifted and didn't meet Derric's gaze.

Exhaling, Derric shoved this information aside and focused on Briskelle. He could feel the magic tethered to him, more powerful than he'd been alone. Shifting closer, he placed his hands on Briskelle, one on her waist and the other up by her neck. She flinched at his touch but made no effort to fight him.

Holding tight to the feeling coursing through him, Derric whispered the spell he'd used on Ygritte and

Drusilla. Heat flooded his hands, tingling every nerve like a kitten's rough tongue on a ticklish foot. Resisting the urge to pull away, Derric said the spell again, this time with more force. Three more times he chanted the incantation until the heat left his hands and the zinging nerves cooled.

As he chanted, he watched as a golden glow engulfed the burned parts of Briskelle's body. New skin grew beneath his fingertips, stretching across and knitting together with the old. He lifted his hands, and Briskelle stirred. From his limited healing knowledge, he'd guess all that remained were the most minimal of burns. Much of her skin was still reddened and even blistered, but long gone was the charred black.

"Heavens and hells," Humphrey whispered, his eyes as wide as saucers.

"Great One," Drisk said, dipping into a bow. "Would you consider healing the others?"

Will you stay with me? Derric asked the magic bound to him. He felt a warm vibration of acceptance from both threads, and he nodded to Drisk.

Over an hour later, Derric sat against the base of the mountain, listening to the funeral songs of the centaur males. Their custom, he'd learned, was to take their dead out into Fangralee where the dead would return to the earth they'd sprung from. It was all very mysterious and magical, but exhaustion overwhelmed Derric, and he'd remained behind.

He'd released both threads as soon as he'd finished healing the wounded. Two had been out of his reach, and they died just as Drusilla had, bringing the count up to nineteen. Gilda's thread felt no different than when he'd drawn it to him, but the thin thread felt thinner still, weaker by the exertion. Dread rumbled in him—had he caused the owner of the thread any pain by his actions?

"Get out of your thoughts, human. You're only hurting yourself."

Jerking around in surprise, Derric saw Ellis standing above him as the redhead again. "What do you mean?"

"The owner of that magic gave it willingly. It was her own burden to bear. If it weakened her, that's her fault."

"If they—she—helped me, I should care about her wellbeing. Especially if I can't thank her."

"Why can't you thank her?" Ellis dropped down to sit by Derric.

"I don't know whose magic it was."

A feline smile twisted the shifter's mouth. "No, I suppose you don't. Oh, I've guessed your suspicions. You're wrong. You'll figure it out. Only you can, after all."

Derric grunted, his fingers digging into his hair. "Why can't you ever give me a straight answer?"

"You may have my name, but I'm still allowed my secrets. You can't force me to be kind to you."

"I didn't force you to give me your name. You could have just left well enough alone."

The woman tilted her head to the side, eyes blank. "You don't pay attention, do you?" Her tone was patronizing, and it set Derric's teeth on edge.

"Why do you keep coming in this form?"

"You don't like it?" Ellis batted its eyelashes.

"No. It's annoying. Besides, it upsets Humphrey."

The catlike grin returned, and Ellis chuckled. "That's why I choose it. I like to upset the prince. Poor soul—a noble sacrifice based in misinformation."

"You like riddles," Derric said, mouth twisting in a begrudging smile.

"I love them." When Derric said nothing, the woman sighed. "If you'd prefer, I'll change form." In a blink, Ellis turned into the hooded man, and Derric's blood turned cold.

"Who is this face?"

"Wouldn't you like to know?" Ellis said with the new man's voice. "Yes, you remember him from your nightmares. Good. Keep remembering him, *Derric*. Your life may depend on it."

At that, Ellis disappeared, leaving Derric alone with his thoughts.

Chapter 34
CEREMONIES AND REALITIES

. . . .

The last few hours had been spent in the Fangralee forest where they were laying the dead to rest. Nysa allowed Sarah and Humphrey to take part in Drusilla's ceremony, the final one to be held, and Maria they allowed to watch.

Standing beside the recovering Briskelle, Maria watched as they laid Drusilla's body between two tree trunks, her head at the base of one and her back hooves at the other, touching the roots of the tree. Nysa directed Humphrey to Drusilla's head and Sarah to her back hooves before having them repeat the words used in the ritual. Where Sarah spoke them, Humphrey turned them into a mournful dirge.

> *From whence we came, to where we return,*
> *We commit you to the land of your birth.*
> *As nature reclaims your earthly vessel,*
> *May your spirit gallop free.*
> *This story ends in a warrior's death.*
> *Our colts will know of your valor.*
> *Though we say goodbye to you,*
> *Your memory will live forever.*
> *From whence we came, to where we return.*
> *Rest in peace, dear sister.*

As he sang, the centaur males joined with a hum resonating from deep within their chests. Maria watched in awe as the roots of the trees pushed up from the earth, wrapping around Drusilla's body. They encircled her form and supported her head with gentle care. When it was finished, no part of Drusilla could be seen. The roots swallowed her up and brought her below ground to rest. Before they'd even left, a tiny sprout sprung up from the place above where Drusilla's heart had rested.

As they returned to the clearing, Maria paid closer attention to the trees near the centaurs' home. The odd way they grouped together hadn't occurred to her before, but now she saw the various clusters.

"Briskelle?" she asked in a whisper. "Those trees Drusilla was buried between . . . were they—were they her family?"

Briskelle, her countenance grim and stoic, nodded. "Her parents, gone to rest before her."

Maria didn't sleep that night. Even when Nysa sent them back to the cave as the clearing started to show the first light of day, Maria's mind was too busy replaying the night's events. It felt like it'd been days since she sat next to Daniel at the fire in their cave, discussing the spells in his journal. So much had happened since their almost-kiss, and in the aftermath he'd avoided any contact with her.

After he'd healed Briskelle, she'd tried to speak to him, but he'd moved on with Drisk, healing those he could. She'd even tried to persuade him, along with Sarah, to join them in the forest for the rituals, but he'd refused without meeting her eye.

When they reached the cave, Daniel already lay tucked into his bedding, asleep. Humphrey and Sarah followed his example, Humphrey's snores filling the space with a rhythmic familiarity. Giving up on any chance of rest, Maria got up and went outside.

The younger centaur, Ygritte, approached her within a few moments of leaving the cave.

"You're supposed to be sleeping, Princess."

"I don't think I can. Too much on my mind."

Ygritte nodded. "Nysa figured you might find it difficult. She told me to watch over your cave in case any of you needed anything."

"She's very kind."

"She's a great leader. Now tell me, what troubles you? Is it the death you witnessed or your conflicting feelings for the Great One?"

Maria pursed her lips and eyed Ygritte. "Shouldn't you already know my innermost secrets? Isn't that why you're saying them out loud for anyone to hear?"

Unembarrassed, Ygritte shook her head. "I'm not yet learned in my culture's most mystical ways. I've just begun my training. I can tell you are troubled, but your emotions are mixed and difficult to read."

"So why did you say what you did?"

"Anyone would assume seeing what we've seen this evening would be upsetting. I am upset. As for the Great One ..." Ygritte spread her hands. "It is easy to see your affection for him, though you are also affectionate toward the prince."

"They're both wonderful young men," Maria conceded, unwilling to offer up anything more. "I'm honored to have them helping me on this journey."

"The Great One is admirable. Were he a centaur, I would make him my mate. Alas, as it is now, we are ill fit for each other. He is whom I would choose if I were you."

"I don't have a choice," Maria said, thinking of her kingdom.

Ygritte cocked her head to the side, squinting at Maria. "No, I suppose you don't. Though, in some ways, none of us do. Things always work out as they should, regardless of our feelings in the matter."

"I guess you're right. What will be, will be."

"When I find a mate, I hope his lips are as soft as the Great One's."

Maria turned so fast a muscle in her neck protested, and she grunted in pain. Ygritte patted her on the back, her brows knit in concern. "Are you all right, Princess?"

"How would you know that? About his lips?" Maria said through gritted teeth, massaging her neck.

"I kissed him." At Maria's incredulous look, Ygritte grinned and continued. "He healed my shoulder after we were attacked by one of the arachnae. I suppose I was caught up in the moment and in my gratitude. I felt it was the one thing that could express my gratitude." Her smile faded, and she leaned closer to Maria. "Please do not tell Nysa. She doesn't approve of cross-breeding. I must keep this hidden deep within me, but it was exhilarating. I recommend it."

A sick feeling swirled in Maria's stomach, twisting it into knots. Was this the reason Daniel wouldn't look at her? Had he been caught up in the moment with her by the fire, and now regretted how close they'd come? Part of her felt she should be angry or feel betrayed, but she couldn't—Daniel hadn't done anything wrong.

Her thoughts shifted to Humphrey, and her stomach gave a guilty flop. He, too, was on this journey for her sake, and here she felt betrayed by the stablehand.

Humphrey. Perhaps he was the reason. Daniel and Humphrey had grown close over the last few days, bonding in a way men do. Perhaps Daniel felt embarrassed for Maria's feelings, knowing she should be focusing her attention on the prince.

The sour sensation in her stomach lingered, and Maria tried to swallow her feelings for Daniel to no avail. She'd have to keep them hidden and not damage the friendship she already had with him. If she couldn't have his romantic affections, she would do whatever was in her power to keep the friendship alive.

Whatever it cost, she had to keep Daniel in her life. The thought of life without him didn't seem possible. No, without him, there wouldn't be anything worth living for.

"I sense turmoil within you. I'm sorry, perhaps I shouldn't have told you." Ygritte shook her beautiful silver mane. "I'm always saying the wrong thing. Nysa says this is what will keep me from growing my emotional senses. Forgive me, Princess. I didn't mean to cause you heartache. You should try to sleep again. I think you need it."

"It isn't your fault, Ygritte. I'm the horrible one who wishes for someone other than my betrothed to sweep me off of my feet and end my troubles."

Ygritte frowned down at her. "I do not understand humans. Why must you wait for a man? End your own troubles, Princess. You are the future ruler of your people—if you can't make decisions for yourself, what makes you think you have the right to make decisions for them?"

"What if I'm not worthy of ruling my people? Humphrey could do a much better job taking care of them. He will be king, and I will stand by his side as he rules. My place isn't on the throne but beside it."

"Humans. Your females are capable of so much, and yet they try to convince you that you are nothing. Without you, the human race couldn't exist. It is about time you start realizing your own amazing talents, Maria Regalla, Princess of Opea, because no one else can give you self-worth."

Maria opened her mouth to reply but couldn't think of anything to say. Ygritte let out a huff.

"Think on these things, Princess. Your country and your future depend upon it." She moved to canter away, but stopped, glancing back over her shoulder. "As for your prince, he isn't as ready to rule as you may think. His heart is troubled. You aren't the only one who dreams of being with another."

Maria sat alone outside the cave long after Ygritte had gone.

A Stolen Kiss

Chapter 35
Focusing on the Future

Derric woke before the others and left the cave, not wanting to wake them. The sun shone down onto the clearing, and from where he stood up the mountain, everything before gleamed like an enlarged version of the golden island. Letting out a soft laugh, Derric soaked in the moment, relishing the warmth. They'd have to go back into the darkness today. The centaurs knew a shortcut out of Fangralee, and he was more than ready to leave it—and everything that had happened here—behind.

"Great One."

He turned as Briskelle approached him. Her skin had improved in the past few hours, no longer as red as just after he'd healed her. Nothing he did, though, would bring back the beautiful blonde hair on either her head or her body. Several bald patches stretched over her lower half, and a few tufts of hair remained on her scalp.

"Nysa is looking for you. She wanted to know when you would be ready to leave."

"The others are still sleeping. As soon as they wake and have a chance to eat something, we can go." He glanced back down at the land below them. Colts played with Leonidas while Cercies the chimera sat nearby, playing the part of a guard dog. "It's funny. You wouldn't even know a battle took place here less than twelve hours ago."

"It is not in our nature to dwell on the past." Briskelle's voice held no contempt or bitterness. "We have mourned those we lost, but they are now with their forebears and feel pain no more. Their spirits continue on in those who stay behind. Our culture believes life is a circle. We are born, we live our earthly lives, and when we go to rest our spirits linger on in the trees surrounding us."

"It's an admirable way to live." Derric cast a sideways look at Briskelle, trying to formulate the right apology.

"There are no apologies necessary, Great One," she said, preempting him in the typical centaur way. "You are new to your magic, and your darker half got the better of you. I do not hold my injuries against you. After all, you were the one who healed them."

"They never should have happened." Bitterness churned in his stomach.

"You're dwelling on the past," Briskelle said with a small smile. "If you focus on your mistakes and your failures, you'll never grow past them. You'll never overcome them. This darker part of you will fester and eat at your soul. I forgive you, Great One, for your mistake last night. You now have to forgive yourself and learn which instincts to trust. After all, because of you, the arachnae were defeated and many centaurs survived. Not a single foal was lost."

"Foal? Why would a foal be lost?"

Briskelle cocked her head to the side, blinking three times before answering him. "Sometimes I forget how narrow human knowledge is. This wasn't the first time the arachnae have attacked. In the past, their goal has been to steal our foals and return to their horde with them. They prefer the taste of young flesh. The few who survived went home hungry last night."

"I didn't realize—"

"No. You did not. I hope knowing will help your heart heal."

"Can you see what lies ahead for us?"

Briskelle sighed and shook her head. "We are knowing creatures, not seeing. I know if you hold onto this darkness, it will consume you. I know it is this darkness that gripped your mother's heart. She was not as pure as you are, and her struggle is unending. I know your friends trust you, but they don't know your darkest secret. I know why you keep it from them, but I do not know if I agree with you. There are dangers ahead. The longer you keep this from them, the more it will hurt in the end."

"Once we find her . . . once the curse is removed—I won't ask them for anything. I want all of this to end. Even if they do find out and hate me for it, it will be worth it if I can give Maria her happy ending."

"You care deeply for her."

"I do. I'm doing it for Humphrey, too. They deserve to live happily ever after like all the other kings and queens of history. I want them to have that chance."

Briskelle chuckled. "It seems no matter what kind of creature we are, we always want what is best for those we love. Unfortunately, all too often they are not honest about what would make them happy."

Derric shook his head, thinking of Maria leaning toward him the night before. "That isn't real. She'll fall in love with Humphrey as soon as she's free from Gilda's curse."

"But will Humphrey fall in love with her?" Briskelle's eyes sparkled as she started down the path. "Come, Great One. Nysa is waiting, and we have talked too long."

They were packed and ready by early afternoon. While the others ate lunch, Derric poured over Gilda's journal.

"Come on," he muttered, flipping through the pages. "You know what I'm looking for. I need something to keep the centaurs safe from any more attacks. Please, there has to be something."

As though reluctant to acquiesce to his request, the pages lazily flipped themselves forward, landing on a page at the end of the journal. Derric read over the information three times before testing the words on his tongue. A spark of fear ignited in his stomach, filling him with dread. What if this was dangerous? He couldn't risk hurting anyone else, especially if he wasn't around to rectify it.

If you focus on your mistakes and your failures, you'll never grow past them.

Briskelle's words quieted his racing thoughts, and he shoved aside the fear. "I'm trusting you," he told the journal. "You'd better be right." Standing, he went to Nysa. She turned her wild dark gaze on him, and before he could say a word, she raised an eyebrow and smiled.

"Interesting thoughts and emotions race through you, Great One. It seems you no longer wish to keep secrets from me."

"I wanted your permission before I acted," Derric said, relieved by her amused tone.

For a moment, she stared at a point somewhere off above his shoulder. Blinking, she returned her attention to him. "This doesn't come from the dark place. We would be honored for you to perform this for us, if you think you are able."

"I think I know how." Derric glanced around at the forest. "Briskelle said there were spirits in the trees. Is there a border where your trees end? Or is all of Fangralee filled with centaur spirits?"

"You did not see the rituals. Your friends could explain." Nysa gave a jerk of her chin. Derric turned to see Humphrey standing a few feet away, watching him. Nysa nudged him forward. "Go. He will help you."

As they walked into the trees, Humphrey told Derric what the centaur burial ritual contained.

"So they're buried between the trees of their parents?"

"Yes. That's why the trees are all gathered so close together."

"What if they have foals and then die? Wouldn't they run out of room?"

"Once two centaurs declare as mates, they form a new

family. Drusilla had no mate, so she was buried between her parents. If she'd had a mate, she would have been buried in a new spot in between the two families, starting a new area. Drisk told me the clearing used to be much larger, but over the centuries they've filled it with their departed."

Derric nodded. "I need to figure out where the centaur trees end and the rest of Fangralee begins."

"Oh, that's easy." Humphrey quickened his pace, and Derric followed. They walked a few moments in silence before Humphrey stopped dead in his tracks. Derric didn't need to ask why.

He hadn't noticed when the centaurs led them in from the other side of Fangralee, but here it stuck out like a stableboy in a ballroom. The closest trees, while darkened by the lack of light, were deep brown in color. They stood tall and proud in clusters of two or more.

Beyond where they stood, trees of black ash twisted up from the forest floor. They reminded Derric of the arachnae skin, and a shiver ran up his spine. He could feel the thick presence of evil amongst them.

"See? Pretty obvious," Humphrey said, eyeing them with narrowed gaze. "Drisk said the half of Fangralee that sits closer to Kyleria is even darker than the part we already went through."

"We're lucky it runs more north to south than it does east to west," Derric mumbled, turning away from the trees.

"So, what are we doing out here? You said you had a plan?"

"Briskelle told me the arachnae have attacked before, which means they'll attack again. I want to make sure they don't have an easy time of it. See this spell?" He handed Humphrey the journal. "It's a barrier spell. I think if I do what I did with the healing spell, I can create enough magic to create a barrier around the centaurs to keep the arachnae out."

"Whoa." Humphrey's eyebrows shot up as he read the

page. "I don't know much about magic, mate, but this looks pretty intense. I mean, yeah, you healed them yesterday, but that was one centaur at a time. You're trying to connect every tree in a wide radius."

"I have to do this." Derric dropped down to his knee and placed one hand on the earth, the other on one of the centaur trees. "It has to work."

Orienting himself within the circle of light came easier the second time. He plucked at his mother's thread, allowing it to pulse around his wrist. He searched for the second thread but couldn't find it.

Come on, I need you. They need you. He spotted it after a minute, and he pulled it up from the web with care. *Will you help me again?*

It wound around his right wrist and gave him a gentle squeeze. Convinced he had enough, Derric started to stand. Both threads turned to dead weight, dropping him back down to his knees in the circle.

I have to go! he thought, attempting to stand and failing.

No, they whispered, tugging him to the edge of the circle. *Not enough.*

Not enough magic? Derric searched the remaining threads in the web for a willing candidate. The swirling colors of blue, white, and black made him dizzy. A sturdy thread that resembled the thin one around his wrist caught his eye. As he reached for it, it lurched the other way. Surprised, Derric pulled back.

Derric followed the retreating thread in search of what caused the struggle. Tugging it in the other direction was a thick, twisted thread. Black as night and round as a small tree trunk, it dragged the other thread away, despite the thread's fight to return to the web.

Without thinking, Derric stretched out his hand and grabbed on to the blue and white thread, pulling it back away from the thick dark enemy. The tug-of-war continued for several moments, Derric pulling with all of his might.

A Stolen Kiss

He could sense the confusion emanating from the black thread, as though it wasn't used to competition. Confusion shifted to intrigue, and it released the smaller thread.

Derric fell back into his circle of light, the third thread struggling against him.

Please, he whispered to it, *I need your help for a moment.*

The thread calmed, soothed by his request, and wrapped around his right wrist. Confident he had enough now, Derric stood and opened his eyes.

Humphrey stared at him, his lip curled and his eyes wide. "You all right?"

"Yeah. It was harder that time." Derric could feel the extra magic pulsing through him. "Will you hold up the page so I can read it while I do this?"

Humphrey complied, and Derric wiped the sweat from his brow before placing each hand on a centaur tree.

"Let's do this."

Chapter 36
THE LAST CENTAUR JOURNEY

. . . .

Maria mounted Verona just as Humphrey and Daniel returned from the forest.

"Where have you two been?" Sarah asked astride her horse on Maria's right.

"We were saving the day." Humphrey stretched and smiled, a new spring in his step. Maria laughed and looked at Daniel. He had his mother's journal in one hand and didn't meet her eye as he put it back into his bag.

"How did you save the day?" Sarah asked Daniel, but Humphrey answered for him.

"Well, I did the manly, brave, heroic, princely thing and held up a book. All my friend here did was some really complex magic that turned the bordering trees into a line of defense to keep the arachnae out." He shook his head at Daniel. "Slacker."

Their guide laughed and swung himself up into his saddle. "I know. Whatever are you going to do with my poor work ethic?"

"Well, I'd fire you, but you can't fire slaves."

Maria's jaw dropped, and Sarah let out a soft gasp, but Daniel threw his head back and laughed. The girls turned to each other, and Maria wondered if Sarah felt the same way she did. Joking about Daniel's slavery? How could they laugh about that?

"Lighten up, you two," Humphrey said to them. "You think the 'Great One' is beyond teasing? I just saw him turn trees into a barricade. I doubt slavery is a big concern for him anymore."

Daniel grinned and shrugged. "It does feel good to feel powerful. I can see how it gets people into trouble."

"Yeah, but not our good ol' boy here." Humphrey socked Daniel in the arm by leaning out from his own steed. "He lets the magic go as soon as he's done."

"Lets it go?" Sarah frowned at her brother. "What does that even mean?"

"Let's head out!" Nysa called, gesturing to the four of them and the centaur procession that would lead them out of this wretched place once and for all.

They started forward, but Sarah didn't give up. "What does that mean?" she asked again as soon as they were at a steady pace.

"I can borrow magic from other sorcerers." Daniel didn't sound proud or smug about his confession but a little bit hesitant. "It's like they lend me their power until I don't need it anymore."

"I've never heard of that. Humphrey, is that common?" Maria turned to the prince, who shook his head.

"I've never heard anything like it, and I—I know a lot of sorcerers. They've never mentioned anything similar, but they also wouldn't have been able to do what I just saw him do."

Ygritte, who marched alongside Daniel, jumped into the conversation. "But sorcerers heal all of the time."

"They heal sicknesses, but so do healers," Humphrey argued. "With potions or the right herbs, most ailments can be taken care of. But burns so black the victim can't feel anything anymore? Or infected wounds to the abdomen as deep as their intestines? No, I've never seen a sorceress heal something so deep and have the person up and walking again the next day."

"Is that why you're the Great One? Because you can borrow magic?" Sarah asked, looking a little disappointed.

"No." Ygritte shook her head. "He healed me without borrowing magic. He's the Great One because he is powerful. His magic is new. It'll grow as he uses it. Besides, no other sorcerer can borrow magic. It is a great power."

The conversation continued, but Maria stopped listening. She watched Daniel, who didn't seem interested in it either. He kept his eyes forward, smiling and replying when necessary, but she could sense his discomfort. If Ygritte wasn't in her way, she'd ride up next to him and see how he felt about what they were saying.

Did he want to be the Great One? Did he believe he was as powerful as they said he was? What made a man great? His power or his heart?

Leonidas pranced alongside Maria, silent except for the occasional caw of affection. Somewhere up ahead of them, Cercies scouted their path, reporting back to Nysa every half hour. It felt funny to think her first meeting with these creatures the day before had been filled with fear, and now she felt safer knowing they kept watch over their troupe. She reached out and stroked Leonidas's head, and he pressed against her palm.

"I'll miss you, too," she told him, her smile wobbling.

"How much shorter is this shortcut?" Sarah swatted at a mosquito as she addressed Nysa.

"Much," Nysa replied, tossing her dark mane. "In truth, it is nonsensical. Any map would tell you it is impossible. However, in Fangralee . . . nothing is impossible."

"It's much like taking a map and folding it, and somehow that makes the distance shorten." Ygritte made motions in the air, pointing out two imaginary plot points and folding them closer together. "Magic can do amazing things."

"Days' worth of journey cut down to a few hours. You might wish to know that Tranchet's Pass can act in a similar way. Tunnels have been known to appear out of nowhere and be a shortcut leading to another location." Nysa gave a wave of her hand. "But be warned, they don't always go where you want them to."

A Stolen Kiss

Cercies stalked back into sight through the trees, his lion's head growling in an unknown language. Nysa replied in kind before nodding and turning to the rest of them.

"It seems our time together has nearly come to an end. Once we pass through this final stretch of trees, you will be in the marsh."

A mix of excitement and dread twisted in Maria's stomach. They were finally leaving Fangralee, but to what new dangers?

"We will rest together tonight. The marsh isn't easy territory, and you will need more light to travel by."

"The marsh has light?" Sarah squealed and threw her head back, staring up into the dark canopy. "Thank you!"

"Make camp here. We'll keep watch over you tonight."

The fire crackled in the center of the small clearing they'd made. Ygritte and a few others had chopped down a few of the Fangralee trees to create the space, and they used the logs for kindling and makeshift benches for the humans to sit. Leonidas and Cercies brought back game to be cleaned and cooked for supper. Somewhere halfway through, Maria transformed.

"I'm going to miss being around such magnificent creatures," Humphrey said, marveling at Cercies.

"Thank you," Nysa said with a wink. "We will miss your presence as well. The marsh isn't as dangerous as Fangralee, but you must keep your wits about you. The melgorns do not appreciate trespassers."

"Melgorns?" Maria glanced at Humphrey, who looked at Sarah.

"I think I've heard of those," she said, squinting her eyes and tapping her chin. "It sounds vaguely familiar."

"Semi-aquatic mud-dwellers that dig holes in the

marsh to trap prey. They eat what they trap by flaying it alive and sucking out the blood before eating the innards."

They all turned to Daniel as he spoke, mouths opening in horror. When he caught their stares, he stopped mid-bite of his dinner.

"What?"

"What?" Sarah's voice hit a new pitch, and Cercies winced. "You say 'what' after telling us the most horrifying thing we've ever heard?"

Daniel ignored her panic. "It's called Mortal Marsh for a reason. Besides, they're way less frightening than a beornach."

All of the centaurs flinched at the mention of the forbidden creature, but Humphrey nodded. "We handled that situation pretty well. I'm sure we'll be fine."

"The trick is just to stay out of the water and keep to the path." Daniel returned to his food. "The marsh won't be anything compared to Fangralee."

"Your confidence is comforting," Sarah said as she rolled her eyes. "But if I end up flayed, I'm blaming you."

Daniel opened his mouth to issue a retort, but Nysa cut him off.

"The time has come for you to rest, my friends. You can worry about melgorns in the morning."

Sarah, Humphrey, and Daniel climbed into their bedding. Maria rested on one foot and tucked her head under her wing. As she drifted off, she felt a fleeting sensation of safety. At least leaving Fangralee meant leaving the real danger behind.

Chapter 37
A Centaur Goodbye

. . . .

"We're going to miss having worthy humans around." Nysa stood straight and stared down at Derric.

"What would you have done if we hadn't been worthy?" he asked, a smile playing across his lips.

"Killed you." Nysa looked to her right. Derric followed her gaze.

They'd reached the edge of the tree line, and Fangralee's exit was just as dramatic as its arrival. The trees came to a sudden stop as though running into an invisible wall. Now, open as far as the eye could see, the marshy wetlands stretched further west.

Though the impenetrable darkness of Fangralee was broken by the marsh, the sunlight wasn't the golden morning beams Derric remembered. Instead, an eerie light permeated the permanent fog, scattering shadows in strange places.

"At least there's some light," Sarah said, shivering and wrapping her arms around herself.

"It's almost winter. Good thing we packed cloaks." Humphrey dug into Sarah's bag and removed hers for her, handing it over. "We're going to need them in there."

"I never felt cold here." Maria mused, glancing around the trees.

"Fangralee doesn't experience winter in the same way as the rest of the lands. The trees prefer a warmer climate." Nysa gestured around. "And now we leave you, for we cannot go into the marshlands." Her gaze fell on Derric. "We wish you safe travels and success on your journey. You will always have a friend in the forest of Fangralee."

"Great One." Ygritte stepped up and stood over a foot taller than him. "I wish you were not leaving us. I will miss you." She placed a palm against his cheek and brushed her thumb against his skin, studying his face.

Embarrassed by her forwardness, Derric fought a blush creeping up his neck and cleared his throat. "It was, um, you're—"

"I know." Ygritte grinned and cast a casual glance over her shoulder at Maria, who looked away. "But a mare can dream." Without warning, she leaned in and kissed him full on the mouth for the second time.

Frozen in place, Derric clenched and unclenched his fists. When she pulled away, he kept his eyes on the ground. Any attempt at words came out in garbled grunts, so he kept quiet.

"Be strong, Princess," Ygritte said, turning to Maria. "Remember what I told you. You can help yourself."

At Humphrey's confused look, Nysa spoke, "It is a centaur custom to leave one with a word of wisdom." She raised an eyebrow at Ygritte. "Usually none so cryptic." Nysa turned to Maria. "Princess, keep your eyes open and remember: people are more than a single layer. They are more than their name or their bloodline."

Out of the corner of his eye, Derric saw Sarah look at him with wide eyes, but he kept his gaze firmly fixed on the centaur. Nysa turned her attention to Humphrey, who swallowed.

"Sacrificing your own happiness for the sake of your kingdom is admirable, little prince, but be warned—your sacrifice might harm as many as you're meaning to help. Sarah, do not let your fear of the dangers in this world consume you. You are capable of great things—your truths are not yet realized."

Grinning, Derric turned to his sister. She opened her

mouth, closed it, and opened it again. When she didn't respond, Nysa turned her wild gaze on Derric.

"Great One, we sense a powerful darkness in Kyleria." She searched Derric's face. "I can sense its presence already in your life. Be careful."

"Thank you for your hospitality and your acceptance," Derric replied, remembering something he'd read in the journal about centaur farewells. "May your hooves be as swift as your arrows."

Nysa dipped her chin in acknowledgement. "And may your magic never escape you and your heart stay pure as gold." She bent her legs just enough to wrap her arms around Derric in an unexpected hug, whispering so only he would hear. "Darkness hides in all of our hearts, Derric Harver, but each of us has the strength to fight it. We need only choose to do so."

When she pulled back, everyone around them remained silent, the centaurs just as surprised by Nysa's actions as Derric's companions. Without saying a word, the chieftainess jerked her head east, and the centaurs disappeared into the darkness.

"Come on," Derric turned and stepped out onto the marsh's path. "We're wasting time."

Chapter 38
OUT OF THE FRYING PAN . . .

. . . .

Maria hadn't realized how wise her idea to buy trousers was until she sank in marshy water knee-deep in her boots.

"Eyuck," Sarah said, sloshing through beside her. "This is so gross."

"Gross?" Humphrey tromped by them, splashing water everywhere as he hopped through. "This is amazing!"

The horses fared better than they did, following on light hooves as they waded through the wet portion between two chunks of grassy, firmer ground.

Daniel, already standing up on the next lot of land with Thumper, stared off into the fog. "We need to keep moving. There has to be a big enough chunk of land for us to rest tonight, and we've got to find it before night falls."

"Why?" Maria accepted Humphrey's arm and allowed him to guide her through the wet mush.

"I don't trust this fog." Daniel frowned and stepped further down the bank as they joined him. He reached out his hand to Maria, and she placed hers in his.

"We'll be fine. Like you said, the megrons are the problem here, and we haven't been in any of the real deep parts." Humphrey stroked his horse's nose and gave a flippant wave of his other hand.

"Melgorns," Sarah corrected. "Are they the only creatures in the marsh?"

"No. I don't think so. Just make sure we all stick close together, all right?"

"We've got the mighty Daniel to protect us," Maria

said, tilting her chin up so she could stare him full in the face. "There's nothing we need to be afraid of."

"I wouldn't be so sure of that," he said softly, holding her gaze.

"How many hours have we even been in here? How do we know we're going the right way?" Sarah stepped in between Maria and her brother, casting a suspicious glance over her shoulder at Daniel.

"I can tell which way Kyleria is." Daniel offered no further explanation.

"We've been in here at least eight hours. We've made so much headway we can't even see Fangralee through the fog anymore." Humphrey stretched and gestured to Maria. "I'd think you'll be a swan in the next hour or two."

"That sounds about right," Maria agreed, moving away from Daniel to stand at Humphrey's side. "We'd best find a spot to rest. I don't know how melgorns feel about swans."

"Just stick close to Humphrey," Daniel said as he stepped past them. "I have a bad feeling about this place."

"What did Nysa say to you?" A sneaking feeling of suspicion twisted up into Maria's thoughts. "Did she tell you something about this place that makes you act this way? This morning you were so confident we wouldn't have any trouble."

"No, she didn't. I can't explain it. I just—I just feel something is wrong here and we need to be careful."

"What do you think she meant when she said I was capable of great things?" Sarah followed after her brother but directed her question to Maria.

"Probably that you could handle the marsh without saying 'Ew' every time you step on something squishy," Daniel shouted back from up ahead. Sarah stuck her tongue out at his back.

"Does it have to mean something?" Maria asked. "They were parting words of wisdom she thought applied to each of us. It doesn't mean it foreshadows something in our lives."

"Yours did."

"What is that supposed to mean?"

"Isn't it obvious?" Humphrey asked, placing himself in between the two young ladies. "You are more than just a princess, just as I am more than just a prince. There are expectations on us based on our titles, but we're more than that."

"Is that why she said you're sacrificing happiness by marrying me, and it will lead to my unhappiness as well?"

Humphrey glowered at her. "Oh yeah? Well maybe you should stop ogling the stableboy if you want our marriage to have any chance at happiness."

"Excuse me?"

"Hey!" Sarah shouted above Maria's next retort, waving her arms. "We're all a little tense. You two are doing the right thing—and Humphrey, don't pretend like we don't notice the way you act every time Ellis turns into that red-headed woman." Humphrey blushed, and Sarah nodded. "Arranged marriages have worked for centuries. Friendship can turn into love. You are going to be fine."

"Where's Daniel?" Maria asked, glancing past Sarah.

"Oh sure, ask where—" Humphrey began.

"No, I'm serious. I don't see him."

The other two turned and searched the mist, but their guide didn't appear.

"Daniel?" Humphrey called. "Hey, mate? Where'd you go?"

"Daniel!" Maria shouted, stepping up on tiptoes as if it would improve her view. "Where could he have gone?"

"I think he was going this way." Sarah started off in one direction.

"No, I thought he was headed over here." Humphrey moved in another. "Wait, didn't he say to stay together?"

Maria.

Startled by the sound of her name, Maria spun around. No owner of the disembodied voice appeared, but she heard it again.

Maria.

"Do you guys hear that?" she asked, stepping away from them.

"Hear what?"

"Someone's calling my name. Daniel?"

Maria, come closer.

"You don't hear it?" She rounded on them, but both Humphrey and Sarah stared back at her with wide eyes.

"I think we should stay together," Sarah said after a nervous glance at the prince.

"I think you're right. Daniel!" Humphrey called with a touch more panic in his voice this time.

Maria, over here! This way. Look!

Maria turned and saw a blue light dancing in the distance, welcoming her. She stepped off of the firm ground and into the water.

Maria, we've been so worried. Are you all right? Please, darling, we're so sorry. Come home.

"It's—it's my mother." Maria's breath came in short, ragged gulps. "I—I don't . . . they must have followed us! Mother! Mother, I'm right here! How did you get through the forest?"

"Maria, stop! Whatever you're hearing isn't there. You have to come back to us now." Humphrey's voice felt closer than the one holding the blue light, but she couldn't obey. She had to get to her parents, and she stepped into deeper water, barely noticing as it rose above her knees and started filling her boots.

"Humphrey, they're here. They came for us! We can't leave them out there without a guide. I'll go get them and bring them back!"

"Maria! Please, come back! It isn't them. It isn't real!" Sarah's words sounded choked, like she might be crying.

Letting out a frustrated grunt, Maria continued on her path. They didn't understand—they weren't listening to her. Her parents were *here*. She mattered enough to them after all.

"NO!" Daniel's shout halted her progress. He'd come back!

"Daniel! My parents are—"

"It's a wisp! It's tricking you. Maria, come back to us. You need to come back."

We're lost. Maria? Are you there? Why can't we get to you?

She turned back to the blue light, determined to get to them and prove the others wrong. Just a few more steps.

A ball of fire shot past her head in the direction of the light, which gave a shriek and vanished. Shocked, Maria jumped back and whirled her arms as her foot stepped where no ground was there to catch her.

Then the world disappeared.

Chapter 39

. . . AND INTO THE FIRE

. . . .

Derric didn't realize they weren't behind him until it was too late. He spun around, but met a thick wall of fog. As he tried to walk through it, it turned solid, preventing him. A whispery giggle echoed through the air, and a shiver crawled up his spine.

"Hello?" Derric peered through the mist and saw a tiny, flickering, blue light bobbing up and down not far from him. A childlike voice called out to him, beckoning him closer.

"Sarah? Humphrey?" he called out and spun around, unable to tell which way he'd come from. "Anyone?" The little light filled him with unease, twisting in his stomach. He had to get out of there.

"You know, when you say 'anyone' it drags me along, too." A bored drawl sent a wave of relief washing over him.

"Ellis." He swiveled around and saw the hooded man standing before him, picking at his fingernails.

"I thought you weren't going to bother me anymore."

"I didn't know calling for 'anyone' meant calling for you."

"Yes, well it seems there are plenty of things you *don't know*, aren't there, Derricus?" The hooded man's voice was deep and oily, leaving Derric wanting a bath after Ellis said his name. "Apparently, what I want is no longer an issue. After all, I didn't want to give you my name. I didn't want to be bound to you and at your beck and call. I had hoped to never cross your path—but then, she didn't give me much of a choice."

"She? She who?" Derric's attention focused on Ellis, forgetting the little blue flame.

"You know, since I'm under contract and forced to do your bidding, I'll never make it easy. I won't give you straight answers. I can always find a loophole." The shapeshifter glanced over its shoulder and noticed the reason Derric had been calling for help. Ellis raised an eyebrow.

"I didn't mean to call you, Ellis. I'm sorry."

"I know you didn't, and that's the reason why I'm going to give you a straight answer on the question you haven't asked." Ellis pointed to the blue light. "It's a will o' the wisp. Misguiding light, if you will. Don't go near it."

"What I want to know is how to get back to the others."

"The wisp is doing this." Ellis gestured to the impenetrable fog. "It will respect magic, though, if you give it a little incentive." The shapeshifter reached out and grabbed Derric's hand, holding it palm up and meeting his gaze with a mischievous glint in its own. "Then, perhaps, you could make it back in time to save your beloved princess. I'd work fast."

Ellis vanished the instant Derric formed a ball of fire in his palm. The wisp gave a shriek and popped out of being. At once, the fog around Derric lessened and voices assaulted his sense.

"Maria! Please, come back! That isn't them. It isn't real!"

He launched in their direction, bounding through the clearing mist until he saw Sarah's and Humphrey's backs. They stared out into the water, tears running down Sarah's cheeks as she grabbed fistfuls of her hair. Out in the water up to her knees, Maria trudged toward a flickering blue wisp.

"NO!" Derric sprang past Sarah and into the water.

"Daniel! My parents are—"

"It's a wisp! It's tricking you. Maria, come back to us. You need to come back."

She ignored him and turned back toward the wisp. Derric could hear it whispering and giggling. Whatever it said to Maria was indiscernible, but she'd reach the wisp before he reached her.

Sucking in a steadying breath, Derric planted his feet and took aim. Forming a ball of fire in his hand, he hurled it through the air, just missing Maria's head. The wisp dispersed, but his action startled Maria, and she jumped to the side. Derric watched in horror as she teetered, a frown flickering across her brow just before she vanished beneath the water.

"Maria!" Sarah's scream sounded far too close, and Derric whirled around to see his sister splashing through the water toward him.

"Sarah, stop now!"

She froze mid-step, Humphrey two paces behind her. Heart racing, Derric moved toward the place Maria had just been. They were all in the water now, the land several feet away from Humphrey, who was closest.

"Maria's fallen into a melgorn hole. I'm going to get her. Humphrey, get Sarah back to land."

Without waiting to see if they were obeying, Derric continued to inch forward, his foot stretched out in front of him. In a few moments, which felt like agonizing hours, the tip of his boot dipped down, having found the lip of the hole.

Throwing aside caution now that he'd found where she was, Derric ducked down and felt inside, hoping she hadn't gone too deep and there wasn't already a melgorn waiting inside. Unable to feel anything other than mud, Derric swore and sat down in the water, dangling his feet into the hole. His boot brushed against something, so he pushed further in until both boots were hooked underneath what he hoped were Maria's arms.

Water slapped at his collarbone, and he struggled to keep himself steady with his hands in the mud on the firmer, underwater floor. With a grunt of effort, he pushed backward, dragging Maria's body up with him. Scrambling around to get his arms around her, he pulled her up out of the water and wiped a layer of slimy mud from her face, clearing out her mouth and nose the best he could.

She coughed and spluttered, spitting out more mud and gagging in her attempt to get air, but her eyes didn't open. Pulling her up as he sat on the muddy marsh floor, he laid her head against his shoulder and oriented his feet back on solid ground. Standing proved difficult with her dead weight in his arms, but he managed to get back to his feet. Just as his heart rate slowed, and he adjusted Maria into a more comfortable position, a blood-curdling screech came from behind.

"Derric!"

Whirling around, he saw Sarah and Humphrey hadn't done as he'd asked. Humphrey had his arms wrapped around Sarah's torso as something pulled her in the opposite direction. The prince's knees were bent, and he leaned back, red-faced with the effort of holding on.

"Sarah!" Derric shouted back, bounding through the water toward them. "Hold on! I'm coming!"

"Hurry up," Humphrey grunted, lurching forward a few steps as Sarah screamed. "I can't hold her much longer!" The thing holding on to Sarah surfaced, and Derric almost fell forward into the water.

Brown and slimy, the melgorn's head was shaped like a malformed infant's, lumpy in all the wrong places. Its black eyes had no whites, and teeth jutted out from its mouth in all directions. A long, razor-sharp tongue flickered out, slicing Sarah's boot. Its webbed hands held tight around her calves. The skin, scaly like a fish but rubbery like a frog, expanded and deflated as though it breathed through every pore.

"Its nose! Smash its nose!" Derric called as he rushed toward them, Maria slowing him down.

"It doesn't have a nose!" Sarah's panicked cry left Derric's mind reeling. It *had* to have a nose. The book said . . .

A Stolen Kiss

Derric watched as the creature lashed out with its tongue again, this time finding a place on Sarah's knee, cutting the fabric and the skin beneath. Sarah cried out in pain, and the tongue slashed the area again.

"Its tongue!" he called, almost to them. "Its sense of smell is in its tongue. Smash the tongue!"

Sarah's legs wiggled, but she couldn't get free of the suctioned grasp of the melgorn. Humphrey, too busy keeping Sarah from going under, wasn't in a position to help any more.

"Sorry, Maria," Derric mumbled, dropping the princess into the water and throwing himself the last few feet at the melgorn.

He hit it hard, wrapping his arms around its middle. The creature didn't release Sarah, but the momentum drove all of them sideways into the water. Surprised but on the defensive, the melgorn lashed its tongue at Derric, who was ready for it. Grabbing hold of the blade-like appendage, Derric lit his hand on fire.

With a yowl of protest, the melgorn sucked in its tongue and released Sarah's legs, its webbed hands flying to its face.

"Run!" Derric cried, pushing himself up and dragging Sarah up with him. "Go! Humphrey, take her."

Without looking back, Derric ran to where he'd dropped Maria and plucked her from out of the water. This time, she didn't cough or gag, but Derric didn't have time to worry about that yet. He could see the melgorn dipping back beneath the water, and the movement of the waves showed it was coming for him.

"Hurry! Get here!" Humphrey and Sarah stood on land with the horses, the prince with his sword drawn.

Derric ran faster than he thought was possible while being slogged down by another person, mud, and water. He dove onto the land just as the melgorn resurfaced, springing at him. Humphrey stepped in with a fierce swipe of his blade, catching the creature in the chest. Yelping in pain, the melgorn lurched back into the water, and Humphrey pulled Derric and Maria up the bank.

"She's not breathing." Sarah leaned in close to Maria's face, her own pale with worry.

"We have to get the water out of her lungs," Humphrey said. "But I don't know how to do that."

Sarah, already having jumped up and rushed to the horses, returned with Gilda's journal. "Save someone from drowning," she told the book, allowing it to fall open. The pages landed, and she shoved it into Derric's hands. "There, go!"

Derric followed the instructions with a mixture of caution and haste, saying the words of the spell and combining them with the necessary hand motions. As he drew his hand above Maria's lungs, motioning up toward her neck and out through her mouth, her chin tilted and a mixture of water and mud exited her mouth.

Maria's eyes opened, and she sucked in a ragged breath. She coughed and wheezed, tears streaming down her face as she clawed for breath in panic.

"You're safe. You're safe now. It's okay." Humphrey gripped Maria's shoulders and tried to calm her, but her hyperventilation increased. She pulled away from him, gripped Derric's shirt, and sputtered, a sob breaking past her lips as she tried to fight her anxiety. Over her shoulder, Derric saw mixture of emotions flicker over the prince's face.

"Sleep," Derric commanded, placing a hand on her shoulder. Much as it had worked on him when Ellis employed it, the princess's eyes fluttered, and she slumped forward in Derric's arms. He lowered her to the ground, and her breathing evened out. "There—when she wakes she should be fine. Sarah, can you get her into dry clothes before she turns into a swan?"

"We should move to wherever we're planning to stay," Sarah said.

A Stolen Kiss

"We're not going anywhere." Humphrey's voice was low and flat, and Derric lifted his chin, tearing his gaze away from Maria.

For a few seconds, the two young men stared at each other. A muscle twitched in Humphrey's jaw, his blue eyes cloudy as he narrowed his gaze.

"She called you Derric." When he didn't deny it, Humphrey pressed on. "Why would she call you that?"

"Probably because it's my name."

Chapter 40
TENSION IN THE BROMANCE

aria shot up a second time, but now her breaths were coming easy and full. Letting out a sigh of relief, she laughed and looked around. Humphrey and Daniel sat on either side of her, and the looks on their faces killed the joy at once.

"What's wrong?" she asked, turning from one to the other. Humphrey glared at Daniel, who stared back, his expression blank. Beside her brother, Sarah's face was pale, and her gaze swiveled back and forth between them. "Daniel? Humphrey? What is it?"

After a long moment of silence, Humphrey exhaled through his nose. "Nothing. Nothing's wrong. We need to find a larger space of land before night falls. I'd bet those little lights get pretty active at night."

Undeterred, Maria grabbed his arm. "Don't lie to me. Something's wrong, and you need to tell me."

He searched her face, a strange glint in his blue eyes. It passed as soon as she noticed it, and when he spoke she lost the tension in her muscles.

"It's nothing. I didn't listen to him when he told us to get back to the island, and Sarah was almost taken by a melgorn."

The looks of surprise on both Daniel's and Sarah's faces led Maria to believe Humphrey hadn't been willing to admit his fault while she slept. "How long have I been out? I remember you coming back and then the fire, but after that . . ." She trailed off, spreading her hands before her.

"You fell into a melgorn trap," Humphrey said, his tone still deadpan. "Dan—he saved you, and then the melgorn attacked Sarah. He also used magic to clear your lungs when you stopped breathing, and used it again when you woke up in a panic."

"That I remember," she said, nodding.

"Well, you slept for about thirty seconds, and here you are now." Humphrey shrugged. "Come on, we need to get to a bigger patch of land." The prince stood, grabbed his horse's reins, and started off into the fog.

Wordlessly and without looking at Maria, Daniel followed suit, leaving the girls to bring up the rear.

"Was the fight that bad?" Maria asked Sarah.

"It was . . . well, it could have been I guess. Things were getting tense, and then you woke up." Sarah didn't meet Maria's eye, and the princess turned her attention back on the young men walking in front of her.

Each held his horse's reins with clenched fists. Both walked with ramrod straight posture, their muscles bunched in their shoulders. Daniel passed Humphrey, gesturing ahead.

"There's a larger spot of land up here. We'll set up camp."

The prince didn't respond, and he didn't look at his friend. Maria's stomach twisted, sour and churning. This fight couldn't last beyond the night. She wouldn't stand for it.

Daniel set up the tent while Humphrey tried his best to start a fire with the kindling they'd brought with them from Fangralee.

"This might go faster if you let Daniel start the fire," Maria suggested, watching Humphrey mash the flint stones together as she sat beside him.

"I can light the damn fire, Maria." The edge in his tone silenced her, and she drew her knees up to her chest.

"Why don't you come help me prepare the supper?"

Ready for something to do, Maria bounded up and over to Sarah's side at the suggestion. They worked in silence, each casting worried glances at Daniel and Humphrey. When the fire crackled hot enough to cook over, Maria studied Sarah's process, absorbing the information.

"Then we'll stir it." Sarah used a spoon to stir the pot their stew cooked in.

"It's amazing what you can do."

"It's not that great," Sarah said, blushing.

"No, I mean it. I've never made a single meal for myself." Maria leaned in closer. "Can I stir?"

"I don't think so." A soft laugh escaped Sarah's lips. "Can you even grab it with wings?"

Glancing down, Maria sighed. Swan time. As she looked back at Sarah, she saw her lady's maid shaking with stifled giggles. Like a contagion, the laughter caught Maria as well, and the two of them snickered over the absurdity of it.

A ball of fire sailed over their heads and off into the distance. Startled, they both looked up, falling silent. Daniel stood straight, eyebrows raised as he pointed in the direction the fire had gone.

"Sorry. I thought I saw a wisp."

A hasty glance at each other was all it took to launch both girls into even more uproarious howls of laughter, continuing until tears streamed from their eyes.

"The look on your face!" Sarah said through gasping breaths, pointing at her brother. "You looked so innocent!"

"Or guilty," Maria said, hyperventilating to find her breath again. "I half expected you to point at Humphrey as though he did it."

"It's not funny," Humphrey snapped, coming over and snatching the spoon from Sarah's hand. "That wisp almost got you killed. Now here. Everyone eat so we can just get to sleep." He handed out bowls full of stew, not looking at Daniel when he passed him his.

Quieting their giggles, Maria and Sarah adopted attitudes of composure, though they snorted into their stew if they caught each other's eye.

When they'd finished, Maria watched Sarah clean out the bowls as best she could without using their drinking water. Daniel and Humphrey agreed the marsh water wouldn't be clean enough to use.

"Go ahead and get some sleep. I'll take the watch, and we'll be up early to get through this place. Shouldn't take more than a day or two's walking, and then we'll be at the pass."

"Oh, no you don't." Humphrey stood and faced off with Daniel. "*I'll* be taking the watch. You get some sleep."

Daniel's eyes narrowed, and he opened his mouth to speak, but Sarah cut him off, jumping up and grabbing his arm.

"That's a good idea. You should sleep. We all know you haven't had much lately. I think everyone would benefit from some rest and time alone." She gave her brother a meaningful look, and he brushed her off.

"Yeah, you're right." He glanced back at Humphrey, but instead of anger, Maria saw sadness and fear in the tight lines around his eyes and mouth. Daniel moved to Thumper, unbound his bedding, and walked to the far side of the stretch of land. Without so much as a good night, he climbed in and turned his back to them.

Humphrey, Maria noticed, watched Daniel with a sort of confusion. He moved toward the other boy, hesitated, and then dropped down next to the fire.

"Come on," Sarah whispered, gesturing toward the tent. "They'll figure it out."

Chapter 41
THE TRUTH WILL OUT

· · · · · · · · · · · · · · · · · · · ·

Derric woke in the middle of the night to someone shaking his shoulder. Rolling over, he looked up and saw Humphrey jerk his head in the direction of the fire. A cold, hard knot formed in the pit of Derric's stomach as he pushed himself up and trudged over. He sat down opposite Humphrey and waited for the prince to speak. For agonizing minutes, Derric fought the urge to squirm while Humphrey stared into the flames.

"Your name is Derric."

"It is."

"Derricus Harver." When Derric didn't deny it, Humphrey nodded, his gaze still on the fire. "Why?"

"My mother named me. I don't know why she chose the name she did."

The prince gave him a withering look and rolled his eyes. "You know that's not what I mean."

"I do," Derric whispered, dropping his focus to the hands he was wringing in his lap. "I would have told you if—"

"If Maria hadn't said your name." It wasn't a question.

"When it happened, I think Sarah panicked. Neither of us knew you, and she'd been trying to convince me to become someone else for a while—to get out of the stables and start a new life without my mother's past haunting me."

"So she called you Daniel."

"And I went with it." Derric nodded. "I think both of us thought that if you knew . . ." he trailed off, not sure how to finish the sentence.

"Well, I did offer to kill Derricus Harver in order to free Maria from the curse." Humphrey's mouth twisted into a sour smile. "I can understand Sarah's decision. She loves you. I wish I was as close to my little sister, Cecily."

Derric straightened, eyebrows rising. "I didn't know you had a sister."

"She's the youngest. Both of us have had our marriages arranged, and she was supposed to be here with me." Humphrey chewed on his lip for a moment before looking Derric full in the face. "Why didn't you tell us after?"

"After?"

"After," Humphrey repeated. "After we started traveling. After we formed a friendship. After I told you about my parents' expectations and how I'd always wanted to act? I mean, come on, mate."

It was Derric's turn to look away and swallow the lump in his throat. The answer wasn't a very good one.

"I didn't want to risk it." He let out an audible sigh. "I liked the way things were going, and I didn't want it to be ruined by the truth."

"Don't you think it's worse the longer I didn't know? I don't even know you, now. You know?"

"Nothing about me has ever been a lie except for my name."

"You didn't tell us you were a sorcerer. You didn't tell us Gilda was your mother or that she's the reason you know so much about magic."

"I didn't know!" Derric shouted, and both he and the prince winced, glancing over at the tent to see if anyone would stir. When no one stirred, he continued. "I didn't know I was a sorcerer, and I did tell you where I learned it all—from my mother's journal."

Humphrey snorted. "Come on. Didn't you know magic can't be gotten rid of? It passes down from parent to child no matter how many non-magic members bleed into the line. It's not like most hereditary traits. Magic is finite. One hundred percent passed down through bloodlines."

"No, I didn't know."

"Oh." Humphrey squirmed, and the scowl returned to his face. "But still, you could have told us. You could have told me."

"And have you acting like you've been acting all evening? No thanks."

"I have the right to be angry. Don't act like I don't."

"Exactly. You don't trust me. You won't let me keep watch or start the fire. You trusted Daniel, and nothing has changed, but you wonder why I didn't want you to know?"

Silence fell again when Humphrey didn't have a ready response. He leaned back and stretched his legs out, glaring at Derric. Derric glared back.

"I did trust Daniel, even though I kind of thought he was trying to steal my fiancée." Humphrey frowned and cocked his head to the side. "But I guess that wasn't it, was it? It's the curse. That's why she's so drawn to you."

Derric nodded.

"But that's not why you're drawn to her," Humphrey said, still watching him. "Are you in love with her?"

"No. I barely know her." Derric rubbed at his nose to give himself something to do other than meet Humphrey's critical eye.

"It doesn't matter though, does it?" Humphrey asked. "Even if you were Daniel Digson and she was who she was, you still couldn't be together. She's still going to marry me and live 'good enough' ever after."

The bitterness in the prince's tone surprised Derric. "You *don't* love her."

"Of course not. The only thing Maria and I have in common is our upbringing and our wishes that we could choose someone else. Don't get me wrong, she's beautiful—and in a way, I do love her, but it feels a lot like how I love my little sister."

"Is that just how royalty works? You're forced into a marriage and have to make it work out for the best?"

"Not always." Humphrey sighed. "My eldest brother fell in love with one of the noblemen's daughters in Dellsby. Since she came from the right family, and since he is the one in line to rule, they were allowed to marry. He didn't have to go through what Maria and I will . . . giving up the one you love for duty."

"So you *did* love someone else then? Someone in Dellsby? It's that redhead Ellis turns into, isn't it?"

"Her name is Alyssa. She's a sorceress in Pendrine, where the palace is. Or at least she was."

"Did—did she die?"

Humphrey shook his head. "She left. I was going to give up the throne and everything it meant for her if my parents wouldn't let us be together. She left me a note saying duty superseded our selfishness, and if I loved her, I would do what was best for Dellsby."

"I'm sorry."

"Me too." Humphrey looked over at him. "Just so you know, I do get it. The more I tried to make you the villain as I was sitting here, the more I remembered everything you've done to try get us to Kyleria. If you were involved in your mother's plot to steal the throne by marrying Maria, you would have confessed who you were and swept her off her feet. I should have realized sooner, though. The clues have been there all along, and I think part of me knew it. Okay, maybe not *it*, but something was off."

"Now you know, and I guess Maria will, too."

Humphrey met Derric's gaze, his blue eyes reflecting firelight. "No, I don't think so. Not unless you tell her, anyway."

A little thrill of hope sparked in Derric's heart, swirling around even as he tried to squelch it. "Really?"

"Really. Everything you've done has been to protect us. I don't know how she'd react if she knew who you were, but my future, the future of my land and hers, rests on this curse being removed."

"True. We can't let her be distracted."

"One last question, though," Humphrey said, throwing a handful of grass into the fire. "What's up with the swan thing?"

Derric blew out an exasperated breath. "I have a confession."

"Another one?"

"When I was young, I thought I could fix the mess my mother created if I broke Maria's curse. So I kissed her when I thought she was under a sleeping spell." It all came out in a rush, how he'd climbed up to her tower, kissed her, and then realized it didn't work, and run back to where Sarah was.

"But then, maybe it *did* work. She didn't turn into a swan for years after that, right?"

"If it had worked, she wouldn't turn into a swan at all anymore. If I'd broken it, she would have been free."

"But maybe that's why she's bound to you. Maybe when you kissed her, you bound her to yourself—you said that could happen, right? Or did I read that when I was snooping in the journal?"

"You snooped in the journal?"

"Hey, when you were being all evil, we used it to save you and then, well, you know . . . it was there."

"Even if my kiss bound her to me, it still should have broken the spell. That's why I think there might be a True Love Clause—or maybe something went wrong."

"Let's think." Humphrey stood and started pacing. "You kiss her when she's about nine years old, and she stops turning into a swan. I kiss her nine years later, and she turns back into a swan again. Seems to me the curse reversed because I kissed her."

"Right." Derric joined him, pacing on the other side of the fire. "But if my kiss accidently bound her to me when I tried to break the curse, it shouldn't have gone dormant."

"Unless your mother never meant for you to kiss her. Perhaps she didn't bind her to you. Maybe your kiss did."

"A Kiss Binding!" Derric exclaimed in a loud whisper, pointing at Humphrey. "A Kiss Binding works to make whoever is kissed fall in love with the person who kissed them."

"Still," Humphrey said, frowning. "Her curse should have broken."

"You're right. So maybe there's no Kiss Binding, but Gilda bound her to me to keep anyone else from taking the throne."

"Still sticky, mate. I mean, why didn't she just kill Maria and put a spell on her parents to make them name her as their successor?"

"I don't know. Maybe we're thinking too dark. Maybe Gilda had another reason. Maybe this was all revenge for something we don't know about and has nothing to do with her wanting power?"

"Is that your honest opinion, or are you saying that because she's your mother?"

"A mother who abandoned me to be a slave in the stables," Derric said with a roll of his eyes. "No, I just . . . I've seen her magic. I can't describe it. I know there's darkness there, but she can't be all evil. She's helped us more times than I could count already."

Humphrey started to rub his temples. "We are never going to figure this out, and I'm exhausted."

"Go ahead and get some sleep. I'll take the second watch—that is, if you trust me to." He raised a brow, and Humphrey grinned.

"Take it. I'm too tired to fight now anyway."

Chapter 42
Just Not My Day

· · · · · · · · · · · · · · · · · · · ·

Maria awoke the next morning surprised to find Daniel and Humphrey interacting as though nothing negative had passed between them. She shot Sarah a questioning glance, but her lady's maid shook her head as if to say "leave it be" and continued to fold up the tent.

"If we hurry, we can be out of here and into the pass by tomorrow morning," Daniel told them, consulting his map. "The marsh, like Fangralee, covers more ground north to south than east to west. I almost think the land *wants* to keep people out of Kyleria. It seems to be its only function."

"Lead the way. The sooner we finish this, the sooner we can head home and my parents can leave to meet up with Cecily."

"Wait, who?" Maria and Sarah said together.

"His sister," Daniel supplied, earning a shocked look from them both.

"You have a sister?" Maria asked. At the same time, Sarah said, "Wait, a sister?" Daniel and Humphrey shared a knowing smile.

"Yes, my little sister. I guess we've been a bit preoccupied, and I hadn't had time to mention her."

Maria let out a groan, throwing her head back. "Humphrey, I'm going to be your *wife*. You should tell me these things. I thought you just had brothers. We can't expect to survive this betrothal if we don't try to get to know each other."

"Survive? So optimistic." He smiled and shot another knowing look at Daniel. "I think once we get this curse thing handled you might be able to think of it as more than just surviving."

Doubtful. Maria eyed Daniel, her heart skipping a beat as his gaze slid her way, the twinkle in his green eyes making her stomach flip. His smile faltered, and he turned away. Embarrassed, Maria looked back to Humphrey. Unlike previous times when he caught her watching Daniel, Humphrey just nodded, still smiling.

"Yeah, we'll survive," he said with a chuckle. "Every marriage has its ups and downs." With a sigh, he gestured wildly into the air. "I'm the third born of four, and my younger sister is traveling south to marry a prince from Myrzel—much like I went west to propose to you.

"The royal family changed the date of her visit to the same week as mine. Mumsy and Dad decided I was the more pressing case, so they sent Cecily on, expecting to make their way down to Myrzel once you and I were properly engaged."

"But you've left *with* me?" Maria asked, eyes widening.

"Cecily is going to be on her own for quite some time." Humphrey stared off, his brows knitting together. "I didn't even think about how it might affect her when we left."

"Will she be all right on her own?"

"Yeah." A small smile played across Humphrey's lips. "She's traveling with her personal guard, a friend of mine who can handle anything thrown at them."

A moment of awkward silence followed until Sarah broke it.

"Don't you think it's weird," she said to Daniel, "how the royals have all of the power, money, and prestige, but we're the ones who can marry whomever we want?"

"Speak for yourself," Daniel said. Maria whirled around to him, and she saw even Humphrey's face had lost a hint of its joviality. "I'm still a slave, remember? No marriage without permission."

He laughed as Sarah's shock turned to annoyance, and

she punched him in the arm. Maria's momentary feeling of elation deflated, and she continued attaching her bedding to Verona's saddle. "We should be going."

"Oh, you have got to be kidding." Maria stared out at the vast expanse of water. "How are we supposed to get through there without running into a melgorn? What about the horses?"

It was late afternoon, and the four of them stood on the last patch of marshy land, the next land mass over thirty meters away.

"Do we just wait until dark and have you swim across and let us know where the traps are?" Humphrey asked, earning a glower from both girls.

"Yes, let's get the whole reason we're on this journey eaten by a melgorn or whatever else is living in that water." Sarah rolled her eyes and turned to her brother. "Is there anything in your journal?"

"The only thing in here about the Mortal Marsh is advice to avoid the melgorns and what they can do. There's also something about the bumbleloch, whatever that is. It didn't even have the will o' the wisps in here. I think I need to add them."

"If there's nothing in the book, we're doomed." Maria dropped down onto the ground, her pants soaking up water from the drenched mossy grass.

"Couldn't you just," Humphrey made a splitting motion with his hands, "—the water, and then we can walk through and see the holes?"

"There's nothing about that in here," Daniel said, frowning down at the journal.

"I didn't ask if the journal had something. I asked if *you* could do it."

Daniel blinked, struck silent for several seconds. "I—I don't know."

"Do you think it's possible?" Sarah moved to Humphrey's side, considering her brother. "I mean, it would require some ingenuity and extreme magic. Maybe you could borrow some."

"No." Humphrey shook his head. "No relying on other magic. I'm saying I think if anyone is capable of doing this, it's you. One hundred percent, remember? You're just as powerful."

Maria frowned up from where she sat, trying to suss out Humphrey's meaning. It made sense to Daniel though, and he nodded and moved to the water's edge.

"You can do this." Humphrey stood behind him and slapped him on the back. "Confidence, mate. Confidence, concentration, and commitment." Daniel shot him a questioning glance, and Humphrey shrugged. "That's what my theatre master always told me."

Maria pushed herself up from the grass, ignoring her soggy trousers as she moved to stand beside Sarah. Her thoughts whirred, bouncing around in her head. Could he do this without any spell? Just on his own power?

Daniel closed his eyes, and she watched his brows contract, giving her the desire to place her hand on his shoulder to comfort him. She resisted, forcing herself just to watch as he brought his hands up to waist height, his fingers spread wide.

At first, she thought it wouldn't work and Humphrey was wrong, but then the water in front of them rippled, disturbed. Awed, Maria's jaw dropped as the water moved like molasses, peeling apart to form a puddled pathway no more than a meter wide.

Sarah sucked in a breath, and Daniel opened his eyes. He let out a soft chuckle of surprise, and Humphrey whooped and leapt into the air.

"I knew you could do it! Off we go! I see a hole up ahead. Okay. Everyone be careful."

"Lead the way," Daniel said. "I'll stay back just to make sure I don't lose this." He spoke through clenched teeth, and Maria wondered how much of his concentration was required to keep the water separated.

She followed Humphrey as he led his horse, Dimple, and Thumper through the path, taking care to march through the waist high water to avoid a hole on the muddy path. Water along the path went up to the ankles of Maria's boots, but she followed Humphrey into the deeper water to avoid the holes made visible by Daniel's magic.

In less than ten minutes, they stood on the other side, drenched from the knees down but giddy with success. Daniel still stood on the bank of the other marshland, his cheeks red from effort.

"Now you come," Humphrey shouted.

"I don't think I can hold back the water and walk at the same time," he said in the same strained tone.

"But—but you have to get across," Maria called as she took a few steps forward. "We can't go on without you."

"I'll have to walk through and hope I don't fall in a hole. I think I remember where they were." Daniel dropped his hands, and the water rushed back into place. He stumbled, and Maria wondered if he'd have the strength to walk through by himself.

"Just hurry." Sarah stood wringing her hands, her attempt at a light tone failing.

"I'll be fine." Daniel stepped into the water and started across. Halfway through, he froze.

"What is it?"

"Daniel, what's wrong?"

"Why did you stop?"

Daniel's gaze met Maria's, and her blood ran cold. Something wasn't right. The water around Daniel rippled and shifted. Something moved beneath the surface. Maria watched in horror as it broke through the water.

A head like a viper, engorged to the size of a bear's head, drew up to a height far above Daniel. Its tongue flicked out of its mouth, hitting Daniel in the face. Instead of the sleek body of a snake, the creature had bulky, scaly shoulders and a broad chest. Four arms stretched out from its torso, one of which reached out and nudged Daniel, who groaned, "You have got to be kidding me."

Chapter 43
The Bumbleloch

· ·

This, he assumed, was a bumbleloch. It looked like a cross between a snake, a bear, and—well, something else. As it blocked his path, he tried to assess his situation. There hadn't been much in the journal about this kind of creature, and he didn't know its weakness—though the broad torso seemed to speak of its physical strength.

It nudged him a second time with one of its four paws, and he met its gaze. The eyes brightened at his attention, and the mouth dropped open, the tongue lolling out.

A dog. Derric blinked in surprise. That's what other creature it reminded him of. The wide, doe-brown eyes reminded him of the palace pups.

The threesome gathered anxiously on the marshland bank didn't make a sound, waiting to see what Derric would do. He took one step to his left. The bumbleloch shifted, staying in his path. Its gaze followed his every move, dropping to his hands and then back up to his face in rapid succession.

"I don't have anything," he said, spreading his hands wide. He felt far too exhausted to bother with this creature, but if it were to get violent ... well, he couldn't drop his guard.

The bumbleloch let out some sort of strange whimper, its snake's head drooping. Derric shuffled left again and caught the lip of a melgorn hole beneath the water. Letting out a yelp, he fell sideways, his leg sinking into it. He threw his hands out to try and catch himself—and found he was several feet in the air.

Twisting in the bumbleloch's arms, Derric realized the creature had gathered him up. Its benevolent expression had turned to a vicious glare.

But it wasn't glaring at him. Turning back, Derric saw a melgorn half-emerged from the water, sucking at the air with its strange gills, its bulbous eyes trained on Derric. A mixture of a growl and a hiss emanated from the bumbleloch, and its two right arms worked together to shift Derric onto its back, where he wrapped his legs around the creature's torso and held on to its shoulders.

The bumbleloch made the strange hiss-growl combination again, advancing on the melgorn.

It wasn't much of a fight, Derric mused as the bumbleloch waded through the water toward Humphrey, Sarah, and Maria—all of whom stared at it with slack-jawed stupefaction. The melgorn had attacked, lashing out with its claws, but the bumbleloch gripped it with all four of its strong paws, squeezed, stretched, and then launched it through the air. The melgorn screeched the whole way, landing much too far away to see through the fog.

"Good bumbleloch," Derric said, rubbing its rough head as it crawled up onto the mossy bank. The longer, lower half of the body had two lizard-like legs and a long tail that wagged when they spoke. Its limbs allowed it to move through the water with ease, but it breathed air.

"What a magnificent creature," Sarah said, moving forward to inspect the bumbleloch. "You're beautiful, aren't you?"

In reply, the creature licked her with its tongue the same way it had Derric. It then proceeded to nuzzle her with its giant snakehead.

"Yes, he's a good boy," Maria said in the same tone

Derric had heard the royals use with their pets. "Such a good boy. Who's a good boy? You's a good boy!"

"I thought you were about to be eaten whole," Humphrey murmured, standing by Derric. "Funny how a little wisp might get you killed, but this brute will probably play fetch."

"Fetch." The bumbleloch spun around to face Humphrey, and the girls squealed in surprise.

"It talks?" Humphrey asked, eyes wide.

"Talks," the bumbleloch repeated in the same deep rumbling voice. It made Derric think of how an earthquake might sound if it could speak.

"Do you have a name?" he asked.

"Tummy." The bumbleloch made a whining noise and wriggled its whole body.

"Tommy?" Maria repeated.

"Tummy." The bumbleloch rolled over onto its back, exposing its long belly.

"I think it wants you to scratch its belly," Derric said with a grin. Sarah and Maria obeyed, rubbing the lizard-like stomach and giggling as the creature's legs kicked in delight.

"Good boy! Boy? Boy." Maria glanced at Sarah, who snorted and shook her head.

"Oi, mate." Humphrey stared down at the creature, leaning over its head. "Whatcha called?"

"Called?" A bemused look spread across the face, and Derric fought back a snort of laughter. The creature opened its mouth, its tongue lolling out to the side as it panted, the giant fangs glinting in the faded light.

"Name? Do you have a name?"

"Burt," the creature rumbled, blinking.

"Burt," Humphrey repeated, drawing out the name in disbelief as he cast a look around at the others.

"Burt," Burt said again. "Burt. Burt. Burt."

"Okay! Yes, we've got it. Your name is Burt."

"Burt."

Sarah giggled. "I like him." She turned to Derric. "Is there much in there about them?"

"It doesn't say they're friendly. It mentions them as something we might run across. Hang on." Derric went through his bag and pulled out the journal again, speaking directly to it. "What do you know about bumblelochs?"

The pages opened to a short paragraph:

> *The bumbleloch (plural–bumblelochs) is a creature of mixed origins and intimidating form. The advice of this writer is to avoid them at all cost. No living soul has ever gotten close enough to a bumbleloch to assess its temperament. These creatures dwell most often in the Mortal Marsh.*

"Wow, that's helpful." Humphrey snorted after Derric finished reading the paragraph aloud. "He's a gentle giant."

"It doesn't seem very accurate." Sarah looked up from where she stood beside Burt. "He speaks rudimentary common tongue and knows how to fetch. I doubt he's never seen a person before."

"That's a good point." Humphrey eyed Gilda's journal. "Maybe that thing isn't as all-knowing as we thought."

"Like I said, it didn't have anything on wisps, so obviously it's fallible." Derric shut the book and shrugged.

"I hope he doesn't eat swans," Maria said, now patting the top of Burt's head as it rested in her lap.

"Plants." Burt grinned up at her, and Derric wondered how something so eerie could be so . . . cute. "Plants. Fishes. Melgorns. No birds."

"Well, he's smart, anyway." Sarah reached over and scratched under his chin. "Maybe he can help us find the best route out?"

"Out?" Burt squirmed into his lower stance, all six limbs on the ground. The muscles that acted a lot like eyebrows danced up and down. "No out. Stay!" The whine in his voice had Maria and Sarah melting beside him.

"Oh, poor Burt." Sarah draped herself across him, and Maria stood and wrapped her arms around his huge head.

"We have to leave," Derric said. "We have to go save Maria."

"Maria?"

"This one." Derric pointed, and Burt's gaze followed. "She needs to get to Kyleria. Past the Tranchet Mountains. Do you know where that is?"

After a hesitant moment, Burt nodded.

"Do you think you could get us there?"

Another pause. Burt nodded again, this time with a reluctant gleam in his eyes.

"Does Burt have to stay here?" Sarah asked, joining Maria at his head. "Couldn't he come with us through the mountains? He'd be wonderful protection."

"Oh, yes, can't we keep him?" Maria rested her head against Burt's.

"Can he survive outside the marsh?" Humphrey asked, folding his arms across his chest. "How are you going to take care of him out of his natural habitat? How will you find what he needs to eat? What if he needs water to keep his skin maintained? What then?"

Sarah and Maria's hopeful smiles drooped, but Derric turned to Burt.

"Burt need to live in water?"

"No." Burt shook his head, smacking into Maria's and earning a sharp "Ouch!"

"Burt need fish and melgorn? Burt need marsh plants?" Derric continued.

"Why are you talking like that?" Humphrey asked in a low tone out the side of his mouth.

"I'm speaking on his level," Derric replied.

"Burt need food." Burt nodded. "Food good."

"Sarah, offer him some of the rations we got from the

centaurs. See if he likes it." At Humphrey's questioning glance, Derric lowered his voice. "We'll have to hunt in the pass anyway. If he likes deer meat and the like, we can let him decide. If he doesn't, he'll have to stay."

Sarah brought back some of their rations and set them before Burt, who sniffed them once before gobbling them up.

"More?" he asked, glancing around and licking his lips.

"So food won't be a problem. Maybe he could even help us hunt."

A half an hour of simple questions later, they'd established Burt could indeed survive outside of the marsh but had lived there because he'd been hatched there.

"We don't have enough food to keep feeding ourselves and him," Derric said with a sigh as Maria and Sarah chattered non-stop in their excitement about Burt's induction into the group.

"Burt. You hunt?" Humphrey asked, adopting Derric's method of simple speech.

"Hunt." Burt nodded and gave a little hop that shook the ground. "Fly to food."

"Wait, what? Fly? How do you fly?"

In response to the prince's question, Burt dropped low, his long body wriggling. The skin on his back writhed and turned, making a sickly, ripping sound as part of it pulled away from the rest. The result was two wings shaped like a bat's but the same color as the rest of Burt's greenish-blue snakeskin.

Pushing off of the mossy ground with all six legs, Burt leapt into the air. The wings caught him, but only temporarily. After a few seconds of flight, he dropped back down to the ground in a spiral, crashing next to Humphrey.

"Whoa! You okay, buddy?" Derric rushed forward faster than the others, checking the brute for injury.

"Ouch!" Burt leapt up and ran away from the spot he'd landed on, as though he could escape the pain. "Hurt."

"You'll be okay, shh." Maria stepped in front of him and placed a hand on each side of his face, murmuring in soothing tones. "Shh." Burt kept his gaze on the spot he'd landed on, as though it still was after him. "Burt, how often do you use your wings?"

"Not." Burt shook his head. "Not use."

"Maybe you should practice with them before you take on anything like that again, okay?" Maria nodded her head, and Burt followed suit, mimicking her nodding. "Okay. You and I will have flight practice, okay? When I'm a swan?"

Burt cocked his head to the side. "Swan?"

"I turn into a swan at night. We'll learn to fly together."

"Together," Burt repeated, smiling and showing his fangs. "Yes."

"Good boy. So do you want to come with us? Burt come to the mountains?"

Burt's eyes grew wide, and he shifted his gaze from Maria to Derric. "Burt come?"

"If Burt wants to, he can come with. He'll have to help get food though." Derric grinned as Burt leapt over Maria and landed in front of him, licking him with his tongue.

"Come! Yes! Come! Good Burt." The bumbleloch's whole body shook with glee. "Leave marsh! Leave marsh! Come. Burt show way."

Chapter 44
"I Love You." "No You Don't."

· ·

Burt proved true to his word, leading them out of the Marsh before they halted for the night. The rapid pace he set meant they ate their supper while traveling, unable to stop. Maria transformed into a swan halfway through Burt's tour, and she felt his urgency increase.

"Faster. Must go faster." Burt eyed Maria and whined. "Bad things here. Must go."

They met solid ground with cheers and whoops of triumph, standing firm on the rocky path just at the base of the Tranchet Mountains.

"This is it," Maria said, her heart beating faster. "We get through this, and we'll be in Kyleria. We'll be almost finished."

"Then we have to come back through it," Daniel said with a grimace. "Think it'll be easier the second time?"

"'Course it will!" Humphrey thumped Daniel on the back. "We'll have you, Burt, and a troupe of centaurs to expedite things. It'll be great. Things are always easier the second time."

"Falling in love isn't," Maria whispered. No one heard her, and she wasn't sure if she was relieved or frustrated.

"Let's set up camp and start through the mountains first thing in the morning," Daniel said, hands on hips as he stared up through the darkness at the peaks arching above them. "Just think, we're going to see real daylight again."

"Isn't it funny how the horses were so bothered by Leonidas, but they don't seem to mind Burt at all?" Sarah mused as she led Dimple and Verona to a spot where they could lie down for the night. A shiver ran up her spine. "It's starting to get cold, now. Will the mountains be worse?"

"They won't be warm. This won't be a short journey, either. The mountains have many twisting paths, and it's easy to get lost. We're up near the Braskey-Opea-Kyleria border." Daniel brought the blankets out for the horses.

"The mountains are what separate Braskey from Opea, isn't that right?" Humphrey asked as he started setting up the tent. "That's what keeps your kingdoms happy?"

"I don't think there's been any interaction with Braskey in over one hundred years," Daniel said. "That's probably because of Tranchet here. It cuts them off from us. I couldn't tell you one thing about them."

"Nor could I," Sarah agreed. "But where the three countries meet, there's the pass. Isn't that right? It's the one place they all interconnect?"

"Yes. Suffice it to say, animals may not be the only thing we run into in there."

"You think we could meet other people?" Maria asked Daniel.

"It's possible." He squinted off in the darkness. "I feel . . . I feel like someone powerful isn't far from us."

"Do you think it's Gilda?" Humphrey asked.

"No. This is something unfamiliar. Something new. It's different from what I sense coming out of Kyleria, which is growing stronger every day. That's dark, and we're going to have to be careful when we get there. Burt, you might have to wait outside the gates of the city."

Burt whimpered and curled up next to Thumper. "No wait."

"We'll see. We don't want you to get hurt, buddy. I'll take the first watch tonight, Humphrey, if that's okay with you." Daniel pulled together a pile of mostly dry brush and lit it on fire.

"Fine by me." Humphrey yawned and stretched. "I want some sleep tonight."

Maria watched as Humphrey got into his bedding and drifted off, Sarah disappearing into the tent. Burt and the horses fell into heavy breathing. Peace and silence settled over the camp while Daniel sat beside the fire, leaning back to stare up at the sky.

"They're beautiful, aren't they?" Maria asked, waddling over to his side and looking up.

"It's nice to see them again. Even if it was just a short while ago we were seeing them with the centaurs, it feels different seeing them in a more open space."

"It does."

They sat in silence until Daniel spoke again. "You should get some rest."

"I'd rather sit with you."

He glanced over at her, frowning. "Do you think that's appropriate?"

Maria feigned innocence. "I'm a swan, it's not like anyone can insinuate anything happened. Besides, who's around to see me doing anything wrong?"

"Maria—" Daniel began, but she cut him off.

"No. It isn't fair. Why does Humphrey get to have his redhead and dream about her, but I can't sit with you?"

"It's different."

"How? How is it different? He's in love with her, isn't he? He doesn't love me, and I don't love him."

"Don't say something you'll regret." Daniel's tone reminded her of his harshness under the beornach's influence.

"I won't regret this," she hissed, glaring up at him. "I'm in love with you. Doesn't that matter? Does what I feel not matter?" She wished she were human, so she could convey her emotions in a proper way. As a swan, crying was difficult and kissing impossible.

"I've been thinking about it, and I think you love me, too. I think that, once I'm free of Derricus Harver, I will end my non-engagement with Humphrey. He'll be free to marry his redhead, and I can be with you. I could allow sorcery back into the kingdom, and you could rule as king. You'd be such a marvelous king. You're fair, kind, wise, and you'd be able to protect the kingdom just like you did the centaurs."

"Maria—" Daniel said again.

"No, please. Just think about it. Don't answer me now, but think about it."

"It wouldn't be what's right for Opea."

"Maybe what's right for Opea is what's right for its ruler. Everyone's so obsessed with doing the right thing, but if you're miserable doing it, how can it be the right thing? How can a miserable king and queen rule?"

Daniel's face contorted, twisting with pain. She reached out a wing toward him, but he shifted away. "Please don't ask this of me. You'll feel differently once your curse is removed."

Maria swallowed the lump in her throat. "The only thing I'll feel differently about is Derricus Harver. You don't understand, but how could you? I dream about him." At his questioning glance, she shook her head. "I don't see his face, I just sense him near. It's so . . . horrible. I can't control the dreams or how I feel in them. The binding—it takes away my freedom. I dream about him and feel like I'm flying. I feel like I'm in love. Then I wake up, and—and I feel awful. I feel like my thoughts have been taken captive. When I'm free of him, I'll love whom I choose." She held his gaze. "I choose you."

"You won't." His jaw clenched, and he turned his gaze to the fire. "You say this because you're cursed. When it's all over, you'll see everything and everyone in a new way."

"Not you."

"Especially me. Please, Maria, don't speak of this again. Just wait until your curse is broken, and then you can make your decisions. Would you do that, for me?"

Maria stared at him. Pain, rejection, and an annoying sense of admiration swirled inside of her. With a curt nod,

A Stolen Kiss

she turned and waddled away, resting on one leg on her bedding with her back to him.

Even as she drifted into an uncomfortable sleep, she couldn't help but feel a sense of glee that she'd soon be free. When she was free, she'd claim Daniel as her own. His resistance made her want him more. His nobility, his wish to do what was best for Opea—it all made her love grow deeper.

She fell asleep, drifting into dreams about Daniel facing off with Derric Harver.

The next day proved Daniel right—about the mountains, anyway. Maria marveled at the pathway up the mountain pass. It turned off in several places, but Daniel guided them straight ahead.

They saw very little life apart from themselves, and when dusk fell the second day, Maria started training Burt to fly. He was a quick learner, and by the time they were looking for a place to rest for the night, their bumbleloch had flown up through the air and disappeared for half an hour. When he returned, it was with a large mountain goat, which he'd killed for their dinner.

"Good boy, Burt." Sarah rubbed his temple, and Burt purred in delight.

"There are caves," Maria said, flying down and landing. She'd separated from Burt in hopes of finding them a place to rest. "All over the mountain, kind of like what the centaurs had. We could use any one of them."

"Perfect!" Humphrey clapped his hands together. "Should we eat first or have Burt carry this up to our campsite?"

"Carry!" Burt exclaimed, picking up the goat and flapping off.

"Oh, I should probably show him where to go. Here, follow that path right there. It will go up the mountain and into the first cave. I'll get Burt." Maria flew off after the creature, bringing him back around to their cave where the others soon met them.

Once they were all around a fire—Burt fetched whole evergreen trees for their use—they put the goat on a spit to roast.

"Are you sure we're heading west?" Humphrey asked, turning one of the maps Daniel had been using. "I feel like we're further north than we should be."

"We're going the right way. I can feel it. It's drawing me this way."

"If you say so, mate." Humphrey frowned and caught the girls' attention. Sarah shrugged, and Maria didn't have anything to add either. How would either of them know the way out of the pass? They should trust Daniel; he would get them out of there so soon that Maria could almost taste freedom.

After all, Daniel's instincts hadn't led them astray yet.

Chapter 45
SHIFTING IN THE PASS

. . . .

On their fifth day in the pass, even Maria had started complaining. Derric ground his teeth in annoyance, glaring down at his map as the other three once again questioned his guidance.

"I mean, I thought we'd be out of here sooner," Humphrey said, in what Derric assumed was meant to be a reassuring tone.

"We're going the wrong way," Maria whined. "We're going to die in these stupid mountains because you won't ask for directions."

"Who do you suggest I ask?"

"Maybe Burt would be a better leader, De—" Sarah started, but Humphrey clapped his hand over her mouth.

"Let's not start name calling," he said in a jovial tone with a stern frown at Sarah. "He's doing the best he can, and we've been traveling together without interruption for too long. How about we all take a few minutes' break and have some quiet time, yeah?"

Nobody argued, and Humphrey shot Derric a warning look. "Yeah, Humphrey's right. Let's do that. Everyone just . . . just rest a moment."

Five minutes of silence felt more splendid than he'd ever thought possible. Derric rubbed his eyes and leaned against a large boulder. What he wouldn't give for time alone. Humphrey walked over to him, resting against the boulder.

"You've got a feeling about this way, right?"

"I just feel . . . drawn this way. I don't know."

"Good. As long as you're feeling good things, I'll trust

it. But hopefully it pans out soon, because I doubt it'll be long before those two decide they'd rather kill us both and continue on alone."

Derric grinned at Humphrey, who showed off his pearly whites in a similar smile.

"What are you two grinning about?" Maria snapped, Sarah glaring at her side.

"Nothing," they said together, pushing off the rock.

"We'd best get going," Humphrey said, gesturing up the path. "Don't want to waste daylight, do we, *darling*?"

"No, I suppose we don't, *cupcake*." Maria sneered back. "Lead the way, oh Great One," she said, pointing at Derric.

They ran into snow halfway through the afternoon. They'd dismounted to stretch their legs when the first flakes began to fall. Sarah danced around in the light flurry, bounding ahead of them all and catching pieces on her tongue.

"Amazing." Humphrey shook his head, walking beside Derric.

"What?"

"After everything we've seen—the darkness of Fangralee, the melgorn attack, Drusilla's death—your sister still remains just as buoyant and optimistic as ever. It's like none of it touched her."

"She's always been that way." Derric let out a soft chuckle. "It's almost like she *knows* something I don't. She has this tendency to say something will happen a certain way—and it does. I envy that about her."

"Yes, it is interesting, isn't it?"

Derric and Humphrey jumped and turned to see Ellis the lynx walking on Derric's other side.

"What are you doing here?" Derric asked.

"Checking in. It's not like you to leave me alone for so long. It's been over a week since you last begged for my help."

"I don't beg."

A Stolen Kiss

"No, I guess that's the princess, isn't it?" The lynx grinned up at them. "You're going through with it, I see. Going all the way to Kyleria."

"Ellis!" Maria appeared with Burt at her side, Sarah coming back laughing. "What advice do you have for us today?"

"How cute." Ellis cocked its head. "You call it advice."

"If it isn't our favorite shifter." Sarah reached down and pet the lynx. Ellis stiffened but didn't push her away.

"Why *are* you here?" Humphrey dropped his hand to his blade, gaze narrowing.

"Can't a creature drop by to check on friends every once in a while?" Ellis's eyes gleamed. "I should think you'd be glad to see me. After all," it shifted into the shape of a bumbleloch; Burt yelped and backed up, growling, "as friendly as your new pet is, he can't tell you you're going the wrong way."

"What?" a chorus of voices rang out as all eyes turned on Derric.

"You're headed north to Braskey, but Kyleria isn't far. Half a day's journey back and two days west." At their incredulous looks, Ellis shrugged. "Don't feel bad. Braskey does this. It pulls outsiders in. If you don't want to be next to die in their civil war, I'd suggest you turn around."

"Why are you doing this for us?" Derric asked, even as they moved to obey. "Why tell us which way to go when you could have let us go the wrong way?"

"Kyleria is going to be too much fun to miss. I want to see the ending—it's going to be big. Besides," he grinned at Maria. "I have to protect my investment."

"What does that mean?"

"It means there are many possible outcomes, and all of them would be worth seeing." Ellis vanished in an instant, and with a groan, they started retracing their steps.

"What does he mean 'investment'?" Derric asked, turning to Maria.

"She owes him a favor," Humphrey said, grimacing. "In order to save your life when you were under the beornach's poison, she agreed to a favor."

Derric shook his head. "That's going to come back to haunt you."

"We'll worry about that *if* it happens." Maria pulled herself up onto her horse. "Come on, we've got ground to cover."

Chapter 46
WELCOME TO KYLERIA

. . . .

The next day they were back in the right direction, and Maria could feel their destination nearly within reach. Burt bounded ahead of them, tromping through the snow and shaking the ground. "Cold! Cold! Cold!"

"Burt, be careful!" Maria called, chasing after him. Her cloak flowed behind her, and she felt the familiar elation of freedom within grasp. As she reached the bumbleloch, he turned and caught her up in his four arms, taking off on his two hind feet.

"Faster! Run, run!"

"Hey! Wait up!" Maria heard Humphrey call behind them. "Bring me back my future wife."

She laughed, looking over Burt's shoulder as the prince chased after them. Sarah, thinking quick on her feet, pulled up onto her horse and galloped off.

"Ah yes, that makes sense," Humphrey shouted as Sarah sailed past him. "Dimple, here boy!"

Soon they all gamboled through the pass, laughing and shouting in their excitement. Even though they'd been in the mountains a whole week, Maria couldn't get over the clean air, the clear visibility, and the endless supply of light. The marsh and Fangralee felt like a distant memory.

They slowed when they came across a fork in the road. Burt set Maria down and sniffed the air with a flick of his tongue. "Left?"

"I don't know. We should wait for Daniel," Humphrey said, looking back the way they'd come. "Maybe we should stop and rest again."

"No," Maria let out a whine. "We have to go. We're so close. We can rest after it's all over."

"So eager to get engaged, Maria?" Humphrey said with a wry smile. "Fine, I'll go—" He stopped. Daniel rounded a corner riding on Thumper's back, Verona's reins in his hands as she trotted alongside them.

"There you are. Do we go right or left? Burt says left." Sarah pointed to the fork, and Daniel nodded.

"Burt's right. It won't be long now."

Two days later, a tingle of fear wriggled its way into Maria's heart and settled there. They exited the pass midway through the morning. Below them, nestled in a valley, was Kyleria's royal city. At the sight, Daniel sucked in a sharp breath.

"What is it?" Sarah asked.

"It's . . . nothing. I just—I dreamed of this place when I was poisoned."

From the look on his face, Maria doubted the dream had been pleasant. She turned her attention back to the land before them. Kyleria gave off no aura of darkness or danger. If she hadn't known this place to be considered the home of her enemy, she'd think it quite picturesque. The hills outside the city rolled with lazy grace, and despite the snow in the mountains, the land still had a lingering green hue.

"Down we go," Humphrey said, taking the lead as he marched down the narrow rocky path. "We've a sorceress to find."

Navigating the treacherous road to Kyleria proved far more difficult than any of them had expected, and several hours passed before they reached the halfway mark. It was almost evening before they could see the city gates again in the distance, barred for the night.

A Stolen Kiss

"We'll camp out here," Daniel said, dismounting from Thumper. "And take that road first thing in the morning. We should get into the city by high noon. It's almost sundown, and I think Maria might draw attention to us."

They all agreed and set up camp. As they all settled down around the fire with bowls of stew, Humphrey set himself down next to Maria.

"Are you still as excited?" he asked in a low voice. Sarah and Daniel sat across the campfire, joking with Burt about his meal.

"I think so," she said. The earth tipped, and she steadied herself, trying to find her breath. "Just dizzy I guess, though I don't know why."

"I feel that, too," Humphrey said, a grimace fixed on his perfect features. "It's like being in Kyleria is throwing me off. I'm glad I'm not the only one."

"Do you think it's Gilda? Maybe she set up some kind of perimeter to keep herself safe, like what Daniel did for the centaurs."

"If that were true, I think we'd be dead, not dizzy." Humphrey took a bite of his deer meat and grimaced. "I'll be thrilled when I'm back home with Cook and can have a first-rate meal again. This wasn't so bad in the beginning, but we haven't the proper tools to summon a real masterpiece of culinary arts."

Maria chuckled. "I've started holding my breath while I'm chewing. I taste less that way."

"Are you ready though? To put all of this behind us and finish what we started?"

"I guess." She sighed. "Are you?"

"I guess."

"Humphrey?"

"Mmm?"

"You don't love me."

Humphrey set down his fork and placed his hand over his heart, eyes widening as he gaped at her in mock-horror.

"Maria? How could you say that to me? Don't know you know I'm a waterfall of desire for you?"

A laugh all the way from her belly escaped her lips, and she smacked him on the arm. "I'm serious."

"Oh, but so am I, my love." Humphrey winked at her. Seeing her sober frown, Humphrey let out a huff of air and nodded. "You're right. I don't love you."

"You love her though, don't you?" Maria pulled out the miniature portrait she'd removed from her bag and handed it to him.

"Where—where did you get that?"

"I fished it out of the pond after you threw it in. I didn't know how to ask you about it, and I was afraid of the answer. But now, after everything, I just want to know who she is."

Humphrey ran his thumb over the smooth glass, his brows knitting together. "Her name's Alyssa."

"Alyssa." Maria tested it and found it beautiful. She'd never heard anything like it before. It felt mysterious and tantalizing. "Why are you here with me instead of with her?"

"I wouldn't be if she hadn't ended things." Humphrey handed the portrait back to Maria. "Keep it. Throw it away. Do whatever you want with it, but don't give it back to me. It's too painful."

"Why did she end it?"

"Duty. Honor. My stupid parents."

"What do you mean?" She slipped it back into her bag.

Humphrey groaned, his food now off to the side, forgotten. Pressing his palms against his eyes, he leaned back to lie in the grass. "They didn't approve and wanted me to marry you. I told Alyssa I would choose her over ruling Opea, and she decided I needed to do what was right for Dellsby and not what I felt was right in my heart."

"You know," Maria said, lying back next to him. "I honestly think arranged marriages are a wonderful idea and

A Stolen Kiss

could work." He turned his head to look at her, and she continued. "No, really. I do. The problem is, I don't think it will work for someone who has already chosen to love someone else."

"I didn't choose to love Alyssa. I fell in love with her. I didn't mean to."

"But you did choose her. You chose to spend time with her, to listen to her, to care for her in a way that was different from everyone else. That's what love is—little choices and big choices, all for the benefit of the other person. You chose to love her, Humphrey, and because of that, loving me is going to be so much harder."

"You didn't choose to love Derric Harver."

"No, but I think I could choose to love someone who isn't you. I think I already have."

"I think you're wrong." Humphrey didn't look at her, but stared up at the sky. The sun drooped ever lower in the evening sky, casting a pink hue.

"I love him, Humphrey. You have to see that."

"No. But you'll know why I disagree. I know what love looks like, Maria, and this isn't quite it. Daniel . . . he's . . . just trust me. Your feelings for him could change."

"I wish everyone would stop saying that to me," Maria grumbled.

"Well, my swan-future-wife," Humphrey said as she transformed. "Maybe we're saying it for a reason."

They rose the next morning and packed quickly, but explaining to Burt why he couldn't come lost them ten minutes.

"Burt, someone in there might hurt you, and we can't risk that." Daniel put a hand on Burt's burly shoulder. "I want you to wait out here where it's safe."

"Keep you safe," Burt whined.

"How about this." Daniel rummaged through his bag and pulled out what looked like a small, silver tube. "If we are in trouble, we'll blow this whistle and you can come save us. Okay?"

Though his posture suggested protest, Burt nodded.

"Good." Humphrey stood next to Daniel. "Can you hide so you don't scare anyone that might come by on this road? Stay close, but don't be seen. Okay?"

"Okay."

"Good boy." Sarah patted his head from up on her saddle. "We'll miss you, and we'll come back for you as soon as the curse is gone. Then, you'll come home with us to Opea."

"Sarah, get down. We're sending the horses with Burt." Daniel reached up, and Sarah allowed him to remove her from her horse.

"Why?"

"I would feel safer if we were on foot. Less conspicuous. Burt, take the horses and hide." He handed the reins to the bumbleloch, who nodded.

"Hide." Burt flicked his tongue and scurried off in the opposite direction of the road, the horses galloping along with him.

"See you soon!" Sarah waved him away. "All right, you lot. Let's do this thing."

Daniel's prediction proved almost right. Since they were on foot, they didn't reach the city gates until midafternoon. No one guarded the gates as they passed. In fact, Maria didn't see a single soul as they walked through the entrance to the town.

"This is creepy," Humphrey muttered, craning his neck to look down side streets. "There's no one here."

"They're up ahead. I can feel them." Daniel's jaw twitched, and his brows sat low on his forehead. Maria could feel the tension coming off of him in waves. Her fear spiked.

As they drew closer to the center of town, Maria started hearing distant voices. They grew louder and louder until she turned the corner. There, in the city square, the entire populace gathered in front of a large platform with three people standing upon it.

"Let's get closer. I want to hear what's going on." Daniel pushed through the outer edge of the crowd, and the others followed him. They didn't stop until they stood in the middle of the crowd, close enough to see the man on the platform.

Though she was sure she'd never seen him before, the man moving to the front of the platform seemed familiar. He wore a cloak, the hood drawn up to cover the upper half of his face, leaving his nose and mouth visible. How then, could she know him?

"Ellis?" Sarah asked, squinting up at the platform.

Maria's mouth fell open, and she kicked herself for forgetting. The man was the form the shapeshifter appeared in on occasion.

"Is that him?" she asked, pushing up onto her tiptoes to try and get a clearer view.

"No." Daniel spoke through clenched teeth, not moving his gaze away from the man. "It's the real man Ellis impersonated."

"Why would Ellis pretend to be this man?"

"As a warning."

Maria, Humphrey, and Sarah all looked at Daniel, and she was glad to see she wasn't the only one taken aback by his assertion.

The man on the platform raised his hands, and the crowd fell silent in an instant.

"My fellow Kylerians," he said, his voice resonating from

deep within his chest. "The Council has considered your request and will now give you our verdict. Through deliberation and the wisdom that comes from our great power, we have decided against your request for a festival."

Soft muttering broke out among the crowd, but it died as soon as the man spoke again.

"It has been deemed too risky to hold a festival. However, in place of your request, the Council has agreed to throw you a masquerade ball—for rich and for poor—tonight in the town square. You will be allowed your festivities for an appropriate amount of time before being sent back to your homes at curfew."

Humphrey and Daniel exchanged a look of worry, and Sarah mouthed the word "curfew." The crowd, however, cheered in delight, clapping and shouting their thanks at the trio on the stage.

The man in the cloak raised his hands, accepting the praise. The other two council members stepped up beside him. The man in the center reached up and pulled back his hood, revealing a silver-haired gentleman in his fifties, still as virile as Humphry. His eyes, so dark they looked almost black from where Maria stood, searched the crowd with hungry greed. She could feel his love of power even from so far away. Still, as she studied his rounded jaw and strong nose, she couldn't help but feel a strange familiarity that had nothing to do with Ellis using his face. He reminded her of someone, but she couldn't put her finger on it.

The man at his left also removed his hood, revealing the younger face of a man in his thirties, not as handsome or commanding. He had flamboyantly-styled, brown hair that crowned his head like a lion's mane.

"I know him," Humphrey said, his words almost drowned by the continued shouts of the crowd. "That's Peranicas. He's a sorcerer my parents once consulted for a spell they weren't sure our palace sorcerer would be capable of handling. Why would my parents consult someone from Kyleria?"

"Daniel, are they dangerous?" Maria asked, tearing her gaze away from the lead council member to look at their guide.

He didn't respond, and he wasn't looking at Peranicas or the man in charge. His gaze fixated on the third member, who had also removed her hood. A woman with hair of gold and eyes green as the grass in springtime.

"Gilda."

Chapter 47
MOTHER AND SON REUNITED

. . . .

He knew her the moment she pulled back her hood. An ache filled him, and he almost called out to her. Though he made no move, he felt the pull of his own magic against hers. The moment he plucked at her thread, she straightened. Her eyes searched the crowd and, within seconds, found his.

The moment their gazes met, a flurry of emotion rushed through Derric's soul. Happiness, anger, fear, disappointment, pride, joy . . . all of it jumbled around.

Wordless communication passed between them. Gilda's eyes shifted to her right, and Derric followed her gaze. A small shop sat empty while the revelry occurred in the streets. With a nod to her, he moved in that direction. He sensed the others following him and didn't stop them.

The shop door didn't offer resistance as he opened it and went inside. He held it open until the other three crossed the threshold and closed it again, looking around.

It was a cobbler's shop. Shoes lined the walls and tables. A counter rested along the back wall where a door led—Derric assumed—to the workspace where the cobbler repaired and designed shoes.

"Wow," Sarah said, mouth open as she stared at all of the footwear. "I don't think I've ever been somewhere so beautiful."

"Why did we come in here?" Humphrey asked, frowning as he picked up a loafer.

"I told him to bring you here."

They all turned toward the door. Gilda stood in her robed glory, the sun shining in from behind and reflecting off her to give her an angelic glow. She closed the door and locked it behind her.

"We don't have much time. They're returning to their homes to prepare for the ball, but the Council will expect me back soon." She whirled around, her focus locked on Derric. "You have to leave."

"What?"

"It isn't safe here. If Tertius finds you, you'll never be free. Go. Now."

"We can't go. We came here for a reason."

Gilda glanced at the other three behind him and bit down on her lip. "Who are these people? They aren't magic."

"No, they're royal." Annoyance pushed aside all other feelings as he watched his mother sneer at his friends. After how many years apart, this was her reaction? "We need your help."

"My help?" Gilda returned her attention to him. "How could I possibly help you?"

"We need you to remove my curse." Maria stepped forward, and Derric shot her a warning look.

"Excuse me?"

"You don't remember me, do you?" Maria continued on her path to stand before Gilda. "I'm Maria Regalla, the princess you cursed to turn into a swan when night falls."

Gilda stiffened and straightened to her full height, which towered over Maria by several inches. "What a brave little princess, traveling all this way in order to beg me for help. Brave but foolish. All you need is to kiss your prince over there, and you'll be just fine."

Maria frowned and glanced at Humphrey, who shrugged. "But that didn't work. You bound me to your son, Derricus, and now I can't accept Humphrey's proposal. Daniel led us all this way so you could fix it and Humphrey and I could get married."

The blood drained from Gilda's face as she listened to Maria. "Would you run that by me one more time?"

Maria launched into a quick explanation—from not turning into a swan all the way to the binding. When she finished, Gilda turned to Derric, her eyes wild. "What did you do?" Without waiting for his response, she grabbed his arm and marched off in the direction of the back room.

"Hey!" Humphrey jumped up, and Gilda waved her arm, sending him flying backward.

"We need a moment."

Derric pulled away from her, moving toward Humphrey. She grabbed at his arm again, and he swung around, forcing her back with his magic. Gilda hit the wall, grunting. "You will not harm my friends." Derric bent down and helped Humphrey up. "If you want to talk, I'll talk, but first you apologize."

He could feel Maria's stupefied gaze, her shock palpable. Sarah gave him a curt nod of approval, and Gilda spoke with deliberation.

"Fine. If that's how you feel about your *friends*." She turned to Humphrey "My apologies, Prince. Now, would you please excuse us while we have a conversation in private?"

Humphrey caught Derric's eye and nodded. "We're out here if you need us."

Derric followed Gilda into the other room. She slammed the door behind her and whirled on Derric. "Derricus Philaneous Harver, you have some explaining to do."

Her voice wasn't raised, and Derric felt confident the door was too thick for the others to hear. "Me? You should explain. You're the one who cursed the princess and left me when I was just a child. You're the one who left me to my father, who sold me into slavery the first chance he got. You're the one who insists *I've* done something wrong. What is this Council thing, anyway? That guy, the big one? He's nasty. I can sense the evil in him. Why are you working with him?"

Gilda's lips pressed into a tight line, and she folded her arms across her chest. "I can't speak of the council, but—" she paused, her eyes searching his face. "Wait. Did you say *slavery?*"

Derric told her his story—the shortest version of it, anyway, starting with the morning after she left and ending with agreeing to take Maria, Humphrey, and Sarah to Kyleria.

"I can't believe that man sold you, even after I told him . . ."

It was Derric's turn not to speak. Gilda placed a hand over her mouth, tears springing into her eyes. "No. No, no, no. This isn't what I wanted." She turned away from him, covering her face with her hands. "This isn't what was supposed to happen."

"What *was* supposed to happen, then, Mother?"

When she turned back to him, the force of her sorrow made him take a step back. It filled the room, wrapping him like wet blanket, suffocating him.

"I always wanted you with me," she whispered, shaking her head. "I left in order to keep you safe—left with every intention of coming back for you once I knew the safest way. I couldn't take you through the forest or the marsh until then." She let out a shuddering sigh and sat down on one of the workbenches.

"I came here seeking refuge, but once here I couldn't leave. He won't let me leave. Derric, you have to know this. I need you to know. I did what I did for you, and all I wanted was to have you with me, by my side. I paid the stablemaster, asking him to keep an eye on you in case Digson mistreated you, but I never meant for him to own you." Her gaze darkened. "If I could get my hands on him, he would know what it means to be a slave."

"You paid him?"

"I gave him a spell, a cure for his ailments. He promised me he would look after you and ensure you had a happy life . . . but then, Digson promised me the same thing. That wretched, lowlife ba—"

"It's not important," Derric said, a strange elation filling him. She *did* want him.

"Not a single day has passed when I haven't thought of you," Gilda said, reaching out and taking his hands in hers. "Especially lately. But it isn't safe for you here. You need to take your friends and go."

"Fine. I will. Once you remove Maria's curse."

The look she gave him was of a withering woman, and he saw past her beauty to the strain underneath. "I can't do that."

"Why not?" He thought over what she'd said and knelt down before her. "How was cursing her protecting me? Why did you bind her to me? You said everything you did, you did for me . . . but that doesn't make any sense."

"My sweet boy." Gilda placed her hand against his cheek. "You were so innocent. You didn't know. I had to protect you."

Before he could answer, the room went dark, and Derric was transported to the past.

Chapter 48
So . . . What's Taking So Long?

· ·

"They're sure taking their time in there," Maria said, frowning at the door to the back. "Do you think he's bargaining with her?"

Humphrey and Sarah exchanged another annoying glance. "Maybe."

Maria drummed her fingers across the table she'd sat down at. "I hope they hurry. I want to get rid of this swan thing before night falls."

"I'm sure they won't be too long." Sarah sounded anything but sure as she looked at the door. "They're probably just catching up."

"Catching up? Why would they need to catch up? They don't know each other."

"Oh, she means," Humphrey said, sitting down across from her, "because they're sorcerers. It happens all of the time in Dellsby. Two sorcerers will meet for the first time and say 'let's catch up' even though they don't know each other. It's just magical slang."

Maria eyed him. "I don't believe you."

"Believe me or not, I don't care."

She turned her attention back to the door. "I wish I knew what they were saying."

Chapter 49
A Blast Through the Past

. . . .

Derric traveled through his mother's memories, reliving her past. The throne room in Edleton in all its opulence materialized before him.

Gilda stood before the king and queen of Opea, a haughty glare fixed on her face.

"I don't understand," the queen said, her hand to her breast. "Why would you do this to us? Why did you curse our child?"

"You betrayed me by asking for a son."

The king glanced at his wife before turning back to Gilda. "You're the palace sorceress. It's your job to perform magic for us. Why would asking for a son cause you to curse our daughter?"

"I gave you Maria," Gilda said with a sneer. "You asked for a child capable to rule, and I gave you what you wanted. Where's my thanks? When your daughter was born, there were no parades, no celebrations. You mourned her femininity as I mourn your stupidity.

"Because of your insolence, your daughter will no longer be just a girl but a swan. May it remind you that your shallow love won't ever be enough to break the curse—but another will have to do what you couldn't. Your throne will remain without an heir until she is freed."

"I'm still young," the queen snapped with a lift of her chin. "I can have a boy without your help."

Gilda's gaze narrowed. "If you hadn't listened to that hack, Digson, you might never have needed my help conceiving. You begat Maria because of the potion I gave you after he gummed things up. But hear me now—you will have no more children," she said, pointing at the queen. "Nor will you." She pointed at the king. "Maria will be your legacy or your downfall."

Without another word, she vanished in a puff of smoke.

The scene shifted, and Derric watched as a mishmash of images flashed before him: Gilda packing everything in her room but leaving her journal behind, kissing Little Derric good night as he slept and telling him she'd come back for him, hastening together her maps and making copies to leave for her son with the wave of her hand, and going to Master Digson and insisting he be ready to take her son in.

"He won't be safe if he's around other people. You have to watch over him."

"I'll do no such thing," Digson said, glaring at Gilda. "He's not my responsibility, and I won't be forced to care for your child."

Gilda's gaze narrowed, and she raised her hand close to his face. "You'll take him in, and you'll care for him as if he's your own. This child has more power than you'll ever understand, and I wouldn't want to be the one that crosses him. I will return for him as soon as I've found somewhere safe for us both. If you harm one hair on his head, I will make sure you suffer the fate I saved you from back when I first met you. And this time, I'll make sure she remembers everything."

Master Digson glanced back over his shoulder to the dark inner rooms of his home. "You wouldn't. She can't know . . . not ever."

"Don't cross me, and she won't," Gilda growled, and he paled. "Keep him safe. Promise it."

"I promise. He'll be safe."

"And you'll keep him away from others."

"Away from others, yes."

"But you'll let him be around Sarah." When Digson hesitated, Gilda pressed. "Say it! He won't hurt her if he loves her. The safest place for Sarah is close to Derric. He needs to have someone in his life who loves him, who looks up to him—someone he can protect. Now promise!"

"I promise."

"And by this binding, I hold you to your words." Gilda grabbed Digson's hand, cut it with her dagger, and pressed her cut palm to his. "Break this bond and die. So may it be."

She left, confident no one would ever know what really happened to the princess.

In the middle of Fangralee, Gilda leapt upon an unsuspecting lynx and placed a dagger to its throat.

"Tell me your name, or you die," she said through gritted teeth.

"Death would be better," it said, its voice young and childish.

"Death will be painful." Gilda pulled tighter. The lynx struggled, and she drew blood. It gave a squeak of submission and stilled.

"Ellis."

Gilda rolled away from it and sheathed her dagger. Her eyes were wild, she seemed too thin, and her hair lay in messy strands around her drawn face. "Ellis, I need help. Find me safe food."

The lynx vanished and returned with an edible plant. "Here," it snapped, dropping the bundle before her. "But that won't save you. You've been slashed by the beornach."

"I know." Gilda let out a low growl, her eyes black as

she glared up at it. "I need to find safety. I can't let it take me." She curled into herself and released a cry of agony.

Ellis watched with a vacant expression. "I feel no pity for you, Gilda Harver. I can see you've always wanted power, and now you'll have it."

Gilda shot a bolt of dark concentrated magic at Ellis, who ducked aside at the last moment. "Help me . . . help me find . . ." She dropped to the dirt, her fingers digging into the earth.

"Can't help you if you don't give me a complete command. It looks like you've already tried and failed at making a cure. Burns, doesn't it?" Ellis said with a grin. A snapping twig in the distance caught its attention. "Must go. Strangers coming. Good luck."

Moments later, a centaur stepped out from the trees and noticed Gilda on the ground.

"Help. Me," Gilda moaned, rolling over onto her back.

Drusilla cocked her head to the side as she surveyed Derric's mother. "Nysa! I have something here . . . something that might interest you."

Gilda lay on her back in a centaur cave, no longer appearing wild—just weak.

"You almost died," Nysa said, staring down at her.

"I wish I had died," Gilda said through clenched teeth. "I can still feel the poison inside of me."

"And you will feel it forever. That darkness is now part of you. I will leave you to rest."

Nysa exited, and Gilda glared into the fire. "Ellis," she hissed.

The shapeshifter appeared before her, this time in the form of eight-year-old Derric. "Yes, Mother?"

"Don't play with me," she said, but Ellis didn't show

any sign of fear. A grin spread across Gilda's face. "You've given me an idea. Ellis, I command you to give my son your name the moment he asks for it, should you ever come upon him."

Ellis's eyes widened, and it stomped its foot. "You can't do that! That's—that takes away my right to secrecy. You're forcing me to be someone's slave without ever even having met them."

"Just like you left me to die, I leave you to your fate."

Ellis's gaze narrowed. "I would have liked you better before the beornach's poison, I think."

"Now we'll never know."

Gilda stepped across the threshold of Kyleria's royal city gates, staring in wonder at the old charm of the buildings. Opean buildings were characteristically uniform, but Kyleria's buildings came in every shape, size, and color. Here she could raise her son. Here, the two of them could lead a normal life away from his mistake and her carelessness. They'd be able to hide here, hide from the royals in Opea and Derric's father, and no one would ever have to know the truth about Maria's curse.

"Excuse me, Miss?" A dark-haired man placed a hand on her arm. "You're a sorceress, aren't you?" Gilda pulled away, eying him through slitted lids. "Don't be frightened. I'm learned in magic as well, and we've been waiting for you. We sensed you'd be coming. My name is Peranicus, and I'm the head of the sorcerers' council here in the royal city of Kyleria. Please, come with me. You look thirsty."

A Stolen Kiss

Gilda stood once again at the gates of the royal city, this time just inside them. Her cheek was red and swollen, her eye blackened. With a tentative, fearful hand, she reached out to the gate. A searing shock ran down her arm and through her body, causing her to yelp.

"I told you," a voice said from behind. "You will never leave me again."

She turned and faced Tertius, the man she'd spent eight years running from—the man whose form Ellis often appeared in. His eyes glittered with a mixture of malice and desire. "Why so ready to run, my love? Are you ready to tell me what was so important you left in the first place?" He ran the back of his fingers down the side of her cheek. "I've waited a long time to have you back by my side—eight long, lonely years. I think you'd better come see what I have planned next."

Flashes of people screaming, a man laughing, and fire all jumbled together and turned to black.

Time warped, moving backwards at a blurring speed. Derric saw himself as a child, running his fingers through the long grass just outside the palace stables. Next to him, Gilda stood with her hands on her hips, dressed in royal palace colors.

"I'm not much for haggling," she said to the stablemaster, an eyebrow quirking higher. Beside her, eight-year-old Derric tugged on her dress.

"Mommy."

"One second, honey. Mommy is working."

Little Derric tugged again. "Can I go play with the princess? She's sitting over by the pond."

A flicker of fear passed over Gilda's face. "Not now, baby. I need you to stay right here with me. Do you hear me, Derric? Stay right here." She turned back to the business transaction, and Little Derric wandered off toward Maria.

A few moments passed, and Gilda realized Derric wasn't beside her. She whirled around, sharp panic in her eyes, and spotted her son speaking to the princess. She ran as fast as her feet could carry her. As she neared, the tail end of her son's words reached her ears.

"—think you're very pretty," Little Derric said, smiling down at the dark haired little princess.

"Thank you," Maria said in a squeaky voice.

"You remind me of a swan," Little Derric said. "I like swans. They're pretty like you." As he said it, he leaned down and kissed the girl on the cheek.

She felt the powerful wave of magic as it pulsed from her son to the girl, and even the grass shifted in the force of the spell.

"No!" Gilda screamed, sliding to her knees in front of the children. "No! Derric? What have you done?" She gripped him by the shoulders, and he started crying. "I told you—I told you never, ever to talk to others without me around to keep you safe. Oh, no. No, no, no."

She waved her hand, and Maria fell backwards, asleep.

"Mommy!" Derric cried, struggling against her to get to Maria.

"Sleep." Gilda waved her hand over her son, and he went limp in her arms. She leaned in next to his ear. "Forget," she whispered. "Forget all of this. Forget Maria Regalla." She moved and did the same to Maria. "Forget."

Rising from the ground, she stared around the grassy area, muttering to herself. "Think. Think." A palace guard rushed toward her, sword drawn.

"What have you done?"

A smile twisted her lips. "I cursed the princess."

A Stolen Kiss

Light returned, piercing through Derric's vision as he pulled away from Gilda's touch and fell to the ground on all fours. His breath came in heavy, ragged spurts.

"I'm sorry," Gilda said, kneeling down beside him. "I should have warned you. Memory sharing is very disorienting. Breathe. Just breathe."

He tried to push her off, but her grip proved stronger than his. Everything in him fought against the vision he'd just seen. It couldn't be real. He couldn't have done that.

"I cursed Maria," he gasped, sitting hard on the floor and drawing his knees in. "I'm the one who cursed her. You were trying to protect me."

"You didn't mean to. You didn't know. You were so young, and your powers were out of control, stronger than any child—and most of the sorcerers I've ever met." Gilda grimaced and placed the back of her hand against his forehead. "What I don't understand is why her prince's kiss didn't end it. It all should have stopped then. What did you do?"

"I kissed her," Derric said, groaning. "I kissed her when we were kids because I thought if I broke the curse, Father would stop treating me like an outcast, and they would let you come home again." He covered his face with his hands.

Gilda sat down beside him, chewing on her lip again. "You can't break your own curse. It's in the contract. When you kissed Maria, your magic must have bound her to you, and because the curse couldn't be broken, it made it dormant. Instead of breaking the curse, the prince's kiss awakened it."

"I can't believe this is all my fault."

"You didn't know." Gilda smoothed back his hair, a sad smile on her face. "But now you know, and now you can fix it. First we have to get you out of here. If Tertius finds you, you'll never be free."

"Who is he? Why does he want to keep you here?"

"We don't have time for this. You need to leave so you can remove the curse."

"How do I remove the curse?" Derric asked, pushing himself to his feet.

"When the time comes, you'll know. Your magic will show you. Come on, we need to get you out of here."

"Mom." Derric planted his feet and didn't budge as she tugged on his arm. Gilda turned, eyes wide. "Please, I don't want to leave you."

He felt like he was eight years old again. Her gaze softened, and she opened her arms. He allowed her to envelope him in a hug, burying his face into her hair.

"I love you," she whispered. "Please forgive me."

"None of this is your fault."

"More than you'll ever know is my fault, including the danger you faced trying to get here." Gilda pulled back, frowning. "I could sense you getting closer. I tried to block your path, delay you, or discourage you. I couldn't let you get here. But it seems my boy is too strong for all of that."

"Did you send Ellis to try to stop us?"

"You've met Ellis?" Gilda blinked, eyebrows arched. "I haven't seen the shifter for ages—I didn't think it safe here with Tertius." A small smile played across her lips. "Ellis was a child when I forced it to give me its name, not much older than you are now."

Derric tried to imagine the shapeshifter as anything other than a full-grown being and failed. "Also, Nysa says hi."

"Nysa! You did follow my path, didn't you?" Gilda looped her arm through his and led him toward the door. "What an interesting female. She and I did butt heads." Her joy dwindled. "I wish I could know more, that you could stay, but—"

A Stolen Kiss

"I don't understand why I have to go. There's nothing for me in Opea. I could stay here with you. Or you could come with me."

"No. You don't know what it's like. Tertius—he's violent. He's wicked. He uses other sorcerers' magic and makes himself more powerful. Until I met him, I didn't even know that was possible. You have such immense power he'd have a well that never ran dry. My stamina's the only reason I've lasted on the council as long as I have. We come from powerful stock."

"You mean, you can't borrow power?"

"No, of course not." Gilda let out a sad little laugh. "If I could, I'd have taken his from him and left here by now. I can feel my magic draining, as though it's being pulled in two different directions. It's worse than normal, and it makes me afraid of what he's planning."

Guilt niggled at Derric. "Uh, I think that might be my fault."

"What?" Gilda paused with her hand on the doorknob.

"I think I might be the one pulling it in the other direction." He pulled at her thread, and she gasped.

"Derric, that's ... that's amazing! I—you—can't— I'm—" She paled and pulled open the door. "Now we really have to get you out of here."

Chapter 50
THE TRUTH ABOUT TERTIUS

· ·

Maria straightened as soon as Daniel returned with Gilda. She'd spent the entire time wringing her hands or twisting her tunic between her fingers. Sarah, who had been trying on various pairs of shoes, leapt to her feet like a soldier at attention. Humphrey continued to clean his blade.

Gilda ignored them, moving past Daniel to peer out the shop windows. "Damn. He's out there." With a flick of her wrist, the shades pulled closed on their own. "You'll have to wait. Once the festivities start, you'll be able to sneak out amidst the crowd. He'll be so satiated with power he shouldn't notice you."

"Who shouldn't notice us? What's going on?" Humphrey sheathed his sword and moved to stand by Daniel. "Why are you in such a rush to get rid of us?"

"Shh," Gilda snapped, covering Humphrey's mouth with her hand. "Not so loud. We mustn't draw any attention to you. Sit."

Humphrey glanced at Daniel, who nodded. With a princely flair, he jutted his chin into the air and moseyed over to his seat.

"Tertius will kill you if he finds you," Gilda said to Humphrey. "He would find nothing sweeter than taking out the future rulers of Opea—it would leave them wide open for domination. What he'll do to you is much worse." She pointed at Daniel. "He'll take your power, sap you of your energy, and never let you leave."

"Is that what happened here? He killed the royal family and took over?" Humphrey asked.

"I don't think you can kill royals and take their crown. I think the right to rule passes to someone else," Sarah said. "Did I read that somewhere?"

Gilda worried her bottom lip, staring off into space for a moment. "Tertius never killed the royals here. He put them in the dungeon to live out their days." She waved it away. "It doesn't matter. You need to leave."

"We'll go as soon as he's distracted," Daniel agreed, his mouth set in a grim line.

"What about my curse?"

They all turned to look at her, and Maria realized she'd shouted, jumping to her feet. Biting back her anger, she spoke in a softer tone. "I'm not leaving until you remove my curse. That's why we came here. That's the whole point."

Gilda surveyed Maria with something that felt like pity. "I'm aware of this. You've come in vain. I can't remove the curse."

It felt like a blow to the stomach. The wind in Maria's lungs vanished as her anger turned to anguish. She sat back down, hard, her head slamming against the top of the chair. Pain pulsed through her skull.

All for nothing.

They'd traveled all this way, faced dangers unexplainable, worried their families—all for nothing. A hand rested on hers, and she looked up. Gilda leaned over the table, her green eyes familiar.

"You're going to be fine. I said I couldn't remove the curse, not that it couldn't be removed. Derric will remove it once you're away from here."

Maria stiffened, her anger resurfacing. "Derric? Well that's just great—and how are we supposed to find him, then? Or is this just another wild goose chase you're sending us on?"

"Find him?" Gilda glanced back at Daniel, who shook his head, eyes wide. Frowning, she turned her attention to Humphrey and Sarah, both tense and waiting. Finally, her gaze returned to Maria. "He'll find you. You don't have to go searching for anyone else. You just need to be safe."

Maria snorted, pulling her hand away from Gilda. "What do you care about my safety? You cursed me in the first place."

"Maria—" Humphrey said through gritted teeth.

"No! No 'Maria.' I'm done with the 'Maria.'" She pushed away from the table, marching off in a huff. "'Don't touch that, Maria.' 'Don't go in there, Maria.' 'It isn't safe, Maria.' 'You don't feel that way, Maria.' 'You can't do that, Mah-ree-uh.'" She whirled around to face them all. "I'm sick of it. I can. I will. I want. I do. I am capable of so much more than you're willing to see."

"When have we ever said you weren't?" Sarah's face crinkled, her eyebrows perched low on her brow. "At what point have we ever told you that you couldn't do something?" She pushed Daniel out of her way and stepped before Maria, grabbing her hands. "You can do anything you believe you can. You're the only one who has ever held you back."

Blinking back tears, Maria shook her head. "No. They've always—"

"They? Who is 'they,' my dear?" Gilda placed a tentative hand on her shoulder.

She couldn't breathe. Everything in her chest hurt and felt tight. Closing her eyes, she forced the words out of her mouth. "My parents. The guards. Those two." She gestured to Humphrey and Daniel.

Glancing back, Sarah rolled her eyes. "Well what do those two know? They're hopelessly oblivious to what being a woman is like."

"They said I couldn't be in love with Daniel."

Sarah opened her mouth and then closed it again. After a second, she raised one shoulder in a half shrug. "Well, you can, and you can't, but that's a question of magical theory, isn't it?"

A Stolen Kiss

"What?"

"Never mind. Listen, Princess, I've served you for some time now, and I can tell you this—you're stronger than you've ever realized. You are the one to control your fate."

"She's right." Gilda squeezed Maria's shoulder. "No journey happens for nothing. You may not have needed to come all this way to see me, but you did need to come. I knew you when you were a little girl, Maria, but I would chance a guess you've grown up more on this trip than you have in the last eight years."

"We all have," Sarah said, smiling up at Gilda. "I don't think any one of us is walking away as the exact same person who left Opea." She turned around and addressed her brother. "I'm glad we had the chance to do this together."

"Me too, little sister." Daniel approached her and wrapped his arms around her, kissing the top of her head. "Even if I spent half the time worrying about your safety in the back of my mind."

"Who are you kidding? You can't get rid of me." Sarah squeezed him and caught Maria's eye. "What do you think?"

"You're right, of course," she said in a dry tone, wiping her eyes. "We all have to grow up sometime."

"But what I still want to know," Humphrey said, still seated, "is why we have to be in such a hurry to leave? Who is this Tertius, and why are you so afraid of him?"

Gilda looked Humphrey up and down, sighed, and moved to sit across from him. Maria, Daniel, and Sarah joined them.

"Tertius Adam is a sorcerer unlike any other." Gilda didn't meet any of their gazes but stared at her hands clasped in front of her. "I met him—when I met him, I was drawn to him, seduced by his power and talent. He was so charming." Her voice faltered, and she closed her eyes. "His true colors shone through, and I realized keeping his company wasn't safe. I left the Myrzellian village we lived in and headed north to get to Opea."

Daniel's eyes widened. "You're from Myrzel?"

"Originally, yes. I traveled through Dellsby and up to Edleton in hopes of finding work as a sorceress. After I left Opea, I knew returning to Myrzel wasn't an option. Tertius would still be there, and I didn't ever want to see him again. I thought Kyleria would be safe, cut off enough from the rest of the lands that I wouldn't be followed. I'd noticed Fangralee's dark turn over the years, but I didn't think much of it until I stepped through the gates of this city. Something in the back of my mind kept wondering why Fangralee had grown dark. Peranicus—the other council member—met me at the gates, recognizing my magical thread. He invited me to a meeting of sorcerers, insisted they had a grand plan to improve the city. When I got there . . ."

"Tertius was waiting," Sarah finished, leaning in to catch every word. Gilda nodded.

"I tried to run as soon as I sensed his presence, but once Tertius knows your magical thread, there's no escaping him. He imprisoned me and many of my kind here, holding us against our will."

"How? How does he do that?" Maria asked.

"Spells more complicated than any other in history. He can control the magic of others, use it to make himself more powerful. Not a single sorcerer in all of creation has ever been able to do this, but Tertius can. He holds us here, he usurps our magic and uses it to cause devastating destruction. In the last year, Kyleria conceded his rule, succumbing to their fate. Now it won't be enough—he'll go after the others: Opea, left without protection by the sorcery ban, and Dellsby, his enemy for rejecting him after he left Myrzel."

"Why did he leave Myrzel?" Daniel asked, frowning at Humphrey.

"It's a young kingdom, a land still finding its way. There have been three significant uprisings since he's taken power here, and each has ended with mass bloodshed as Tertius publicly executed those involved."

"But," Humphrey frowned at Daniel. "But he isn't the only one. There are others who can do what he does."

"Yes, there is another." Gilda turned to Daniel as well. "But you are so young. There's no way you could stand against his power. The safest thing for you to do is leave."

"What about this Peranicas?" Daniel asked. "Is he a threat?"

"I've seen him before," Humphrey told Gilda. "He consulted with my parents in Dellsby not long before I left for Opea."

Gilda glared and shook her head. "If he was there, it wasn't anything good. Peranicas left for a short time not long ago, on an errand to cause mayhem, no doubt. His magic is never used for the good of anyone other than himself."

"So he's a threat," Daniel affirmed. "Someone we need to be cautious of when we make our exit."

"The sun will set not long after the festivities begin," Humphrey said, having stood while Gilda was talking and moved to the window to peer through the shades. "Maria will draw attention if we don't leave before then." He walked back to her side and placed a hand on her shoulder. "Maybe if Derric could find us sooner than later," he said with a steady gaze fixed on Daniel, "we could get ourselves out of this mess. Ow!" He leapt back away from Maria, rubbing his hand. "What was that?"

"Magic," Gilda and Daniel said together, standing in eerie synchronicity.

"Which one of you has powers?" Gilda asked Maria and Humphrey. Both shook their heads. The sorceress narrowed her gaze. "I can sense it. It's faint, but it's there. One of you has power."

"No," Maria insisted. "It isn't me."

"Step away from her." Gilda gestured to Humphrey, and he backed up. She leaned over Maria, and the princess leaned away.

"I swear, I don't have any magic," she said. Gilda wasn't cruel, but having her this close felt . . . unnerving.

"It's coming from you."

Daniel stepped up beside Gilda, frowning down at Maria. "You're right. I never . . . I never noticed that before, but I know the magic."

"The magical trace from Maria's curse was hiding it, but this magic doesn't want to be hidden anymore." Gilda considered Maria. "Do you have anything on you? Anything that might have magical properties?"

"I don't think so." Maria reached in the small satchel she'd carried with her into town and removed the contents that weren't clothing. She laid out the necklace she'd been wearing when they left, a comb, and the small portrait of Alyssa.

Daniel picked up the portrait and frowned. "I've never seen this." He handed it to Gilda. "Do you feel that?"

She nodded. "This is it. Step back." She set the portrait on the floor, raised her foot, and brought the heel of her boot down hard on the glass.

"No!" Maria and Humphrey shouted together, moving for the picture. A blast of energy burst forth and knocked them both backward onto the ground. When Maria sat up, she let out a gasp of surprise.

Where the portrait had been, a young woman now sat on the floor, her red hair mussed, no longer in the coifed bun from the picture. She even wore the same dress.

"Alyssa?"

Chapter 51
ALYSSA'S RETURN

. . . .

Derric stared down at the girl on the floor of the shop. She sneered up at him but not in ill humor.

"It's about bloody time," she said, reaching out her hand. Derric grasped it and pulled her to her feet. "I've been trying to get your attention for weeks now. It's a lot harder to do when you're stuck inside a satchel day in and day out." She whirled around as Humphrey helped Maria to her feet.

"And you," she said, pointing at the both of them. "How thick-skulled can you be?" She moved with a fluid grace, crossing the room in three strides and throwing her arms around Humphrey. Her lips met his, and Derric turned away to give them privacy—not that they seemed to care if they had it.

"Alyssa!" Humphrey said, breathless as he pulled away from her. "What—how—why—I don't—"

"It's like watching a play," Sarah said, sinking down into one of the chairs again. "Every time you think you understand what's going on, poof!"

"How are you here?" Maria asked, eyes wide as she stared at the other woman.

"I've been trapped in that blasted portrait for at least a month." Alyssa pointed to the shards of glass and pewter on the ground. "I was cursed there by your adoring parents." She glared at Humphrey, who held up his hands in defense.

"I had no idea."

"I know that, you adorable nincompoop." She smacked his cheek with light affection. "You threw my portrait away! You threw me in the pond! If this darling creature hadn't gone in after me, I'd still be sitting at the bottom of that blasted waterbed."

Derric ran his fingers through his hair as the realization hit him. "Of course. You're the other one who's been changing Maria back from a swan. You did it when she was in the pond."

"I was so glad *someone* had come for me. I tried to get her attention the way I'd tried with Humphrey—by the way, my darling, you need to pay closer attention."

"Every time I changed back it was either because Daniel touched me or ... or when I was digging in my bag." Maria shook her head. "I can't believe I didn't realize it was connected to you."

"I'm so sorry if I caused you trouble. There wasn't a lot I could do with my power in my cursed state. Little jolts were all I had." Alyssa placed a hand on Maria's shoulder. Derric felt an instant appreciation for her—she was almost as tall as Humphrey and sturdy in frame. He couldn't image anyone brave enough to curse her.

"Who did this to you?" he asked.

Alyssa turned to Humphrey. "Do you remember that sorcerer your parents invited for consultation? The fluffy-headed one? I'm going about my own business, and I'm summoned to the throne room. I expected this, of course," she said to the room at large, gesturing with her hands as she spoke, "because Humphrey wasn't going to go to Opea, but was going to marry me—a sorceress—instead. So anyway, I go to the throne room, and your mum is all fidgety, and your father says something like, 'the good of the country is more important than the happiness of two young people,' and out of nowhere that stupid man comes up and just zaps me from behind. I had no chance to defend myself. Completely caught off guard.

"Then, the bastard plucks me up off the floor and hands me to your dad. He says he's sorry and how it's for the best, and he hopes I understand, but the sorcerer told them there's no way I would go quietly. Like hell I'd go quietly! I couldn't get out, but I still had a touch of my magic, so I zapped your dad, and he dropped me. Then that steeyupid sorcerer conjures up a letter in my handwriting and takes me and the letter up to your room to leave for you to find."

She spoke so fast Derric almost didn't catch her story. All at once she softened and had eyes only for Humphrey.

"There's nothing worse in this world than to watch the one you love fall apart. I had to sit and watch your heart break as you read my letter, and I couldn't do anything about it. I tried so hard to get you to realize I was still there, but nothing worked."

"I always thought it was me—wishful thinking and all that, missing you. That's why I kept feeling little sparks when I'd pick up your portrait." Humphrey wrapped his arms around her and kissed her forehead. "I've missed you so much."

"You lent me your magic," Derric said, drawing their attention away from each other. "You're the other thread."

"I've never seen anyone with magic like yours. I kept willing someone to bring me out and show me to you. I knew you'd know what I was. You saw me once, when she pulled me out of the pond, but you weren't ready yet. Your magic wasn't in use."

"Wait, so all of this time it was interacting with sorcerers that changed me back from swan to human?" Maria pressed a hand to her temple, massaging the right side. "No. Don't try to explain it to me. I don't care. I'm so beyond caring by now."

"I need to leave." Gilda moved to Derric's side, taking his hands in hers. "He'll notice if I stay away any longer. You all must stay here until I return for you. It will be an hour now."

"But—" Derric began, holding fast to her.

"Don't worry. I'll be back soon." She vanished in a puff of smoke.

"Now *that* I want to learn how to do," Derric said, walking through the space she'd just occupied.

"Me too." Alyssa stepped forward, eyes wide with delight. "Oh, by the by, here's me being formal. Alyssa Pendergan."

"D . . ." Derric stumbled over his words, and Alyssa waved it away.

"I know who you are. So, how long do we have to wait before this party gets under way and we can slip out?" At their surprised looks, she grinned. "You'd be surprised how much you can hear through the fabric of a bag."

Humphrey hadn't taken his eyes away from Alyssa, but at her mention of leaving, he turned to Derric. "A word? In private, please?"

Derric nodded and followed the prince into the back room. Humphrey closed the door behind them.

"You have to break the curse?" he asked, eyebrows rising.

"I'm surprised you managed to leave Alyssa out there with Maria just to ask me that."

"Alyssa isn't going anywhere," Humphrey said, his jaw set firm. "We are still in imminent danger, and I think getting her killed would be a cruel twist of fate on my part."

Derric sighed and rubbed his neck, his whole body feeling the fatigue of the journey. "I cursed Maria."

"You *what?*"

"I didn't know it. She—Gilda—made us forget. I was young, and I didn't know how to control my magic."

"So you have to be the one to remove it."

"Yup."

"How do you do that?"

"I have no idea. I'm trying to figure that out, but first I think we need to get out of Kyleria."

"Agreed. Okay. Let's think." Humphrey began pacing.

A Stolen Kiss

"Between your and Alyssa's magic, we'll draw a lot of attention. Then again, we'll also have a better chance of getting back through the forest with both of you by our sides. So we sneak out and then—what? Make a run for it?"

"Go as fast as we can, to get as far as we can, before stopping for a rest." Derric nodded in agreement.

"Good. That's good. But we don't have a horse for Alyssa."

"She can ride Burt. Or one of us can, and she can take a horse."

"Smart thinking, mate."

"There's just one thing I can't figure out," Derric said, crossing his arms.

"Which is?"

"If my mother grew up in Myrzel, how did she know my father when she was young?"

"What?" Humphrey blinked, caught off guard.

"Whenever I asked her to tell me stories about my father, she told me about how she knew him when she was young, that they were both idealists who wanted what was best for the kingdom, but he changed."

"Well, she doesn't seem old, mate. She was probably pretty young when she had you—she got to Edleton, met your dad, and all the rest is history."

"Maybe. There's just something about it that seems—"
"HUMPHREY!"

Chapter 52
Impossible Revenge

. . . .

Daniel and Humphrey shut the door behind them, and Maria stared at Alyssa, still in shock from her arrival. After a few moments, she moved to a chair and sank into it.

"I guess that solves my problem of marrying someone I don't love."

"Not really." Sarah sighed. "Your parents will just find a new prince."

"Gee, thank you for your emotional support, Sarah. So now I'll be cursed forever *and* forced to marry someone I don't even know if I can tolerate. At least I knew Humphrey and I would get on all right as friends."

Sarah's lips quirked up at the sides. She moved out of her seat and knelt before Maria, taking her hands in her own and holding her gaze.

"We still have time. We'll find a way to get out of this without you having to marry anyone. Once your curse is broken, we can—"

"Pah!" Maria balked, laughing. "My curse? There's no way my curse will ever be broken. You heard Gilda: she can't remove it. Only Derric can, and even if we found him, what's to stop him from deciding he wants the power of the throne for himself?"

"He won't."

"You don't know that."

"Yes I do."

"How? How could you possibly know that?"

Sarah hesitated, biting her lip. "Because . . . because I know Derric Harver."

"You *what?* You know Derric Harver?"

"You don't?" Alyssa asked, pointing at Maria.

"No! Do you?"

"I thought everyone knew."

"Good for everyone, but no. I. Do. Not. Know. Him."

Alyssa held up her hands and walked away. "Don't take it out on me, love."

"Maria." Sarah squeezed her hands. "I didn't tell you because, because I didn't want you to worry or to feel afraid. The truth is, I know he will remove the curse. I know he'll help us because he isn't evil—not any more than Gilda is. You've seen her, spoken with her. She might not be all good, but she isn't wicked."

Maria looked away, tears threatening to spill from her eyes. As much as she hated to admit it, Sarah was right. Gilda wasn't the enemy—she was helping them, trying to keep them safe. Surely, if she knew right from wrong, her son would too.

"He's good?"

"He's wonderful." Sarah's lips spread into a wide smile. "I don't know anyone more amazing, wonderful, or noble. He'll help you."

A zing of cursed jealousy zipped its way through Maria's heart. "You seem very smitten with him," she said in a terse tone she knew she didn't mean. "I'm sorry. I don't . . . I don't mean to."

"I know." Sarah patted her hands and released them. "I do love him. I really do, Maria. And if you weren't cursed, I would suggest you do the same. He's the most wonderful man I know, and I want you to remember that when he reveals himself to you. I want you to remember his goodness before you hate him for his actions."

"That doesn't make any sense. What actions?"

Sarah squirmed and focused her gaze elsewhere. "If he's the only one who can remove the curse, that means he's the one who cursed you in the first place."

"What?"

"Only the sorcerer who casts the curse can remove it," Alyssa said from the other side of the shop where she'd been pretending not to listen. "A curse can be broken by whosoever fits the clause, but it can only be terminated by the creator."

"But . . . but Gilda's so young. Derric couldn't have been more than a child when I was cursed. Why would a little boy curse me?"

"Maybe he didn't mean to."

"Seems like a rather malicious accident." Maria could hear the bitterness in her words but couldn't work around them. How could any child cast a curse as strong as hers? It was unbreakable. What had she done to this little boy to make him hate her enough to curse her?

"Just remember what I said," Sarah said, brushing a strand of Maria's hair away from her face.

"Sarah, where do you fit into all of this?" Alyssa kicked off the shoes she was wearing and put on some that had been out on display.

"Beg your pardon?"

"Why are you here? Maria's cursed, Humphrey's responsible for her as her intended, and the sorcerer is the one who led you all here safely. Why are *you* here? You're a child and can't be more than twelve. You don't seem to serve a purpose. It seems the whole journey could have happened without you."

Sarah blinked, her face paling. Though Maria knew Alyssa hadn't meant her words to hurt, the harsh and blunt delivery had stabbed deep. A tear ran down Sarah's cheek, and she brushed it away with haste.

"Blast." Alyssa brought one hand to her face. "I've gummed it up. I always do this. I say things without thinking of how they'll sound. I'm sorry. I didn't mean—"

"You're right." Sarah's voice caught, and she cleared her throat before continuing. "I don't belong, do I? If we were to ask everyone we've met along the way who their favorite was, it wouldn't be me. I thought this would be just a fun adventure with my brother. I'm always pestering him, and he puts up with it, but I'm not even *his* favorite. I've just been in the way this whole time. He didn't even want me to come."

"Sarah, don't say that." Maria leapt up and moved to her side, but Sarah pulled away.

"It's true. If I hadn't been so helpless, Drusilla wouldn't have died. If I hadn't been in the marsh, the melgorn wouldn't have had anyone to attack, and you would have been saved sooner. If I'd had my way, we'd have stayed in the centaur cave and been eaten by the arachnae."

"You killed that arachnae." Maria reminded her.

"On accident." Sarah pressed her hands to her eyes, her shoulders shaking as she started to cry in earnest. "I—I've been nothing but in the way. I just w-wanted to be brave like you. I wanted to have an adventure. I wanted to show D-d-d . . . I wanted to show my brother I wasn't like my mother and father, but I am. I'm just like them. I'm selfish and careless. I don't belong here." She dropped down on a chair. "I wish I hadn't come."

"Sarah!" It was Maria's turn to kneel before her friend. "You need to stop talking like this. It isn't true. The melgorn went for you and Humphrey. Otherwise, it would have come after Daniel while he was still carrying me. You killed that spider—I don't care if it was an accident, it counts. You sang the loudest in Fangralee and made the darkness lift. You were the one who had the wit to check Daniel's journal for a cure to the beornach's poison." She gripped her hands. "I wouldn't have made it through this journey without you. Every time I've doubted—every time I've questioned myself, you've been there to remind me who I am. Humphrey might be the muscle, and Daniel the power—but you're the heart."

"He's a slave," Sarah whispered, staring at one of the

shuttered windows. "My brother has been in slavery most of his life, and I never noticed. I never once noticed. Do you remember what he said—that he was sick of me?"

"He didn't mean that. He was under the effect of the poison. Dry your eyes."

Sarah wiped at her face, sniffling as she spoke to Alyssa. "By the way, I'm fourteen."

"Well la-tee-da." Alyssa moved to the window, and Maria wrapped Sarah in a hug. "It looks like people are starting to gather out there." Alyssa peeked through the curtain. "We'll be able to leave soon, and all of this can be behind us. We'll . . . wait. What?"

"What?" Sarah and Maria said together, turning to Alyssa.

"Peranicas," she hissed.

"Bless you," Maria said, turning her attention back to Sarah, who sat rigid and alert.

"No." Sarah shoved her away and rushed for the door at the same time as Alyssa. Sarah's tiny frame crashed into Alyssa's broader, stronger one.

"Out of my way!" Alyssa shouldered into Sarah, her eyes wild.

"No! You can't go out there!" Sarah pushed back, wedging herself against the door.

"That man put me into a picture to live out eternity in agony!"

"Alyssa, please. You'll get us all killed!"

"You think I can't move you?"

"HUMPHREY!"

Chapter 53
A Kylerian Party

. . . .

At the sound of Sarah's shout, Humphrey and Derric launched themselves toward the door of the back room. After a moment's struggle of hands, arms, and doorknobs, they poured out into the main shop.

Shoes were scattered everywhere, one of the displays knocked sideways. Sarah and Maria had their arms around Alyssa who, being much stronger, struggled with the partially opened shop door.

"No!" Humphrey threw himself forward, dragging Alyssa, Sarah, and Maria away as Derric shut the door and locked it.

"What were you thinking?" Derric gasped, dropping to the floor and leaning against the door.

Humphrey and the women were a tangle of limbs. "He's out there!" Alyssa's voice came muffled from the bottom of the pile "Peranicas!"

"Ah, yes." Humphrey wriggled free. "Now, darling . . ."

"You knew?" She shoved Maria and Sarah off and sat up with a huff. "You knew, and you didn't tell me!"

"I couldn't risk you going out there!"

"I *will* have my revenge."

"Yes, everybody will get revenge on everyone they hate," Sarah snapped, pushing up to her feet. "But not until we're away from the psychotic sorcerer out there who can *steal your power and use it for himself.* Or weren't you paying attention to that part from inside your little picture?"

Alyssa's lower lip pouted out, but she didn't argue.

Humphrey helped her stand while Sarah got Maria to her feet.

"I think I've been knocked to the ground more times on this trip than in all my life before it." Maria dusted off her trousers.

"Once again, I'm thankful for the pants. Good call." Sarah twisted her slacks back into place. "But this is no way to be dressed for a ball. We'll stick out like sore thumbs."

"I hadn't thought of that," Derric said, his head still resting against the door. "How are we going—"

"I already thought that through." Gilda appeared out of nowhere, a bundle of fabric in her arms. "I'll have you incognito in no time." She glanced around the room, her brows knitting together. "What in the hells happened here?"

Half an hour later they all stood dressed in the finest clothes Derric had ever seen. The royals and Alyssa were at home in their finery, but he couldn't help fingering his silky jacket and marveling at its softness. Sarah kept twirling in her dress, admiring its beauty.

"Put these masks on." Gilda handed around colorful pieces of a hard material.

"These? Why?" Alyssa turned hers over and held it up to her face. It had holes for the eyes and covered the top of her nose. The color matched her gown.

"It's a masquerade, a Kylerian tradition. This way, no one can see who you are. Everyone will be wearing masks."

"Masquerade," Maria repeated, grinning down at her disguise. "We must have one of these when—" she stopped, turning her attention away from Humphrey. "Well, you and Alyssa must come when I have one of these in Opea."

Alyssa's mouth twisted into a lopsided grin. "It's weird, isn't it? Changing your expectations."

"Yes, but I'm not disappointed or heartbroken . . . yet." She glanced at Derric, and he felt a mingled sense of elation and dread wash over him. He still had no idea how to tell her who he was, let alone how to remove the curse once he'd done so.

"All right, I think enough people have gathered for you to slip out into the crowd now." Gilda gestured for them to join her at the door. "Act casual, and don't draw attention to yourselves. Mingle through the crowd until you can slip away unnoticed. Don't do anything stupid." She glanced at Alyssa, who avoided eye contact.

"One final thing. Avoiding Tertius and Peranicas is obvious, but there are others in Kyleria that could present a danger to you." Gilda sighed, her hand on the doorknob. "Some who crossed the council were cursed for it. Don't touch any stranger's hands unless you want to turn into gold. And do not, under any circumstances, wish for anything out loud."

"Why not?" Sarah asked, still twisting from side to side in her dress.

"Let's just say, in Kyleria, wishes come true and being careful for what you wish for has never been so important."

Sarah glanced at Derric, and he shook his head. No doubt someone had been struck with a genie curse. Those were dangerous; if their contract hadn't been specific, a genie would be required to grant any wish given within earshot.

One by one, they slipped out the door of the shop and into the bustling crowd of partygoers. Derric held back, stopping Gilda. "Who cast the genie curse?"

She didn't meet his gaze, her eyes hidden behind the mask. "Don't ask questions you don't want to know the answer to."

With a nod, he moved out the door behind the others.

Derric let out a low whistle at the sight of such frivolity. Lanterns hung on strings, lighting up the center of the town. Festive music, played by an orchestra, piped through the square. Sounds and smells, several clearly magical in origin, wafted by.

"This is amazing," Sarah whispered beside him, holding her mask up to her face by a thin stick clutched in her hand, her blue dress billowing about her.

"Did you ever think the two of us would end up someplace like this?" Derric murmured back. She grinned up at him.

"Never. We've come a long way, brother of mine."

"I wouldn't want anyone else here beside me."

Even through the mask he could see her eyes were wide with surprise. "Really?"

"Really," he said. "No one else has ever believed in me like you have. You always told me I could be something more, and you were right. Thank you, Sarah."

She didn't reply but followed close beside him through the crowd, mimicking his casual pace. If they could get to the edge of the gathering before—

"My friends!" The magnified voice of Tertius Adam echoed through the assembly. The people cheered, and all eyes turned to the platform where the Council stood just as they had earlier that day. Tertius held up his hands for silence.

"We celebrate tonight our eighth year of peaceful Council reign."

"Peaceful, yeah right," someone muttered behind Derric. He didn't dare turn to see who spoke.

"Together we have created a better country. It all started here, in Kyleria Capital, when you accepted us as your humble leaders, and we ended the turmoil of the prior reign."

"Turmoil? Try a few bumps in the road for a king trying to teach his children to rule."

It was the same voice as before; Derric itched to turn and see his face. Despite the cheers, it seemed Kyleria was just as disenchanted with Tertius as Gilda was.

"Let us enjoy tonight as we celebrate," Tertius said, still beaming at the crowd. "But let us not get out of hand. Curfew is still in effect, and consequences will not be halted for the sake of merriment."

A little shiver ran through the crowd, and Derric wondered what "consequences" might mean.

"Know this is just the beginning. Kyleria is now a safe and happy place to live, but the other countries need us! We will move forward into Opea and Dellsby, Myrzel and Braskey. We will unite the world!" More cheering, though little sincerity showed in the faces of those gathered. "Let's strike the music up once more. Everyone enjoy your evening."

"Daniel," Maria whispered, tugging on Derric's sleeve as she appeared at his side. "We need to—"

Whatever they needed to do, he didn't find out. The band began to play, and the crowd parted to create space for dancing, leaving Derric and Maria standing in the center of the dance floor. Couples joined them, forming a line and waiting for an invisible cue Derric wouldn't recognize.

Maria must have seen the panic on his face, because she started mouthing instructions to him each time they were meant to move. His movements were far from graceful and often a second behind everyone else's, but he watched her with intent focus for each guided step. Down at the end of the line, Humphrey and Alyssa danced with ease, accustomed to partnering together, though Derric saw Alyssa step on the prince's feet several times.

When the song ended, Derric grabbed Maria's elbow and ushered her to the refreshment table, panting from the exertion.

"You were marvelous," she said with a laugh. "Was that your first time dancing?"

"Sarah tried to teach me steps in the stable when we were younger, but it didn't go well." He peered around. "Where is she?"

"Right here."

Derric jumped and turned around. Sarah stood beside Gilda just behind them.

"We need to find Humphrey and Alyssa and make our way out of here," Derric said, speaking in low tones as a young woman with vivid blue hair moved to the table to obtain a drink. Gilda stiffened. Behind her mask, she watched the newcomer.

"Why is her hair—" he began just as Maria spoke.

"I love it when you take command," she said, grinning up at him. "Your father might have sold you to the stables, but I wish he could be here now to see what a strong leader you've become."

"NO!" Gilda shouted. "Don't!"

The girl getting the drink straightened, her back rigid as she turned to Maria with a mournful downturn of her lips. "Your wish is granted." She snapped her fingers and disappeared into the crowd.

"Do you know what you've done?" Gilda asked, ripping off her mask.

"Was that her? Was that a genie?" Derric asked, staring after the girl as she disappeared into the crowd.

Before Gilda could answer his question, a soft pop signaled the arrival of sunset and Maria turning into a swan.

"Oh no," Gilda groaned as people turned to look at the large, black swan standing at the refreshment table.

"What's going on?" Humphrey and Alyssa appeared at Sarah's side. Their eyes widened at the sight of Maria. "Fix it!"

Derric leaned down and stroked Maria's head with a casual, but quick gesture. She promptly launched back into full human form, her pink dress puffing out and tripping a man who was walking by.

"You!" Alyssa screeched, and Derric recognized him as Peranicas. At the sight of Alyssa, he backed up, stumbling again into Maria's voluminous dress. Caught in her crinoline, he forced Maria backward into the refreshment table, which went belly-up and crashed to the ground, taking Maria with it.

Chapter 54
Derric's Father

. . . .

Maria hit the ground hard, landing on her elbow and sending shooting pain up through her arm. The zing of magic whirled around above her.

"Here, I've got you." Sarah stepped through the mess and batted aside Maria's many layers of ball gown. "I forgot how ridiculous these things are."

"I miss pants," Maria agreed, grunting as she struggled into a standing position. Just in front of her, Alyssa hurled balls of ice at Peranicas.

"You weasel of a man!" she shouted, launching another one at him. "Attacking me from behind! Coward!"

"You have to stop!" Gilda cried. She turned to Daniel, just a few feet away from Maria and Sarah. "Go, go now. He'll be here any second, and if he finds you . . . I couldn't bear it."

Before any of them could move an inch, a harsh booming growl had them covering their ears with their hands.

"*Who is disrupting my celebration?*"

Peranicas ran for Tertius as soon as he appeared, hiding behind the stronger sorcerer as he approached Alyssa. "It's the one from Dellsby—the sorceress I put into the portrait."

"You didn't do a very good job," Tertius hissed, glowering at Alyssa. Though she glared back, a tremble passed through her body.

"What a feisty little thing you are," Tertius said with a sneer. "You've got gumption. Yes, I think you'll make a wonderful citizen of Kyleria."

"I'm not staying." Alyssa turned away to make her point but froze mid-step.

Tertius, his hand raised, flicked his wrist, and Alyssa dropped to the ground, crying out in pain. Humphrey started forward, but Sarah blocked his path.

"Even the strongest can be broken," Tertius said in a soothing tone. "You'll learn your place here. Your magic will serve us well." He blinked and looked up, searching the crowd around the mess where Alyssa lay, twitching. "I sense something else . . . something bigger."

Gilda shifted in front of Daniel, but Tertius noticed the movement. His gaze locked on Daniel, and he approached them. Maria watched in horror as a look of mad glee lit up Tertius's face.

"This is a treat," he said, staring at Daniel with hunger in his eyes. "I can feel it . . . I thought I sensed it before, but now—now I know. What a wonderful surprise."

"Tertius—"

"Now, now, Gilda." He grabbed her arm and yanked her out of his way.

"Hey!" Daniel moved toward her, but Tertius blocked his path, his fingers still wrapped around Gilda's arm.

"Now I know what was so important you had to leave Myrzel," Tertius said, still staring at Daniel. "Now I know why you fought so hard to get away from me here."

The crowd waited, not a murmur to be heard. Daniel and Tertius stood in the middle of an open space, Gilda at Tertius's side, Sarah and Maria not far from them. Humphrey knelt beside Alyssa, forgotten a little ways away.

"It's not what you think," Gilda said, still struggling in Tertius's grasp.

"It's exactly what I think." He reached up and pulled off Daniel's mask. A sick comprehension filled Maria with dread as the final puzzle piece clicked into place. She realized why Tertius felt so familiar to her.

Tertius ran the back of his fingers down Daniel's cheek. "So this is Derricus Harver." He glanced back at Gilda. "Did you really think I wouldn't know my own son?"

Chapter 55
Revelations

The world stilled. Though the words penetrated Derric's brain and he knew what each one meant, stringing them together didn't make any sense. Tertius grinned. Gilda paled. People whispered. None of it made any sense.

"He's not your son."

Sarah's assertion broke through the haze in Derric's mind. He blinked and shifted his focus to his sister—or to the girl he'd always thought was his sister. She stood just behind Tertius, hands on her hips, glaring up at the back of his head.

Tertius turned, one eyebrow cocked high. "Be gone, girl. This doesn't concern you."

"It most certainly does!" Sarah said. "This is my brother, Daniel Digson, son of Charles Digson. He is of no relation to you."

"Yes, I know what Gilda has claimed." Tertius winked at the sorceress, her arm still in his vice grip. "She told me some time ago she had a son with a man in the city of Edleton, though his name was Derricus Harver. She may have told him Digson had fathered him, but she lied, and now he knows. There's no denying it." He turned back to Derric. "You can sense it, can't you? The power? The energy? The three of us together could conquer the world."

Bile churned in Derric's stomach. He *could* sense it. He could feel the similarities, hovering in the air between them, the electricity before a lightning bolt strikes. He looked to Sarah again. Her eyes filled with tears as she shook her head.

"Run." His voice cracked. She cocked her head to the side in question. Humphrey obeyed Derric's order and pulled Alyssa from the ground. He grabbed Sarah by the arm and tugged as Derric shouted. "RUN!"

Tertius raised a hand to stop them, but Gilda shoved her body into his, throwing them both off balance and into Derric. He wrapped his arms around Tertius, absorbing all the energy the sorcerer intended for the escapees. Light flashed, and his whole body went rigid. He held Tertius in his immovable grasp. The sorcerer cursed, struggling against Derric's arms.

"Let them go," Gilda said from somewhere on the other side of Tertius. "They're nothing. We're together now. Let them go."

"Not all of them!"

Peranicas's voice rose in pitch, but Derric couldn't see him from his frozen position. Tertius cursed again and muttered the counter jinx, releasing Derric. Tertius pushed away from them and stood, commending Peranicas on his quick thinking.

As Derric shifted to see, his heart sank. An unconscious Maria lay slumped against Peranicas, who fought to keep her upright. Tertius fingered her hair, a dark look overtaking his face.

"Good. Bring her. We're all going to take a little trip to the castle." To the crowd at large, he roared, "The ball is over! Back to your homes this instant!"

Kylerians moved to obey. Gilda pulled Derric to his feet, her voice low and intent as she spoke. "Do as he says. The best we can do now is cooperate. We'll figure out a way out of this later. Just do as he says, and no one will get hurt."

Still too stunned to do much else, Derric nodded. He followed Gilda as they fell into Tertius's wake, Peranicas ahead of them, Maria now floating at his side by magic.

At least the others got away. They'll be safe. I'll figure this out for Maria, but at least Sarah is safe. Derric couldn't stomach the thought of something happening to Sarah. Humphrey would take care of her.

Someone ran into Derric, jostling him backwards. He had the impression of height, dark hair, and skin as light as his own.

"Take this." He shoved something into Derric's hand, and for a fleeting moment, he had the sense this was the person behind him during Tertius's speech. Slipping the object into his pocket, Derric followed behind Gilda as though nothing had happened.

The Kylerian castle didn't have the turrets and towers the Opean castle had. Instead, a large, square, stone monument loomed over the capital city. From the inside, Derric wondered how anyone stayed warm. Everything about the decor, even in the throne room where he now sat, seemed cold and dark. Torches lit the walls, and tapestries in earthy colors hung in between the windows. Night reigned in this place, and Derric had an eerie feeling like he was back in Fangralee.

He sat against a stone wall, holding Maria. There were no signs of immediate danger, but he didn't trust Tertius anywhere near her.

The sorcerer in question sat on the golden throne not far away, his focus on Gilda, who stood before him. If they hadn't been discussing him, Derric would have thought they'd forgotten he was there.

"When you left Myrzel, did you know then you were pregnant?" Though Tertius's tone remained light, a forbidding bite and crispness lingered in his enunciation.

"I did." Gilda kept her eyes downcast, her hands folded in front of her. She looked bored.

"You took my child from me and didn't even have the

decency to tell me he existed?" This time, Tertius's fists clenched, and he shot a bolt of black energy at the wall. Derric winced, but Gilda remained unmoved.

"I wasn't going to allow my child to be raised by a monster." Her eyes snapped open. "I saw what you were becoming, and while I hadn't been willing to leave for myself—despite all of the abuse I'd endured—I was willing to leave for the baby. I knew he wouldn't stand a chance once you realized his power. I wanted him to have a life worth living—to laugh, play, and enjoy his youth." Gilda's gaze flickered to Derric. "I failed him, but at least he didn't grow up with you."

Tertius slammed his fist onto the armrest. "You found me so vile, Gilda? You haven't seen what I'm capable of, what I plan to do to you for what you've done." He glared down at her, his jaw set. "But not until you answer all of my questions. How did you convince the other man he was the father? You must have been well along by the time you reached Edleton."

"He came to me when Derric was two years old, before I was employed at the palace. He was betrothed to a woman of wealth but had taken a peasant girl into his bed when he discovered his future wife would be barren. The girl, with child and madly in love with him, was threatening to tell his fiancée everything. He begged me to make the girl forget—to get rid of her by whatever means necessary to save his future marriage. His bride already suspected his infidelity, and I had to help her forget as well. Twice the magic, and he wasn't willing to pay me.

"I told him I would help him on one condition . . . he allow me any favor I asked. He agreed, and I used my favor to force him to claim my son as his own, to keep Derric safe from you. He was resistant, but I told him if he didn't keep quiet, I would tell his wife he'd come to me for help, I'd gotten rid of the other girl, she was barren, and the child she claimed as her daughter wasn't her own."

A Stolen Kiss

Tertius cocked his head, intrigued. "You mean that little girl who insisted Derric was her brother isn't even legitimate?"

"I kept the peasant with me until she gave birth to a daughter," Gilda said, glancing at Derric again. "I erased her memory of the affair and her child and sent her to a different country. I gave the child to Digson and altered his new wife's memory, convincing her their marriage—six months in by that time—had been in haste because of the newborn babe she now held. Her child."

"And how did she come to terms with Digson claiming Derric as his son?"

"They weren't even betrothed when Derric was born. When the time came for her to know—after I'd given them the other woman's child—Digson passed it off as an affair before he met her. Knowing I'm a sorceress, his wife was convinced I'd seduced him. She was the one who suspected Derric wasn't Charles's son. Either way, she never realized the truth about her daughter."

"All of this just to keep him from me? Do you hate me so much?"

"I hate what you've become." Gilda lifted her chin, her gaze back on Derric. "I wanted my son to be more than you. I wanted him to be *good*, unlike us. To care for others and protect them, not use them for his own gain. I didn't want him to be forced to do the wicked things you've forced me to do." Her brow creased. "Or the things I've done all by myself."

Derric could feel her pride in him, and he swallowed the lump in his throat, knowing he was going to fail her. There was no way he was going to get out of this without people getting hurt.

Chapter 56
Sarah's Choice

. . . .

No one stopped Sarah, Humphrey, and Alyssa. They ran until they reached the city gates, but Sarah stopped dead in her tracks before crossing the threshold.

"What are you doing?" Alyssa asked, skidding to a halt.

"We can't." Sarah's heart raced while she beseeched Humphrey. "We can't leave them there. They have my brother! We have to go back."

"What are we supposed to do?" Alyssa asked, raking a hand through her disheveled tresses. "How are we going to fight someone that powerful? You didn't experience what I did—he can cause pain like you've never known by barely lifting a finger. We can't fight him."

"We have to try." Sarah turned away from them, looking back the way they'd come. "You don't have to come with me, but I'm not leaving here without my brother."

"You heard Tertius, didn't you? That's his father—he isn't even your real bro—"

Sarah rounded on Alyssa, shaking her fist in her face. "Derric is, and will always be, my brother. Blood does not make a family. Family is made up of the people who love you no matter what."

"What are we supposed to do?"

"I don't know, but Derric is the best and greatest person in my life, and I am not going to let him down now."

"You're right." Humphrey shifted to stand beside Sarah, casting a pleading gaze at Alyssa. "I feel closer to Derric than I do to either of my own brothers. I'm not going to leave him behind."

"Then we go, but not alone." Sarah reached down the front of her dress and pulled out the silver whistle.

"Where did you get that?" Humphrey asked, eyes widening.

"Derric gave it to me before we left the shop. We felt I should be the one to carry it." Sarah held the whistle to her lips and blew. A piercing note shrieked, high-pitched, almost impossible to hear.

Within moments a monstrous figure soared through the night sky, descending upon them. Alyssa shrieked and jumped backward, her arms raised in preparation for a fight.

"This is Burt!" Humphrey said as the bumbleloch assessed them.

"Wow." Alyssa approached him with tiny steps. "I heard you talk about him, but I never saw—he'll do."

"Do? Do what?" Burt bounced around on his six limbs. "Where others? Where they?"

"They're in trouble," Sarah said, holding Burt's massive face between her hands. "We need your help to save them."

"Save. Yes. Burt save." He nodded, his face growing fierce. "Where? We go. Now."

"Hang on." Humphrey rubbed his hands together. "First, we need a plan."

Chapter 57
Maria's Reaction

. . . .

Derric's mind spun in a jumble of directions as he tried to think of a way out. Tertius and Gilda still conversed, and as long as she had him talking, Derric had time to think. He lowered Maria to the floor and fished out the item the man outside had given him. It was a slip of paper rolled up in a masculine, silver ring.

Setting the ring aside, Derric read the hastily scrawled and barely legible note.

Derric read the note three times trying to understand what it meant. It had been signed "Prince Shen." Gilda said all the royals were in the dungeons of the castle—was it possible one still walked among the people? Derric studied the ring and saw it appeared to be the Kylerian royal crest, the same one adorning the coat of arms hanging on the wall opposite him. He slipped it on his finger, afraid he might lose it otherwise.

Beside him, Maria groaned, her eyes fluttering open.

"Maria?" he whispered, glancing over at the throne to make sure Tertius still focused on Gilda. Not far from them, Peranicas picked at his nails, ignoring everyone.

"I think I fainted," she moaned. He hushed her, and she sat bolt upright. "Where are we?"

"The throne room."

She blinked, her face paling as she pushed away from him, her mouth set in a grim line.

"He's your father."

"Yes, I think so."

She nodded and opened her mouth, then closed it again to think for a moment more. "Your name . . . your name is Derric Harver."

"It is."

Another chunk of time passed as she stared at him. He could almost see the thoughts racing around in her mind.

"I see," she said, her eyes filling with tears.

"I'm so sorry. I never wanted to hurt you or lie to—"

She held up a hand to silence him, staring at the ground. "Don't. I need . . . I need to think." She pressed a hand to her face and shook her head. Several moments passed in silence. "I can't think. I'm angry, and I'm elated. I'm sad, and I'm antsy. Part of me really wants to hate you, to claw your eyes out and finally have my revenge for everything you've taken from me. But a greater part of me just wants to throw my arms around you and never let you go."

"Maria—"

"I'm so stupid. Everyone kept trying to tell me. All of you kept hinting at it, like you wanted me to know. How did I miss all the signs?" She sighed and leaned back against the wall next to him, not looking at him. "So I suppose this is why I feel the way I do about you."

"Yes."

"And that's why you kept insisting I didn't actually love you."

"Yes."

She chewed on her bottom lip for a moment. "But this curse isn't why you are in love with me."

"Who said I'm—"

"I'm saying it." She turned and gave him a level stare. "You didn't tell me because you were afraid of what I'd do if I knew you were the son of Gilda Harver. Then you kept it a secret because you cared about me—about Humphrey—and didn't want to lose the relationships you'd formed with us."

"Humphrey knows."

Maria reared back as though she'd been slapped. Then she snorted. "That explains a lot." She shook her head again as though trying to clear it of a fog. "I can't . . . I can't tell how I feel about this."

"That's because you're still under the spell," Derric said, trying to fight off the misery that overwhelmed him. "There's more."

Maria's gaze narrowed. "How can there be more?"

"I'm the one who cursed you, not Gilda." Before she could respond he continued. "I didn't know—she removed the memory from me, from both of us, so she could take the blame. She was trying to protect me."

"Good. She's awake."

They both turned and saw all three members of the Council looking at them.

"My dear, if you don't mind, I'd like a word with my son." Tertius raised his hand and beckoned for Derric to come forward.

Though he intended to ignore this order, Derric realized Tertius wasn't giving him a choice. Both he and Maria were dragged across the floor, stopping at the steps before the throne.

"Stand." Tertius clapped his hands, and both of them launched up to their feet. "You, here." He pointed at Maria, and she lurched forward, coming to kneel beside him. He grabbed her by the neck from behind, and she squeaked.

"Don't hurt her," Derric said, taking a step forward.

"I won't as long as you be a good boy and do as you're told. Now, Derric, I know all of this must be confusing and overwhelming for you. I admit it's an emotional time for me. But think of what an amazing gift this is. You have my blood running through your veins. You, as my son, will be the second most powerful sorcerer the world has ever seen. Together we can rule the world."

"And if I decline?" Derric asked, holding Tertius's gaze.

"You have no such option. You will rule with me, or you will watch everything you love burn."

Derric closed his eyes—he'd heard those words before when he'd dreamed about Tertius under the beornach's poison. "What would ruling entail?"

"Ah ha! I had hoped you'd be accommodating. Very well. By my side, you will have more power than you could ever dream of. You will be revered, feared, and loved by all. We will take Opea, then Dellsby, and then turn our sights on Braskey. Myrzel will be the easiest. It's of no concern at the present time."

A flicker of desire sparked in the deepest part of Derric's heart. If he accepted, he'd be part of a family—his true family. He'd have endless power and could do whatever he wished. As the thought appeared, one thought extinguished it.

He'd lose Sarah, Maria, and Humphrey.

"No." Derric squared his shoulders and glared at Tertius. "I won't join you."

Tertius's countenance darkened, and he bared his teeth in a jeer. "You don't think I'm capable of making you agree? Your mother used to feel that way, but now she works beside me. You'll soon see our way is best—pain is a magnificent teacher."

"I won't let you do this to him." Gilda glared up at Tertius with tears in her eyes. "I won't let you turn him into a replica of you."

Tertius sucked in a breath, reeling back as though slapped. "You love me. You will do as I say, and so will our son."

"He may be your blood, but he isn't your son." Gilda stepped in front of Derric. "I won't let you hurt him. I won't let you break him the way you broke me."

"Then you are no longer of use to me." A bolt of energy shot from Tertius's hand, striking Gilda in the chest. She let out a gasp, her face frozen in shock.

"No!" Derric caught her as she fell backward, lowering her to the ground. "Mom, no!"

Gilda's green eyes homed in on his, tears leaking out from the corners. "Derr-Derric. Don't let him . . . don't be like him. Don't be—be like me. Y-you are good. I'm so sorry I wasn't there for you. I'm—I'm so sorry."

"No, please. Don't talk. You're going to be okay. It's okay."

"Don't lie to her, son. She knows what's happening." Tertius's glee made Derric want to launch at him, but he couldn't. Not when she needed him.

"He's right," she gasped, clutching him. "Derric, I love you. Don't let him . . . don't let him change you. Don't give in to . . . to the darkne—"

She let out a shuddering final breath. Her head dropped back, her eyes deadening. Her thread of magic vanished, leaving emptiness inside him. Derric pulled her close, a choked sob escaping him as he clutched her lifeless body. He shook, tried to suck in a breath, and failed. He chanted the spell to return the lost.

"What has been lost, now return. From beyond, now to rest. Return the life to this broken vessel."

Gilda remained still as the grave. Derric repeated it over and over again, and nothing happened. His father knelt beside him, staring down at her.

"It won't work. You don't have the power to bring back life—no sorcerer does." For a moment Derric thought he heard regret in Tertius's voice, but when he turned to look at him, his father grinned and stood, Maria still struggling in his grip. "It's not like she was ever much to you. You barely knew her. Be a man and stand up before I make you."

A whimper from Maria brought Derric to his feet. He lowered Gilda to the floor with gentle care and forced himself to rise. His mind felt like mush, and he couldn't focus.

"We can do this the hard way or the easy way." Tertius lifted Maria off the floor. She clawed at his fingers, fighting for air, but since he stood behind her, she couldn't find purchase.

"Stop!" Derric shouted, moving forward. Tertius lifted his other hand, and Derric ran against an invisible wall.

"Tsk tsk. You aren't learning, my boy." He started to laugh and then let out a yell, dropping Maria. She hit the ground hard and rolled away from him. His hand bled where she'd cut into him with her nails.

"Maybe you're the one who needs to learn a thing or two," she gasped as she scrambled to Derric's side. "I'm not some helpless damsel in distress."

"How quaint." Tertius cocked one eyebrow. "I suppose she will die just like your mother. How many do I have to kill before you realize the only way out is to join me?"

"You'll have to kill me along with them."

Before Tertius could retort, the door to the throne room burst open, and Burt charged through, three people clinging to his back.

No. Derric didn't want to believe it. They couldn't be there. Not now.

"Attack!" Humphrey yelled from just behind Sarah, who leapt off of Burt's back and hit the ground with a roll. She was dressed once again in trousers, her eyes wild and her hair tied back.

"Give me back my brother, you bastard."

"Feisty one, isn't she?" Tertius said. "Peranicas, the girl."

"Fetch, Burt!" Alyssa directed the bumbleloch after Peranicas, cackling. He screamed and tried to run but was no match for Burt's speed. The sickening crunch that signified the sorcerer's end forced Derric to turn away.

"I feel better," Alyssa said, sliding off Burt's back and coming to stand beside Derric. "It seems your Council is down to one."

Tertius's mouth twisted into a grin. "One is all I need."

Alyssa turned in a jerky motion and shot an ice ball at Derric. Her scream enabled him to duck just in time.

"What are you doing?"

"Like puppets on a string." Tertius laughed. "You think you can play with the big dogs, Derric? This is what happens when you come against me. You lose."

Alyssa continued her forced assault on them until Humphrey tackled her from behind. The prince continued to struggle with her as she fought against him, apologizing as she punched and kicked him.

Burt ran for Tertius, but the sorcerer shot another bolt of energy at the creature, knocking him to the ground with a loud whimper. Maria rushed to his side.

"No! Stop!" Derric raised his hands in surrender.

"Disobedience will not be tolerated," Tertius said, snatching Sarah by the scruff of her shirt as she, too, ran for Burt. She wriggled in his grasp, kicking out and buckling his knees. Tertius let out a cry of pain and pulled her in closer, one hand around her throat and the other hovering over her chest.

"No!" Derric dropped to his knees, eyes wide. "Don't hurt her." His plea felt weak, a child with no strength to defend himself.

"Ah." Tertius's dark eyes glittered with triumph. "Have I found something worth bargaining for?" He glanced at Maria. "It looks like you weren't quite enough, but this one here . . ."

"I'll do whatever you want. Just let her go."

"This is where you learn, boy," Tertius hissed, his eyes wide and maniacal. "No one crosses me. No one says no to me. You will do exactly what I say when I say it."

"Yes. I will. Please." Derric's vision clouded, and a voice whispered from somewhere inside him, just like the one he'd heard in Fangralee. *We're with you.*

"You have to learn what happens when you disobey me."

A Stolen Kiss

You don't fight alone.

Everything in Derric fought to focus on Sarah, to do whatever Tertius said in order to keep her safe.

You are stronger than you know. Use us.

"This is your punishment, Derric. This is your fault." Tertius slammed his hand against Sarah's chest, and a bright blue light blazed from his palm into her, lighting up her stunned face. He released her, and she fell, her lifeless body crumpling to the ground.

Her sightless eyes stared beyond him. The one thing Derric had always tried to protect—the one person who had always believed in him—was gone.

Something inside him snapped.

Chapter 58
The Great One

. . . .

It all happened so fast, and yet Maria saw each second as though it was an eternity. Just as he had with Gilda, Tertius blasted Sarah, stealing her young life away. Maria's closest friend dropped to the floor, dead. Air sucked out of Maria's lungs. She couldn't breathe.

Derric, on his hands and knees inches from Sarah, let out a scream. Maria covered her ears. The windows shattered, spraying the room with glass. The chandelier high above them rattled, burst into flame, and then fell to the floor not ten feet behind Tertius.

The sorcerer jumped, spinning around. For the first time, fear registered on his face. He turned and paled. Maria followed his gaze. Light poured from Derric. It encircled his body, emanated from his fingertips, and shone from his eyes.

Behind him, Alyssa knelt on the ground, her forehead pressed to the stone floor, still as a statue. Burt, injured but alive, stooped into the same stance.

"What . . . what is this?" Tertius asked.

When Derric spoke, it was with many voices, not just his own.

"The Great One."

Chapter 59
Retribution

Threads of sorcerers surrounded Derric. Without his having to ask, they clung to him, wrapping around him, surging him with power. They pulsated, clinging to him and chanting.

We are with you. You are not alone. Fight. Fight. Fight.

Thousands stood with him as he rose to his feet, his gaze fixed on Tertius.

"The Great One?" Tertius stumbled backward. "I—I don't understand."

"We are one," Derric said, the many voices of those fighting with him echoing in his words. "You have reigned through fear, and the time has come to deliver justice. Your tyranny is over."

Tertius regained his composure, his face hardening. He stretched out his arms, and Derric felt the tug of the threads as Tertius pulled them. In his mind's eye he could see Tertius's thick black thread drawing all those with dark magic to himself. Tertius's body stiffened, his eyes blackening until no iris, no whites remained. His fingers grew claws, and his teeth shaped into fangs.

"I am the Great One here," he growled. His words sounded like they reverberated off steel. "No man can defeat me."

Together. Derric mentally plucked at the threads with him. *We will do this together.*

"I am not one man." At the final word, Derric threw up his arms and released the pent up energy inside. Tertius mirrored his actions.

Golden fire collided with black lightning, filling the

room with flickering shadows. The cruel force pushed Derric, but he held his ground, pressing against Tertius's magic.

Together.

Tertius screamed in frustration. The evil grew in the room, forcing out the light. Derric focused his thoughts on Sarah and Gilda, Humphrey and Maria. Losing wasn't an option.

Amidst the chaos, the pain shooting up his arms, and the growing fatigue, a voice sang. Another joined it, and somewhere in the back of his mind he knew it was Humphrey and Maria. He knew the words. Though he couldn't break his concentration to sing aloud, he thought the words with them, and many of the threads joined in.

> *Though the winter winds blow fierce and cold,*
> *And all my love has gone,*
> *I will be both brave and bold.*
> *Yes, I will carry on.*

"What is this?" Tertius's cry gave Derric the strength to take another step forward and regain ground. "Stop! What is this singing?"

> *When darkness sets its grip on me*
> *And fear starts to descend,*
> *I'll hold on to the light of old*
> *Until the very end.*

Several steps more, forcing Tertius on the defensive. He struggled against Derric's flow of golden light as it crept through the blackness and wrapped tendrils around his arms.

"No! What is this?"

> *I will bid the darkness flee*
> *And tell death to be gone.*
> *It hasn't strength nor hold on me.*
> *My light will carry on.*

A Stolen Kiss

The golden light wrapped around Tertius's body, engulfing him in a blinding, violent light. Derric turned away. Agonized screams echoed through the chamber, reverberating to a high pitch, and vanishing at once.

When he turned back, no sign of Tertius remained but a scorch mark in the stone floor.

Exhaustion clutched at Derric with savage ferocity, but he didn't have time for that—not yet.

Stay with me just a bit longer, please, he asked the others. Though he could feel their fatigue, they remained with him as he crossed to Sarah, dropping down before her.

Please, help me do this. I need you.

Derric rolled Sarah over onto her back. Her lifeless eyes stared up into nothing. Placing a hand over the blackened spot on her chest, Derric closed his eyes and gathered the borrowed magic.

"What has been lost, now return. From beyond, now to rest. Return the life to this broken vessel."

The golden glow pulsed from his fingertips, entering Sarah's chest and wrapping around her. Every ounce of energy Derric had left, he focused on her. Blood or not, she would always be his little sister. He watched, waiting for a sign of life, and repeated the spell.

In the second before he passed out, Sarah's eyes closed and reopened, her lips parting to suck in breath.

Derric awoke in a comfortable bed surrounded by strangers.

"He's awake," a girl said, eyes widening. "I'll go tell the others." She dashed out of sight. With great effort, Derric turned his head.

"We weren't sure if you were going to return to us,

m'boy." A wrinkly, white-haired man grinned down at him. "It was a bit touch and go there for a few days."

Days?

"He's going to recover, isn't he, Healer Mantis?" A tall young man stood on the other side of the healer, his arms folded across his chest.

"Yes, Your Majesty. I believe he will. If he'd like to prove it, though, a few words wouldn't hurt."

He didn't have the energy to speak, but the young man reached out with his own magic, strengthening Derric for a moment until he recognized it—it was the thread he'd pulled while creating the barrier in Fangralee. He'd used Alyssa's, Gilda's, and . . .

"Shen?" Derric mumbled, staring at the lean, raven-haired royal.

"See? I told you he got my note." Shen smacked another individual who stood beside him. "You got my note! That's why you called us all, right?"

"Called?"

"The sorcerers. You pulled all of our threads together. That's what the note meant—we would fight with you."

Derric glanced down at his hand. The signet ring still encircled his finger. He lifted it in gesture of return, but Shen shook his head.

"No, that's yours. Let it be a symbol to all that you are a friend to the royal city of Kyleria. You've freed us from two decades of slavery to a tyrant."

"Derric!" Humphrey bounded into the room and gave a whoop of delight. "You're awake, mate! We were worried about you."

Seeing Humphrey brought everything back. Derric's aching bones no longer mattered. He sat up and threw his legs over the side of the mattress.

"Sarah? Is Sarah—" he didn't need to finish his sentence. His little sister dashed into the room after the prince, a smile lighting up her face.

A Stolen Kiss

"Derric!" she cried, leaping up into his arms and rolling him backward.

"Now, now, missy." Healer Mantis grabbed Sarah around the middle and dragged her back. "This young man is in a fragile state!"

"He's fine," Sarah said with a dismissive wave of her hand. "Look at him—he's a normal color now and everything."

"I'm sore glad you're back." Alyssa approached the bed. "This one has been nothing but a pacing, worried mess while you've been out." She thumped Humphrey on the back.

"How long have I been asleep?"

"Four days. Alyssa was out for one of them." Humphrey shoved her, grinning.

"Hey, it takes a lot of energy to bring back the dead." She shrugged. "All of the sorcerers in Kyleria needed a rest after standing with you."

Sarah sat down on the bed beside him, resting her head on his shoulder. "Don't ever do that again."

"As long as you don't ever get yourself killed by a crazy sorcerer again."

"Deal."

Derric glanced up and saw another figure in the doorway. Maria leaned against the doorjamb, arms folded tight across her body. She didn't smile, nor did she approach. Seeing he was awake, she nodded and disappeared out the door.

"She's been coming to terms with your identity while you were out," Sarah whispered. "We've talked to her, and while she isn't happy, she does understand why you did it." To the room at large, Sarah started making shooing noises. "Go on. He needs his rest. He doesn't need six maids and this many valets watching over him. You, of course, can stay, Your Majesty." She curtsied at Shen, who laughed.

"I'll obey orders, Miss Sarah. Great One. Fellow royal."

He gave a respectful nod to Humphrey, who returned it, and then left the room.

"He's been on the run for ages," Humphrey said, answering Derric's unspoken question. "His family is out of the dungeons now, but they're in bad shape after the way they were treated. He's going to be the one responsible for running this place until his father and older sister improve." Humphrey shook his head. "I don't envy him. I don't think he's looking forward to it."

Something shifted in Derric's mind, and he leaned back against his pillows. "My mother is dead."

The other three exchanged worried glances. "Yes. She is." Alyssa leaned against the bedpost. "Maria says she died because she wasn't going to let Tertius use you."

"She didn't even have a chance to defend herself." Tears pressed against the corners of his eyes. "I finally found her again, and she's gone."

"She's never gone."

Derric looked at Sarah, and her mouth quirked in a small smile.

"It's true. I—I don't know how to explain what happens after, but . . . you don't turn into nothing. There's more out there, and I know Gilda will always be with you. There's something about the heavens. They're real."

A great sense of comfort washed over Derric, and he bit down on his tongue to try to keep from crying.

"Hey, mate, don't fight it." Humphrey, now up by the head of the bed, patted his shoulder. "Deal with the emotions. Don't bottle them. Crying is the manly thing to do."

"He cries way more than I do." Alyssa smiled and wrapped an arm around Humphrey's waist. "Now you need to get better so you can come to Dellsby for our wedding. That is, once we've explained it to his and Maria's parents."

Chapter 60
Tumbling Emotions

· ·

Maria sat on a bench out in the courtyard, enjoying the warmth of the Kylerian winter. The royal city wasn't far from the coast. Part of her wanted to see the ocean for the first time, but she knew they needed to get back to Opea. Humphrey had sent a carrier pigeon with a letter for their parents as soon as things had calmed down, but that wouldn't be enough to ease their worry.

Derric had been awake for a few days, and she hadn't gone to see him. It still felt strange even to *think* of him as Derric and not Daniel. He'd lied to her. He'd pretended. She could look back and see so many moments where he'd been trying to tell her without saying it. She understood his actions, of course—that wasn't why she was avoiding him.

She felt foolish. She'd professed her love and pined for him. For weeks she'd planned on getting the curse removed so she could claim him as her betrothed and marry him instead. Yet none of it was real. Closing her eyes, Maria rested her head against the back of the bench, letting out a sigh of frustration.

"Am I disturbing you?"

She jumped, eyes snapping open at the sound of Derric's voice. He stood off to the side, his hands held at a weird angle like he wasn't sure what to do with them.

"No, of course not. Please, sit." She patted the space beside her, and he settled into it. For several moments, neither of them said anything. "So, I suppose you're ready to leave tomorrow?"

He hesitated, not looking at her. "I'm not going with you."

"What?"

"I'm not going back to Opea."

She stared at him, her mouth agape. "I . . . but . . . why?"

"Prince Shen has asked me to stay and help him sort things out here. I told him I would."

"Only for a little while, though."

"I'm not sure." Derric stared down at his hands. "I might stay in Kyleria."

"But what about your home, your family, and your friends?"

Derric chuckled, but there wasn't any humor in it. "My family is dead. My father killed my mother, and I killed my father. The man I always thought was my father is, in fact, just some poor jerk forced into pretending I belonged to him. No, Opea is not my home. Here, I can help. Back there, I'm a slave."

"But you won't be a slave, not anymore." She grabbed hold of his arm, but he still didn't look at her. "You won't. I mean it. You'll be free. I'm going to lift the ban on sorcery. I think . . . I think you should be the palace sorcerer. You'll be able to keep Opea safe. It's a wonderful idea."

"I don't think your parents would be thrilled to have the person who cursed you be their sorcerer, especially if he's the son of the woman who made sure they'd never have any more children."

"They'll get over it. It won't matter." Maria waved his concern away, her heart racing. "You have to come back. How else will we get through Fangralee?"

"You're going to have Alyssa and Burt with you. I've also spoken to Ellis about keeping an eye on you, should anything go wrong."

She sucked on air, finding it difficult to draw breath. Maria tugged at his arm with new ferocity. "Derric."

At the sound of his name, he looked at her. She realized

it was the first time she'd said it out loud. For a moment, they held each other's gaze.

"What about me?" she asked, holding back tears.

"I'll remove the curse. You'll be free from me, and you'll never have to be a swan again."

"I don't want you to."

His eyebrows arched, and he straightened. "What?"

"I don't want you to remove the curse." She let out a shuddering sigh. "I've thought a lot about this, and I don't want it removed. I would rather keep loving you. I want to be with you. Think of all the good you could do in Opea. You would be an amazing king. You would—stop shaking your head!"

He stood and stepped away from her. "Maria, I can't. You can't."

"Can't what?"

"I can't be king. I can't rule for you. You can't keep hiding from your responsibilities. You're strong enough to be the queen of Opea without any help."

"Then don't be king. Come back and just be mine." She hated how desperate she sounded, but she couldn't let him go.

"I can't." His voice softened, and he turned away from her. "You love me because of the binding."

"I don't care!"

"I do." He faced her again, kneeling down before her. "I want to be loved for the person I am, not the power I have over you." He moved to sit down again, taking her hands in his. "It's because I love you I'm doing this for you. No one should have to live their whole life in a lie, and I don't want to see you every day and know all of this was my fault."

"What? No, it isn't. You can't be blamed for anything that happened here—you've only ever tried to save—"

"If I hadn't kissed you and cursed you when I was a child, my mother would still be alive. She and I would be together in Opea. You never would have been cursed, and your parents might have had a son to rule so you wouldn't have to. Humphrey wouldn't have had to choose between you and Alyssa. Sarah never would have been in any danger . . . all of this is my fault."

"Derric."

Before she could protest, he leaned forward and pressed his lips against hers in a gentle caress. As he pulled away, he whispered her release. "Maria, I set you free."

She blinked. "That's it?"

He nodded. "My mother told me I'd know what to do when the time was right. A stolen kiss started it, and a stolen kiss finishes it. You're free. You'll never have to see me again."

Chapter 61
A Broken Goodbye

Derric helped them saddle up their horses and rubbed Burt's head.

"Take good care of Thumper," he told Alyssa. She would be riding him back to the stables where he belonged.

"I'm very good to horses." She grinned and hugged him. He might not know her well, but he could see why she and Humphrey were so right for each other.

Sarah wrapped her arms around him next. "You promise to write?"

"Promise."

"And," she lowered her voice, "you will come back and see me?"

"Of course." He kissed the top of her head and squeezed her extra tight. "You'll never get rid of me."

"Well, mate." Humphrey put his hands on his hips and looked Derric up and down. "I guess it's goodbye until the wedding?"

"Write me to let me know when it is. I don't want to miss it."

"You can't miss it. You're going to be right beside me." He slapped Derric on the back and sobered. "Are you sure you won't come with us?"

"I'm needed here. My parents created a mess that I want to help clean up."

"Right, but . . ." Humphrey glanced over his shoulder at Maria as she played with Burt.

"She's not under the curse anymore. Having me around would be confusing."

"If you say so." Humphrey pulled Derric into a hug. "Keep safe."

"You too."

Maria didn't approach him. She pulled up onto Verona's saddle and turned her attention his way. Her brow flickered. He could sense the conflict within her. The remnants of the curse might remind her of the feelings she had before, but she would already be seeing him for what he was.

No one.

"Goodbye, Derric," she said, a note of bemusement in her tone.

"Goodbye, Maria."

A Stolen Kiss

Chapter 62
THE MASQUERADE

. . . .

Six Months Later

Maria stood behind the curtain beside her mother, waiting to be announced. She could feel the queen's gaze on her every few seconds. Biting back a sigh, Maria straightened her petticoat and made sure her mask was in place.

Ever since she'd returned, her parents had walked on eggshells around her. Her first order of business, after informing them her curse was removed and she wouldn't be marrying Humphrey, was to tell them she didn't need a man by her side to rule her kingdom.

"When I take the crown," she'd said, her chin high and her hands on her hips. "I will do it as your daughter and rightful heir. I will not worry about whether or not I'm married, and if I do get married, that man will not be the king, but the prince regent. He will work with me to rule our people, but I will have the proper say. I will carry the scepter."

It had taken them some time to come to terms with her assertion, but they'd realized she was far more capable than they'd ever given her credit for—having Burt stand beside her as her constant protector might have helped a little.

"Now, you *will* dance with the young men tonight, won't you, dear?" her mother asked, fussing over her own dress.

On Maria's other side, Sarah chuckled. Upon returning, Maria elevated her to the highest lady-in-waiting position, declaring Sarah a noble. She didn't extend this title to Sarah's parents.

"Yes, mother. I will dance with the gentlemen and will walk away tonight without feeling the urge to marry any of them."

"I'm allowed to hope." The queen gave her daughter a small smile, and Maria returned it.

She dreaded dancing. Though she'd been the one to advocate for a masquerade ball during Humphrey and Alyssa's visit, she hadn't danced since she was in Kyleria with Derric. Despite what he'd said, she'd never forgotten him. Though, she no longer felt the urgent need to be by his side or in his arms. On occasion, she'd asked Sarah how things were going for him in Kyleria. Sarah always answered with a sly smile.

"You should enjoy tonight, Maria," Sarah whispered. "After all, you missed Humphrey and Alyssa's wedding, and you're doing this for them, so you should have fun with it."

"I will."

"Don't let thoughts of the past drag you down."

"I won't."

"Maybe you'll meet your happily-ever-after tonight."

Maria rolled her eyes. "Oh, not you too."

"I have a feeling. I just think it might be nice for you to fall in love."

"I've already been in love," Maria retorted, lips pressing into a thin line. "Once was enough."

"You just say that because of the circumstances. If you could trust me, I'm telling you that tonight you'll—"

"Presenting Lady Sarah Digson of Edleton."

At the herald's voice, Maria pushed Sarah through the curtain without waiting to hear the rest. After a few seconds, he heralded again.

"Princess Maria Andelle Regalla, future ruler of Opea."

Maria stepped out into the light and descended the stairs, smiling at her masked subjects. A thrill went through her. At the bottom of the stairs, she spotted Humphrey and Alyssa conversing with Sarah. She'd recognize them anywhere.

"Your Highness." Humphrey bowed with flair as soon as she reached them, his arms overdramatizing the effect. "Might I have the first dance?"

One eyebrow rising, Maria glanced at Alyssa. The newlywed princess nodded her approval. Taking Humphrey's proffered hand, she followed him out onto the dance floor. As she was opening the ball, all eyes were on them as the orchestra struck the first note.

"Now this is dancing," Humphrey said, whirling Maria across the floor in an elegant waltz. "Alyssa has two left feet, I swear it. She spends most of the time on my toes."

Maria chuckled. Somehow she found no difficulty picturing the feisty, hot-headed Alyssa tromping along on her husband's feet while dancing with little grace. Their trip back to Opea had been filled with Alyssa's falls and klutzy blunders. More couples joined them on the dance floor.

"How's Sarah?" he asked. The flicker of concern in Humphrey's eyes filled Maria with affection for him.

"She's doing well, I think. Far more subdued than she used to be—doesn't give her opinion always or insist she's in the right every single argument. I think she's becoming quite a humble, empathetic young woman. It's funny, she's even more insightful than before."

"Death could do that to you, I suppose."

"Death, the family you thought you knew being destroyed, watching others die for you, and leaving your brother behind . . . that's a lot for a fourteen-year-old girl to handle."

"She's fifteen now, isn't she?"

"Yes. Just last week."

"Did she hear from Derric?"

The mention of his name sent a flutter through Maria's stomach, but she feigned indifference. "I think he sent her a letter with a gift, yes." It was a necklace crafted by the jewelers in Kyleria and imbued with protective magic specifically for Sarah. But again, Maria didn't want to show how much attention she paid to all things Derric. With a casual glance around the room, Maria continued. "Have you seen him lately?"

"He was at the wedding, and we write pretty regularly." One thick eyebrow arched as the corners of Humphrey's mouth twitched in amusement. "Why do you ask?"

"Just curious." Maria caught sight of a man standing by the open double doors leading out to the garden. He was tall, blond, and wearing a mask that covered most of his face. Grunting in frustration, Maria turned her head away.

"Something wrong?"

"It's Ellis."

"Ellis?" Humphrey glanced around the room, searching for the shapeshifter.

"Over by the outer doors." Maria gestured to the man with her chin. "It keeps coming to me in that form—has been for the last two months. Always with cryptic messages and shrewd smiles."

"Sounds like Ellis." Humphrey chortled, focused on the figure. "Why has it been visiting you at all? You're not its master."

"Just checking up on me—that's what it always says, anyway. One of these days, it's going to request the favor I owe." Deep in her heart, Maria loved Ellis's visits. Part of her hoped it was Derric who sent Ellis to her, making sure she was still safe and well.

"Always that same figure?" Humphrey asked, spinning Maria around to get a second look at Ellis. Maria nodded. "Seems familiar, but it's hard to tell with the mask covering that much of his face."

"Its face," Maria corrected. "I should go and see what it wants."

"I don't know." Humphrey's brows knit together, his lips forming a thin line. "Ellis came to us as people he was telling us something about: Alyssa, Tertius, Sarah's father . . ." Humphrey paused on the dance floor. "Maybe it's warning you about someone real here at the ball—someone to be afraid of."

"I don't think so. After all, it also came to us as a lynx. I'll just be a moment. I'll see what it wants and then return." When Humphrey opened his mouth to reply, Maria held up a hand. "Burt is waiting in the garden, watching the perimeter. No one can harm me when he's near."

She beckoned Alyssa from the outskirts of the dance floor and swapped places with her, leaving Humphrey to dance with his wife. Sarah stepped up to Maria's side, a soft smile on her face.

"I see Ellis is here," she said, eyes twinkling as she glanced over at the doorway. "I suppose you'd like a moment to speak with our friend without maternal interruption?" Sarah gestured to where the queen stood, watching Maria and worrying her lower lip.

"That would be best. Although, in the current form, she might think I've found a young man worth my attention."

"Maybe you will have. Go. I'll stop her if I need to." Sarah fiddled with her new necklace. "I could engage her in a conversation about the centaurs. She loves talking about Nysa."

"She did leave quite an impression on Mother when the herd was here." Maria thanked Sarah and made her way toward the doors. Ellis slipped out ahead of her. As she walked, she smiled and nodded at the nobles who'd attended, twice stopping to engage in polite conversation.

The garden, blooming in the early weeks of spring, had a dim glow in the light emanating from the ballroom. Maria spotted Ellis straight away, its back to her as it pet Burt.

With a forced sigh of impatience, Maria approached the shapeshifter, her heartbeat quickening. "Well? What message have you for me this time?"

Ellis turned, and though she couldn't see the details of the face it used, she sensed its surprise at the less-than-cordial greeting.

"Message?"

"Message, missive, cryptic note." She ticked off options on her fingers. "Whatever riddle or puzzle you expect me to solve today."

Ellis glanced at Burt, who shook his head, eyes wide. "You're not pleased to see me. Perhaps I should go."

Maria took a step back. "Really? You'd give up so easily?" Pausing, Ellis turned its head, giving Maria a curious side stare. "You never give up. Usually you pester me for at least the better part of an hour—always wearing that mask."

"This mask?"

She folded her arms, waiting for an explanation that didn't come. "I wish you wouldn't come to me in this form. It hurts to have him so near and yet know it isn't him. You speak with his voice and make me feel like . . . like he's here, and I would rather you didn't."

He hesitated and took a step forward. "Who exactly do you think I am?"

"Ellis," she said, doubting her answer for the first time and wondering if Humphrey was right.

Chapter 63
A Stolen Kiss

. . . .

Ellis? Derric would have laughed but was too surprised. "Ellis," he repeated, staring down at her. She nodded, peering up at him, trying to see behind the mask. A mixture of relief and frustration collided in him. Ellis had been posing as him when checking on Maria? Not just any Derric, but this exact outfit and mask?

"That explains why you followed me out here," he said, trying to fight the melancholy sweeping over him. "You thought I was someone else."

"You didn't want me to follow you, then?" Her quiet voice challenged him.

"I came here to see for myself that you were all right." He shifted, his back to her. "At first, I thought you assumed I was one of your guard, dressed up to move about the party unseen, and you wanted a report of some kind. Then I figured you knew who I was and were trying to tell me to leave you alone."

"Derric?"

"Yes?" He turned to her.

"You're Derric," she repeated, pointing at him.

"Last I checked." He frowned, trying to understand the wild look in her eye.

"Why?"

He paused. "I've always been Derric."

"No, why are you here?"

"I just told you. I wanted to see you were doing well. When you weren't at Humphrey's wedding . . ." He trailed off, fiddling with the edges of his tailored jacket. Shen had given him a luxurious new suit as a parting gift. One of many.

Maria sidestepped him, stopping next to Burt to scratch under his chin. "I didn't think I could face you again."

Derric's stomach dropped. This was why he hadn't planned on speaking to her. He wasn't sure he could handle her open rebuke. "I understand."

"I don't think you do." She didn't look at him but cupped Burt's massive face in her hands. "I didn't go because I didn't want to admit I was in love with someone who didn't want me."

Derric opened his mouth and closed it again, trying to understand what she meant. Someone who didn't want her? "Humphrey?"

She let out a huff of air, her lips pursing together. "No. You."

What?

"You . . . you're still in love with me?" At her annoyed glare, he spluttered forth, "I'msosorryMaria." He took a breath and slowed down. "I had no idea—I thought . . . I thought I'd removed the curse. I never meant for you to still be suffering the effects of the binding."

She lifted up her mask, her eyebrows contracting. "I'm not. You removed the binding."

"But if you're still—"

"I love Humphrey," she said, her hands on her hips. "Yes, I will marry Roger. I am in love with Steven. I hate Derric. I love Derric. See? Not under the binding." She dropped her arms to her side. "Would you just please remove that mask?"

"Oh, sorry." He pulled the mask up and off, rubbing his face with the other hand before looking at her again. Her eyes widened, and she took a step back. Heart beating faster, Derric tried to hide his disappointment. "You don't recognize me, do you?"

He knew it was possible. A magical binding would alter her vision to see the perfect man, to reinforce the love imposed upon her. Once the binding wore off, she'd see him for who he really was—her dream image would be broken.

"I—I don't," she confessed, taking a step closer and squinting at him. He stood still as she studied him, a crease forming at the bridge of her nose. After a few moments, their eyes met, and a smile spread across her face. "There you are. Your eyes are the same. Your jaw is squarer, and I never noticed your cheekbones were so defined. Have you always been this rugged?" She reached up and placed her palm against his cheek, running her fingers along his jaw.

"Maybe? It's been six months. Maybe I've changed."

The joy in her face dimmed, and she dropped her hand. "Maybe we've both changed." She looked away, the chords in her neck strained. "I suppose you'll need to go back to Kyleria now you've seen for yourself I'm free."

"Actually, no." He sighed. "Kyleria is getting back on its feet. Shen's done so much, and his family is back to full health. I would have been back sooner, but there was a bit of a snag early on caused by a young woman named Kida whom Gilda had cursed . . ." He waved his hand dismissively. "Anyway, everything worked out."

"What are you going to do now?"

Derric didn't answer her. He'd just noticed her dress, and it, if anything, sparked hope in him. "Where did you find that dress?"

Caught off guard by the change of subject, Maria glanced down at her black and white gown. It was tight at the waist and then flowed out in layers of tulle, silk, and petticoats. With her dark hair pinned up in the back, and the mask shaped the way it was . . . could it have been an accident?

"I had it made by my personal seamstress. I sketched out what I wanted it to look like, and she put this together."

"You look like a swan in it."

A soft blush pinked her caramel skin. "I know."

"After all of those years of feathers, you wanted to go back to it when you were finally free?"

She ran her hands over the skirt. "Do you remember what you said to me right before you lifted the curse? That if you hadn't cursed me in the first place, everyone would still be alive and happy? But that was all Gilda's fault because she hid it from you. What you should have focused on was the second kiss."

His gaze narrowed, curious where she would take this.

"You see, if you'd never stolen a kiss when I was sleeping, I never would have been bound to you. Without the binding, I never would have met you. Humphrey would have broken the curse, and we would have gotten married as planned. Alyssa would have forever been trapped in her picture, and Humphrey would have been miserable with me for his wife—which, in turn, would leave me feeling the same.

"You never would have discovered the true potential of your powers but would have stayed a slave in the barn until the day you died. Sarah wouldn't have amounted to anything other than a maid. You never would have seen your mother again, and speaking of Gilda—" Maria paused for dramatic effect. "She would have been trapped in Kyleria at the hands of Tertius for as long as she lived, as would the rest of Kyleria.

"If you hadn't stolen that kiss, Derric Harver . . . there wouldn't be one happy ending to our miserable tale." She stood as close as her dress would allow now, her fierce gaze fixed on his face. "Do you love me, Derric?"

He swallowed the lump in his throat. "I do."

"Then why didn't you come for me?"

"I thought, once the binding disappeared, you'd never want to see me again."

"The truth?" she said, one eyebrow arched. Derric nodded for her to continue. "I did hate you. All the way back through the pass, I hated every bit of you. It was empowering to know I *could* hate Derricus Harver. I relished the feeling—clung to it." Her gaze dropped, and she pulled her mask the rest of the way off. "Then, about halfway through Fangralee, when the centaurs stayed up late listening to the stories of the Great One from Sarah and Humphrey and telling their own tales to Alyssa and Burt, I realized I only hated you because I thought I was supposed to.

"I listened to the tales of the Great One, and I felt proud of the man who'd done such amazing things. I could remember every time you did something to protect someone else, every time you were gentle with me or Sarah. I couldn't help but fall in love with you all over again. The binding made it easy the first time, but you being yourself made it just as simple the second."

Dizziness threatened to overwhelm him as he listened. He felt giddy and short of breath, and he cleared his throat when she finished speaking. "You know, technically I still belong to the crown of Opea." Her head snapped up, eyes wide. "I, uh, never was freed."

Maria's mouth twitched, and he could tell she had to fight to keep from smiling. "That's true. You've been a very naughty slave. I should order you to stay."

"I suppose so. I'd be powerless to refuse."

"I could even order you to marry me." She reached up and wrapped her arms around his neck, a devilish grin spreading across her face.

"You could."

"Right now," she whispered, her face inching closer. "I order you to kiss me."

"Mm." He moved to close the gap, but she jerked back.

"Wait." She pressed a finger to his lips, a mischievous glint in her eye. "Nothing's going to happen to me if I kiss you, is it? No feathers . . . no turning into a frog or anything?"

Relief washed through Derric, and he chuckled, pulling her hand away and kissing the tender skin of her wrist.

"Nothing like that. I've got it all under control now." He tightened his arm around her waist until she was pressed against him, her voluminous dress squished between them.

"I like a man with a bit of control." She slid her arm back out of his grip and around his neck, her fingers running up into his hair.

He pressed his lips to hers, relishing the sensation. They spent several moments entwined together, and when they parted, she looked down at her body. At his questioning glance, she winked.

"Just making sure. Still human."

"I told you, I have it under control." He leaned in again. "At least, I think I do." After another long moment spent savoring the feel of her kiss, he pulled away, a bit breathless. "Should we go back?"

Maria nodded, looping her arm through his and walking at his side as they returned. He couldn't take his eyes off of her and ran right into a shrub.

"You're almost as graceful as Alyssa," Maria said with a snort of laughter, pulling him out of harm's way. "What are you thinking about?"

Derric stared down into her beautiful dark eyes. "I'm just so glad I liked swans."

She laughed, throwing her head back. "I'm glad you're the type of rogue to steal a kiss."

They reentered the ballroom hand in hand.

The End

MAGICAL CLAUSES

. . . .

An excerpt from Gilda Harver's journal

Curse Clauses:

Kiss Clause—A kiss is required to break the spell. Any kiss from any member of the opposite sex will do. Often mistaken for True Love's Kiss Clause, leading the fulfillment of many standard Kiss Clauses to end in marriage.

True Love's Kiss Clause—A kiss of true love is required to break the curse. Much harder to come by, as true love depends upon trust and choice, not merely attraction.

Royalty Clause—The curse can only be broken by a member of a royal family. Conflicts with True Love's Kiss as there's no guarantee the cursed will fall in love with a royal (e.g. when the daughter of the Sultan fell in love with a street rat.)

*Loophole: Find a genie or another sorcerer and have them make the True Love a prince/princess.

Permanence Clause—In a cruel twist of fate, magic can put an expiration on happiness and a permanence on sorrow. A Permanence Clause often befalls the cursed when they do not fulfill the required task in the time allotted (e.g.: Princess Aileen Dubios was given 100 years to find someone to love her, despite her hideous, monstrous nature. Many are given until their 16th or 21st birthday to succeed at breaking a spell). If the cursed doesn't succeed in fulfilling the required task, their curse becomes permanent (forever a swan at night, forever a monster, forever asleep, etc.).

334

Spell Clauses:

Happily-Ever-After Clause—Often used as motivation. When a spell is cast, the caster will often require an action in order to make the spell stick (e.g. a kiss by the third day, being back by midnight, etc.). If the action is met in the allotted time, the castee will receive a "happily-ever-after" to their story.

Expiration Clause—Opposite of a curse's Permanence Clause, the expiration denotes a time when the magic will end and payment is due. This is used by a socerer(ess) with ill intentions (e.g. sea witches and dark fairies, although some godmothers are limited by these clauses). Often the chosen time is up to three days, though many will end at midnight.

Fulfillment is demanded as soon as time has passed—the firstborn must be given, or the soul of the castee is owned by the sorcerer(ess) who cast the spell.

*Loophole: Time traveling potion.

Love Spells:

Love at First Sight—The man or woman who has been put under a love spell will attach to the first person they see. Literally, they will fall in love (magically) at first sight. Not necessarily a spell used to ensnare two individuals. Often, the one cast will fall in love at first sight, but the person they've seen might need more convincing. The second party is usually won over by the outpouring of love from the first.

This clause is often used to undermine the desires of the one who cast the spell (e.g. When sorcerer Edwin McGill was commanded to put a love spell on his own sister for a selfish king, McGill added a Love at First Sight clause and his sister, Fiona, fell in love with the ogre who saved her. They lived happily ever after).

Love at First Kiss—The spell isn't complete until a kiss is exchanged. Upon the exchange of a kiss, the two parties will fall in love. This binding needs only be cast upon one person to affect both.

Often attached to a Standard Kiss Clause by a well-meaning fairy in an attempt to foil a sorceress's plot (e.g. The sleeping princess fell in love with the young man who kissed her, even though it had been 100 years since she'd fallen asleep, and she didn't know him).

Love at First Fight—An odd spell and an old magic, this explains how two individuals who so obviously hate each other actually have chemistry. Sure they don't get along, but from the first fight there's suddenly a sexual tension undercurrent.

Does it make any sense for two people who loathe each other to actually fall desperately in love? Of course not! How does it happen?

Magic.

Often used to undermine a relationship already in place, (e.g. Any time a scruffy knight is coerced into helping a princess get to her prince in order to save/marry/ understand him. And/or when the frog prince turned an ordinary servant girl into a frog as well (Royalty Clause!) and they had to work together to find a royal to save them both, despite hating each other).

Bindings:

Bound by Name—This rare binding is used to attach the cursed or enchanted to a specific individual. Their enchantment/curse can only be removed/fulfilled by the person they are bound to. Bindings are more dangerous than love spells, as a person bound to another cannot see past the binding to the person's faults. Someone bound is fated to accept all treatment from the one they are bound to, never questioning their motives.

*Loophole: If you have a careless sorcerer(ess), they will bind the cursed/enchanted to a name without specifying a person (e.g. the sorcerer Roflind Trill cursed a prince to spend his existence as a frog with a Kiss Clause and bound him to the name Aubrielle—the name of Trill's niece. Unfortunately for Trill and his niece, the frog prince met another Aubrielle, and she was able to break the curse).

Bound by Heredity—A particularly malevolent use of magic, the binding by heredity is often used to trick the offspring of a powerful figure into usurping their parent's power. The sorcerer will offer the child (often rebellious) what they selfishly want most, adding into the contract an Expiration Clause and a Heredity Binding. When the offspring fails (as they always do), the Heredity Binding offers a way for the parent to take their child's place in fulfilling the contract (paying with their soul, becoming a slave, etc.).

(e.g. When the daughter of the King of the Sea failed at getting a human prince to fall in love with her, her father, the king, offered himself in her place to the Sea Witch, giving the witch his soul.)

Bound by Blood—The darkest magical binding, Blood Bindings connect two individuals' fates together.

Anything that happens to one happens to the other—both positive and negative. Dark sorcerers most often use this magic, though on special occasions, light sorcerers have used it to prevent war between countries.

Blood bindings almost always result in the deaths of both parties.

Acknowledgements

This is the part of the book where I fall down on my face, profusely thanking those who got me here. So, in no particular order, here are the people who have kept me from jumping off a three-foot cliff or eating my weight in Ben & Jerry's Triple Caramel Chunk Ice Cream.

Thank you to my mother, who always had a positive attitude and encouraging word when I felt like I'd never see my book in print. Also, thanks for that whole giving me life thing.

This story wouldn't be what it is if it wasn't for two super powerful writers who answered my call when I hit a wall in the story. Rachelle Dekker and Katie Cross, thank you for being my rocks when I turned to jelly, my sounding boards when I'd gone deaf, and my sisters when I felt alone.

To Clone and Buttercup—you make the world a better place. Your encouragement means everything, and there aren't enough words to express my love for you.

To my editors at Quill Pen Editorial . . . let's be honest, you make me look good. Everybody take a moment to realize that this was a team effort, because first drafts should never be seen by the public eye.

Thank you to Jenny at Seedlings Design, Kella Campbell at E-Books Done Right, and Chris Bell from Atthis Arts for their amazing design work, both inside and out. Also, thank you to my publisher for holding my hand the whole way.

Finally, thank you to the Blue Monkeys and the Musers, the Wattpadians and the Swans. They say it takes a village to raise a child. Well, it takes a community to make an author. I couldn't have done it without you.

www.ingramcontent.com/pod-product-compliance
Lightning Source LLC
Chambersburg PA
CBHW031313210726
48287CB00005B/1531